Floater in the Baltimore Harbor

B A SMITH

ALSO BY B A SMITH

FICTION

DEATH AT PAINTED CAVE

GREEN GROWS THE GRASS

Floater In The Baltimore Harbor

NONFICTION

THE PSYCHOLOGY OF SEX AND GENDER

Floater in the Baltimore Harbor

B A SMITH

A ROBIN CRANE MYSTERY

An Imprint of Rough Waters Press
www.robincranemysteries.com

Copyright © 2015 B A Smith
ISBN-13: 9780692547717
ISBN-10: 0692547711

Dedication

For my beloved granddaughter
Rachel Marie Smith

Prologue

Dr. Bernard J. Manning, a celebrated Johns Hopkins surgeon, took his Irish setter for an early morning walk on the Stony Run Trail. When he reached the point where they usually returned home, the dog tugged hard against her leash and darted off at full speed. That was the final straw for the good doctor. The divorce had sucked him dry physically and emotionally but the greatest damage, he complained to his friends, was financial. Though early, sometimes others were out walking their dogs. It would be a sure lawsuit if his pet tangled with another animal, never mind bit its owner—in affluent Roland Park, lawyers were by no means in short supply. Also problematic would be the subsequent delay in getting to his first surgery of the day; he'd left his cell phone on his briefcase by the front door. Dr. Manning went after the dog, yelling as he ran. To no avail.

The doctor discovered Red Dog—hackles up, barking and whining—at the entrance of the culvert passing under Wyndhurst Road. Dressed for work (wearing his newly purchased Ferragamo shoes), Manning hesitated before going into the creek. Once he had hold of the dog, he peered inside. After his eyes had adjusted to the low light, he made out a small body lying on a slab of cement installed at the bottom of the pipe. Dr. Manning wrapped the whining dog's leash around his hand and moved closer.

Chapter 1

Patrolling the Streets of Baltimore

The radio crackled and the dispatcher came on the line. "Rossi, Crane, gotta possible domestic: 2044 Eastern Avenue. Anonymous. No previous calls for the address. Out."

"Affirmative. Will comply. Out."

Greg flipped his lit cigarette out of the window, and we sped through the darkened but not quiet streets of Baltimore toward Fells Point. After closing the windows, I fastened my seatbelt. Rossi never used his. Cameras, blue lights flashing, kept a careful lookout over the kids clustered on the corners—I wondered how often the lights served for target practice.

As had happened to me before, a call for a domestic elicited a painful flashback of Doug's investigation of Roberto Ortega. I missed my old partner and friend, but pulled myself back to the present. "Hey Rossi, I noticed quite a few city detectives using marked cars. What's going on? In Santa Barbara we used unmarked cars."

"Yeah, our detectives did, too, until a few months ago when an order came down from the brass requiring increased use of patrol cars."

"Why?"

"I guess the powers that be are trying to keep the community mollified—the city council is demanding transparency and visibility. The Commissioner went along with it."

"Sure gives the bad guys the advantage. There's also the safety of the public and their detectives to be worried about."

"Yeah, well now you're in Baltimore not California. This won't be the first thing to make you scratch that pretty head of yours—blonde hair, blue eyes, and *hot*—you're certainly going to be a stand-out on the streets I patrol."

Shades of Sonia, I thought. So much for the East Coast-West Coast distinction regarding political correctness, or the lack thereof, which had given Doug and me some good laughs. I'd moved to the West Coast with the belief they were all about political correctness, unlike the East Coast. Sonia put that belief to rest—the SB dispatcher, known for her inappropriate comments, frequently referred to the detectives with sobriquets related to her colleague's physical characteristics—flakita, gordito, chinito. She also provided nuggets, such as a repeated advisory for me to watch my backside, when sending me out on a call. Greg Rossi, from Brooklyn, New York, and Sonia Rodriguez from Santa Barbara, California, would make interesting partners—for me, each had been a problem. One ride-along and Ken O'Donnell would set Rossi straight in a millisecond. Since it was unlikely my old friend and colleague was coming to Maryland anytime soon, there was always the option of requesting a transfer. That, however, was a less than optimal way to begin my career of choice in a new city. Still, I was in no mood for overt sexism on the job. Baltimore presented sufficient challenges without last century personnel issues. It took me a full minute to realize I was being ridiculous—as the kids say, I needed to chill.

After introducing myself to my new partner—tall and a bit paunchy, with curly gray hair cut short, he, in turn, had given me the once-over. I knew from another colleague that this old-time tough and impatient cop had twenty-two years on the job—fourteen of them in Baltimore, the remainder in Brooklyn. His face reflected those years: a rigid jaw, worry lines that had metamorphosed into deep furrows, and sagging jowls dared anyone to cross him. Sarge assigned us to the part of Southeastern that included quirky Fells Point—often a smorgasbord of problems.

In the car, Rossi described his expectations. Pretty clearly at that. Given his self-proclaimed seniority and tactical know-how, he insisted on being first in with me as back-up. Training or experience did not count for much I thought irritably as he continued to set limits, in considerable detail, for every conceivable situation. "Partner-in-training" was how he repeatedly referred to me, though I definitely understood how to work a scene. He definitely was going to be a pain!

My partner pulled up to the address given by the complainant and parked in front of a darkened house two doors down. I did *not* need him to tell me the obvious: "It never pays to be in the line of fire." Once out of the car, the blues and reds flashing, we heard a man and a woman yelling at each other inside 2044. Despite the volume, not a single neighbor was in evidence. Well, as far as I could tell.

The mayor, intent on building up the tax base of the city, had recruited Latin American families from the DC area. Aware of the high concentration of Latinos living in this neighborhood, I spoke up, "Greg, an FYI—I speak Spanish and understand more."

"Good, but follow my lead."

"Of course." It was all I could do not to add a sardonic "*Sir*."

Once on the landing, Rossi whispered, "I don't know how you're used to policing; in Baltimore we put an ear to the window before knocking. That way we can listen to what's going on inside. The guys call the front door the fatal funnel … and gals." He threw the last two words into the mix with only the barest hint of sarcasm. *More subtlety than I expected.*

"Request an additional unit—sounds pretty fucking heated—tell dispatch it's for officer safety. We'll wait for reinforcements to arrive before we go in. Dealing with domestics can be a friggin' nightmare. I'll take gangbangers any day—they're more predictable."

He was right there—I moved to the sidewalk and called in. Less than five minutes later, a patrol car pulled up and I rejoined my partner.

"Okay, let's see what's up. Those two can stay out here." Rossi signaled the newly arrived officers accordingly, and positioned himself to the left side of the door. I stood to the right. We drew our weapons.

Greg rapped hard on the door and stepped back. "Baltimore City police. Open the door—that's an order!"

Nobody answered. "Go ahead," he said, with a thrust of his jaw in the direction of the door.

I knocked. "Baltimore police here—Officer Robin Crane. Please open the door; we just want to talk with you."

I pulled back, ambivalent about the overhead light. The yelling had stopped, which could mean about anything. During those tense moments, a discussion with Matt one night over dinner came to mind. Though he'd never been to Baltimore, he *had* seen the television series, *The Wire*. I laughed at the time, telling him the popular show did not exactly represent Baltimore as so many people had come to believe. Later, I discovered the man who was now my husband had seen the series *twice*. He was pushing for us to watch it together. As I waited to find out what was going on behind the closed door, I figured I might want to take back my assessment of the program. It seemed a long time before the lock turned, though it was probably less than a minute.

The door opened to reveal a terrified couple—pupils dilated, mouths clenched, and body stances rigid. The man standing in front of me was cleaning wire-rimmed glasses, his expression strained. Under other circumstances, his was almost certainly a pleasant face. Dressed in a long-sleeved purple Flacco football jersey—number five on the front—faded blue jeans, and Nike shoes, he was slim, clean-shaven, with straight black hair on the longish side. The woman was shorter but also thin. Childish barrettes held curly hair back from her face. She appeared Latin American with her brown eyes and dark skin. The woman was breathing rapidly and focusing on the floor. We reholstered our firearms.

"Come with me, sir!" Greg's voice boomed out an order rather than a request. "We've had a noise complaint for this address."

"We're sorry, Officers. *Nothing* wrong is going on here, just a normal husband-wife disagreement," the man insisted. He moved a few steps forward and then stopped at the threshold with arms crossed, and resolutely stared over our heads.

"Sir, I'm not saying anything is wrong. We want to keep things that way, so how about you come outside and talk." My partner, contrary to departmental protocol, took hold of the tense man's elbow and firmly led him out of his house to the small seating area near the front stoop.

Rossi signaled to the officers standing by their car. "Davis, remain with Crane. Santiago, you stay put."

After Rossi had finished hollering orders, I directed my attention to the scared woman who now stood alone in the doorway biting the cuticle of her left thumb. "Ma'am, I'm Officer Crane." I showed her my badge. She didn't look up. "No need to be scared—you're not in any trouble, we just want to make sure everything is all right. Do you mind if we come in?"

She barely nodded her head, but I took the slight movement as assent. Davis and I entered the tiny foyer. Steep narrow stairs went to the second floor. To the left, I saw a living room and figured the dining room was located further back.

"Ma'am, why don't we sit down and talk?" Without waiting for an answer, I led the way. I passed through the front room and stood to the side until the woman was seated. I surreptitiously looked around the dimly lit room. The only other piece of furniture was a mahogany sideboard with three slim drawers above two cabinets. On top sat a clear glass vase of purple silk irises and several framed photographs. From my jacket pocket, I removed a notebook and pen. A nonchalant Davis remained leaning against the wall. He said nothing.

"Let's begin with your name, why don't we?" I asked the question gently and for the first time she looked at me directly.

"Marisol Jimenez. Officers, can I get you anything to drink?" By now, her thumb was beginning to bleed where she'd been chewing it.

"No thank you," I said. She glanced in Davis' direction; he shook his head.

"Ms Jimenez, we received a call about a fight coming from your home. Are you okay?"

"Yes, of course. I'm sorry, Officer—I guess we got kinda loud."

"Ma'am, do you mind telling me what's been going on? We'll be on our way, but we don't want to return. You should know that if multiple calls come in over time for this address, there is a possibility responding officers would issue a citation for acting in a disorderly manner that disturbs public peace. Not so good—the ticket is five hundred dollars and the police can fine the property owner. Another report comes in and the City can double the charge to a thousand; then the landlord will have a problem on his or her hands. But first, ma'am, are there children in the house?"

"No, just us. Me and Johnny, my husband."

"Are you hurt in any way?"

"Hurt—no way! Johnny would *never* hurt me," she said vehemently, with a fierce glare.

"Well, ma'am, I want to believe you. I do. But if that's the case, why the yelling?"

"We're married. Officer, married people fight," Marisol said tersely through pursed lips. She began chewing on the cuticle of her other thumb.

"True, Ms Jimenez, but not usually loud enough for a 911 call."

"Sorry," she said apologetically. "I guess I lost my temper."

I tried again. "Anything you want to tell us?"

"Not really." Marisol sighed. The woman took almost a minute to make up her mind about something. "We don't have any children but what I didn't tell you was that Johnny's sister and her daughter were living with us. My sister-in-law is a problem and always has been, but

I put up with her because she's family. Brenda's daughter, now that's a different story—I love my niece. In any case, Brenda wanted money and I did *not* want him to give it to her. At first, my husband sided with me, which made her furious. Officer, when she gets angry, it's something else. I'm surprised someone didn't call 911 then. *That* would have made my day."

Now that Marisol had started talking, I remained quiet to see where it took us. When she'd finished, however, the reason for the fight remained unclear. I caught Davis' eye and he shrugged.

Something was up, so I continued to probe. "And where are your sister-in-law and niece now? By the way, ma'am, what are their names?"

"Brenda and Joey. Well, most of the yelling tonight was about them. When her mother said she was leaving, Joey started crying— she's happy living with us; her science project is due in a couple of days. Brenda screamed at Johnny, telling him in no uncertain terms that any brother who threw his sister and niece out on the street was a son-of-a-bitch because he knew she didn't have any money."

"Was he throwing his sister out or was she threatening to leave?"

"My husband was *not* throwing Brenda out! He loves his family, so what did the dumb lug do?" Without waiting for my answer, Marisol continued, "I'll tell you what he did. Johnny gave Brenda most of our rent money! I swear she'll put it up her nose."

"Okay, ma'am, I guess I understand. Do you know where Brenda and Joey went? By the way, is Joey a nickname?"

"Yes. Her name is Josephine but everyone calls her Joey. I have no idea where they went but, Officer Crane, they wouldn't go far. Johnny's family moved here from DC and that's where her ex lives."

I wasn't sure why this woman was so worried. Or why I should be concerned—well, unless there was a drug problem contributing to child abuse. With that in mind, I decided to take a full report—you can never tell where things might lead. "Brenda's last name?"

"Same as Johnny's, Jimenez—but they don't write the accent over the first *e*. My family came from El Salvador; my father says there is an accent. Johnny says, 'Forget it'—he's American."

17

"Why don't you give me a description of your niece? Let's start with her age."

"Eleven."

"Physical description?"

"Really pretty brown eyes with long lashes. Joey has light hair—more blonde than brown; she likes it cut above her shoulder and insists on not having bangs."

"Good. Height?"

"Let's see, she is about 5-foot-2, maybe a little more because she's gone through a growth spurt. I'm not sure how much she weighs; I doubt it's more than a hundred pounds—she's very thin."

I wrote down the description, a habit I had acquired from Doug. "Thank you for your cooperation, Ms Jimenez. Please give me a minute—Officer Davis will keep you company while I go outside to talk with my partner." Despite my relief that the woman had calmed down—well at least she was no longer trembling—I felt unaccountably concerned, perhaps because a child was involved. I've always hated abuse cases—somehow, as a society, we must to do a better job of protecting our children.

Outside, I was surprised by the sight of a relaxed Rossi sitting on a lawn chair, smoking. Also at ease, Johnny sat on a step, feet propped on a cracked clay planter housing dead pansies. Smoking. I quickly understood that I had interrupted an enthusiastic dissection of the Orioles' win against the Red Sox. Davis' partner was leaning against their car.

"Hey, Crane, guess the sister's responsible for the ruckus. Well, indirectly. Anyway, all's okay with my pal, here."

"And my wife," Johnny added.

"Mr. Jimenez, please remain seated while I talk with Officer Rossi. It'll just take us a minute."

"Sure. Just don't want charges. We didn't do nothing."

"I understand, sir. Greg, can I see you for a minute?"

He followed me far enough from the house that we couldn't be overheard; I said quietly to my now unconcerned partner, "Are we in agreement about what is going on here? This isn't a domestic. According to the wife, most of the fighting happened before the sister took off with their niece *and* the rent money—the latter, more or less freely given. The noise called in was between a frustrated wife and her husband—maybe somebody became worried because of the loud arguing that had taken place earlier. I saw nothing indicating physical violence. No previous calls from this address."

"I agree, California. We're done here. After all, this is Baltimore—plenty of places to go, people to see."

"Rossi, what about the young girl the sister is dragging through the streets of Baltimore in the middle of the night? Marisol thinks Brenda is out to score drugs now that she has money."

"The mother is an adult and the girl is her daughter. There's no evidence she's an abusive parent or is using—just an angry sister-in-law's suspicions. You don't even know they're on the streets. Anyhow, it's too hot to be wandering around the city—I guarantee they're at a friend's house. California, we're *done* here." Though said in a tone brooking no argument, he laughed. We went back to the house.

"Johnny, my man, you can rejoin your wife but do me a favor and keep the racket down—aggravating relative or not." Without waiting for an answer, Rossi walked up the stairs, poked his head through the doorway and yelled for Davis. He turned around and headed to the car.

With the husband in tow, I returned to the dining room. "Thanks, I'll be just a second," I said to the departing officer.

"Yes, ma'am."

Johnny sat down next to his wife at the table and took her hand. "Hon, it's okay. I'm sorry about this." "Mr. and Mrs. Jimenez, we appreciate your cooperation." I handed a card to each of them. "Please call if I can be of any help. Have a good night."

"Good night," Johnny said. "I apologize," he added, studiously cleaning his glasses, again, all the while avoiding looking at me. Still, he sounded contrite.

Marisol smiled in my direction, silently mouthing a thank-you. Her husband put his glasses back on and they trailed me to the door, closing it gently behind me without saying anything more.

I expected no further calls that night, but was sure this would not be the end of trouble for the people living in this rowhouse. When I got into the car, I started to put my notebook into the glove compartment, but then thought to add a reminder to check into the policies of the Child Protective Services and maybe the state Child Recovery Unit. What I did know was that we didn't have anything warranting a referral to CPS.

———

Although things remained quiet for the rest of the evening, it was well past midnight when Rossi finally got around to talking about more than his expectations of me as his "partner-in-training." He took a pack of cigarettes out of his vest pocket, removed one and lighted up before rolling down the window and blowing out a long thoughtful trail of smoke.

"Crane, I heard you were on the job in Santa Barbara before coming east. Do I have it right?"

"Boy, word gets around quickly! Yeah, that's right," I said, thoroughly distracted—I could hardly believe my partner smoked in a patrol car. Despite the heat—it felt more like summer than spring—I flipped off the air conditioning and rolled down my window.

He laughed. "Yep, word *does* get around, but you should know that—you're a Bawlmer girl! Seriously, the locals seem to use a special method of communication when it comes to their own." He took another drag on his cigarette.

"Rossi, I left Baltimore years ago! In truth, it's been over a decade and I'm probably as much of an outsider as you are—being from Brooklyn and all."

"C'mon, Crane, you'll never be an outsider—this isn't really a city—Baltimore's a small town. Besides which, *hon*, it doesn't matter because I have learned to interpret the chatter. The reason I asked was I've lost track of two buddies from my NYPD days. Last I knew, both were on the job in California, though they might be retired by now; I hate to admit it but we're all winding down. A long shot, but I wondered whether you'd heard of Tony Martinelli or Kenny O'Donnell."

"O'Donnell! *Absolutely!* Not Tony Martinelli—sorry, I'm not familiar with that name, but Ken is a good friend of mine. In fact, he's the Chief of the Santa Barbara PD." I didn't bother mentioning the groans accompanying Ken's promotion when the Department's beloved Chief Bartolo retired early and took off with his wife and daughter on his boat, *Crime Fighter*.

"Well, I'll be damned ... O'Donnell's a friggin' Chief? Goddamn, isn't that something!"

I was surprised at his emotional response and taken aback by the knowledge my partner was acquainted with a friend of mine. "Boy, what a small world. I'll give you his contact information when we get back to the house. Rossi, I'm concerned about the girl."

"Girl. What girl?"

"The domestic. The sister-in-law and niece."

"For now, there's nothing to follow-up; if we need to, we'll get right on it. *Bawlmer* has plenty going on to keep us busy. Trust me on this."

"Rossi, she's a child, we must be able to do something."

"California, why expend our already limited resources on a girl who is safe and sound in somebody else's house? Anyway, they're probably in DC and well out of our jurisdiction. Cool it."

The phrase, "famous last words," ran through my mind. "Well, I'll just do that."

He must have heard the edge in my voice.

"If you're so concerned, keep your eyes open. There are a lot of street kids around here—see if one of them knows anything. Make an effort to establish a relationship or two; you might acquire a useful confidential informant—but be sure your CI is over eighteen and go through the necessary channels."

"Thanks for the idea," I said and meant it.

"Why are you making such a big deal out of this? There's nothing to say the sister isn't taking care of her child. The sister-in-law sure as hell doesn't want the Jimenez broad around, so why would the woman leave her daughter behind? Makes no sense. Crane, you've certainly got enough experience to realize that emotional involvement in a case seldom pays off."

"Probably, but—"

"But what?"

"Rossi, to be honest—"

"By all means, be honest—"

"I will, if you'll give me a minute of uninterrupted time and an open mind."

"Snitty, are we?"

"Seriously, Greg, I want to find the girl."

"California, there is *nothing* to say she's lost."

Chapter 2

Hangin' at Fells Point

I arrived in Baltimore in October of 2013 to take the Civil Service Test before undergoing BPD's required interviews, polygraph, background investigation, and medical and psychological exams. Once cleared, I began the police academy program.

Six months later, the field training began: the Major paired me up with Greg Rossi in the Southeastern District for ninety days. When I raised the possibility of working in Homicide, I learned my next detail would be with the Gangs and Guns Unit. At that point, he assured me he would make some calls on my behalf regarding Homicide. Unbelievably complicated, given the years I'd already spent as a detective in Santa Barbara. Still, I needed his support. Matt was not thrilled with the plan.

After a week on the job with Rossi, I again made a conscious decision to lighten up, deal with my partner's eccentricities and concentrate on learning what policing the Baltimore streets meant.

———

"Hey, Greg, I didn't get much sleep after last night's shift—how about some coffee? We took Sean to the doctor this morning—he has an ear infection. God forbid there's trouble on the streets tonight." I would soon learn that it was a wish thrown out to the universe the people of Baltimore would roundly ignore.

"Good idea—I'll take a Coke. I can't understand the hot coffee. *Iced* coffee would make more sense in this damn heat. How about a stop at Jimmy's? At the same time you can pick up an order of fries for me—ketchup, salt, plenty of napkins."

"I drink hot coffee—stronger that way—for the same reason you consume an inordinate amount of fries: fuel."

Rossi turned up Broadway and stopped in front of the popular diner located in the heart of Fells Point. After a hefty delay, I placed my order. While waiting for my change, I scanned the room bustling with activity despite it being after midnight. At the far end of the room, seated at a corner table, was the couple from the domestic dispute we'd responded to on Eastern two weeks ago. Curious about the outcome, I decided to chance approaching them. Could be I wouldn't be welcome, but they didn't seem the type to make a public fuss.

"Mr. and Mrs. Jimenez, what a surprise running into you." I lowered my voice to a whisper when neither responded. "Robin Crane—"

"How can we forget—why are you here?" Johnny asked quietly, the muscles rippling in his jaw. He took off his glasses and concentrated on cleaning the lenses.

Marisol glanced from her husband to me and then back again. "Hi, Officer Crane, what *are* you doing here?"

"Just making a caffeine run. My son has an ear infection and I didn't get much sleep before the evening shift began. *And* my partner needs his fries." I laughed, hoping to calm Johnny. It seemed to work; the facial muscles relaxed and he stopped fiddling with his glasses and put them back on.

"Johnny, remember Joey's horrendous ear infections?"

"*Nobody* in the house slept! I hate it when she gets sick," he said fondly.

Marisol gave me a beseeching look and I decided to take Johnny's recollections as an opening. "Have you seen your niece lately?"

They looked at each other. He redirected his attention to the menu, and his wife replied instead. "We tried to reach Brenda to smooth things over but had no luck. Officer Crane, I want to apologize. Joey is only a child, and I was worried." She began picking at a cuticle. I avoided eye contact with her husband, who remained occupied with the menu. When he finally set it down, Johnny covered his wife's hand with his. "Don't worry, they'll be back; you'll see, she's okay. Hon, you've got to know that even if Brenda has her problems, she loves her daughter."

"I hope so," she mumbled, not looking convinced. "Sorry again, about everything."

I barely heard her over the noise in the restaurant. Surprisingly, nobody appeared interested in our conversation, but I noticed the cashier trying to get my attention before I could say anything else. "I think my order's ready. You have my card."

Marisol smiled. "We'd better figure out what we want—the place is busy tonight. Good night, Officer."

"Thanks. You too."

I left without looking back. Despite the heavy traffic, Rossi had remained double-parked in front of the restaurant. I threaded my way across the crowded sidewalk, handed the drinks and food through the open window and got in.

"Hey, girl, Jimmy's taken to growing and grinding the beans? Or, did you demand a fresh pot?"

"No, wise guy, it was your fries that took the time! Well … and … Rossi, I ran into that couple from the Fells Point domestic we responded to a few weeks ago."

"Who?"

"Johnny and Marisol Jimenez—fight with the sister, *missing* niece."

"Oh, that call. Yeah, what about it?"

"I guess they're feeling remorseful about us showing up on their doorstep. More importantly, I think the wife is concerned about her niece and wants to make amends with her sister-in-law."

"So they should get it together. What's the big deal?—families fight." Rossi popped a cluster of fries into his mouth. Ketchup settled on his chin.

"They *are* willing to work out their problems but can't locate Johnny's sister. This time, he didn't pooh-pooh his wife's concerns. I had the sense that something's going on that worries them both."

"Well, California, there's not much of anything we can do. We are *not* social workers. People want us to raise their children—no can do, not part of my job description."

I figured I would back off, at least for the present. "How's your Coke—sugar and all? Let's not forget your fries—fat and all!"

"Fries, I tell you, are a necessity when working night shift. Anyway, what's the point of those no sugar, no caffeine drinks?" Rossi didn't wait for my answer; instead, he slurped his drink and ate the fries as quickly as he could drag them through the ketchup.

"Let's park by the pier, so I can keep an eye on the square. There has been a string of complaints from shop owners about street kids intimidating tourists. As *you* suggested, maybe I can make contact with some of the teens who hang out around here."

Rossi snorted and pulled into a spot in front of the area where the city kept the water taxis docked. I understood why there had been complaints: some panhandled on the sidewalk; despite the honking, others migrated into the road when cars approached. Driving on cobblestones was difficult enough without dodging kids.

The group quieted down after we pulled up, but after ten minutes of a police cruiser in their midst they resumed their activities. One or two continued hitting up pedestrians for money; it seemed their idea of a compromise was to stay out of the road.

Although using a young CI would be problematic, it wouldn't hurt to try—at least short-term. "Rossi, I'm going to go chat them up. They sure don't look like bangers to me. A few may be street kids, but my guess is most of them are from the burbs—I can't imagine what they're doing downtown at this hour."

"Go for it, California. I'll notify dispatch." He pulled out a cigarette.

I got out of the car, coffee in hand. The volume of the music and their rowdy voices lowered noticeably as I approached. An older kid, perhaps early twenties, took off. A couple of them jammed their hands into their pockets. I laughed to myself, hoping nobody would set his or her pants on fire—there was probably a burned finger or two at play.

"Officer, can we help you?" a boy sitting on the back of a bench asked nonchalantly. When I had watched from the car, he'd been clowning around—now this preppy-looking boy with longish dark hair sat there stiffly, definitely on guard—eyes darting between the cruiser and me. I guessed him to be about 16 or 17; tall, athletic (probably a lacrosse player), dressed in khakis, white shirt and a loosened tie—he went to a private school for sure. I had gone to a local Catholic school, but not one of the well-heeled north Baltimore schools this kid surely attended. His bravado drew titters from two of the girls, which caused him to preen and further play to his audience. I decided to give him his two minutes.

When they quieted, I introduced myself. "Hi, I'm Officer Crane. You?" I put my hand out to shake his.

He hesitated for a couple of seconds, pulled himself together and stood up. "Anthony … well, Tony," he corrected, extending his hand. I gave the boy credit for a firm handshake and meeting my eyes directly.

"Hi, Tony, I'm new to the area, getting to know Fells Point. Looked like you were having a good time, so I figured I'd introduce myself." That did the trick. Everyone seemed to relax.

"Where did you work before you came here?" one of the girls asked, actually sounding interested. Maybe a year or two younger than Tony, the slight, pretty girl was also wearing a uniform—it would be worth learning which schools require which uniforms. Slung over her shoulder was a worn backpack on which she'd pinned political and social buttons.

"California."

Tony visibly perked up at that information. "Where?"

"Santa Barbara. You know California?"

"Yeah, my aunt lives in San Diego—she taught me to surf. *Nobody* gets bored there. A bunch of actors and musicians live in Santa Barbara—pretty cool!"

"Why would you leave to come to *Baltimore*?" another uniformed girl asked incredulously.

"Well, as I'm sure you know—things happen. I was originally from here, and as you are probably aware, most Bawlmoreans return to Bawlmer."

I got a laugh with that comment or perhaps the blue-collar accent, who knows. After answering more questions, I figured it was time to move along; I hoped that I had established some sort of connection with the kids—they appeared at ease. I tossed my cup into the trash-can. "Good to meet you all."

"Same," responded Tony.

"Bye, Officer Crane," said the girl who could not imagine why I had left California for Baltimore, now that she knew actors and musicians really *did* live in Santa Barbara and, of equal importance, that the city was located on the coast.

"Good night, kids. Stay safe." Without looking back, I returned to the car and knocked on the window. Rossi unlocked the door and I got in.

"Jeez, Rossi. There has to be a policy about smoking in public vehicles. Don't you know anything about the evils of secondhand smoke? At least roll down the window."

"It's too damn hot to worry about ridiculous regulations. Anyhow, wouldn't be good for the air conditioner."

"Well, if you're not going to crack the window, don't smoke. Best of all, quit smoking. Even those kids would show better sense!" I dialed things back. "Never mind, Rossi, I'll open the door."

"Have it your way." He rolled down the windows but left the air conditioner running.

"Thanks, partner."

"How'd the social work effort go?" he asked snidely, thrusting his jaw in the direction of the plaza.

"Just getting to know the natives. Rossi, give me a break, you were the one who suggested I make some contacts. Any idea where they're from?"

"Some are escapees from north of the city, neighborhoods where I'm sure the parents have absolutely no clue that their precious kids are in *Fells Point* at this time of night."

"What are they doing down here?"

"What do you think? Scoring some weed or pills, hanging out— dabbling in the forbidden. After several hours they get into their expensive cars, drive to expensive homes and climb into comfortable beds. In the morning, the bozos put on their uniforms and head off to private schools. Then there are kids who actually live in the neighborhood and several who are runaways or throwaways. Some dealing drugs."

"Dabbling in the forbidden, great. Where do the homeless kids go at night?"

"Depends. Some crash at a friend's house. If the weather isn't too bad there are plenty of abandoned houses in the city, but staying in one of those can be dangerous because drug dealers and junkies use them—sometimes they serve as body dumps."

"Body dumps—like in *The Wire*?"

"Yep. Some simply kill onsite; others use them to dispose of bodies. They help the decomp process along by pouring bags of lime over the corpses. In any case, back to your question: Yes, there are shelters."

"Pretty sad situation."

"Not our concern, California—like I said, save it for the social workers. Are you sure that you're in the right line of work? Anyhow, enough of that. Now that we're done here, we'll see what kinda crime's goin' down in Upper Fells Point. Let dispatch know we're outta here."

"On it." Before I did anything, the radio crackled.

"Rossi, Crane, I've got a call for you. Homeless man on the promenade between the Marriott and the footbridge crossing over to Pier Six Pavilion. He was hassling tourists, one of whom didn't take it so well when the guy almost ran over the wife with his bike, cursing a blue streak as he pedaled. He's combative; bicycle patrol officers on the scene asking for back-up."

"We're on it," I responded. "Out." Rossi rolled up the windows, turned on the reds and blues, and we headed to the scene. Cars cleared a reluctant path on the narrow streets. Once there, we found a tall, emaciated man wearing a torn jacket and navy blue watch cap, a filthy backpack slung over his shoulder. He was hanging onto a battered bicycle with one hand and waving the other in the general direction of two police officers. Behind them stood a man and a woman who appeared to be the victims. As dispatch had reported, the husband was aggravated; the woman, whom I assumed to be his wife because they wore wedding rings and matching shirts, was obviously anxious. Rossi and one of the officers moved away a short distance and spoke quietly for several minutes before returning.

"Sir, I'm sorry for what happened here," Rossi said to the husband in a friendly tone I seldom heard. "We apologize for the inconvenience and upset you experienced. My colleague will take your information and then you might like to go over to McCormick's and relax for a bit on the patio—there are some excellent, very reasonably priced specials today." He pointed in the direction of the restaurant.

"Thank you," was all the man had to say, the wind now out of his sails. His wife continued clutching her husband's hand.

"You there, take our friends here to that bench so they can sit down." The young officer walked off with the couple, probably relieved to increase the distance between themselves and the mentally ill man who continued to curse. With the tourists out of range, Rossi tried to talk him down, but in short order the guy let loose with an expletive and a right hook that missed by a mile. With that, my partner cuffed him.

"California, put the backpack in the trunk. I'm not going to stand around waiting for the wagon to arrive." Gingerly, Rossi took the man by the elbow and put him in the back seat of our vehicle for the short drive to Central Booking. "Buddy, take care of the bike," he told the remaining officer.

"Sure thing, Rossi. Thanks for the help. It's been busy—bunch of loons out tonight."

Greg Rossi might have his faults but his experience showed when it mattered; well, other than his unwillingness to wait around for transportation. "This might be a mistake, Rossi. We're liable to have to go clean the car after leaving him off."

"C'mon, buddy, shut the hell up—they're taking care of your bike. Might even put some air in your tires. Yeah, California, I might regret this but I'm not standing around all night. I'm sweating, and the mayor will be all kinds of pissed if tourists complain about a poor police response or do that damn blogging and Facebooking about Baltimore City crime. Better to get the douche outta here. The complainants won't run into him again, our friend has a bunk for the night and some grub, and we go home without some stupid ass problem hanging over our heads."

We pulled into the parking lot a few minutes later and took our prisoner into Booking. As I waited for our guy to be processed, I spotted a boy who had been in Fells Point earlier that evening. While chatting with the others, he'd remained panhandling on the sidewalk. He was definitely not one of the kids who, at the end of the night, got into an expensive car and went home, unless it was with a john, I thought sadly.

I walked over to where the boy sat on a bench. "Hi there, weren't you on Broadway with some other kids earlier? Officer Crane—you remember me?"

"Sure. The Santa Barbara cop."

"Yep, that's me. Why are you here—at Central Booking? Were you picked up for panhandling?"

"No. The others left," he mumbled.

I was confused. "So, why are you here?" If I remembered correctly, he was one of the kids who had put his hands in his pockets when I approached the group. Maybe he got popped. All the same, nobody seemed to be paying him any mind, and I doubt he'd been holding much.

"Stopped by is all. Ain't done nothing wrong."

"Didn't say you did. Where are you sleeping tonight? I hope not on that bench. If that's what you had in mind, it looks pretty uncomfortable."

"I'm on my way to the shelter."

"That's good. What's your name?"

"Seth."

Noting his dilated pupils, I avoided asking his surname. "Well, Seth, is there a room for you?"

"Yeah. Already took care of it."

"Sure?"

"Signed up earlier at the Fellowship."

"Hey, California, our buddy's all set," my partner called out, his expression turning uncharacteristically surly at the sight of Seth. "We've got a call. Let's *go*."

"Good night, Seth—be sure to stay safe."

"Yeah, I'll like do that," he laughed and plunked himself back down.

I wondered what was really going on. I hoped that Joey Jimenez was not in a similar predicament although, in reality, a homeless kid was probably safer hanging out in Booking than walking the streets all night. Be that as it may, despite the chaos in the place, I was sure he wouldn't be allowed to hang around there indefinitely.

"What was that about?"

"Just chatting."

Chapter 3

Still in Transition

As **I pulled** into the driveway of the home Matt and I purchased in Mt. Washington, I thought of nothing more than a shower and a nap. A realist, I was confident I would get the shower but no sleep. If so, I would attack some of our still packed boxes.

Close to the Montessori School Sean now attended, and the beltway, the house was a great find and the timing had been right—housing prices had fallen. With Matt out of work, we were fortunate that we had enough money for the down payment and closing costs, mostly because of what he'd saved while living in a cabin in the mountains of Santa Barbara provided to him by the Park Service. I love my parents but after residing with them for a few months, I discovered myself regressing to adolescence and what comes with that and my mother and father reverting to cranky parenthood—not a good combination. Though they denied it, they were probably as relieved as I was when the time came to move into my own home and they had theirs back to themselves.

A glassed-in porch, the large and sun-filled family room, and the spacious living room provided beautiful views of the trees surrounding the house. Best of all, I loved the kitchen with its cooking island and multiple skylights. I carried in the groceries and made a fresh pot of coffee. It was quiet: Sean was at camp and Matt had a meeting about a possible job.

After a long hot shower, I headed back downstairs. Annoyingly present were the boxes. I told myself that after a bit of down time, I would finish at least one. Mug in hand, I fled to the patio, placed my cup on the table and scooped seeds out of the covered storage container we kept in the woodbin. I settled into a rocker enjoying the flurry of activity as birds and squirrels scrambled for the food.

Living with my parents had compounded my discomfort with the decision I made to leave Santa Barbara. Despite my university education and previous policing experience, I was essentially starting all over. The rationale for further instruction of experienced police was that new hires needed to learn the laws and policies of Baltimore City and Maryland, as well as familiarize themselves with the city's geography, culture, and history. Perhaps that was all true, but nothing so far had persuaded me that they needed so much extra training. Nonetheless, I found myself intrigued by Baltimore's past.

Although a native *Bawlmer girl*, I quickly learned how little I knew regarding the evolution of my city, particularly as it related to race and law enforcement. Established in 1853, the Baltimore Police Department, comprising ten districts, was one of the oldest departments in the country. Historically, like many others on the Eastern seaboard, Irish American men dominated the BPD. Not until 1937 did they hire the first African American, who I was surprised to learn had been a woman, Violet Hill Whyte.

The landing of a flock of noisy starlings interrupted my train of thought. I gave them a few minutes to forage and then shushed them off.

While sipping my coffee, I resumed thinking about policing in Baltimore. A year after Whyte's hiring, the city proceeded to bring four African American men onto the force. The Command assigned them to the streets in plainclothes. It took five more years before they were in uniform. I was taken aback to read that the BPD had remained segregated until 1966, not *that* long before I was born. Even then, African Americans couldn't use squad cars; rather, white supervisors continued assigning them to foot patrols. Quarantined in rank and barred from working in white neighborhoods, perhaps the most insidious discrimination of all was the racial harassment by co-workers. In 1968, after the death of Martin Luther King, riots tore Baltimore apart, leaving 6 dead, 700 injured, 5800 arrested, and even deeper rifts in the citizenry.

Despite improved social conditions, I was acutely aware of the racially charged concerns around me while growing up in Maryland. Claims of discrimination, biased policing methods, and high crime rates in some neighborhoods persisted during the years I lived in California. It was no surprise to learn departmental functioning and local politics reflected those issues. If I had not been aware of it when I returned, it became crystal clear while engaged in field training that Baltimore would be a far more difficult city to police than Santa Barbara.

As I watched two squirrels munching on sunflower seeds, husks flying, my thoughts turned to my husband. I met Matt Webster, a Park Services ranger, in the mountains of Santa Barbara while working the Painted Cave case—an investigation into the senseless death of a promising young graduate student. Matt and I began seeing each other at that time, but life went awry and I backed off. It wasn't until one moonlit night when he laughingly pulled me, *fully clothed*, into the ocean that I imagined a future with the man whom Sonia Rodriguez, the SBPD dispatcher, had described as the "Marlboro man for the 21st Century"—this descriptor, by the way, of a man who does not smoke.

Stunned by Matt's proposal, it took me more than a month to accept. When we told my then eight-year-old son, Sean, he responded with squeals of excitement, jumping into a grinning Matt's open arms. The wedding, we agreed over celebratory pizza and root beer, would take place back east.

One night while discussing our future, Matt broached the idea of moving to Maryland. The decision to marry had been difficult; the thought of a cross country move left me further disoriented, and I asked for time to think. We eventually settled on investigating jobs, neighborhoods, and schools while in Baltimore for our June wedding.

———

Instead of going on a honeymoon after our small ceremony, the three of us—now a family—explored Baltimore and Washington, DC. Afterward, Matt and I checked out the region's professional possibilities. There was a plethora of opportunities for me; unfortunately, Matt was unable to find *anything* in the area. Available Park Service positions were located in DC or rural Maryland or Pennsylvania, any of which meant considerable travel. Despite concerns with the commute, we both believed it important to settle down close to my parents who live in Baltimore. On a whim, before returning to California, I submitted an application to the city police department.

A few weeks later, I was surprised to receive an offer from the BPD. Our concerns were no longer theoretical—we began to confront the mound of practical matters involved in a decision to move. After our late night discussions became increasingly stressful, Matt suggested it would be less disruptive for Sean to transfer schools midyear—during Christmas vacation. If we moved him right away, he wouldn't have the opportunity to say goodbye to teachers and friends—to transition more gradually. Matt proposed taking on the role of a stay-at-home dad as we adjusted to all the changes. That, he added, would give him more time to tie things up in Santa Barbara and to explore his own options, and for me to make sure the BPD was what I wanted. For me, his most convincing argument was that the arrangement would be a "good bonding experience" for Sean and him.

I left for Maryland, anxious despite Matt's assurance that the time would pass swiftly and his reminder that we live in an age of FaceTime and texting. And there's always the telephone. I would return to California for a couple of long weekends and Thanksgiving vacation, and then we'd pack up the house and the whole family would move at Christmas, celebrating the New Year in our new home. It was during one of those frequent long-distance conversations that I became cognizant of my difficulty in referring to *our* son, an issue I knew Matt must have registered, but one to which he never referred.

My coffee cold, the squirrels and birds returning to their respective nests, I went inside, poured another cup and headed upstairs to confront the boxes on the landing. Opening the first one, I thought back to how I came to be at peace once we chose to leave California. That is, *until* I arrived in Maryland. Quickly, I came to believe the move had been a mistake: I missed Matt and Sean, missed my Santa Barbara colleagues, and missed the West Coast. Policing the Baltimore streets was significantly different from what I had done, and I began to think of changing careers. Before my graduate forensics program and the Los Angeles Police Academy, I had focused on the educational needs of autistic children. When I called Matt one sleepless night, he pointed out that if I wanted to return to my previous profession of psychology, given the number of universities here, there would be plenty of opportunities. An option identified, I continued with my training.

As I unpacked one of my son's boxes, I remembered the kid I'd spoken with at Central Booking—Seth, who seemed relieved to have a bed in a homeless shelter; Seth, who couldn't be more than fifteen or sixteen, not that much older than my own son. I could not imagine what the boy was doing out on the streets. Next tour, I figured I would return on my own and look for him. I clearly needed to learn more about the services available for street kids in my city. *My city—well, that's an interesting shift.*

———

Evening was fast approaching when my cell rang. "Hi, Matt. How's it going?"

"Good. I'm calling to see whether I can talk you into pizza for dinner. If it's a go, I'll throw in a quality bottle of wine or root beer, your choice."

"Boy, you sure know how to turn a girl's head! How about you pick up the wine. I'll add root beer to the pizza order."

"You've got it, sweetie."

After we hung up, I dialed Pizza Boli and ordered the root beer, a Greek salad and two medium pizzas: one cheese and a mushroom and pepperoni. Thoughts of more unpacking happily on hold, I went downstairs and set the table. Tonight we were going to discuss going on a vacation.

Chapter 4

Gangs & Guns

Once detailed to the Gangs and Guns Unit, I found myself partnered with Tyrell Wilson, a Baltimore native. Married, Ty had three kids who, he assured me first night out, would put him in his grave long before any gang member managed to do so. Tonight, we were discussing the problems his teenage son had *last* year with an "unreasonable" math teacher when his cell phone rang.

He listened for what seemed a long time without interrupting and then patiently replied, "Hon, I'm working. We need the overtime. *You* know that."

Even though I had quickly looked away, there was no pretending I couldn't hear his wife's response. She was pissed: it was *supposed* to be Tyrell's day off. I was embarrassed, though he didn't seem bothered at having an audience to the dispute. I had been answerable only to my son until I married Matt. For the *first* time it occurred to me that we should discuss, in greater depth, the stresses asscciated with my new job.

"Hey, hon, what 'ya want me to say, we've got bills to pay. Gotta go. Love ya, babe." Tyrell hung up.

"Wife's not happy—this job doesn't do shift for a marriage, but I guess that's pretty obvious!" He laughed and emptied his drink container.

I had nothing to say.

"What does your old man do?" Tyrell asked, all the while crunching his mouthful of ice.

"Well, in California, he was a ranger with the Park Service. Since we moved to Baltimore last December, Matt has been staying home with our son. That's coming to an end—Matt is actively searching for a job but there doesn't seem to be much in the immediate area, so I'm afraid there's a commute in our future."

The phrase, *our son*, still did not come without conscious though; still, I liked to believe it was becoming easier to say. More importantly, I was starting to buy into what I was saying. We had even discussed the possibility of Matt adopting Sean, which meant that my son's biological father, Stewart, would need to give up his parental rights. Never enamored of fatherhood, Stewart delighted in making me miserable, so I anticipated a long difficult road ahead to remove him from our lives. Matt had asked whether money might make a difference. It was a thought.

"Househusband—*sweet* deal for your old man," Tyrell commented, interrupting my reverie.

"It's been great. For all of us. How about you—how long have you been with this unit?"

"Always. Well, since I finished training." He laughed and added, "Back then we weren't required to go through the street gig before getting on to the real stuff!"

I was going to like working with Ty—he seemed an upbeat sort. And he didn't smoke. "I wish I'd arrived before that policy change."

"Who were you partnering with on patrol?"

"Greg Rossi."

"Oh, that explains it. The time has come for Rossi to retire—he's been on the force too long for everyone's good, including his own. Still, you've got to give him some credit—the man knows the job."

"He does. To be honest, and this stays between us, he made me crazy in the beginning, but I got used to his ways. In retrospect, I learned a lot about Baltimore law enforcement from him. What about this unit?"

"What about it?"

"You like it?"

"Me? Yeah, it's my second home. Some days my first."

I was surprised—G & G was considered by everyone I had spoken with to be high risk and, as a result, especially stressful. There was a high turnover. I thought back to his phone conversation of a few minutes ago and wondered how fond his wife was of what he was doing. Probably not so much. I was well aware that I didn't have much experience with the effects of a policing career on a relationship, but could see I would learn soon enough.

"How many years do you have with the unit?"

"Twelve plus."

"You like day or night tour better?"

"Nights but the bosses switch us around all the time. Still, I've been on the job long enough to be realistic about the hazards at night."

"I suppose you get used to them." At least, I hoped so.

"If you lose your edge, Crane, it's time to leave. Don't ever forget that. Believe me, I'm aware of the risk every day I go to work and, honestly, it's a good part of the problem with my wife."

"Ty, I understand what we do puts us at risk from the knuckle-heads; now, I'm learning that quite a few cops are pretty unhappy with the indecisive leadership."

"What I've learned over the years is that there are always those who'll complain, no matter what. Like with anything else, there are problems in G & G, some serious—I wouldn't say otherwise. Still, this is a good unit, though I preferred wearing civvies and driving an unmarked car—dumb shit changes make policing even riskier. In spite of the budget cuts, we go out in two pairs as much as possible, which is a good thing. *Always* keep your radio turned up, Crane—this advertising of ourselves is fuckin' ridiculous."

"Thanks. There's something else I've been curious about—how do the night and day tours coordinate in this unit when there's an overlap on a case or between them?"

"Great question—we work long hours, but at some point we go home and, with some cases, others pick up the investigation. I'll grant you, it can be tough. Even so, a level of cooperation is necessary if we're going to bring in the bad guys. To be honest, Crane, there are often problems because we're a hardass competitive bunch. More importantly, everyone is plenty aware of the rivalry that comes into play when arrest stats mean the next promotion." He laughed. "Or the lack of one, never mind the dreaded demotion."

"So—"

"—hey, there's a tail light out. Let's go!" Tyrell exclaimed cheerfully, flipping on siren and lights. With tires squealing, he took out after a black SUV sporting only one rear light.

"Ty, this is a gang unit … why are we worrying about malfunctioning tail lights?" I asked in disbelief.

"Well, California, you've got a lot to learn about Baltimore. We're in a high crime area. After we pull a questionable over, we look for anything out of place. Then with the license and registration we can determine whether the car is stolen or if there are outstanding warrants in the system."

Concerned at our speed, I concentrated on the Lexus GX 460 with its darkened windows. The driver hadn't shown any signs of slowing down.

Tyrell sped up. "Hey, California, we definitely have a good stop here! Not only is the tail light out, the tint is dark as shit, and *now* an evasion. You'll quickly learn vehicle stops work for us—that's when these guys are at their weakest and we're most likely to find something. First thing is to get the front windows down, but be careful of what's going on in the back, particularly with the tinting. Lots of guns on the Baltimore streets, no doubt about it." He shifted his focus. "Enter the plate so we have an idea of what we're dealing with."

I was feeling edgy as Ty squealed around a corner, two cars barely making it out of our way. What was I doing working in a large urban area with a serious crime problem? In Santa Barbara, there were two murders in a city with a population of 90,000 in 2013. In Baltimore, the same year, there were 235 homicides in a population of 622,000. Using the same ratio, there should have been only 14 murders for the year in this city. An unimaginable figure! I told myself it wasn't that I was searching for an adrenaline high, which seemed to be the case with some of my colleagues. *It's not the time to be thinking about Doug.* I focused and tapped the enter key; the computer sprang to life and I began inputting the make, model, and license of the vehicle. As I keyed in the last numbers, the SUV pulled over—midway between two streetlights.

The driver turned off the lights but kept the car running—billows of exhaust showed white in the night air. Tyrell had positioned our car at an angle to the rear of the Lexus, left the red and blues on, as well as the high beams. He waited while I pulled up the information, hoping we wouldn't be peeling out after a fleeing vehicle.

"What do we find?" Tyrell asked, not taking his eyes off the idling vehicle in front of us.

"Ran the tag number through the MVA database. The SVU has a valid registration and is insured—belongs to a Leroy Nichols. Lives on the east side.

"Glad to hear Mr. Nichols is a good boy but, unfortunately for him, his tail light is out and the tinting is excessive. Let's do it," declared my partner.

We got out and approached the SUV, guns hot, mag lights in hand, staying well behind the tinted front windows. The driver had turned off his vehicle. Leery of the unknown, I broke into a sweat.

Ty rapped once on the darkened window with his baton. "Sir, please roll down your windows." Our duty weapons were held in a ready fast position; as the windows ever so slowly opened, we raised them—I was sure Ty could see that I was shaking. At least a minute passed before they fully came down to reveal a skinny man looking everywhere except at the police officers standing on each side of his SVU. His hands jumped off the wheel. The pungent herb smell of burnt marijuana lingered in the air.

"Sir, please keep your hands on the steering wheel where I can see them," I ordered tersely. We pointed our weapons in his direction.

He complied. "Sir, who am I speaking with?"

"Leroy Nichols."

There was no passenger in the front seat, which certainly didn't rule out someone hiding in the back. I glanced down at the floor. "Tyrell, I've got something here."

The driver moved in my direction with a sudden and suspicious movement.

"Sir, don't even think about it." Hand on my weapon, I demanded, "Roll down the back windows and then step out."

He hesitated, still leaning over the center console.

"Sir, sit up straight and roll down the windows! *Now*."

The man I assumed was the driver of record, Leroy Nichols, sat up straight and shot me a nasty look. "Cain't get out with my hands on the wheel," he said mockingly.

For good measure, Tyrell barked, "Sir, please exit the vehicle slowly."

"You got no reason to stop me, Officer," he said sarcastically, shifting his baleful glare in Ty's direction. He still hadn't opened the back windows. "Judge will agree with my lawyer—'illegal stop!'"

I figured it was going to be a long night. What Ty said next confirmed that thought.

"Sir, you're not under arrest, but you're acting pretty suspicious and getting shot isn't on my bucket list. Smells like you just smoked a joint. You're twitching as if in need of a fix. Officer Crane, you know what we got here?"

"No, Detective Tyrell." Not sure where this was going, I was willing to play along. "What do we have here?"

"Well, Officer Crane, what we got us here is probable cause and we'll need to search the vehicle for contraband." He directed his full attention to the suspect. "Been partying, my man?"

The driver must have had second thoughts about the stance he had taken. He shrugged. "Ya got it wrong, man—just me in here and I weren't smoking nothin'. Officer, don' want me no trouble—got me a family. Without another word, the back windows came down.

"Crane, call for back-up."

Glad for my vest, I would feel even better when another car arrived. I radioed in; reinforcements would show shortly: "10-16." Finished, I left the radio turned up per Ty's suggestion. There had been vague talk about body cams—I was all for them. I opened the door and looked inside but didn't see anyone. There was just a pile of trash in the back, though I knew that given the lack of light I could be missing someone hidden further back. "Tyrell, ask him to open the back."

"You heard the lady, roll down the hatch window." The man tried to get out without acquiescing, but Ty put a restraining hand on the door. "Before you come out of the vehicle, man, I want you to unlock *all* the doors. Are you sure you're alone?"

"Yeah, yeah. Man, cain't get out, keep my hands on the wheel, be rolling down windows and opening doors at the same time," he protested irritably, before proceeding to do as asked.

Gun drawn, I approached the rear of the vehicle from the side. "All clear."

"Okay, take it easy, sir," Ty said, opening the driver's door fully. "*Now*, I want you to get out … slowly." Despite the caution, the man appeared likely to tumble right out onto the street.

I marveled at the shape our suspect was in—it was difficult to believe he had actually been driving through the streets of Baltimore and hadn't injured anyone. No wonder there are so many hit and run accidents in the city.

Tyrell reiterated his earlier warning. "*Leroy*, please calm down, we don't want you to hurt yourself."

I hadn't been able to check the MVA photo against the driver when I looked up the plate. "Sir, you are Leroy Nichols, aren't you?"

"What of it?"

"Sir, please hand your driver's license to the lady here."

I waited while he dug it out of a wallet crammed with hundred dollar bills. "Mr. Nichols, how about you sit on the curb while we examine your vehicle. I'm sure you don't mind, do you?" He asked the question in a solicitous tone, though I recognized my partner was not really giving him an option.

"Guess I got me no choice."

Ty frisked him before helping him sit down on the curb. "*Now*, you need to cross your legs."

Leroy complied, put his head in his arms and promptly nodded off. His head bobbed but his eyes remained closed.

"Crane, how about you keep our friend here company while I check things out."

"You got it." I stood by the man, prepared for trouble but less tense. Police were always at a disadvantage—the suspect knew the score, the cops seldom did. Ty disappeared into the vehicle, mumbling as he rummaged around. Leroy began to snore and I was afraid that before long he would pitch over into the gutter.

"Officer, I got me a bag of what appears to be marijuana and a baggie of pills from the floor in front of the passenger seat—could've rolled out. In the console we have paraphernalia—papers, a pipe, and some other stuff. What is this, Leroy?" asked Ty. "My, oh my, we've got something *else* here."

Leroy was on the nod or not interested in replying. I was relieved to make out an approaching patrol car—the stop had clearly escalated from "a rear light out."

Two detectives pulled alongside the SUV and angled across the front of the vehicle. They were out in a matter of seconds.

"California, guy got priors?" Trem asked.

"Hey there, Trem. Now that you're here, I'm going check. Ty's searching the car now. So far, we found weed, pills, and an unknown substance. Mr. Nichols here seems to be having problems."

"Hey, guys," Tyrell called out to them. "Our buddy stashed some serious bucks in here—a couple of thousand, at least. In addition to what was up front, there are several bags of what appears to be cocaine in the back seat map pockets—sandwiched between folded American flags, which I'll bet are from O'Malley's 1812 celebration. Regular drugstore and bank going on. Trem, Al, met Robin Crane?"

"Yeah, we've met." The officer I knew only as Tremor smiled. "What can we do for you guys? You seem to have the situation under control."

"Would appreciate your calling in for a report number—controlled dangerous substance violation. We weren't exactly sure what we had when we first made the stop; another team's needed for this one. Trem, come check out the goodies. Al, can you keep an eye on our friend here while Crane runs his paper? Here's the registration," he said to me. He handed a pair of gloves to Trem.

Al and I traded places and I left to enter the details into the laptop. People were beginning to gather. The Soundex number indicated the man driving the vehicle, Leroy Nichols, was the legal owner—license, registration, photo ID, and name all matched. There was nothing about gang affiliations but Nichols was on probation and did have an open drug distribution charge. I finished up and returned to the others.

From the rear of the vehicle, Trem called out triumphantly. "Well whadaya know. GUNS!"

Tyrell strode over to where Nichols sat and immediately yanked him up to a standing position. "Com'n, man, help me out here and stand up straight. Nichols knew the drill—he placed his hands behind his back, palms facing outward with thumbs up; Ty applied the cuffs. He lowered the prisoner back down to the curb, had him cross his legs, and returned to the vehicle. Al remained in place.

"California, we got us some heavy ass guns back here: dozen handguns … 40s and 9s. Two AKs. Ammo. Found the stuff where the spare's supposed to be—somebody with considerable talent built out the area."

"Hey, Leroy, what happens if your tire goes flat?" Tyrell asked the forlorn man slumped over, head in his arms.

At that, Nichols raised his head with an unexpected snap. "Man, I got some *good* tires on my ride; ain't going to be no damn flat."

I had gotten out of the cruiser just in time to hear that gem and burst out laughing. "Well, Mr. Nichols, you got me beat!" He looked at me, confused.

People were beginning to gather and not one of *them* was laughing. A few were videotaping the stop with their cells—everyone was now aware of their constitutional rights after some interactions turned out less than optimally for the police. YouTube was a definite draw. There were jeers concerning cops setting up poor blacks. Racism. I figured we had better wrap this up or call in another unit for crowd control.

"California, you run this guy?" He glanced around and saw what I had just seen. "We need to get a move on."

"Yeah, I see … get that. Ty, he *is* the owner of the vehicle. He's out on probation; the only open charge against him is for drug distribution. Other than going heavy with the window tinting and not replacing a tail light, he's been law-abiding about his vehicle—license and registration are up-to-date."

"Okay, why don't you guys take Mr. Nichols to Headquarters? And remember, bro," Tyrell laughed and punched Trem's shoulder, "it's our bust."

"Sure, man." Trem helped the unsteady man up from the curb. "Al, advise him of his rights."

The tall thin officer with a pockmarked face and thinning hair removed a card from his shirt pocket. "C'mon, Mr. Nichols, you need to listen: You have the right to remain silent. Anything you say can and will be used against you in a court of law. You have a right to an attorney—"

"Save your breath—I knows all that. Man, stuff ain't mine. I'm tellin' ya, Cuz took my ride to DC. He be using it a lot."

"Yep, Ty," said Al, "this is one good boy we got us here in custody. Beats me how he's been driving 'cause he's not doing so well on his feet."

"Took definite notice of that. We'll inventory the vehicle in prep to tow it to the city yard."

"Sir, pay attention to what I'm saying," Al demanded of the prisoner.

"No need to be talking so damn loud, man. Got me a hell of a headache and y'all making it worse. I was on my way to get me a cup of coffee when you flashed them lights—didn' see 'em. Listen to the peoples, man—racist bullshit!"

"Sorry about that," Al said soothingly, still focused on reading the words off the card he was holding. "Sir, please, I need for you to concentrate, whether you've heard this before or not. You have the right to remain silent, and anything you say can and will be used against you in a court of law; you have the right to consult with an attorney and to have an attorney present during questioning. If you are indigent, an attorney will be provided at no cost to represent you. Sir, do you want a lawyer?"

"Yo, told you, man, I didn' do nothin', so I don' be needing no damn lawyer—causes more troubles and costs me money I don' have." He lowered his voice, "I'm telling you, Cuz be having my ride—cain't blame me for what the bro's been up to. Kid's no good, always in some kin' of trouble."

Al laughed and said, "Okay, my man, you've been Mirandized."

"I heard them rights before. Don' wan' me no damn lawyer."

"Leroy, my man, let's go back to the district for a chat. There, you'll be comfortable while we get this straightened out," Al assured him.

"Man, I'm telling you, I don't know where them guns come from. Sure not be mine. Cuz and his frien' be using my car. An' them drugs in the back—only thing be mine is a bit of weed in the front. A few pills from the doctor. Man, I'm sick and need them pills. Damn, don' you know the weed goin' be legal any day? Why you wan' to do paperwork on that?"

I chuckled to myself. The man had a point about the marijuana. And the pills could have been prescribed—I have a friend who keeps some in the car in case she forgets to take one at home. I looked over at my partner who had snorted at the comment. "Mr. Leroy, you first said you were with your cousin. Now, Cuz has a friend. Can you give us some names? I'm sure we could help you out here."

"Cain't give you no names, Officer. Never said I would—he'll hurt me, my family. Cain't be snitchin' in Bawlmer."

"Okay. Trem, I think you'd better take him in," I said. A crowd was gathering. Big ears. Too many cell phones. Next, they'll be distributing flyers with our pictures—not so good for those working undercover. *Still, Doug would have liked working the streets of Baltimore!*

"You got some aspirins?" Leroy asked of nobody in particular.

"Sure, Mr. Nichols, we'll see what we can do for you," Al reassured him. "You're our new best friend," he whispered while helping the prisoner into the back seat.

"Would appreciate that, Officer Al." He settled down and it appeared as if he was going back to sleep.

Trem pulled out with his overhead lights on but no siren. Fun over, the crowd began to disperse. A few individuals let loose comments about police harassment but soon were on their way.

"Well, Crane, that was a good bust," Tyrell declared. "Late night stops can suck—never know what you're going to run into. There's just no way we've found to keep on top of these gangs. I'll take wild animals over them any day. C'mon, let's finish this up—too much going on with this vehicle; called for Crime Scene and they should be here any minute. I want to interview Leroy and find out what's going on here—I hate to say this, but he seemed surprised about the arms and the cash."

"Ty, why aren't our cars equipped with gun safes? If we go in as back-up for, say a shooting—we take the evidence with us, park the car, and some kid comes along, pops the trunk and takes off with the stash. Commits a crime with one of the guns. Not only that, the first bust is down the tube."

"You're right, it makes no f'ing sense. Just another one of those ill-considered budget issues—a mayor up for election. Folks want the shootings to stop, numbers to come down, but they think it's going to be taken care of by a miracle—never enough money for more police and equipment."

"Sounds like a war."

"Yeah, some days. Let's tie things up, so we can find out what the douche bag has for us."

"Okay, boss!" I laughed. I was beginning to feel that I would eventually belong.

Chapter 5

Snitchin'

Okay, Crane. We are *done* here," said my partner as he started up the car. Let's head back before Trem and Al screw up a good bust." We slowly made our way across town, dodging jaywalking pedestrians as we went.

"Ty, I was thinking about something you said earlier."

"Which was?"

"About the job and relationships—I'm curious as to how you make it all work—me being a *newlywed* and all." I laughed and hastily added, "Not necessarily yours."

"Ask away," he said distractedly, stopping for an apparently homeless woman crossing Fayette by the post office, her shopping cart brimming with an array of bags.

"For instance, what happens after a rough night, you walk through the door and into a wife who had her own bad day?"

"Good question—not an uncommon occurrence as I'm sure you'll discover if you haven't already. I'll tell you, Robin, it's not easy balancing home and the job. Work is tough to shut off just because it's the end of shift, particularly when things go south—we don't get the bad guy or one of the good guys gets hurt."

"How do you cope?"

"It helps to grab breakfast with some of the guys before heading home. A few chill out in a bar—drink too much. I'm not one of the boozers. Others go to the gym—sweat it off, take a shower and go home. Some focus on hobbies—biking, home improvement. From my experience, when a shift doesn't go well, the worst thing to do is start a heavy conversation about *anything* right after you walk through the door. Still, it's important to keep talking—though that's definitely easier said than done and—

"—well here we are," he said, without finishing his thought.

"I appreciate the advice."

"Anytime. Robin, why don't we get the families together sometime? I'll talk with Janie."

"That would be great—let me know."

Ty took a left onto Baltimore Street, drove for a block and pulled up at Central District. I wondered whether there was enough time to run over to Crazy John's for a sandwich but just as quickly changed my mind. Maybe later—the probability was high that Ty was also hungry. He didn't quite have Doug's appetite but, like my SB partner, he didn't much like missing a meal.

I followed him into the building. The blinds down but opened, the safety screens across the windows and door gave the room a secretive feel. Furniture more suitable for the dump sharply contrasted with the marble walls. We ran into Sarge at the elevator: shaved head, tall, heavy, reeking of nicotine, old time Irish, with a great smile and ready laugh belied by a conspicuous scar running down his left cheek and another just as prominent slicing through his eyebrow on the same side. Remarkably, nobody knew how he'd come to be injured.

"Hey, you two! Word is you got yourselves a busy night."

"Seems like it," Tyrell said cheerfully. "We'll know more after having a go at him."

"Roger. Keep me posted," he said, stroking the scar on his cheek with his forefinger, a habit of his. I tried, unsuccessfully, to maintain eye contact. Without saying anything else, he left with a smirk.

"Will do, sir," Ty said to Sarge's retreating back. "Crane, I'll be back in five."

"I'll be at my desk. Any idea what we're looking at time-wise?"

"Late—maybe nine, most likely after that. Depends on the suspect—think we're going to have to work for it tonight—he's been in the system."

"All right, then. I'm going to call Matt and tell him what's up."

"Got it."

It was with trepidation that I called home. Just when I thought I had gotten away with leaving a message, my husband answered.

"Hi babe," he said, obviously half asleep. "Good timing, I was just thinking about mixing up pancakes for tomorrow. The fruit is already washed and cut up. Thought we could sit down for breakfast together before I drop Sean off and go take care of my own stuff. The house will be quiet and I'm hoping you'll get a good morning's sleep. What's the ETA?"

I cringed, hesitating for a long minute before giving him the bad news. "Hon, you shouldn't wait for me. It's going to be a late shift—don't see myself getting out of here and home before you leave. Earliest will be nine, but Ty figures later. Either way, on time or not, I'll be caught up in the rush hour traffic."

"Robin, there's no doubt about it; a 14-hour plus day makes absolutely no sense. You must understand it's not safe, never mind healthy. What happens if you're called into court in the morning to testify and need to go back?"

"Matt, I can't talk now. Sorry, but there's nothing I can do about it—we have a good collar and it will take awhile to process. Just the nature of the job. *You* know that."

"Not really, Robin. Patrolling the hills of Santa Barbara and polic-ing downtown Baltimore are altogether different things. You know *that*. What about court?"

"Please, not now. I promise we'll talk. Anyhow, I'm pretty sure nothing's coming up for court."

"Well, stay safe. I'll take care of Sean. By the way, I arranged for the sitter to pick him up later, but if you leave for work at five and don't get back until seven or eight next morning—sometime after he's already left for camp or school—"

I interrupted him, not wanting to hear the rest of it. "Matt, I understand."

"Honey, it's time for a serious talk. Sean is not seeing enough of you. Period. Don't worry, he and I are doing well—we have fun and, for the most part, he respects my rules—but I am *not* his mother. This has been a huge change for him. Bottom line is he needs to see more of you."

"I understand, I do, but I can't discuss our personal lives now." As I said it, I recognized Matt's need to talk, but instead told him about the bust. By the time I had to hang up, he still wasn't happy but had managed to say he loved me. I knew that he did. We'd decided that any disagreements would not spill over into either of our jobs—a simple pact to agree to, but one not always easy to respect. Especially when a child is involved.

Just as I hung up, my partner poked his head over the top of the cubicle. "Crane, our boy is in interrogation—Boyd's keeping him com-pany." He laughed. "Not sure who's going to give up first, Boyd or the tweaker. My bet's on Boyd! They never make it easy on the newbies."

"Not too much of a newbie," I remarked. "At least I don't think he was in my class."

"The one before yours? Anyhow, the boy doesn't have your talents."

"Thanks, but I've probably got experience over him. Now what?" I asked. "What did Trem and Al get from him?"

"Nothing. Another call came in so they parked him in the room with Boyd and left. All for the better, but first I need to package the stuff and take it to Evidence Control. I'll see about some help so that we get to the tweak before he crashes. Crane, the suspect has an open distribution charge, right? Out on probation."

"Correct."

"Let me see his sheet before we question him. He apparently told Boyd he's got something important to give up, but will only talk with us … 'the brother and the ice queen,' as he put it." Ty laughed, and I couldn't help but join in—he had an infectious laugh, deep and resonant. It eased some of the stress from the conversation with Matt.

"The dude's got us down to a twitter handle!"

"Sounds like it. Anyhow, Boyd says despite Leroy's bullshit, he thinks he might actually have something."

"I'll print out his record. Shoot me a text when you're ready."

"Good. I'm going to get started—it won't take too long."

I returned several calls and had no more than reexamined Leroy's history when I heard from Ty. I went downstairs. "Here, you go—we definitely have enough to use as leverage."

"Appreciate it." He spent a few minutes reviewing the record. "Okay, Crane, let's go talk to Leroy Nichols before he crashes and wakes up with no memory of anything except his Miranda rights."

"I'd be surprised if he's not *already* dead asleep! He wasn't doing too well last I saw him and that was hours ago."

"I'm hoping that Leroy is jumping out of his skin by now, which would make him more likely to deal. C'mon, partner, let's do it."

We walked up the dimly lit corridor discussing strategies. Tyrell opened the door to the interrogation room, windowless except for a small observational opening in the door. Handcuffs were bolted to a wall where a bench was positioned. He ushered me inside and then slammed the door. The sound reverberated in the perpetually dank concrete room, no more than twelve feet square.

The noise had the desired effect—our suspect startled. "Damn, yo, I been waitin' too long and now why you makin' a racket?" Leroy lifted his head up out of his arms, sat back and, instead of another groan, grinned from ear to ear. He finally had his audience—"the brother and the ice queen."

"My head be hurtin', man. Needs more of them aspirins from Officer Al. Now that polices be treatin' me right."

"Sorry, Leroy, but we can't be dispensing drugs of any kind. Thanks, Boyd, I appreciate you keeping our friend company. We'll take it from here." Without a word or even a nod in our direction, the big man with a shaved head, broad forehead, strong jaw, and a thick carpet of reddish hair on his arms and at his throat, left the room, closing the door quietly behind him. I wondered whether Boyd and Sarge were related.

I turned on the recording equipment, checked to see if the red light outside the room was lit (it wasn't always functional), and then locked the door from inside. Tyrell and I each took a "soft" seat, which could be moved around, whereas the suspect's chair was bolted to the floor and we could handcuff him or her to the table. We made ourselves comfortable without saying anything.

"Hey, guys, I don' got all day. What's been takin' y'all so damn long?"

"Well, Mr. Nichols, we sure don't mean to inconvenience you," I said. "But before we can start, we need to Mirandize you; have you sign an explanation and waiver of rights form." Though the suspect is Mirandized in the field, we routinely do it again before an interrogation to reduce the chances of a case going down the tubes.

"Already done heard it."

"Well, sir, we just want to be sure we are doing our job correctly, so we're going to film this conversation. Is that okay with you, Mr. Nichols?"

"Don' wan' no lawyer. Don' wan' to be in this room—too damn cold. Chair be too damn hard."

"I guess it's time to leave if you aren't interested in signing this paper. It took a while, but what do I say?—you had a lot of stuff we needed to put to bed. I don't know, man," said Ty, shaking his head.

Leroy laughed appreciatively at Ty's sally. "Ain't be mine, Officer Tyrell. Yo, tol' you Cuz and his friend used my ride. Don' you get it?—marijuana's legal. I wan' me a deal."

"Sure you do, but we can't be talking with you without your signature. Without you saying 'Yes, I understand what you've told me about my rights.'"

"Gimme that damn paper!" Ty handed him the pen and waiver form. Leroy scrawled his name and pushed it across the table. "I unerstan' what you tol' me 'bout my rights. *Now*, I wanna talk 'bout a deal."

"Well, then, Mr. Nichols," I began, "why don't you give us your cousin's real name—his friend's? Phone numbers and addresses would be good. We could give them a call and get together for a chat—Leroy, you can trust us, we won't give up *your* name. That way you will only be facing a bit of time for pot and a few pills. We might even be able to make those go away if you give us something important."

"No way, Miss. I'm not a snitch. I don' know nothin' 'bout no guns and money. I work. *Officer Miss*, this be Bawlmer!" he said in a tone that suggested I was at best an idiot if I did not understand the ways of his city. At worst, I was trying to get him knocked off intentionally.

"Well, then, I guess me and the 'Ice Queen' will need to book you," Ty said as he sat back in his chair and stretched his legs out in front of him. Arms crossed, my partner didn't appear to have a care in the world.

"Leroy, it seems to me there's big trouble coming up the road," I said, pulling out my notebook and pen without breaking eye contact. The smile was gone.

"Officers, how we be goin' to fix this? I can help ya some but ain't goin' to do no snitchin'."

Ty leaned forward, elbows on the table, fingers laced. "Leroy, my friend, we took a good look at your record. Man, I could paper a room with your sheet! *Now*, guns, ammo, a drugstore, thousands of dollars *and* an outstanding warrant for drug distribution. Out on probation! Not cool, Leroy. Not cool at all. This shit's not going to bring a smile to your mama's face."

"Ain' no mama and leave Gramma outta this! Life been damn hard—no daddy either."

"Leroy, we all have sad stories—fathers are pretty slippery creatures and we just gotta deal with it. Officer Boyd seemed to think you have valuable information for us. That true?" I asked. "We read your rap sheet and you need to know we're backin' five years for a violation of probation."

Ty sat up straight and locked eyes with Nichols. "Officer Crane is right, man—you're in some deep *sheeit* tonight. How about we conduct some business?"

"Yeah, Miss, I can give you information but I ain't gonna talk widout a deal. I want me a *fine* deal," he said, shifting his attention to Tyrell.

I guess that as the "Ice Queen," I was not quite up-to-snuff if he was going to manipulate the system successfully.

The two men locked eyes. "Man, ya gotta take care of me—these are some heavy hitters and I don' want to end up in the Bawlmer Harbor." He giggled nervously and sat back. "Water not be cleaned yet!"

Neither of us joined in, though I have to admit that I appreciated the man's sense of humor.

"Seriously, what you got for us, Leroy?" asked Ty. "It better be damn good because you got some bad shit going on here—enough to put you in Hagerstown for a *long* time. We want to help you. We honestly do. But we can't just bring guns, money, and drugs to Fayette Street, log them in, and *somebody* doesn't pay. Yo, my partner and I are working stiffs—we have a boss and he wants evidence. I'm sure you understand how bosses are."

"Yeah." he responded with a nod. "Detective Tyrell, I can deal—I promise I got some good stuff. Jus don' wan' my gramma losin' her baby boy. Goin' be killed in jail if I gotta go back—las' time be bad. Drugs, guns—they don' be mine. I got somethin' good—*huge*. Detective, you twos will be famous—in the news, the movies."

"Give it up, Leroy. We'll do what we can—you got our word. Officer Crane and I have parents—we sure don't want any part of a grandmother losing her boy," Tyrell said reassuringly, again sitting back. I nodded my head in agreement but remained quiet, not wanting to interrupt the connection that Ty had managed to establish with our suspect.

Leroy's eyes rolled up. He sighed, closed them, and settled his head back in his arms.

We glanced at each other and waited. I hoped our suspect was giving the offer some thought and hadn't crashed. Two or three minutes later, I spoke up. "Well, Ty, guess it's time to go home to our kids—my old man's not so happy I'm late. Just doesn't seem like anything is going to happen here."

"I agree. The wife's going to be totally bent out of shape if I don't show my pretty face soon." Ty began to get up, and I followed suit, intentionally scraping my chair against the floor for good effect.

Without a word, Nichols raised his head and shook it slowly from side to side several times. I thought it was over; he was going to ask for a lawyer.

All of a sudden, Leroy blurted out, "*Girls.*"

"Girls?" I repeated.

"Whores—thots."

"That's what you got for us—prostitutes?" Disappointed, I sighed, sat back and stretched my own legs out to the side. It was going to be a long night and I could picture an unhappy Matt sitting down at the breakfast table to eat pancakes with a child asking for his mother. I wasn't looking forward to the conversation that would take place next time we were together.

"A prostitution ring?" Tyrell's laugh bounced off the walls, reverberating around the room. He got up, leaned against the door and glanced over at me with a waggle of eyebrows before directing his attention back to Leroy. "Damn, bro, that's nothing new. The city's full of whores—Baltimore could give Reno a run for its money."

"No. I tol' you, what I got is good. I don' wanna go back to Hagerstown."

"Sorry to tell you this, my friend, but prostitution ain't going to keep you out of there. Might shave off a year or so, but not much more—my man, you want a lawyer?"

That question surprised me—I couldn't understand why Ty raised the possibility of legal representation. I had no idea what happened to Nichols at Hagerstown but whatever it was, it was working in our favor.

"No damn lawyer. Listen here, Detective: I be talkin' 'bout *more'n* prostitution."

"Well, give it up then," said Ty, darting a glance my way.

I figured my partner must know what he was doing and so continued doodling. "Leroy, you need to trust someone and it might as well be us." I looked up. "Sir, we *will* come through for you, but only if you have something substantial for us. This was a big bust we made tonight, so we need big info to take to our boss and the prosecutor to get you that 'fine deal' you want."

"Ma'am, y'all goin' to be interested in *this*. Don' be letting me down—I be trustin' ya. Y'all need to move us out of the city—like you did for my frien'."

This sounded serious. I put down my pen and glanced at my partner.

Ty nodded. "Leroy, give us some solid information to take to the state's attorney and we'll have your back," I said.

"Sex traffickin' of kids." He said each of the four words slowly, with a distinct air of confidence, and then sat back and crossed his arms. There was *nothing* tired or drugged out about the man now.

Ty and I looked at each other. He cocked an eyebrow and leaned forward. It occurred to me that the tweaker sitting in front of us believed he was stuck talking to two idiots. I certainly felt like one. "In Baltimore?" I asked, trying to buy time while gathering my thoughts.

"Baltimore–DC–Philly," he said triumphantly. "They moves the kids roun'." Aware he had hit a home run, Leroy grinned from ear to ear, twitching away and picking at a sore on his neck. It was beginning to bleed. I glanced at my partner.

Ty continued from where I left off. "That's good, Leroy. That is *very* good information. I think you *might* have intelligence that will get you to that deal you want. What do you think, Officer Crane?"

"I agree that Leroy, here, may have something important for us. Detective Tyrell, I think that we should be able to help him *if* his info pans out."

"Yeah, Leroy, we just might be able to do something with what you got. Man, you seem ready to jump out of your skin. Can we get you a soda, a coffee with a bunch of sugar? Don't mind getting you a sandwich."

"I don' want to do no time. Are you hearin' me?"

"I'm hearin' you. My partner hears you. Want a drink, man?"

"Yeah, one of them Mountain Dews. And blanket. It be cold in here!"

"Sorry about that. The city has its difficulties—air conditioning does what it wants. Officer Crane, do you mind?"

"No problem, I'll be back in a few minutes." I left to get a drink, though not at all sure it would do the job given the shape Nichols seemed to be in. The blanket might help, even though the owner was bound to be pissed when discovering it was gone. I ran into Sarge at the soda machine.

"Hey, Crane, how's it coming?" he asked, worrying the scar on his cheek.

"Fine. Suspect may actually give up something useful. Tyrell is good at this. Patient. Persistent. Understands how to gain the suspect's trust."

"Tyrell is a damn fine detective. Your partner has been on the job for a long time and not one citizen complaint," he said, tearing open a bag of Skittles. "In Baltimore, that's a miracle. Some days, with the lawsuits, it feels like we're an ATM machine—all legal has to say is that it's not worth the court fight," he mumbled. "Keep me in the loop."

"Will do, Sarge." After he left, I began dropping coins into the slot; after the last one, out rolled the green and yellow can of Mountain Dew, landing with a thud. For good measure, I purchased a Coke for my partner. I hesitated before feeding in a five-dollar bill and pressing the button for a Milky Way and another for an Almond Joy. After retrieving the change, I stopped by my desk to pick up a bottle of water before snatching a blanket from the sleeping quarters and returning to the interview room.

I opened the door to complete silence. After all the enthusiasm, Leroy's head was again cradled in his arms. This time our suspect, snoring up a storm, was definitely asleep. An exhausted Tyrell was leaning back in his chair, eyes almost closed and long legs extended to the side of the table.

"Hey boys! Naptime?"

My partner sat up straight. Leroy didn't move. "Aren't you two lively!"

"Hi, Robin, our friend here was fading. We decided to wait for you, oh Ice Queen, to bring some sugar before continuing the interview."

I walked to the other side of the table. "Well, Leroy, I got you the Mountain Dew, but you've got to wake up to drink it." I set the can down in front of him with a bang. "And a bonus." I laid the candy bar next to his soda. "Tyrell, why don't you take this? Hate to say it, but you really do seem to be fading; got to get you home in one piece." I set the Milky Way and Coke in front of my partner. He popped open the soda and dropped the tab into the can.

Our suspect suddenly came alive and grabbed for the Almond Joy with one hand while snatching Ty's Milky Way with the other.

"Hey man, that's my damn candy bar," protested Ty.

I suppose that to be sure he was going to keep them, Leroy put both on his lap. *Good move!* Neither of us would touch that candy now, no matter how hungry and tired we were.

"Well, Leroy, now that you've taken your nap and Officer Crane has kindly brought you all sorts of goodies, we need information to take to the prosecutor before we go much further with this."

"Like what? Yo, I already gave you somethin'."

"Like a name would be good. You know the drill, bro—we need specifics."

"Y'all get a name when I got me my deal. Not that I don' trust ya, man." With that, Leroy calmly drank his Mountain Dew while removing the wrapper from the Milky Way. He bit off a large chunk, rescuing the trailing caramel with his tongue. I knew that once home, I would head for the shower before anything else. Before breakfast. Before bed.

Ty had enough—I'd been in two other interviews with him and though he generally exercised a great deal of patience to arrive at his goal, he had less when being jerked around by an arrestee—it was clear he was annoyed.

"Put up now, Leroy, or it's over. My word is good, but if you can't accept that, my partner here will back you up."

I nodded. "I will."

"Hey man, it's been a long night and I need to go home or the old lady is going to relieve me of my head if not another body part."

Leroy Nichols laughed, spraying soda in our direction. I was about done and my face must have shown it.

"It's not funny, Mr. Nichols—we're tired and don't have the time or the desire to sit around chitchatting with a badass running guns and dealing serious drugs. Carrying a lot of money. What do you think, Officer Crane? Nichols, I bet the state's attorney will charge you with violating banking laws. That will bring the feds down on you—man, they are always on the lookout for terrorists. No drinks, candy, or deals with those dudes—man, they will *fry* your skinny ass without a second thought. Probably waterboard you good."

Before my partner went any further, I interrupted, "What I think Detective Wilson is saying is that you're in a whole boatload of trouble!"

Leroy squinted from me to Wilson and took another gulp of his soda. "I'll get you a gun."

"Say what?" Ty responded.

"I'll lay down a gun in the alley for you, so you can get the stat."

I responded. "Thanks, but no thanks, Mr. Nichols. We would need an arrest to go with that gun."

"Okay, okay—I can maybe get you somethin' better, but my family *can' be* staying in Bawlmer, not even a safe house—them places ain't so safe!" He guffawed, gulped down more Mountain Dew, and then began talking. "I may know this nigga workin' some kids up at a motel in southeast. I heard he's got the kids on Backpage, advertising them out. They's pickin' up a kid in one city and brings 'em to a different city. Kids trickin' at motels—they stays in different ones for a few days before movin' on. They work roun' here."

"That's very good, Leroy. A good start. What do you think, partner?"

"Ty, if he keeps this up, I see a deal in our friend's future." What I did not say was that I couldn't understand why he would give up so much without a solid guarantee. Must have been bad for him inside.

"What cities are we talking about?" asked Tyrell.

"Sometimes stays in Bawlmer. Or Bawlmer to Philly. Back to Bawlmer and to DC. And to New York or Wilmington. Atlantic City."

"Keep it up, Leroy, and any major charges related to this bust should take a walk. Officer Crane, you getting this?"

"I am."

"What 'bout them other charges?" Nichols asked.

Ty nodded and I said, "We'll have to take another look at them but if what you have proves to be legitimate information, I'm sure the prosecutor will be willing to work with us *if* and only *if* you have no direct connection to the guns. Kids … that is what you said before. Not adults. Mr. Leroy, how old are the kids?" I asked the question, confident we were finally going to get somewhere but figuring, hoping, that by "kids" he did not mean young children. I sure hoped Ty was right about the state's attorney's office working with us on this case. We would owe Leroy Nichols.

"Guess they be mostly runaways—high school, might some be younger."

Well, he had answered my unspoken question. Despite the plethora of charges that Leroy might be facing, we should be able to bring the prosecutor on board for a case involving the sex trafficking of children.

"Girls, boys?"

"Don' matter none. Peoples got differen' tastes, Detective Miss. Sure you know that in your line of work."

I continued taking notes, unsure whether the camera in this particular room was functioning dependably. In fact, it frequently malfunctioned; shit was going to hit the fan one day when somebody lost a big case because of it—I hoped to God that it would not be one of ours. On the one hand, a suspect could level an accusation of misconduct against the cops. Alternatively, as my partner pointed out, the lack of a camera gave the police a little more leeway.

Tyrell ignored Leroy's sarcastic comment about our "line of work," and continued. "Hey man, how did you come by this information? Your cousin?"

"Cuz needs hisself a nigga to drive with him to DC. I went. Came back same day."

"When was this?" I asked.

"Yesterday."

Ty appeared confused. I *was* confused. He asked, "I thought a friend went with your cousin and you were in Baltimore. Isn't that what you understood, Officer?"

"I did."

"Didn' know you were goin' to cut me no deal!" At that, Leroy began laughing uproariously. When he quieted down, he said, "Not my *actual* cuzin—the bro we be talkin' 'bout calls hisself Cuz."

Ty sighed and settled back in his chair. "We get it."

I looked at Tyrell and shrugged. "Okay, Mr. Nichols, how about telling us where you guys went?"

"Somewhere on 16th. Could be by Oklahoma. Cuz made me get out—I waited 'bout an hour before he came back."

"He left you to wait on some block in DC for an hour? On 16th. C'mon, man!" His voice thick with ridicule, Ty leaned back and sipped his soda.

Nichols' chin shot up and his dark eyes narrowed. "That's how things goed down. Calling me a liar?"

They were headed for a pissing contest. "No, he's not calling you a liar," I assured Leroy. "It just seems strange. It was raining yesterday—where did you wait?"

"Weren't rainin' in DC. Cuz got a friend."

"Can we confirm your story with the friend?" I asked.

"Man wasn't home. I watched television."

"If he wasn't there, how'd you get in?"

"Door open, yo." He looked at my partner as if he was flat out stupid.

"You must remember the address." I prompted.

"Nope. Don' remember."

Though I didn't believe him, I figured we'd better drop that line of questioning before we lost him. "Leroy, did Cuz come back to Baltimore by himself? Other than traveling with you, I mean."

"Man, you the polices. Polices ain't to be trusted—they all cruddy. Except you, yo. I be trustin' y'all. I'll be givin' you somethin' if you let me go. Detective Miss, I needs me a deal or I got nothin' more to say." He made the pronouncement with the assurance of someone who believed he'd had a revelation, and then pulled the blanket more tightly around him. I was surprised that he hadn't thought to ask for a pillow.

"Just one more thing and I'll make the call," Ty assured him. "You *know* we can't cut make an arrangement without sufficient information." He nodded in my direction.

"Leroy, did Cuz bring a child back with him to Baltimore?" I asked the question emphasizing the 'with him,' hoping not to alienate the man. It would be a big break if we could manage to keep him on board and break a human trafficking ring. *Doug always said there should be a special place in hell for anyone causing pain to a child.*

66

"No shit, Detectives. I ain't sayin' it agin. No more till I got me somethin' in writing, yo."

"We can't give you anything in writing, Leroy, but I can look you in the eye and shake your hand like a man—not a knocker or the police—and talk with the prosecutor on your behalf," said Ty leaning forward and locking eyes with the guy. Mr. Nichols, we've got a machine downstairs with food. Officer Crane might be willing to get you a sandwich while I put in a call to the prosecutor. Need to warn you though, it's early; we might not be able to reach anyone right away."

What kind of sub do you want?" I asked, hoping to distract him. "Never mind, instead of the machine, I'll go over to *Crazy John's*. I guess we could use some food."

"Good idea, I'm famished," Ty said convincingly.

Our suspect chimed in and leaned forward. "One of them block burgers, well done with extra cheese an' mayo. 'Nother Mountain Dew." He sat back and leered, toasting me with the empty can.

Abruptly, he turned his attention to Tyrell. "Yo! Let me take a piss."

"Okay, Leroy, hang on a minute and an officer will accompany you to the bathroom. Robin, on your way out would you send Boyd in? I want to call the prosecutor."

"Sure."

"Can't wait for no dumb lug to come. Gotta take a piss, yo! Don' wanna be spoilin' no good blanket."

"That's enough, numb nuts. Let's quiet down, why don't we? When Officer Boyd arrives, I'll see what kind of deal we can get you. Eat your candy."

Chapter 6

Domestic Distress

Sean's asleep. Matt, can we get back to the conversation we started while I was at work?"

"Remind me, Robin."

Finding it difficult to believe that my husband was unable to remember why we'd been having words earlier, I swallowed an indignant *What?* "You were pretty upset about the amount of time I'm at work and told me, in no uncertain terms, that our son needs *more* of his mother. Now you're telling me you're not sure which conversation I'm referring to?" I probably sounded irritated. I suppose I was.

"Sure, Robin, I remember, but let's not start this conversation with a fight. How about we sit outside on the patio by the fire pit—would you like a glass of wine?"

"Sounds good. I'm sorry, Matt. It's been a tough week."

"Red or white? I've got a fine Merlot."

He had ignored my apology. "Whatever you're drinking, hon."

"Robin, I'm drinking a *beer*," he said toasting me with the Natty Boh he was holding.

"The Merlot would be great. Thanks. Tell you what, I'll head outside and catch my breath." Hoping the whole issue of my work hours would go away or I could at least bring down the emotional temperature, I laughed self-servingly and left for the patio.

Matt eventually joined me, bringing with him a glass of red wine and another beer. "Sorry, I had a call."

"No problem—it's peaceful out here."

Instead of sitting down, he handed me my wine and proceeded to build up the fire, which he then continued stoking thoughtfully. The silence between us hung heavy.

"Finally, he pulled a chair closer to the pit. The fire crackled. "There's something I need to say. I'm not sure I have the right words but here goes."

"Okay, Matt, but you sound rather intimidating."

"Sorry, don't mean to. Robin, night shift is bad enough. The thought of you dealing with Baltimore gangs is even more difficult. And turning around and going to court a few hours after you come off a long shift only makes things worse. To be honest, this feels like an impossible situation. I have absolutely no idea how single parents manage because we're certainly having problems as a two-parent household."

"Well, that was a lot of negatives." I tried to laugh, despite not finding any of what he had to say in the least amusing. "Hon, why don't you come closer?" When he did, I leaned over and gave him a kiss. "This is an exceptional wine. Matt, you are aware I'm grateful for all you do, aren't you?"

"Robin, don't try to change the subject. This is not about my feeling unappreciated. As much as I would like to sit here and make out like the newlyweds we are, I want to understand what's up with you. If you're not conscious of the problem, I sure am."

"What are you talking about, exactly? I have a difficult job, I'll grant you that, but why are you so angry?"

"You're not listening, Robin. This isn't about being angry; I'm concerned—you don't sleep well, all the tossing and turning. Honestly, it's like sleeping in a damn blender. You're stressed. You are *very* stressed. Often. You snap at Sean and me for what appears to be no good reason. Sweetie, I need to understand what's going on. Whatever it is, we can't keep sweeping it under the rug. This is something we have to deal with."

I sat stunned, avoidant, transfixed by the fire. I finished my wine while I thought about our marriage. I had not understood how troubled my husband was until this very moment. There was no way out of this conversation. A dog barked in the distance.

"I'm really sorry, Matt. I didn't understand how upset you've been. Frankly, I'm not sure what's going on. I guess it's just been such a big change—the move, the job, being married. Mostly the job, I think. Hon, policing in the city is nothing like what I was doing before. It's not that bad things didn't happen there … you *know* they did. But so much goes on here—I don't know, it just feels like we'll never make a difference; these streets feel more dangerous, despite what happened back home—"

"Back *home*? Robin, do you regret leaving California? If so, I'm sorry."

"You're sorry. For what?"

"Well … after all, it was my idea. Honey, the highway goes both ways—we can always return to California. Ken would welcome you back at the SBPD with open arms."

"I know. I know, but that's not what I want. We were starting a new life together and making new memories—a good idea. I think we should try this but will keep your offer in mind."

"Good," he said, with some hesitancy.

This was as far as I could go right now. "Matt, I'm really tired. I'm still not convinced whether or not I want to be on the job—maybe I ought to go back to psychology. Remember, you brought the option up when I was looking for a job and having trouble working with Rossi. Both times I considered different graduate programs and clinical possibilities, but for now I want to put in another request for Homicide."

"Maybe I'm missing something here, I don't know. Robin, I'll let it go for now, but I'm not sure how switching from gangs to homicide is going to help matters."

"I'm not sure, either, Matt—I guess I feel like I need to give it a try."

"We've talked about this before—there wouldn't be as much danger, a good thing—no, a great thing. But, Robin, the hours would be worse—you'd be on call all the time. You can't expect me to think *that's* a good thing?"

"Matt, we can talk more, it's just that tonight isn't so good—I really am exhausted. We're working a tough case."

"Come sit on my lap, babe. You're right, we've been at this long enough—it's late and I've been missing you."

I put down my glass. "*That* sounds good. Matt, honey, I promise to do better." When he wrapped his arms around me and whispered words of love into my ear, I felt an inordinate sense of relief.

Chapter 7

Floater in the Harbor

I parked my car on narrow Albemarle Street in Little Italy. After my walk, I figured I would stop by Vaccaro's to pick up a sandwich. Besides the food, Ana, the woman behind the counter, inevitably put a smile on my face. I checked for messages before powering off my cell and slipping it under the front seat. Car locked, I headed in the direction of the harbor.

There had been little enough sun for the last week or two—I missed the California sunshine and wrapped Matt's scarf more tightly around my neck. In any event, now that my head was together—well, relatively so—walks were how I kept it that way. It was the one time during the day that I was just Robin rather than mother, wife, or police officer. The anonymity of blending in with the runners and walkers dotting the promenade at that hour afforded me some peace.

Crossing President Street with its six lanes of traffic was tedious, but I successfully reached the other side after several light changes. I passed McCormick's and the lighthouse, crossed the bridge leading to the inner harbor and wove my way through clusters of chattering school children arriving for a visit to the aquarium, their teachers making a mighty effort to herd them into a coherent whole.

At Baltimore's World Trade Center, the workers were still on the job cleaning glass heavily streaked with city grime. When I'd passed the previous day, the wind was whipping their platform back and forth at a crazy angle, sudsy water splashing over unsuspecting pedestrians. I was pleased to see they had made *some* accommodation for the weather: yellow tape now sealed off the work area. The question of the workers' well-being persisted, however. No longer positioned as high, the platform nonetheless swayed alarmingly. Oddly, only one man clutched the rope; typically, they worked in pairs. There was nothing to do but laugh at myself, wrapped up as I was in the safety analysis of window washing. I went to check out the bird sanctuary.

The Waterfront Partnership had developed nesting sites for the waterfowl; I enjoyed watching the ducks—they provided balance for the surfeit of commerce in the area. Unfortunately, not one was in sight; instead, debris from Saturday night revelers remained trapped in the grasses.

I was passing by the memorial to the Maryland victims of the 9/11 tragedy in New York City when one of the window washers I'd seen the day before almost bowled me over as he dashed toward the BPD permanently parked in the circular drop-off area. I kept walking, despite the approaching sirens. Lights flashing, three royal blue and white electric police cars sped past me in the direction of the Trade Center, effectively scattering walkers, runners, and bicyclists alike. Not on the job, I strode briskly along the brick promenade that follows the curve of the harbor. After a mile, I came to the Sorso Café. I felt like a lizard as I basked below a heat lamp on the patio, drinking coffee and reading Le Carré's *Smiley's People*, absorbed in the Cold War travails of the enigmatic spy.

An hour later, I refilled my cup and left. The sun had come out and the water sparkled, a magical sight I loved. Approaching the Trade Center, I saw yellow crime tape strung around the circumference of the building. A body covered by a large white plastic sheet lay on the pier where the dragon boats were moored. Faint, overwhelmed by the memory of *another* body lying dead and abandoned, I dropped to the nearest bench, lowering my head and concentrating on catching my breath. After a few minutes, I steeled myself and peered upward—this time, both window washers were hard at work. A little late, actually a lot late, I realized that one of them had probably spotted the body from his elevated vantage point and, in a panic, had hurried to inform the police who were routinely stationed below.

I wondered about the person who now lay under the sheet, his or her life over. I figured the victim to be tall and heavy, although drowning victims can become disturbingly bloated depending on how long they've been submerged. Patrol officers and detectives milled about on the dock, probably waiting for the medical examiner. I recognized Greg Rossi and hesitated for a split second, but kept my head down and continued to my car. Soon enough I would be on duty. Vaccaro's wasn't too crowded and I had plenty of time before my tour began, so I ordered a sandwich and salad for later and then made my way to Fayette Street.

———

Ty met me as I got off the elevator.

"Hey, Crane, a call came in while *you* were out stretching your legs. We've got shots fired at Pratt, off Broadway."

"Our shift hasn't even begun!"

"Just giving you shit. It's early but we need to move it."

"Give me five to change—I'll meet you at the car."

When we arrived at the scene, one of the officers moved a couple of orange cones and Ty pulled in. Adrenaline coursing through my body, I released my seatbelt and checked my gun—the key to having "an edge," I guess.

Mostly police cruisers were in the immediate area under investigation. Two unmarked cars I figured for detectives, three others probably belonged to residents. A few locals were milling around, talking in hushed whispers, kept out by yellow caution tape, a series of traffic cones, and two patrol officers.

"Hey, Ramirez!"

"Bro, it's been too long." Tyrell and an unfamiliar man exchanged bear hugs, without a doubt glad to run into each other. "California, meet Justin Ramirez. My old buddy here has got himself quite the record," my partner said seriously, but then broke out laughing, probably in response to the puzzled look on my face.

"Ramirez, nice to meet you. What's the record for?" I asked the good-looking man with a cleft chin and full moustache who I figured could easily be either a criminal or a dedicated detective. Tattoo sleeves on his arms and ink on the back of his neck, he wore aviator shades, jeans, black tee shirt, and a backwards Orioles cap—the net effect was convincing if he was an undercover detective hanging around with the criminal class. He tossed his leather jacket through the open window of a black Escalade. I wondered why I hadn't run into him before. If I had, I would have remembered—the man definitely had presence.

"Just ignore the jerk!" He extended a hand, and we shook.

"Robin Crane."

"My man, Crane's my new partner—though sorry to say she's a temp. Our girl, who came to us from the Golden State, is aiming for your job. California, word to the wise, you do not want to partner with my friend here. He's got at least three wrecks under his belt—one carried with it a suspension. Yo, my boy, he's a star, that's who he is. Been laying off the gas?—no evidence of any shenanigans lately."

As the men continued their banter, Sarge and the patrol supervisor drove up and parked in the alley. That put an end to the horsing around. The Irishman lumbered over to the group and lit up a cigarette. "Hey, Sarge," Ramirez greeted the big man.

"Hey there—get yourself some remedial lessons yet?" His belligerent laugh let *everyone* know he'd arrived.

"Give me a car that's actually built for what we do and there won't be any problems from my end. Outgunned, outmuscled, outdriven—not much else to say, Sarge!"

I joined in the laughter. *Well, maybe not outmuscled.*

The big man guffawed but almost immediately got serious. "Okay, boys, what have we got here? Heard there's a discharging incident. Commish will be down next. Deadly shootings are over the 180 mark and there are two more months until we head into the new year. Mayor doesn't like this shit and, believe me, I do *not* like working with an unhappy boss. Worse, I don't like interacting with the press."

"That's something we *all* understand. Sarge, plenty of shots fired—at least a dozen in all. Witnesses agree that the shooter ran through the alley and along the side of that house but didn't get a good look at him with the hoodie and all." Ramirez pointed toward the rundown rowhouse three lots from where we stood. Boarded up, it appeared uninhabited, like so many in the city.

"Anybody hit?" asked Sarge.

"No, the intended target was in the house, but her car is well-ventilated. The lack of a shooting victim is more likely due to luck or bad aim than to a generous heart. Or, they were trying to scare her. Seven hits to the woman's car, but it's not talking. Or driving, either—two of the tires are flattened."

"Could be that a knife was used," Ty suggested. "Bullets shouldn't take the air out so quickly. Crime Scene can answer that."

"Good point," said Ramirez. "The woman was definitely targeted but she's not going to say anything here—we'll arrange something else." He surreptitiously indicated a heavyset African American woman sitting in the back seat of one of the cruisers. Grey-haired, the woman might be in her early sixties.

"Ask Boyd and his partner to take her to the hospital to be checked out before the media arrives," Sarge said to nobody in particular. "Tell them to use a cell to tape any conversation—with her permission, of course. Crane, be sure to get her name and contact information before they leave."

"Will do," I said. Ty left to talk with Boyd.

"Ramirez, you're familiar with this neighborhood. What about the victim—any idea what's going on?" He asked the question in what was a thick Irish brogue, despite decades in the States. "She's not our typical target."

"Sort of. An ongoing problem, most likely related to drugs. Actually, the intended target is not clear—the woman living in the house or someone else. And there's always the wrong address," Ramirez said.

Sarge laughed regretfully. "An unwarranted shooting—definitely willing to give her that. You got a description of the shooter?"

"Not much, but she might give Boyd some information once she's out of here. We need to provide more patrols—don't want her shot after we leave. A legitimate worry given what's happened."

"Crane, let someone know we're taking the woman to the hospital—that might help relieve her of any suspicion regarding snitching."

"Yes, sir." I headed over to a small cluster of anxious-looking women. One had been crying. I introduced myself and asked several questions. I then explained that we were concerned about their friend and wanted a doctor to examine her; an officer would remain with her at Hopkins, and then bring her home when they release her. Nobody protested, so I rejoined the others.

"Sarge, I told the women what's going on. Our victim's daughter isn't home, but if she arrives before Boyd returns with her mother, they'll inform her as to what's up. Ramirez, what's the 'neighborhood problem' about?" I asked. "One mentioned ongoing problems, which 'the cops *never* take seriously.'"

"Probably drugs. If she or the neighbor is reluctant to give up any specific information, my guess is that we can figure it out from a review of the 911 calls and reports that have come in from here. Anyhow, my understanding is that the woman, who I *again* want to emphasize is worried about her safety, is angry because some gangbangers are dealing out of one of the abandoned houses. There have been some real bad characters going down her alley for the last several months, including 'a white kid in an expensive car.' She's lived here all of her life and is scared for her grandchildren; wants them to be able to play outside but is afraid they'll be hurt even if she's out there with them, so she keeps them inside. What a bunch of shit!" he said angrily.

"Well, I guess all of them have good reason for not talking with us. I can't imagine how we can protect her," I said, looking around at what were desolate lots to the left; less than a block away was bustling Broadway, with the Rumba Club on the corner. Nobody responded. Everyone knew we needed an improved witness protection program to triumph in what was essentially an urban war—the overworked prosecutor, who was carrying almost two hundred cases, was *still* trying to work out secure housing for Leroy Nichols, now out on bail. Complicating matters, Nichols didn't consider what was available to be safe, so he insisted on staying put for the time being—I wondered if the prosecutor had investigated his present living situation.

Ty rejoined the group. "All's good, Sarge. I think more than anything she's angry, but it's a good call to have her checked out. I'm pretty sure she'll talk once we get her out of here, *if* she knows anything."

"Okay, you guys. A couple of you speak to the other neighbors so we don't leave the woman with a bull's-eye on her back. Put it out as a random incident, neighbor caught in the crossfire—unknown assailant, etc. Keep it low-key. Those of you not taking witness statements should begin canvassing the area, though by now the shooters almost certainly in the wind. I can send more units if they're needed. Meantime, people, keep me posted and watch your backs. Ramirez, avoid the light poles!"

With that rat-a-tat-tat sequence of cautionary notes, Sarge and the patrol supervisor (who had not said a word, at least while I was there) left. Both lit cigarettes before getting into the car—I thought of Rossi and his smoking habit. No wonder he didn't care whether he was violating departmental policy. They took off, lights still flashing. Siren off. Windows up.

My partner came over. "Anything?" I asked. "I was told that the first guys on the scene checked out the house over there but didn't find anybody. He must be long gone by now."

"Don't fool yourself—there are knockers—"

"Knockers?"

"Local pronunciation of narcos," Ty laughed. "Anyhow, there are knockers hanging out—they'll make him feel safe and then move in. Crane, maybe Baltimore is a far cry from Santa Barbara, maybe not, but bear with me as I'm going to take this training bit seriously for all of two minutes. Part of the reason so many cars arrived once the call came in is that one of the first things we do is to control access to the surrounding streets; we want to keep anyone else from joining the fray. Believe me, there is always someone out there with an itchy finger. Cops aren't so popular these days." Ty said wryly. "Once the area has been sealed off—well, as best as we can, we surround the house. By locking down the area we can better control the threat level and, to be honest, so witnesses don't leave before we get their information. Mostly, we seem to miss a perfectly good arrest or successful prosecution because of the lack of witnesses. People bail like greased lightning—as Leroy Nichols made clear, the *no snitch* culture is alive and well in Baltimore City. By the way, we should check in on the status of his case tomorrow."

"Good, I was just thinking about him—guaranteeing safety is difficult. What's next?"

"If we don't find the shooter, we'll begin canvassing in tandem, meaning dispatch will make sure the specialized units can easily link up with a patrol if they see anything suspicious. Crane, we'll engage in *proactive* enforcement—car stops, checking out people in alleys and kids on bicycles. I sure would like to find this guy during our tour. If we don't locate him in the next day or two, he'll probably get away with it. This time, at least. Priority is keeping our witnesses safe. *Nothing* better happen to this grandmother for trying to give her family a decent life—nobody wants a repeat of the Dawson case."

"God forbid." The deaths of the Dawson family had rocked the city to its core—a grandmother trying to rid her neighborhood of drug dealers had been burned to death in her home with her grandchildren. "Ty, it's difficult to believe that people live under such horrible conditions. Makes me glad to do what we do. Grateful for my own life."

"I know where you're at, California. Let's get out of here; Ramirez has the scene under control. We'll cruise around and see if anything is out of place—check in with Boyd later to see what's up at the hospital."

Just as I was going to contact dispatch, the radio came to life. "Wilson, Crane, got a call, can they spare you?"

"Wilson, here. Yeah, we're pretty much done … at least for now—Ramirez is on it. You can check with him, but there's probably no need for our boots on the ground. What do you have for us?"

"Patrol on the scene. White male beating on white female." The dispatcher gave us the address in Upper Fells Point.

"Got it. Out." Tyrell turned on the lights and took off, tires squealing. The others barely gave us a glance. Urban policing, I figured. I clicked on my seatbelt.

We pulled up next to the cruiser. I rolled down my window. "What's up?" I asked the officer.

Eyes twinkling, smirking, he was doing his best to hold back a laugh. "Have to give these two *something* for originality. Neither wanted to press charges. The female already had a bruise brewing on her face but denied the male hit her. He denied hitting her. She was the passenger—the injury was to the left side of her face. He was right-handed. She claimed … man, you gotta hear this … female got out of the van to rescue a cat. So, she's in the middle of the street and *fell over the cat*." He gave up and emitted a full-throated laugh. "According to her, she fucking tripped across the cat when it took off! No cat in evidence for what appeared to be a second-degree assault. Anyway, we gave her a pamphlet listing local shelters and were just getting ready to leave when you pulled up. I'm sure we'll be seeing her another day."

"So, why were we called?" asked a confused Tyrell.

"Dispatch, the Sarge, *somebody* was not impressed with the outcome. My guess is someone who had run across your partner recently thought a female might get through to the victim."

"And where are they?" I asked, looking around for the van.

"Sorry, couldn't hold them. Tried, but they took off."

"No problem," I assured him.

"Later," he said.

"Ty sighed. Well, partner, off we go. If the beginning of this shift is any indication, it's going to be a long day."

I couldn't keep from laughing. "Ty, you have to give the woman credit for an inventive story. I saw cats all over the place when Rossi and I walked the streets and never managed to trip over a one … but I guess it was a possibility. On second thought, I'd better not say anything—wouldn't want to jinx myself."

Tyrell called in to the dispatcher. "10-4, all set at this address."

———

Sarge was concerned about the number of shootings that had taken place during the previous week—we were once again on night shift. Ty picked up his cup, opened the top, sucked in a mouthful of ice and crunched away.

I took a sip of my coffee but it was cold. "Ty, how about making a pit stop?"

"Yeah, I'm down to ice and about outta that."

"How would I know that? You're going to break a tooth while chewing on the stuff."

"Let's refuel at the Royal Farms on Fleet." Five minutes later, we pulled up in front of the busy store.

"I'll run in," I volunteered. Dispatch came over the radio. "All units engaged—anyone near Boston can take a call?"

Ty responded. "Wilson and Crane. Just stopped for coffee at Eastern and Fleet."

"Received a drag racing complaint from an anonymous caller—south Clinton, off Boston."

"We've got it. C'mon Crane, forget about the java."

"Shit." We headed up Boston Street, passing the Korean Veterans Memorial. At Canton Crossing, Ty turned right onto Clinton. Just ahead was a car doing donuts. Our lights were flashing, but the motorist pulled the car out of a spin and drove down the road for another twenty-five yards without slowing down, long enough that we were concerned about having a chase on our hands. It took another seventy-five yards before he pulled over and shut off the vehicle, leaving the lights on. I called in the stop before we got out. My partner approached the driver's side of the car and indicated that the kid should roll down the window. "Sir, please give me your license and registration."

I remained on the passenger side, wondering what he was doing out here at this time of night if not drag racing. Nobody else was in the immediate area, although I had seen retreating tail lights about two hundred yards away.

"Why you hassling me, man? Didn't do nothing." The kid failed to comply.

"Sir, you know why we stopped you? If you're going to lie, forget it. What should we think you're doing with this totally tricked out ride, if not racing? A noise complaint was called in by a business back there." Ty held his hand out.

"Hey, I'm no damn mind reader. Here's my license and registration. It's not against the law to take good care of my car. Not against the law to drive it, either."

"Well, son, I see you live in Dundalk. What are you doing in this neck of the woods?"

"I have a *right* to be here."

"True. But, Darren Antek, are your parents aware of where you are at this time of night?"

"Sure," he responded sullenly, but a hair less belligerently.

His attitude made me hope that Sean would remain *forever* young. Sullen, sarcastic, snippy ... I could go on and on. Unlike Rossi, Ty was great at not letting kids get under his skin.

"Well, why don't we check in with them?" I asked.

With that suggestion, I was able to establish eye contact—we now had his attention. He sat up straight, clutching the steering wheel tightly. "Their phone number, please." I requested the information knowing there was no reason he had to give it to me. I was pretty sure he didn't know that. Ty raised an eyebrow and managed not to smile.

"*No!* You can't. My mom is sick. Officer," he looked at me—guess he picked up on that unmistakable *maternal* tone, "I promise to head home right now. Please don't call."

"Sounds like a good idea. I'm sure your parents don't want to hear that you're in trouble, particularly if your mom is sick." Then, it occurred to me why he seemed familiar. "Darren, didn't I see you in Fells Point one night a few months ago? You were hanging out with some other kids but took off."

His face froze at the question and he reached for his documents. "I don't need to talk to you, lady."

"No, you don't and, Darren, there's no reason to be rude—I was new to the area and just being friendly. You all seemed to be enjoying yourselves. You go down to Fells Point a lot?"

He was tense, an attitude solidly in place. "Not so much. Sometimes, what of it?"

"Just interested. Darren, you aren't in any trouble here," I assured him.

"Sorry."

"Nothing to apologize for," I said, though he did not sound sorry at all. "I just thought you might be able to help me out before you go on your way." Ty appeared confused but remained silent.

"I guess."

"Since you're down there sometimes, I wondered ... do you know a girl named Joey Jimenez?"

"Nope."

"About 5-foot 2 or 3, thin; medium length blonde hair and brown eyes. She and her mom were staying with an aunt and uncle who live in the area."

"I said, *nope*." He glanced at my partner. "Can I go now?"

"You can but I don't want to hear of any more drag racing around here. Darren, if we get a call again, you're in for a very expensive ticket."

"*Fine.*"

Before we even got into our vehicle, the kid had taken off. He was going a little too fast but not so much that we were inclined to go after him.

"Fluid stop, Ty? I'm so in need of caffeine."

"What was that all about, Robin? The Fells Point thing."

"I thought I saw Darren one night when I was working the streets with Rossi. We had a possible domestic dispute—turned out there was nothing much to it, but a child was involved. Saw the aunt later and she didn't know where the girl and her mother were. I wondered if they'd returned, though even if they had that doesn't mean she hangs out down there—Joey Jimenez is only eleven."

"Got it. I guess."

"Ty, you saw Darren's license. How old is he?

"Seventeen, why?"

"I don't know. At the time, I guess I thought he was older. He was the only one to take off when I approached."

He sighed. "Who knows what's going on with these kids? Call dispatch; let's hit the 7-11."

Chapter 8

Satisfied Customers

"**Okay, boys, quiet** down," Sarge hollered as he entered the room. Everyone did so on a dime, and he began to read off shift assignments. "Before you head out," the big Irishman cautioned, "keep a serious eye out for trouble—there are two Black Guerrilla Family funerals taking place in the Western District and we need to be concerned about the grandmother in Southeast who served as target practice for a punk who, unfortunately, is still at large. *Everyone* is to remain available for other units needing support. Crane, we would have appreciated you California folks keeping the BGF in the sunshine state!" Had to give Sarge his just due, he could be pretty funny in an understated sort of way. "Okay, hit the streets—remain on your toes and stay safe."

I was mulling over the possible origins of "remain on your toes." I must have missed something my partner said because when I looked around for him, he was on his way out of the room and calling to me over his shoulder.

"Earth to *Robin Crane!*"

I wove my way across the room. "Sorry, Ty. What's up?"

"I received an interesting voice mail. An old CI of mine says he has information I'm going to want."

"Got any idea what it is?"

"The informant is in need of a favor, a *big* one—don't ask," he said, before I could. "In return, he says he'll give up something *big*." He laughed. "The guy he's willing to sell out is almost certainly someone who crossed him."

"Why you?"

"Probably because he's pretty sure he can get a *big* favor out of me—you know what a soft touch I am! Plus the cash is good. Crane, he owes me one—I kept him out of jail but, more importantly, he understands his identity is safe with me. Anyway, I put the word out on the street that we're looking for the guy who tried to off the grandmother; I'm hoping it concerns that case. I agreed to meet him in the parking lot under the Cross Keys Inn in Roland Park."

"Why there?"

"Fewer prying eyes in yuppieland."

"Well, then, let's go pass some time with the guy. Ty, I can't understand what kind of person thinks of killing a grandmother. Not only gives thought to the idea; actually attempts to *murder a grandmother*. Damn."

"My bet is it's someone who intends to keep tight control of his drug business, that's who," Ty said glumly. "CI dropped a hint about a rich white kid, which is probably why he's willing to snitch—payback won't be such a bitch."

"I'll call in and advise dispatch. Shouldn't we switch out cars?"

"Nah, we're good. There'll be a few security vehicles, so we'll blend in just fine," my partner said confidently. "On second thought, let's get another car."

Ty pulled into the garage, parked in an isolated corner and popped the locks. In less than a minute, someone got into the back seat. We had decided I would remain facing forward.

"Hey man, my partner here doesn't know who you are. We can talk while she's upstairs."

"Well, guys, better make it quick because the hotel is going to wonder why a cop is decorating their lobby."

"Will do. My boy and me, we got a thing going—won't take us more than ten."

Although I wasn't sure about leaving Ty alone, he'd insisted on maintaining his CI's anonymity. Too often, a hump got one killed. I walked across the garage until I reached the elevator. My concern about hanging out in the lobby without raising an eyebrow or two replaced any worry for my partner.

After being approached, first by the manager and then by hotel security to see what the problem was, I quickly used the restroom and retraced my steps to the garage. True to my word, I returned in under fifteen minutes, which included the time it took to look at the conveniently posted bar menu—a garlicky pizza sauce had caught my attention.

Once I in the car, I was relieved to hear my partner on the phone engaged in an animated conversation. When I got in, he signed off with a "Later, babe."

"Well, that was fast, Ty. Took less time than the drive here. Get anything?"

"Told you it wouldn't take long. He knew what he wanted, I knew what I wanted—a bing bang bong—two satisfied customers! It's Bawlmer. Doesn't do him any good to hang with the cops." He laughed heartily and put his phone away. "Figured you decided to stay for dinner—good bar food here."

"Tempted—I smelled a pizza calling my name. What gives?"

"Patience, patience, Crane—where's the mellow Californian in you? Anyhow, my CI has knowledge of an individual who sold a gun to 'a rich white boy.' Rumor floating around is that the kid, not one of the local gangs, shot up the grandmother's place and her car. Unfortunately, the rumor does not include an explanation or a name."

"Wow, he did have something 'big' for you. What did you give up for that piece of information?"

"Don't worry about it. If it's no good, I know where to find the punk. Let's go! This is a new development, a *white* kid shooting up the 'hood. Info should make Sarge's day!"

Chapter 9

Snitchin' Means Stitchin', or Worse

We were engaged in some community-friendly patrolling. In the process, we hoped to acquire information that would lead us to the shooter in the grandmother case, as we'd taken to calling it. It was quiet and I expected it to stay that way. The Leroy Nichols' investigation was on hold for now while we waited for a decision from the prosecutor's office; so far, they hadn't been especially forthcoming. The shift from nights to days had been a relief, mostly because things had settled down with Matt. At least I hoped they had.

"Ty, I was downtown when a worker at the Trade Center reported a body in the harbor. There was a brief comment or two on the news but not much since. Know anything about the case?"

"Spotted by a guy washing windows?"

"That's the one."

"Still unidentified but between you and me, he probably rolled into the water one night after one drink too many. On the other hand, could be he got into a fight and splash! Why?"

"Just curious—"

The radio crackled: "Anonymous caller reports discharge of firearms—one adult black male down. Possibly gang related. Deceased victim is currently out on bail—distribution and multiple possession charges, including firearms. Not going anywhere now. Officers at discharging scene report other injuries; one individual, critical, is also out on bail—aggravated assault with firearm." She went on to give the address and other relevant details. Ty turned the car around.

"Crane and Wilson—ETA five minutes depending on traffic."

———

"I wonder what's going on with the anonymous complainant. Must be a neighbor—gang members aren't going to be calling for our help—they'll take care of whatever is going on themselves, which guarantees no end to this shit. Crane, if these gangsters were just shooting each other that would be one thing, but innocents are routinely caught up in the crossfire."

Then, it dawned on me. "Damn, Ty. Isn't that the address for the grandmother's house?"

"Shit, shit. Shit!"

After his outburst, quiet pervaded the car. Active shooter calls typically engender ubiquitous feelings of anxiety. Tyrell's philosophy is that fear is normal—it facilitates the concentration needed to do the job and walk through my front door at the end of the day. Maybe he's right, but I like to corral it so I don't get tripped up.

We pulled in behind two squad cars at the scene and headed into the general confusion created by the shooting. The grandmother stood on the sidewalk in front of the house—two women barely supporting her. "They shot my baby!" The sheer volume of her scream drove chills right through me.

I put on my jacket as I approached. "Ma'am, are you hurt?"

"They *killed* my grandson!"

"Was she hit?" I asked the other women. Both mouthed "No." I remembered from our previous visit that she had a daughter. "Either of you her daughter?"

"Daughter's at work," one of the woman responded.

"Is she the dead man's mother?"

"His mother left when he was jus' a little thing."

I redirected my attention to the still screaming woman. "Ma'am, please, we need your help if we're going to find the person who killed your grandson."

I turned to the other two women and gestured in Ty's direction. "I would appreciate it if you would give my partner contact information for your friend's daughter. I'll take good care of her, I promise." Skepticism was written all over their faces, but they complied.

I helped the distraught woman put on her sweater and then took her arm and moved a bit further away from the house. "Ma'am, let's sit on these steps and talk." She followed suit with considerable effort. The grieving woman sat hunched over and weeping but, thankfully, no longer screaming. One of the friends, her face tear-stained and creased with worry, glanced our way. Tyrell managed to keep her engaged.

"Ma'am, can you tell me your name?" Even though I had asked the question, I knew the answer.

"Sherry Earle," she said through sobs.

"Miss Earle, I am so sorry for your loss. We want to find out who killed your grandson, but need your help. Can you tell me what happened?"

"How can you ask me questions? *Now!* My baby, my baby—I raised him from a baby," she said, pulling away.

"Here," I said, handing her a small packet of Kleenex.

She pulled out a few and blew her nose before balling up the tissues, which she clutched in her fist. "Didn't see nobody, but—"

A shriek from a woman stumbling down the porch stairs, an officer close behind, drowned out Sherry Earle's answer. "That be his girl."

The woman began to push herself up, but I gently restrained her, worried she would collapse in the process. Concerned there would be no other chance of getting her to open up. "Ma'am, my partner will take care of her. Please sit here until you feel a little better—I don't want you to hurt yourself."

Out of the corner of my eye, I saw Tyrell approach the screaming woman. Sherry Earle's two friends now assisted *her*. In a couple of minutes, he had moved everyone far enough down the sidewalk that I could resume questioning my witness without being disturbed.

"Ma'am, do you feel any better?"

"A little."

"That's good. Ma'am, do you know who shot your grandson?"

"Don' know nothin'," she said, her voice rising perilously high.

"Can you tell me whether he came from outside? Or, was he already in the house?"

"I told you. I don' know nothin'." She sat stone-faced, no longer weeping.

"Take your time, ma'am. It can be extremely difficult to remember details of a trauma. Still, I want you to think carefully—Miss Earle, we want to find the person who did this to your grandson."

She sniffled and blew her nose. Pulled hard at her hair. Through halting sobs, she mumbled, "The doorbell rang and my baby went to see who it was … there were shots."

At least she was talking. "Miss Earle, where were you and the others when you heard the bell?"

"People were at the table or in the kitchen. His girl must'a been asleep in the bedroom upstairs. Me and my grandson were in the kitchen."

"And which door did he answer?"

"Front door."

"What room is that—nobody was in that part of the house? I asked, not wanting to believe there wasn't at least one witness to multiple shootings that had taken place in, or just outside, a house full of people.

"The front hall. We were eating at the back of the house. Like I *tol'* you, we were in the kitchen and dining room." My witness stopped talking; her eyes widened. What had happened must have sunk in because she began screaming again. "They killed my grandson. Oh, Lord! Oh, may the good Lord help me!"

Though I struggled to keep her from completely crumpling, gravity was rapidly winning the battle. "Hey, I need help over here!" I yelled.

An officer came running; between the two of us, we managed to save the grief-stricken woman from sliding down the steps. "Miss Earle, we're going to take you to the car so that you're more comfortable." A good thought, yet a different story when we tried to take her over there. Out of the corner of my eye, I saw Greg Rossi pull up along the curb, window down. "Hey, buddy, can you give me some help here?" He parked and moved more quickly than he usually did.

"Hey, California, how's it going?" he whispered.

"It would be better with some assistance," I hissed. "We're trying to get the grandmother of one of the victims to the car. Rossi, someone needs to examine her—she keeps breaking down. And it's chilly out here."

After we made it to the car, an unexpectedly compassionate Rossi said, "Ma'am, let me help you into the back seat—we'll keep the door open. An EMT will check you out and determine whether you need medical attention. I'm sure this has been a terrible shock," he added soothingly.

I surveyed the area; there were now easily half a dozen cruisers all with lights going; several of the patrol officers were keeping back curious onlookers from Broadway. A number of wide-eyed children watched the activity, while others played down the street as if nothing had happened. Certain parts of the city are war zones but, even then, life appears to go on. Ironically, it made me feel less guilty about the complications I had introduced into my son's life. She was now leaning against the back of the seat, eyes closed—her breathing slowly becoming more regular, or at least I wanted to believe that was the case.

"Got it under control, California?" Rossi asked.

"Thank you. She seems to be feeling better. How are you? It's been awhile."

"I heard you put in a request for homicide. Give me a call when you get the assignment, and we'll go for a beer to celebrate. I'll buy! And bring your partner with you."

I laughed, surprised *and* pleased. "How'd you hear that? Never mind. Thanks for the invite."

"Well, I've got to shove off, but I'll send the med tech over before you have another victim; she appears good for a coronary. Probably should use the second bus to get her over to Hopkins."

"Thanks."

"See you for that beer!"

The EMT came over and asked my witness for her name, basic contact information, and permission to examine her. Not encountering any resistance, he removed a cuff from his bag and took her blood pressure. After that, he proceeded to scrutinize her pupils and listen to her breathing. "Ma'am, did you drink or take any drugs today?" he asked matter-of-factly, putting away the stethoscope.

That got her attention: she stared at him and then at me. I didn't understand what the problem was. She began to say something but then must have thought better of it.

"*Ma'am?*"

"Would you ask such a question of an older white lady?"

She had a point. "Miss Earle, we want to make sure you're okay," I said, hoping to smooth things over. "Please understand we're not interested in whether you took anything—we're here to find out who shot your grandson."

"Ma'am, I'm sorry. I didn't mean to sound disrespectful," said the young tech, flushing through his freckles. "I ask that of *all* my patients—I need the information so we can care for you appropriately."

"How old are you, Miss Earle?" I asked.

"Fifty-six."

The emergency technician continued. "Ma'am, do you have any health problems that you know of?"

"Doctor says I must be careful of my pressure."

The tech tried again. "Do you take any medications? You were at a party—that's why I asked about alcohol. Ma'am, some medicines interact badly with alcohol."

She appeared to be thinking that through. "Yes," she replied, less indignantly this time. "Pills for my pressure and diabetes. All I drank was sweet tea. It was a birthday party."

"Well, ma'am, I think we need to take you to a doctor for a complete examination. Your blood pressure is pretty high," the EMT repeated with measured concern. He shifted his attention to me. "Officer, can you remain with Miss Earle while I bring the bus closer."

"No problem."

———

It was a relief when the ambulance pulled out. The crowd had thinned and I headed over to where Ty stood talking with some of the others. He left the group and joined me.

"What's happening?"

"EMT took the victim's grandmother to Hopkins to be checked out. She—Sherry Earle—said someone rang the bell, her grandson went to answer the door in the front hallway, and she heard shots. Supposedly, everyone was in the kitchen or dining room—girl in a bedroom, so there were no witnesses. She did say "they" rather than a shooter, so I don't know. Ty, once the hospital releases her, I'd like to go inside the house and map it out—find out who could see what."

"Was I wrong, Crane—there are five victims, not four? The grandmother is injured?"

"No, though she might be a possible coronary. Turns out Rossi wasn't far off base: middle age, heavy with high blood pressure, the med tech wanted her seen by a doctor. What about the girlfriend?"

"She was asleep upstairs until a detective knocked on her door—claims she doesn't know anything. Crane we didn't catch this case—it's been assigned to Ramirez and his partner."

"Too bad. What about the victims—the grandson on the porch?" I asked.

"Dead—adult black male. According to the witnesses I spoke with, that victim answered the door. When shot, he must have fallen over the threshold. Nobody admits to seeing him—the killer, I mean. If it *was* a him. The grandmother give you the deceased's name?"

"No. Sorry, Ty, I didn't get much. She wasn't in such good shape."

"Crane, you're not going to like this."

"Not like what?"

"Witnesses said the dead man is Leroy Nichols."

"Shit, I *don't* believe it! Are you sure, Ty?"

"Yeah, the ME let me take a look at the body. It's Leroy, all right. An unintended consequence of the bail system."

"The bail system? Ty, *we* were supposed to keep him safe. Damn! Damn! Damn! Nichols was right—snitchin' in Baltimore is a dangerous business. I wonder how Cuz found out—*he* had to have put this in motion. He must have been behind the shooting up of her car. Then what was the role of the white shooter?—maybe you should talk to your CI again. Somebody knows who's responsible for what's happened here."

"I agree," said Ty dejectedly. "Good idea to touch base with my CI. I shared some of our info with Ramirez, but I'm going to talk with Sarge and the prosecutor—they need to know we lost Nichols. Robin, Ramirez caught the case but we'll probably end up working it together."

"We ought to be able to work it—can't imagine Sarge will have a problem with that. More immediately, although the EMT was sufficiently worried about the grandmother to want her examined at JHH, she's capable of answering questions. I figured it was better not to push her any further, but with it being Leroy who was murdered, all bets are off. I think we should talk with her—this victim was *our* collar and we made promises to him. What else do we have?"

"Three others were hit. The young black male—he has a long sheet—was found at the side of the house and is in critical condition.

Also hit were an older woman and another young black male, both inside. There had to be more than one shooter and, of course, one or more of the victims may be the shooter or shooters. As usual, nobody's talking; Crane, we're not even sure who was at the party."

"Sheer chaos and no witnesses; the scene gets changed around—no wonder the arrest rate in Baltimore is such a problem. We got a gun, Ty?"

"Nothing's turned up."

"It makes no sense why there are so many victims if Sherry's grandson was the only one in the front hallway and everyone else was in the dining room or kitchen. I can't imagine the shooter just stood at the doorway and waited for others to come out to see what was going on, unless he was in the house for the party and something went bad. Anyone admit to being on the porch or in the yard?"

"Robin, Ramirez is taking over from here, at least for now. *He's* going to do the interviews. I'll give him a call to find out whether he wants you to speak with Earle, since you have a connection."

"Thanks. Ty, why don't you and I canvass the neighborhood—see if we can find someone to talk with us. Leroy's death must be payback related to the information he gave us. Or, could be the stuff in the van we confiscated. The vehicle belonged to him on paper, but maybe it wasn't his to use."

"There sure is a lot of activity around here, but you're probably right and this is payback. Still, Sherry Earle was convinced the first shooting was drug-related."

"Well, could be the two things are connected. Crane, I'm not aware of anything suggesting a link between Cuz, drug running, the initial warning, and Nichols' murder. You?"

"No. Ty, I feel bad about Leroy—he must have been hyperalert to threats, but obviously not alert enough."

I thought about the kids exposed to gunfire, screaming women, sirens, strobe lights, and dead and injured hauled away on stretchers, some not to return. I couldn't imagine how it had progressed from an afternoon party to a shootout. I assumed the children knew some of the people involved. Might even know the shooter. I pushed back intruding thoughts of Sean and what would happen if I were shot—even with my parents and Matt there for him. He had already experienced enough loss in his young life. I never asked Leroy if he had children—he had just spoken of his concern for his grandmother and, honestly, I hadn't been too concerned about her. Who would be crying for today's victims?

"Let's go," said my partner. "We're off, boys."

"Later, Wilson, Crane."

I waved and we left. An officer moved several cones and Ty pulled out. "I hate the transition from nights to days," he sighed. "I'm cold and need a hot cup of coffee—let's head over to the 7-Eleven on Fleet. Then we can see who's up and about."

"I agree—transitions can be a problem, but I particularly don't like nights when we need to testify in the morning. There has to be a correlation between lack of sleep and safety concerns on the job. Then, frequently, the prosecutors aren't prepared—they carry too many cases. My hat's off to you—I've no idea how you've been doing this for twelve years. So far, it's been pretty depressing—most days it's difficult to imagine that we're making a difference. Today, it looks like we got someone killed."

"No argument there. Yeah, it's really a bunch of shit some days! Robin, somebody's gotta do it and I'm all right with that. My woman—not so much."

"You said you had friends who run with the gangs. How did you escape the life?"

"I think about that sometimes. Mostly, I guess, it was my grandmother who made the difference when it came to a *career choice*—gangsta' or cop."

"She must be a wonderful lady."

"She is. Robin, bring that husband and son of yours over some weekend—Grandmom loves children and I'm a mean man with the grill. Speaking of which, I could use a couple of Big Bites—lots of onions and relish, dash of ketchup. And a big gulp."

"Bloomberg says no big gulps—I'll stick with coffee and a bottle of water."

He pulled into a spot and we got out. "That's New York City, Crane. Baltimore's good with extra sugar. Thrives on it!"

We went inside the crowded store and rummaged through the aisles searching for whatever it was that would satisfy our respective food cravings. Once back in the car, Tyrell amped up the heat. We ate in silence.

Ty sighed with satisfaction. "That hit the spot. Time to get on with it and discover what's up in the 'hood." We hadn't gone even a block when we saw a boy, maybe fifteen, walking by himself. He wore a black hoodie, no belt—the waist of his jeans heading toward his knees, a Ravens hat on backwards and mirrored sunglasses despite the weather being overcast.

Tyrell pulled up next to the curb, slightly in front of the boy. I rolled down my window. "Hey, man, can you come over here?" my partner called out.

You had to admire Tyrell's timing—we were now almost exactly parallel with the kid. Though stopped, he remained where he was, too far away to carry on a conversation.

The distance didn't stop Ty. "Hey man, you hear gunshots an hour or so ago?" he yelled out across me.

That brought the kid over to the car. "Didn't hear nothin'," he replied with plenty of attitude.

"There was a shooting over on Pratt, a block off Broadway. Man, the guy's dead at his *grandmother's* house. At a birthday party."

"Don't know nothin' about no shooting, man." He took a few steps forward, but turned and with a fair amount of attitude, declared, "I told you, yo! Don't know nothin' 'bout no shootin'."

"Okay, okay. Man, why you geekin'?—here's something for food." Tyrell handed me a five, which I raised high enough for the kid to see. He snatched the bill and walked off without a change of expression or even a word.

We continued patrolling streets and alleys, but it remained quiet.

"Ty, back to the question I asked yesterday or the other day. How is it you've been doing this for so long?"

"Stupid."

"No, really? I've asked this before but never get a straight answer."

"Seriously?"

I nodded, and this time he appeared to give the question some thought.

"Well, I suppose that despite the years and what's come with them, I still feel I make a difference. Robin, these are *my* streets and this is *my* city—too many of my friends are dead. I was lucky; I had my mother and grandmother, went to college. I guess *that's* why I do what I do—still, Leroy had his grandmother and *he's* dead. I just don't know."

"Do you live here—in the city?"

"No … I hesitated because you do and I'm also aware some on the city council are pushing for cops to live here. Anyhow, I'm going to answer your question truthfully. I don't live in the city and unless I have to, I don't even come here when I'm off. Folks recognize those of us working the neighborhoods. We live in the county but, even so, I've run into trouble. Once at the Towson Town Center, on the down escalator, a teenager going up spotted me and loudly informed my daughter I was 'a dick.' Crane, he could just as well have pulled a gun on us. That was it for the mall. Since then, Janie and I have discussed moving to PA. When the communities make noise about the police, they never think about how the job affects our personal lives or how bad things would be without law enforcement. All you hear is one mother's son, who shot a rival—another mother's son—in the head, is innocent and the police are picking on *their* baby. On top of that, there's a constant threat of lawsuits. Some rotten apples? Absolutely, but most of us are just trying to do our jobs. Enough of that—didn't mean to start whining. Crane, I know you're only with me for training purposes—still hankering for Homicide? Or do you figure on continuing this wandering life of yours?"

I laughed—Ty might have my number. "I'm still thinking Homicide. I guess I like the science of it—the painstaking and methodical work solving a murder demands. To be honest, Ty, the work you do is so fast-paced and dangerous—I've spent too much time worrying about Sean if I end up wounded or, worse, dead. I don't mean to sound dramatic—"

"I get it, Robin. I live for the job, but I want to be here for my kids and hopefully my grandkids. I'd like to stay with a woman for life and policing makes a relationship difficult. But back to Leroy Nichols—when we talk to Sarge about the case, we should double-check about the extra patrols. There's bound to be retaliation over the shooting, which is sure to be about territory, *broadly* defined." He looked at his watch. "Hey, we'd better move it."

Tyrell drove around, orienting me to the particularities of the neighborhood and identifying landmarks as he threw out historical nuggets. Though kids should be in school, we passed far too many who, for the most part, began to all look the same to me with their hoodies and athletic gear. In contrast, my partner could instantly name the kids, their friends, and provide a few personal observations. In several instances, their criminal histories. I was impressed—no wonder he stuck with the job.

Ty slowed the car down. "See the kid leaning against the pole? The one with the white cap turned backward, dark blue jacket. Smoking. Probably a joint," he laughed and waved. The boy flashed the peace sign before taking a drag off whatever he was smoking and blowing it in our direction.

"What's up with him? Like most of the kids we've driven by, he looks like he should be in school."

"Name is Dontay Macklin and what I can promise is he's seldom, if ever, in school. I went to school with Stanley Macklin, Dontay's older brother—we played on the same basketball team in high school and I'm the godfather to his eldest child. My friend is dead, yet here's his little brother hangin' on the corner—I wonder how long it'll be before I'm attending another funeral and, again, struggling to comfort Miss Rosie. She has always worked hard and tried to protect her boys, but the streets keep swallowing up our kids."

"What happened to Stanley?" I asked.

"Like so many of my classmates, Stan the Man was shot over a drug deal—he left behind a pregnant girl and three small kids. Robin, I guess what keeps me here is the knowledge that I could just as easily have been my friend."

I waited for more but none came. "What was the finding?"

"Wasn't one. Homicide took over, which is usually the case, but the investigation went cold, like so many others—we don't prosecute even fifty percent of the shootings and homicides. Robin, it's up to this unit to keep a lid on things—get the bad guys before someone is hurt, keep the drugs off the streets, stop the trafficking of children—that's what makes the job difficult, but rewarding. C'mon let's head back before I get more discouraged."

I glanced at my watch. "Maybe, for a change, we'll be home early enough to do something with the kids."

He laughed. "Janie appreciates you!"

"What?"

"She likes that I'm working with a married woman and mother."

The sun was setting and rush hour traffic was increasing. A distinctly different Baltimore would be coming alive. Soon, I would be home closing the blinds.

Suddenly, a jarring high-pitched voice filled the car. "To all units. Suspect in Pratt Street shootings is a young black male: thin, tall—6'2" to 6'4", wearing a black hoodie, dark sweats and white air maxes. Last seen heading north from the harbor—728 calling for back-up." Dispatch repeated: "Suspected shooter, considered armed and dangerous, on foot running north—last seen south of Fayette."

"That's Ramirez and his partner. Let's go, Crane."

"357 responding. Ty, maybe we can get justice for Leroy after all." But before we had gone more than a couple of blocks, something had changed—dispatch confirmed 728 had dropped the pursuit at Fayette. Location of possible shooter unknown.

Ty drove into the Kennedy Krieger parking lot minutes later. I took my glasses out of the console and looked around but didn't see anyone of interest. "I wonder how they came up with a suspect."

"Got me, Robin. Here's Ramirez—let's ask him."

Justin Ramirez pulled up alongside our vehicle and got out, leaving his door open. "Hey, guys, we lost the little shit—see anything?" he asked, leaning against his vehicle and lighting up.

At least he doesn't smoke in the car. "Hey, nobody with dispatch's description running or looking suspicious—we came up here from east Baltimore via Broadway. Where was the guy when you last had eyes on him?"

"Flushed him out of an abandoned house on Pratt. Last I saw he was heading south between the H & S Bakery buildings. We continued searching south to the Waterfront Kitchen, Smith Barney, etc. and through the Harbor East area. Nothing on the streets after the first glimpse; nobody splashing in the water. Then a call of a suspicious male running north came in, but nothing came out of that. Oh, here comes my partner! Be prepared."

The three of us watched as the cop approached ... *on foot*, obviously pissed.

"Ramirez, what happened back there? We could have gotten the SOB! Damn, I had him in my sights. Why didn't you continue the pursuit?"

"Get your act straight, buddy—it wasn't the same guy. You're fucked up and it shows. I'm not putting civilians at risk. If you want to hot dog it, find yourself another partner. You've had two questionable shootings in the past year; one excessive force—even the Union complained. I don't want to be involved in that shit. There's enough trouble going down in Baltimore and I've got enough on me with that suspension."

Radios in both cars crackled and put an end to the tirade. "Suspect for the Pratt shooting spotted in the vicinity of Asquith and Prospect. All available units respond."

We headed for our respective vehicles. "Shit, how'd he make it so far north?" Ramirez's partner asked of nobody.

"Bro, I said you were drawing on the wrong guy—c'mon let's get the right one. Later," Justin called out of the open window of the moving car.

We took off behind them with sirens blaring, lights flashing. "357 in pursuit," I reported to dispatch. "Hey, partner, why don't we turn off the reds and blues? We can't be tearing around in this traffic and, besides, we're signaling our location."

We spent the next ten minutes weaving our way through alleys. It was when coming out of one that I saw a suspicious individual fitting the description we had. "That might be him—to the east, 50 meters." I called in the sighting and requested that dispatch notify Ramirez of our location.

Ty took a hard right; the tall, thin suspect, spotting us, raced across the street and into a weedy trash-filled lot. "*Stop the car!*" He braked. I bailed and ran to the clump of bushes where I thought I saw the guy ditch something.

It didn't take long. "I got it!" I bagged a Glock 50.

My partner pulled over. "Ty, you see where he went?"

"Over there, I think," he said, pointing at a house four properties down. "Though he might have gone out the back." The two-story house looked uninhabited; the roof of the porch was collapsing and all visible windows boarded up. Still, it had a new black iron gate at the front door. Ty locked the weapon in the trunk. "It's completely ridiculous not to install gun safes in the vehicles," I groused … again.

"I'll give you that. C'mon, Crane, let's go check out the house before we lose him."

There was a name on the mailbox. We stood to each side of the doorway, guns hot, and I knocked. Nothing. I knocked again and waited; this time the door cracked open, although nobody was visible. "What do you want?" a male voice demanded.

"Mr. Martinez, it's the police. We were hoping you could help us." The ploy didn't work. The door closed, the latch clicked into place, and all we could hear was the sound of running feet.

Ty pounded down the wooden stairs. "It must be him in there. Keep an eye on the front—I'm going around the back."

Seconds later, I heard my partner screaming at the suspect to stop. "Crane, back here!"

I raced around the house to the rear and joined the chase. Tyrell was more than a block ahead, but the guy I'd seen toss the gun was visible. Ramirez came out of nowhere. At about the time I caught up with the two men, Ty had vaulted over a metal fence. Ramirez followed suit. I saw an open gate and ran up a narrow alley and out onto the street. *Nobody* was in sight. Just as I decided we'd lost the suspect, he dashed across the street—hat gone, but wearing the white shoes. "Police," I yelled, quickly closing the distance. "Stop where you are; go down on your knees—my gun's drawn and locked. C'mon Mr. Martinez, or whatever your name is, don't make this any more difficult than it needs to be. Show me both your hands." He took a few hesitant steps.

Out of breath, heart pounding, I needed help if he was going to make a run for it. *"Stop right now!"*

"You'd better listen to the lady," Tyrell, approaching from behind me, said in a low angry growl. "Yo, California, here, will shoot you dead if you even blink."

"And if she doesn't, I sure as hell will," Ramirez threatened, moving in from the front.

One foot went forward. "Don't even think of taking another step," I said. "Get on the ground. Now." Siren screaming, Ramirez' partner pulled up with a squeal.

———

"I'm interested in what comes out of *that* interrogation. Tyrell, I need to work out more—for a minute I thought I would stop breathing. I guess I've let myself go with the family here. Plus, not to make excuses, but I'm unfamiliar with these neighborhoods—I'm more likely to get killed by a fence, garbage can, piles of trash, pit bull, or a car than the bad guy. Sheer luck I spotted the open gate."

"I understand. The streets are remarkably hazardous but, seriously, *never* forget these gangs are dangerous as hell. Don't give them an inch, 'cause they'll get you every time. I lost a partner to one of those pieces of shit."

"Sorry, Ty. I lost a partner and it still hurts."

"Yeah, I know what you mean."

Chapter 10

Homicide in Roland Park

The news of my detail to Homicide came through unexpectedly; after 90 days, if approved, I would have my promotion to detective. I quickly shelved my excitement when I learned my first assignment involved a dead child. Matt for the umpteenth time suggested I consider another profession. I insisted that I would continue considering my options, but it was becoming increasingly clear he'd about had it with my feeble assurances. In such doubt-laden moments, I missed Doug.

In sharp contrast to the never ending drug, gun, and gang problems downtown, big deals in Roland Park, where the boy's body had been discovered, were misdemeanor crimes—garage break-ins and teenagers with no parents in evidence, running amuck and slashing tires or keying cars late at night after too many beers. The report of a suspected homicide had shocked the community. And they were, without a doubt, frightened. Although violent crime was highly unusual, over the years there'd been several robberies, two armed; one woman put in a car trunk after an ATM withdrawal, as well as a home invasion involving a rape. Nonetheless, Baltimore City crime stats show the neighborhood is one of the safest in the city. All of that is why the discovery of a young boy's body by a physician walking his dog on the 9th of November was completely out of character for Roland Park.

It was my first day on the job with Detective Erica Moreno. When I called Ken in Santa Barbara about the detail to Homicide, he teased me about not being able to keep my partners straight. He had a point—she would be my *third* since I began working for the BPD.

"Ready to go?" Erica asked over her shoulder, headed for the door. I doubt she'd even seen me in the cubicle. Her stride as she left the room said "tough."

"Give me a sec." I saved my work and logged off the computer, put on my regulation jacket and, though a good seven inches taller, *hustled* to catch up with the short woman, a bit on the heavy side. When the Lieutenant introduced us, I was struck by Erica's exotic features, which were emphasized by dark hair so tightly pulled into a braid that it tugged at her scalp. Her skin was creamy brown and her eyes a piercing coal-black with stern eyebrows reminding me of Frida Kahlo.

I caught up with Erica at the car. "What's going on—a call come in?"

"No call, California. I want to recheck the scene where the boy's body was found—Stony Run Park. We are *nowhere* with this investigation. How in the hell can we have a dead child and nobody has come forward to identify him? *Carajo!* Too many days have gone by since his body was discovered."

"I understand." Once we were on our way, she seemed calmer and I asked the question that had been on my mind since the reassignment. "Erica, given the intense concern over this case, what happened to your partner?"

She continued gazing straight ahead, but by the time it occurred to me I'd stepped in it, she answered. "My previous partner, a *good* guy by the way, was promoted and transferred to Northwest. They've got problems—a cop dealing heroin in the district's parking lot, if you can believe that! Another protecting a drug dealer—giving him a heads-up when detectives had him made. I do not know which is worse! To be honest, I miss my boy, but he will make a difference there. Crane, when they transferred your Sarge from downtown to Northern during the shake-up, my old supervisor suggested 'a fresh set of eyes on the case might be helpful.' He brought you with him. I heard through the grapevine you are good police."

Well, *that* answered several questions. Her response also implied that she was reluctant to take me on, though that could be unwarranted paranoia. "How would anybody here know anything about me?" I asked, surprised at the unexpected bit of news.

"No big deal. Rossi spoke with an old friend of his in California and passed along the information to another friend who works out of Northern."

"You're kidding me! Is nothing sacred?"

"Not really, so you had better get used to it. I've been fortunate—Costa Rica is too far for the gossip mill."

"Lucky you!" I laughed.

"Never mind all that now; let me catch you up with the case. California, you and I are going to catch the shit who did this! Killing a child—I take that personally and I intend to roast his ass."

The implication of Erica's rant sank in and I put aside thoughts of Santa Barbara. "Well, let's get back to business. A second examination of the park sounds like a good idea, especially since I don't know the area. I've only heard bits and pieces about this case, so why don't you fill me in on the way? What *is* clear to me is that the boy's death is a real anomaly in this neighborhood, which I understand to be a relatively safe oasis in an urban area with an exceptionally high murder rate. Do I have that right?"

She regarded me curiously. "I thought you came from Baltimore?"

"True, but I lived here years ago … and when I did, my home was a *long* way from Roland Park. Mine, Erica, are blue-collar roots—I grew up in Dundalk. No reason to be up here. Anyhow, there've been a lot of changes since I left for California, changes which even seem to be coming to my former neighborhood."

"That's what I hear—I guess your old stomping ground will become yuppieized, which seems to be true for much of the city. Not sure that's the correct word but you know what I mean."

"I do. I've seen it for myself."

"Anyhow, you're right, this is definitely one of the safest neighborhoods in Baltimore, if not *the* safest, so the murder of an unknown child threw Roland Park into a state of turmoil. There is serious pressure to get it solved."

"Meaning?"

"Meaning nothing to me," she laughed. "Politics are for the leadership; I do not involve myself in that kind of shit. Word to the wise, California, you should stay out of anything political. It has taken me awhile but I've finally learned Baltimore is less of a city and more of a conglomeration of neighborhoods with competing needs, lots and lots of history, and *very* long memories accompanied by exceptional grudges. The politics are complicated beyond belief."

"Sounds like excellent advice. What do you know so far?"

"Not much, I am sorry to say. What we have, based on the teeth and bone analysis, is that he was between age 10 and 11 at time of death. Probably closer to 11, though the boy was on the small side. The ME has not yet determined cause of death—might have been asphyxiated, no evidence of strangulation."

"Any ideas how it could have been done?"

"Perhaps a pillow. No evidence of malnutrition and dehydration."

"What about sexual abuse?"

"No evidence of sexual abuse, which was a real surprise. A relief. Robin, what I find strange is the lack of a report for a missing child fitting his description. We released a sketch, a good one, but nothing helpful has come in. The FBI and the National Center for Missing and Exploited Children has nothing for us. One of the posters is in the glove compartment."

I removed and unfolded the paper. Staring out at me was a boy a little older than Sean but not by much. The child had close cut brown hair, light-colored eyes and seemed to be of mixed race or else deeply tanned. There was a smattering of freckles across his cheeks and nose. "A cute kid—somebody must be missing him. What a tragedy. Do you have any children, Erica?"

"I do. A daughter and a son; she is 14 and he is 12."

"Where do they go to school?"

"They live with their grandmother in Costa Rica. Abita, we call her—short for Abuelita."

I didn't respond, not understanding for the life of me why her two children lived in a different country and hardly knowing her well enough to ask. Her English was excellent and she had only a slight accent. I changed the subject. "*Somebody's* child is missing—it's strange nobody recognized him with all the publicity—he appears well cared for. My boy is about the same age, although if the ME is correct, Sean is younger. While in Santa Barbara, I worked a case involving the murder of a pregnant graduate student. The devastation her parents experienced will stay with me always."

"The Blessed Virgin knows that I am with you—I dread making those death notifications. Even so, I would rather tell the parents their son has passed than to go home each night knowing a child is lying unclaimed in the morgue. Unless they were involved in his death— *that* would be a possible explanation. Okay, almost there."

Erica drove down a hilly street, Oakdale, and pulled into a small parking apron fronted by a low stone wall. We got out and went around the barrier. To our right was a sign declaring the grassy area thick with trees to be Stony Run Park. In addition to a map and drawings of foliage with biological notations, tacked to the board was a request to pick up after one's dog, followed by emphatic exclamation points. Someone had nailed a wooden box stuffed with plastic grocery bags to the post. Curious, I scanned the other notices: one concerning a Roland Park Association meeting and two describing lost cats and the heartache owners suffered in their absence. On the rise above the border of the park were large, beautiful and what I figured for very expensive homes with generous lawns and meticulous landscaping that managed to blend in with the less controlled foliage below. Fifty or sixty yards from the road was a creek lined with tall trees.

We walked north along a well-packed dirt pathway running about twenty feet from the edge of the creek at the beginning and increasingly closer as we continued. I thought of the doctor simply out walking his dog before work and then the horror he must have experienced at the discovery of a dead child. It was obvious those of our ilk were not regulars in the park, mostly because of the number of loose dogs and startled looks—one woman hastily attached a leash to her retriever's collar and, without looking at us, kept going. Police are not always so popular in urban areas; I wanted to think that those living in the immediate area were relieved at our presence. We hadn't passed any children, but then none was outside playing when we drove through the neighborhood.

After walking for about five minutes, Erica stopped so abruptly I bumped into her. "What's the matter?"

"Crane, here is where Dr. Manning found the boy's body." She pointed to a culvert running under a narrow but relatively busy street fronting a cluster of small stores. High on one of the buildings facing the street was an archetypal wooden sign declaring it to be Wyndhurst Station, 1901, in gold lettering.

"The body was discovered a couple of feet inside. From where you are standing, can you see the cement slab running off the edge of the base to the left?" Without waiting for my response, Erica continued. "It was on that shelf the boy was found. He was dressed in jeans, a long-sleeved Orioles tee shirt, and a dark blue winter Timberland jacket. The shirt suggests he is local, which is why I am surprised there is no report of a missing child."

"Why such a heavy jacket? Sean has one and in Maryland it's good for only about three months—December through February."

"You are right, but remember we had that freak early snowfall. He was wearing white athletic socks, which by the way were clean. Nike sneakers. No useful forensics on any of the clothing. All brand names and none of it, including the shoes, showed any wear. No identification, although that is not a surprise given his age."

"What do you know about the doctor who found him?"

"Dr. Bernard J. Manning, a hot shot at Hopkins, is not such a bad sort. The doctor's Irish setter likes to run; appropriately named Red Dog, she somehow got loose, took off and headed this direction. When Manning finally caught up with her, the dog was standing at the opening of the culvert barking and whining. Curious as to what had upset the animal he looked inside and that's when he saw the body. Manning checked the boy's pulse. There was none."

"Time of death?"

"The ME estimates the boy was dead between 10 to 14 hours, which put time of death between 6 and 10 the night before. But you know how unreliable TOD can be—plus it was cold that night."

"Yeah. Is the doctor clean—could he alibi out?"

"An alibi. Not really, yet so far there is nothing suggesting he's a suspect. Manning lives alone. The previous night it was just him with his dog at home. Said he was reading a medical journal in the den. No phone calls and not on the computer. He went to bed at 10 and watched television before going to sleep. *Thinks* he turned it off when the news came on at 11. Nobody saw him outside after he came into the house for the night. No evidence he used the car; the boy was small but it would be a long walk carrying a body—the doc lives four blocks from here. Could have driven from his house, but it is likely he would have been seen. Manning had an early morning surgery—7:30, which explains why he was out so early; it was a little after six. Cutting it close if you ask me—he needed to get back to the house, drive over to east Baltimore, park, and scrub up. What's more, he did not remember passing anyone while walking his dog. Or, seeing anyone on the other side of the creek, even though he and others said local residents are often out at that hour."

"Certainly none of that eliminates him as a suspect. Does he have a record?"

"No record of any kind. Well, other than a few speeding tickets, which everyone in Baltimore has received given malfunctioning speed cameras. Robin, we asked for anybody who was out at that time or earlier to give us a call. Nothing helpful came in, so we didn't rule out Dr. Manning. I spoke with neighbors, but nobody reported seeing him the next morning. We can bring Manning in again when there is evidence pointing us in his direction."

"I assume the scene was searched thoroughly—are you looking for something in particular today?"

"Not really. Well, nothing more than what I have told you." Erica hesitated. She carefully smoothed back hair with nowhere to go. Thirty or forty seconds later, she sighed and said, "Well, California, I guess there is one more thing. The snow came the day before Manning discovered the body. It has warmed up since then. She paused. "Obviously," she added sarcastically. "In any event, on my way to work this morning I was thinking it might be worth looking again—no snow, new partner. Robin, I do not know if you are religious, but I am praying we will locate evidence I missed the first time."

She seemed embarrassed; I kept things light. "Makes sense. How do you want to do this?"

"Not that I want to start off on the wrong foot with you, but would you object to taking the area under and around the culvert? I searched it pretty thoroughly, so *fresh* eyes might help, even if it is only for my peace of mind. Meantime, I will take another look at the surrounding area."

"Sure." Though dreading the wet feet sure to follow, I headed over to the culvert. If I had known what was on the schedule for today, I would have brought waders.

Erica must've caught the slightly sarcastic undertone. "Hate to tell you, but there is more."

I pulled up abruptly. "More?"

"Don't worry; it does not involve more sloshing about in the water. I was hoping we could walk both pathways—this one and the one on the other side of the creek. Keep an eye open for *anything*; this is a pretty trash-free zone—here are a few evidence bags and some gloves."

"Thanks," I said, pocketing them. I began by examining the area around the culvert. The flow of water seemed strong for a creek, although there'd been plenty of rain and even the unexpected snow. I wondered whether it had once been a river, yet that seemed improbable given the location of old growth trees in the park. Out of place for Maryland was the bamboo—several flourishing clumps, which I figured would be out of control in no time at all because of the shade and constant water flow. I zipped up my jacket and scanned the immediate area while making some notes about the physical layout and the vegetation. Nothing in particular caught my attention. I put away the notebook and picked my way across the stones, stopping to remove gloves from my pocket.

After I reached the opening, I bent over and cautiously entered the clammy cold area under the roadway. Water coming from the north flowed through a culvert perhaps eight feet in diameter before rejoining the creek. I hunched down and began a closer examination. Once I finished, I commenced turning over rocks washed inside by the water. Not surprisingly, given how much time had passed, I couldn't find anything that didn't belong.

I shifted my attention to the concrete slabs reinforcing the structure, and then scrutinized the sections above the waterline. There was evidence of animal activity on the slab to the right—(although I was hardly an expert on avian fecal matter); also rotting leaves and some twigs. I poked around carefully but found no obviously human debris. To the left, where they'd discovered the boy's body, a few stray leaves and bird droppings littered the cement. I would have to remember to ask Erica when the police removed the crime tape and how long they had watched the crime scene after discovering the body. I was also interested in knowing where the creek originated and how far north they searched beyond Wyndhurst.

After taking a last look, I backed up and surveyed the area but didn't spot anything out of place. Using my cell, I took photos inside and outside of the culvert.

Despite having made every effort to remain on the rocks, water seeped into my shoes at every step and my feet were unbearably cold. In any event, I continued poking around with a stick and turning over rocks, looking for anything that might provide evidence as to the identity of the dead child and, if lucky, some explanation for what happened to him.

Feet frozen and my mind blank, I sighed, finally admitting to myself that I needed some heat and dry footwear. I was taking a last look when the cement archway captured my attention. On closer examination, what I first thought to be tagging included an elaborate painting. Then I saw it! I had missed it completely—it was like playing *Where's Waldo* with Sean after a long day. Once he or I locate Waldo, it's always difficult to understand why the search takes so long. Cold feet slipped from my mind.

I called out, while trying to dampen my excitement, "Erica, can you come over here?"

"Sure, but give me a minute, Robin. I want to finish this section—it has been slow; I am recording as I go."

It took what seemed an impossibly long five minutes before she returned to the culvert. "Damn, California, I have not found anything and I mean *anything*. What happened to the fine art of littering?—folks are not aware of what a good time they are missing. Got something interesting?" She looked at my feet as I stood in the creek and laughed. "Besides cold feet that is. Sorry, I know it is not funny because I have literally been where you are right now—with snow added to the mix."

"Well, it's hard to tell—I guess I'm not sure given the amount of time that's passed since the boy was found. Erica, how long was an officer posted here?"

"I don't know. Probably when the ME and Crime Scene techs had finished up. Hmmm ... maybe a few hours—Robin, we are chronically short-staffed and there was no justification for leaving a car here. Why?"

"What about the crime tape?"

"Would have been taken down when the officers left, though it wouldn't have kept anyone out if up. In this neighborhood, I am sure they removed the tape. Why the procedural questions? There are plenty of photos of the area if you want to review them. Anyhow, we should set up a board. Sounded like you had something. Give it up, California!"

"Well, I was thinking that since we had no eyes on the area, someone may have been curious and … it might not be anything at all. Erica, there's been a lot of tagging, both on the outside of the concrete archway, as well as inside the culvert. The graffiti seem out-of-place given the nature of this neighborhood: as you pointed out, there is a definite lack of litter and crime in the area.

"Initially, I thought that maybe what we had here was an *artiste* from one of the high schools but then wondered whether someone had been here after the body was discovered—I guess we'll know better after reviewing the photographs. In any case, disregard that concern for now and concentrate on the far side of the archway over the culvert. Originally, it seems this was a nature mural; subsequent tagging then overlapped with that: so, forget the graffiti and focus on the two flying geese at the top, which I assume are part of the mural. Follow the painted stairs. They seem weird and out of place, so they might be a kid's contribution to the mural rather than graffiti *per se*. Anyhow, those are what I want you to look at." I looked from the painting to my partner; she simply looked confused.

"Hang on, Moreno." I picked my way back across the creek until I was close enough to indicate the geese and the zigzag line I interpreted as stairs. "Follow my finger downward; see the small turtle on the lowest stair—line—whatever?" I asked, pointing at the amphibian. "Are you with me?"

"Yeah, I think one of the guys said that the local neighborhood association paid for the mural when some work to shore up the sides of the creek was completed. Afterward, I guess kids came along with a spray can, although I agree the stairs look strange. Too bad—the tagger's work certainly fails to measure up. Robin, why so much interest in the local artwork?"

"Like I said, Erica, ignore the tagging. Concentrate on the original painting—specifically, the turtle. Now, look below and beyond the turtle and tell me what you see?"

She stepped back and concentrated on the painting. I remained quiet.

"Ay, Dios. *Damn*, Chica! I see it," she said in disbelief.

I walked over to the turtle and slowly traced a line a little further into the culvert and stopped at the painting of a small teddy bear. "I don't know how well you can see it from there, but this bear looks to have been done *after* the original mural, and isn't the same color or style of any of the tagging. I'm thinking that it was done fairly recently."

"Why?" she asked uncertainly.

"Well, the colors seem pretty vibrant relative to the rest of the artwork. Still, it's small, so I wouldn't swear to it."

While we stared at the painting, Erica rubbed her temples as if she had a headache. "You are right. That figure does appear to be more recent than the rest of the paintings. Well at least to me, us. I guess CS will be able to tell us."

"*That's* not all. Here's the corker—but you've got to come closer."

Cold forgotten, we were inches from a small bear someone had painted standing up, arms outstretched. On one sash of the red ribbon around its neck were the letters *RIP* in fine white lettering, as if written with a calligraphy pen. On the other was a date, 11/8/14. I took a series of shots and then moved further back to include the rest of the mural. I glanced over at my partner who had remained standing in the water, her face a tight mask of fury, dark eyes flashing.

"Son-of-a-bitch!" said an angry Erica finally. "The bastard who did this killed a little boy and abandoned his body in a culvert and *then* took the time to paint a damn teddy bear. What was he doing even bringing paint to the scene? He would have needed a light. *Then* he had the balls to add a damn message. ¡Carajo!" She sighed. "And we missed it," she added regretfully.

"Don't do that to yourself. The painting is small and easy to miss given the rest of the stuff. After all, you were coping with the discovery of a dead child. The boy looked well cared for—somebody has to be missing him. Erica, I want to look at the staging photos—this has the smell of something personal all over it."

"¡Caramba! Robin, please call this in—tell them to get the Crime Scene Unit out here, *now*—have D come with them. He's a top-notch detective. Let them know we are at the body dump site. Wilmslow is the street to the west side of the park running off Wyndhurst. It is a one-way going north for only a block. Better, tell them to park across the street at Wyndhurst Station. Make sure they bring plenty of crime scene tape and some cones. Meantime, I'll take photographs."

"Will do. Erica, we should search the creek above the culvert. Is it possible to get boots?"

"You're right. A pair of size 5s for me. By the way, Crane—you have a good eye; I am glad to be working with you."

"Thanks, but it was your idea to revisit the scene. Moreno, it might take us awhile but we *will* find the doer."

Chapter 11

The Teddy Bear

Sirens sliced through the quiet of Roland Park. Despite my directions, only one of two police vehicles parked in the small area in front of Wyndhurst Station. The other, a mobile van, pulled the wrong way into Wilmslow and jumped the curb onto the grass, narrowly clipping a pair of trees. The driver got out and approached us at what I thought, given his entrance, was a pretty relaxed saunter. He wasn't a CS tech; I had seen him at roll call and figured him for D.

"Gotta love the speed at which you pull into a one-way lane the wrong way, D—not even in your own vehicle!" called out Erica, who was still searching the creek. "Now you stroll along like you have all the time in the world."

"Hey Moreno, cut the crap! The California newbie told dispatch you had something and there were no available cars. CS was glad for my driving expertise!" He laughed; the technicians, focused on their equipment, paid him no mind.

"She is not a newbie, came here as a detective. Thanks to Officer Crane, soon to be *Detective* Crane, we do have something—that is if *you* don't screw things up. Come over here you idiot, and let her show you what we have."

It was a good feeling to know that my new partner already had my back. I complied, pointing in the general direction of the cement archway. "Fair warning, your shoes are going to get wet."

D made his way over but stopped at the point there were no more large rocks. "You're going to have come a little closer." He failed to move and I began to laugh. By then my own feet were done for. "Afraid of water?"

He hesitated, but reluctantly approached. I moved nearer to the culvert opening and glanced at Erica, who was trying to hide a smile. "Okay, Detective, keep an eye on my finger ... now, follow the geese down the zig-zig until you reach the turtle—small, odd-looking, but that's what it is. Anyhow, I want you to concentrate on the turtle and look a bit further back into the culvert—see the painting of the teddy bear?" I stopped and made sure he was with me rather than backtracking out of the stream at a rapid clip. He nodded affirmatively, and like my partner, at first didn't seem to be registering what he was inspecting. Erica was watching D instead of looking at the painting.

"Okay, the painting of the bear is directly across from where the boy's body was positioned and didn't appear to have been there all that long. See it?" He still wasn't paying a lot of attention.

"Focus! D, what you're seeing is some sort of staging," said Erica.

"*Holy shit!*"

"That's about right! CS needs to start ASAP," my partner said. "We are going to need more people out here for crowd control, especially with you wheeling in," she said acidly. "Good bet that the media will be here in no time—you know who is still on top of this story."

"He groaned. "Shit, I hope not."

I wondered whom they were concerned about—he or she seemed to strike the fear of God into the two detectives, neither the fearful type.

"D, who's across the street in the other car?"

"Smith and Hall followed your instructions, *Princess*."

"I'm glad someone listens. They may need to call for another unit—we're going to search further upstream. The child was light enough that the doer, if he was a large man, might have carried him in from a more isolated part of the trail. This is an active area. Even at night, someone would most likely notice an individual pulling up in a car, removing a body and then carrying it into the creek. You bring the boots?"

"Yo boss," D said. "Come with me."

"C'mon, Crane, let's grab the stuff and leave these guys to do their thing. Pay him no mind—trash talking is what he does. You would not know it, but he is absolutely the best when it comes to forensics—D just cannot help himself. He is a *Bawlmer* boy, what can I say? We'll head north; there are schools up that way and a small shopping center. A library. D, do not let this get screwed up!"

"Never. Moreno, we want the suspect every bit as much as you," the now serious detective said while taking the boots out of the back of the mobile unit. "See what a good guy I am! Even brought you the right sizes," he chuckled, handing us each of a pair. "And because I'm such a damn decent colleague, I'll tell you what I'm going to do for you and California—dry socks!" Still laughing, he bowed, while waving four unexpected pairs in our direction.

I reached for the socks. "Thanks, D, *frozen* does not begin to describe the state of my feet."

"I figured," he said, tossing them to me with a wink. "I'm going to change mine. Here are the keys; enjoy warming up the old tootsies. Let me know if a massage is in order." He turned to go. "Put the keys behind the visor—no need to be searching the damn creek for them." Suddenly serious, he said, "Now, leave us to our work."

"Don't let us stop you; under the visor I'll put them. Much obliged for the socks! C'mon, Robin, let's clear out of here. Meantime, we can dry out."

A few minutes after starting the van, Erica set the heat on medium and directed the air toward our feet. By then our shoes were off—the sopping wet-grayish socks in a bag, and we began drying our feet under the vent blasting out hot air. In the beginning, the sensation was one of piercing needles; five minutes later, our feet dry and warm, we put on the clean socks and dry boots and walked across Wyndhurst.

"Hey, Smith and Hall!" Erica greeted the two men in the car parked at the side of the low wood building.

The cop in the driver's seat rolled down his window: "Going to eat, Moreno?"

"Some of us have work to do, Hall—cannot sit around looking pretty like you two. Hey, Smith."

"What's going on? Heard you got yourself a new partner. This the one?" Smith indicated me with an upward thrust of the chin.

Erica made the introductions and updated the two men. I was anxious to get going. It was hard to believe that someone not only murdered a little boy, but had also planned the crime with such precision that he thought to bring paint and a brush to leave his message and thumb his nose at the police. Thus far, he had been successful. Well, it was probably a man, though depending on how the drop-off had occurred, the killer could have been a woman. Or a couple.

"Good work, Crane," Smith said appreciatively, pulling me back to the present.

"Thanks," I smiled—nothing else came to mind as a reply. Erica glanced at me and continued walking. I saw a few people peeking through the windows of the shops and, despite the chilly weather, others had gathered in the small parking lot and on the sidewalk passing over the culvert.

"We're beginning to attract some attention."

She scanned the area and nodded. "Our car is at the entrance off Oakdale, can you drive it over?" She dropped the keys through Smith's open window without waiting for an answer. "We are going to search the creek upstream."

"No problem." He waved us off and rolled up the window.

I followed my partner past the shopping center, giving a nod to the curious onlookers. To our left flowed the small creek.

"Are you good with me taking the far side, and you this path, including this end of the culvert?"

"Sure." I watched while Erica picked her way across the boulders, which were larger in this area. I then began to search the culvert, but found nothing. A careful search of the creek also yielded nothing. The walk back was relatively more fruitful; we found the occasional water bottle and plenty of cigarette butts. Given the number of people living in this neighborhood, it was difficult to believe how little litter we found.

"Erica, you didn't search here before?"

"Not this far up. Chica, I was thinking that we should drive a few blocks north to another small shopping center. We can work the path down from there. No reason to go back into the water unless we see something."

"I'm game." When we got back to the culvert, no civilians were watching the activity. There *were* several officers milling about and nursing coffee cups. I guess dispatch had taken a request for crowd control seriously. We were lucky that it was lunchtime—people were probably concerned about their stomachs.

"Hey, D, how is it going?" Moreno called out as we approached. The technicians were inspecting the cement archway.

"It's going, it's going—we're taking our time, Moreno, knowing our balls will be in a vise if we don't get it right! Spitfire tica!"

"You know it! Better tone down the volume, dude—there is sure to be someone in the vicinity with a working cell, but without our sense of humor."

"True. True. Life is not as much fun with all the technology and PC requirements. Seriously, they've taken the photos, done the paint scrapings, and are dusting for fingerprints. The prints may be an iffy proposition given the time that has passed since the doctor discovered the body, the weather conditions, and the number of people who use this park, never mind wildlife. Rich here had a good idea—he sprayed a protective coating over the relevant surface in case one of the local artists wants to decorate the culvert."

"Good idea, Rich. Thanks. D, apart from what is going on here, is there anything else new on the case?"

"Nah, nothing useful on the clothes. The FBI is now processing them. Good job, you two—what we've got here seems damn promising."

"Is that what you picked up?" asked Rich.

Erica handed him the evidence bag. "A few plastic bottles and cigarette butts—maybe DNA will show up that is consistent with the body or anything in the culvert and steers us to a suspect. Anyhow, we are going to Deepdene Road and will work our way down the creek. After that, back to the house. Well, not that quick, we need to check out a lead for Manny—his floater case."

"What's the deal?" D asked. "I thought the guy was drunk and fell in."

"Nope. He was clean—no drugs, no alcohol, pricey clothes, and expensive dental work. No ID."

"So what's the lead?"

"Probably nothing. Someone up this way *thought* he had seen the victim in DC before he turned up in our harbor. Manny figures anything will be helpful at this point and asked us to interview him."

"Good luck. I guess we'll investigate some more while the spray sets—make sure we don't need to come back *again* because we've missed something," he said, darting a glance in my direction that he followed up with a wink. "If the big man approves the request we'll leave up the tape for now and station a marked unit here for a few hours. Some trouble up by the methadone clinic off York but otherwise things are fairly quiet."

"Thanks, guys," Erica said. "Ready, Crane?"

"I am."

"Let's go." We walked back across the street, got into our vehicle and, again, went through the drying out routine. Once we arrived at the small shopping area on Roland Ave, Erica parked in the garage under the bank.

"Now that my feet are in recovery mode, my stomach's acting up. What about lunch before the detecting?"

"Great idea, Chica. One of the week's specials at Eddie's is a shrimp salad sandwich—such a deal! How about I buy the sandwiches, while you get the coffee?—black, double shot for me. Grab a table while you are at it."

"Will do—see you in a few. I'll take mine on a Kaiser roll with lettuce, tomato, and onions."

"Onions?" She looked surprised but said, "Sure, if that is what you want."

At Starbucks I stood in a ridiculously long line, paid for the coffee (doctored mine) and headed outside where there were plenty of tables. Apparently, it was too cold for the good citizens of Roland Park. Most customers were sitting inside, excepting one elderly man reading his paper, a golden retriever at his feet. Though chilly, I sat down.

A good fifteen minutes later I glanced up from my phone and saw my partner approaching, blue plastic bag in hand. "Erica, it's too cold to sit outside and noisy inside. How about parking close by to where you want to search. We can eat in the car—with the heat on."

"That is fine with me. Besides, somebody is bound to complain of wasted tax dollars if we're seen hanging out at Starbucks, particularly given the seriousness of this crime. On the other hand, by parking in the neighborhood we might get some kudos in the *Baltimore Patch*, especially since D and the CS crew are so visible. This case has dragged on too long; people want results."

"Can't say I blame them."

Erica pulled out of the garage and drove the couple of blocks to the end of Deepdene. "Well, Chica, here we are—I am so ready for this sandwich! I got us each a bag of chips—figured we can walk or at least shiver off the calories." She grinned and laughed. "Well, *I* need to walk them off; I probably should have gotten you *two* bags," she said, her dark eyes twinkling.

"Nope, trust me—there's stuff going on—I'm just taller and the impending doom is spread around. Besides, what's a sandwich without chips?"

Erica took the food out of the bag and divvied it up. I opened my water and took a long swallow. "That looks delicious—how long's the special?"

"A week," she said, crunching on a chip. "Ay, Dios, I cannot believe winter is almost here."

"I'm with you—I never missed the cold in California. Do you go back to Costa Rica often?" I asked, still curious as to how Erica came to Maryland and why she lived apart from her kids.

"I take my vacation there when it is winter here. If the prices are decent, I go another time or two during the year. If I cannot get the time off, my children come here."

"I'd love to meet them next time they visit. I was thinking that maybe we could go to Hershey Park."

"Thank you. They would love it—after a day or two, my children are tired of hanging out with me and begin missing their friends."

"Sean would be happy. He's been begging to go back, hoping he'll be tall enough for some of the rides he couldn't get on last time." The coffee, though tepid, was strong and I felt reenergized. We ate in silence—Roland Park was aptly named: even leafless, the trees have a calming effect.

Once we were finished, Erica busied herself putting our lunch trash into a plastic bag, which she tossed over her shoulder onto the back seat. "Well, Chica, it is time to leave our comfy car; there has to be something that will tell us who the boy is, so let's get busy and find it. I want to find the bastard who killed him *and* discover why nobody seems to be missing this child. I am beginning to think that one thing is related to the other."

"Erica, we may need to look further than Maryland." I then added hastily, "If you haven't done so already." I removed evidence bags and several pairs of gloves from the trunk, tucked some into my jacket pocket and handed a couple to Erica.

"We have," Moreno said, shooting me a smile. She locked the car and clipped the keys to her belt loop. "We can talk more about that later. We should go."

From the street, I followed Erica along a small overgrown path that linked up with a trail running parallel to the creek. On the far side were large grassy playing fields, all empty. The sun was still out but billowing pale gray clouds were slowly moving in from the south. It was getting cooler and in short order would become more so.

"Is that a school over there?" I said pointing toward the cluster of low stone buildings beyond the playing fields.

"It is. There are several schools in the area. Straight ahead is Friends, which fronts onto North Charles. Farther up Charles, on the same side of the street, is Cathedral. If you turn to your left, you will see Gilman, a boys' school fronting on Roland Avenue. The road you see through the trees is Northern Parkway, which I am sure you know runs east-west; Charles runs north-south. On the other side of Northern is another school, Bryn Mawr—a girls' school. Across Roland from Gilman is Roland Park Country, another girls' school. All are private."

"Seems to me that's a lot of private schools in just this one neighborhood."

"Bueno, I never gave any thought to how many there were—I guess it was because people wanted boys and girls educated separately, and the rich people who lived in this area didn't want their kids going to school with the "riff raff." She laughed and added, "If Latinos had been here, they probably wouldn't have wanted to go to school with them either. Robin, somebody else told me that that the private school system continued to exist because of some law about education passed in the fifties. Anyhow, not *all* schools are private—I forgot the one public school, which is located between the bank where we parked and Gilman. Students come from all over the city, many on public buses, to attend Roland Park Public, *if* they can get in. I don't come over this way at 2:30 or 3 when schools start letting out—there are kids and cars everywhere, a total mess."

"I assume the private school students don't usually take public transportation."

Erica laughed. "You have that right!"

"Were flyers posted on the buses providing transportation to the public school?"

"Good idea, Chica, but the answer is no. Now that I think about it, reaching out to the schools again probably would not hurt. We did that by telephone right after the body was discovered, but there is nothing to lose by making a personal visit."

"Makes sense. What about residents walking their dogs at this end of the creek—anybody report anything suspicious?"

"Nothing. Fewer dog walkers come up here because most of the homes are in the other direction. This is a more commercial area. And the schools, as you now know."

"Erica, how about we cover the pathways first and examine the creek on our way back? I'm damn sure going to appreciate a hot shower when I get home tonight!"

"I'm with you there. Chica, you will probably need to put gloves on because we will find more litter in this area—the school kids are not nearly as conscientious as the older population on the other side of Wyndhurst."

"Got it." I was relieved to cross the creek without getting my feet wet; from there, I walked south while scanning the area in silence. There *was* more rubbish up here: cigarette butts, bottles, candy and sandwich wrappers, blue plastic bags, Starbucks refuse, and even a couple of condom wrappers—items easy to spot because of the lack of bushes or trees on this side. I bagged it all.

"California, over here!"

I crossed and joined her in the stand of trees where she was holding up the end of a sizable branch. Dried and leafless, it had snapped off long ago.

"Could belong to some kid skipping school, prepared to show back up when Mom, Dad, or the babysitter comes to pick him or her up. Robin, maybe, just maybe, we have something here. Did you bring one of the big evidence bags?"

"Here." I removed one of the larger plastic bags from my pocket and handed it to her.

"Hold on to this branch, will you?"

Confused, I did what she asked of me. "Shit, this is heavy ... oh my God, I see it!" I said, spotting the dark green backpack tucked under a bush over which the branch had come to rest, or more likely, someone had placed it. "Good find, Moreno!"

"I hope it's relevant to the case and not just a kid ditching school for the day. On second thought, we had better contact D and ask the CS folks to come over here. They get annoyed when we handle the evidence; claim we don't change gloves and cross-contaminate, etc. I will flag the area and take photos. You call."

———

After the discovery of the pack, I renewed searching from the point where I'd left off. Erica continued combing through the trees along the pathway but like me, found nothing more than evidence of trips to Eddie's, Starbucks, and the Tuxedo pharmacy.

"Robin, given the backpack, once the techs arrive let's return by way of the creek and then head out."

"Okay," I replied ruefully, not at all happy about the prospect. This was ridiculous, I was going to get some heavy-duty waders this week-end—Matt and Sean would enjoy a trip to Dick's Sporting Goods. Regardless, I headed back into the creek, turning over rocks as we came back to our starting point. For all our efforts, we didn't find anything else.

———

"Bueno, California, we can go now that Crime Scene is here. For a city waterway, it is pristine. You should see Costa Rica—litter is a huge problem in my country." She flushed and said, "Sorry, this is my country, too. I've lived here for a long time and my father was American."

Erica uttered the last words as she walked off. Caught off guard by the personal revelation, I didn't say anything and continued the search.

By the time we returned to the car, any sensation in my feet had long since disappeared. I went to the back of the car where Erica removed dry Nikes and two pairs of socks from a black athletic bag. She handed me my still damp shoes and a pair of the socks. We hustled inside. "Damn," I said, as the blast of cold air hit my feet. I shut off the heat while the engine warmed up. A few minutes later, I tried again. All I felt was pain … until, finally, the luxurious rush of warm air.

"Shit! Look at the time! We need to interview Manny's potential witness. I should let him know we are running late."

"Sounds good. I'll go in for caffeine while you make the call."

So, Erica, who are we going to talk with?"

"Ted Moore is the name of the guy. He called early this morning— I guess he had been traveling and was catching up with his newspapers when he saw the sketch of the man found floating in the harbor. Moore could not shake the feeling he was somehow familiar. Later, it occurred to him that he might have seen the man when he was in DC at the end of October. Though Moore is not sure it is the same person, he was sufficiently concerned to call. You interested in the case?"

"I happened to be walking by the Trade Center when a window washer spotted the body. I don't know why the incident stuck with me. How many people end up in the harbor anyhow?"

"They have fished out about a dozen bodies over the last year. Not too long ago, a man was out partying and he fell off the Fells Point dock after his friends left. Sad case, he had a little boy. Nothing comes to mind about anybody else recently, although I think a homeless man who sleeps on one of the wharfs fell in. Gracias a Dios, the Harbor Patrol rescued him. There are also fights and somebody ends up getting pushed in. And then we have gangs who periodically dispose of a body in the harbor—not just our locals; the DC hooligans occasionally drive someone they've offed up to Charm City to cause problems for the Baltimore boys." Unexpectedly, Erica laughed. "I am sure from your time with Tyrell Wilson that you are aware of the competitive spirit among Baltimore, DC, Philly, and New York gangs. Sometimes members of BGF, Crips, Bloods, DMI, and others cooperate, but they are mostly at each other's throats. Lately, that seems to be about lots of adulterated heroin." Appearing perplexed, she asked, "Robin, you care about this man's death because you were downtown at the time?"

I had asked myself the same question more than once, and found it tough to answer. "I don't know, but whatever the reason, I think of the dead man at the strangest times. Then, when I can actually dig into the case, it slips my mind. I'm sure a psychologist could help!" Although not funny, I laughed.

"You are not asking for my advice, but I think you have enough on your plate without bothering about a case that is not yours. We are only involved now because someone living in our neck-of-the-woods might give us something, and I wanted to help out a friend."

I couldn't stop myself. "What do they know about the victim?"

"What they do *not* think is that a drunk passed out too close to the water and fell in, or a gang member met his end in our beloved harbor. According to the ME, the death is a homicide. An identification is complicated because somebody cut off the victim's fingers. Manny thinks the shredded ropes dangling from his torso were used to weigh down his body. CS believes a propeller tore the body loose and it floated to the surface."

"Anybody missing in the area with a similar description?" I asked.

"Unh, unh. It has been a challenge getting a fix on him. The fish and crabs had "quite a go at the body," which is why Manny doesn't expect to get much from the caller. Anyhow, he asked me to check him out—boss approved it, so that is what we will do. But, Robin, we should focus on our own case—a dead child trumps anything else, at least in my mind."

"Amen to that. The ME is right; we need to get that poor boy out of the morgue and home to his loved ones. Last question, Erica: What does Manny think happened?"

"He believes someone killed the guy and tossed him from a passing ship. That is difficult to follow up for obvious reasons."

"Race? Age?"

"That's the reason he's thinking this is not a gang murder. Manny does not figure him for a stowaway: for a change, the vic is white, blonde and blue eyed. Good teeth—bueno, those that remain. CS said he was wearing expensive clothes, also what was left. Anyhow, he has been checking with the cruise lines—it would not be the first case of a missing passenger. Okay, Chica, let's go talk with the caller."

She turned down a shady road and parked in front of a lovely forest green Craftsman home with brown trim. When I got out of the car, I took a minute to appreciate the lush garden—I needed to put more time into ours. The property reminded me of Santa Barbara.

Chapter 12

DUAL INVESTIGATIONS

Exhausted, I slumped into the chair next to Erica during roll call. Sean had a doozey of a cold and it'd been a rough night—Matt eventually went downstairs to sleep; he stayed home with him today. Given I had a sick son and I'd been mucking about in the creek the day before, it was only a matter of time before I'd be in sickbay. My parents would help out tomorrow.

Sarge was speaking, but nothing registered until I heard my name—I felt like a kid caught daydreaming. A professor demonstrating the "cocktail party" phenomenon flashed across my mind—test subjects were oblivious to what was being said in their vicinity, until *their* name came up. The subjects' attention then shifted to that particular conversation. I was proof of the pudding—we may not appear to be focused but s*ome* part of the brain is engaged.

"Listen up, guys. Moreno and Crane, here," he said pointing in our direction—all eyes following suit—"stepped forward and helped Manny with his case; *even though* they spent hours yesterday wading through a cold creek on their own. It seems we might have something on the victim in the harbor. Despite the poor quality of the sketch, the caller believed he saw the deceased in DC on the 27th or 28th of October. The guy caught his attention because 'he was dragging around luggage and looked frazzled.' Manny's here today to follow up with the witness."

"Thanks, Sarge," Manny took a bow and saluted in our direction. "Much appreciated, Moreno, Crane."

"We'll collect." Erica laughed.

"I expect no less!"

"That's enough!" And with that, Sarge put an end to the banter in the room. "As you know, Moreno has been investigating the death of the young male found in Roland Park. Glad to have you on board, Crane. In addition, hats off to D and the guys from CS for some outstanding forensics work. There could be some movement with this case. Moreno and Crane are visiting schools in the area today and will be posting flyers requesting information on the buses servicing the area. Give 'em a hand if you can. Manny, see me before the interview. Okay, that's it for now. Roll out and be safe, guys."

No offers of assistance came out way—only the daily dose of harassment that goes with the job in the name of camaraderie. "Let's go, Moreno. If we want to get this done, we need to do it ourselves. Which school should we start with?"

"Bueno, first to the public school, I think. We can post the flyers in the buses later; doing both will get us more exposure."

"Do you think we'll get some help?"

"Yeah, Chica, let's see how many want to help—not *any* is my guess," Erica said sarcastically. "We can wait for another ten minutes— I could use the caffeine."

She was correct; it was a wasted ten minutes. We went to the car, threaded our way through the traffic, almost getting hit by a driver unwilling to stop at a red light, and headed north on 83, exiting at Northern. Erica pulled into the full lot of the Roland Park Public School, barely managing to tuck the vehicle into a corner close to the building.

A green decorative fence with a creative fish motif had been installed on each side of the uphill pathway leading to the school. We rang the security bell across from the front entrance. After identifying ourselves, a slight click indicated the door had been unlocked. Inside, the highly polished floors and pastel walls covered with artwork brought back memories of my years in elementary and middle school. A large sign from the state congratulated RPPS for having earned a Blue Ribbon of Academic Excellence. Though the assistant appeared concerned about police on the premises, at Erica's request she made a quick call and offered to escort us to the principal. After explaining why we were there and learning he had no useful information but would certainly contact us if he did, we thanked the harried man and departed.

"Robin, how about we go to a couple of more schools in the area and then get some lunch? I overslept and missed breakfast."

"Okay. Which ones?"

"After Gilman, we can head over to Bryn Mawr."

"Sounds like a plan. I was up a good part of the night with Sean and didn't eat either."

"What's wrong with the muchachito?"

"Still battling a cold. *None* of us is getting any sleep."

"*Pobrecitos. Una sopa de pollito*, my grandmother would say— chicken soup. Now, I hear scientists have proof for her medicine. California, you up for a walk? Gilman is next door and from there Bryn Mawr is only a few blocks. It is not so cold and a tour of the neighborhood will give you a better sense of the lay of the land. The car is safe here. Perhaps we will find some more tagging, which could get us to a particular school—I sure would like to identify that kid."

"Walking's fine by me. Moreno, it's pretty put together around here—I would be shocked if we found graffiti at *any* of these schools. I went online last night looking at tuitions for Baltimore private schools. Any errant kid would be out in a flash."

"Probably. Robin, the difference with the private schools is that we will need to meet with the heads of the upper, middle, and lower schools—this is bound to take awhile. I was thinking we could show them the photograph—all they have seen is the sketch."

"Makes sense."

The receptionist ushered us into the office of Gilman's upper school headmaster. He gave Erica his full attention, but once she asked for his cooperation he said nothing, and I worried we weren't going to get the help we needed. What seemed like a good suggestion—reaching out to the schools for help—might prove to be a waste of time. I glanced at my partner, but she remained focused on the headmaster, who now appeared uncomfortable. I looked around the plush well-appointed room and wondered whether I might want to teach. Through the open door, a stream of students changing classes passed by. On second thought, detecting might be easier than dealing with a school full of teenage boys set to be unleashed on the world.

Just as I was ready to break the silence, the headmaster spoke up. "What a tragedy that nobody has reported the child missing. I'm hesitating, I guess, because I thought the police identified the child but were keeping their findings quiet for investigative reasons. Detectives, believe me when I tell you this—I'm sure that if the dead boy has a direct link to Gilman, we would know almost immediately that one of our students was missing. An indirect link—well, I thought we would have heard something by now, but I'll make some inquiries. If you want, we can send a letter to our parents. I'll talk with the other headmasters—can I get your contact information?"

"Thank you," I said, "here's my card. Sir, we would appreciate it if you would email us a copy of whatever you intend to distribute before you do that."

He was visibly taken aback by my request.

I explained, "It's only that we're in the middle of an active investigation and need to be careful about what information gets to the public. Still, we want to identify the child."

At that, he appeared to relax. "It's really no problem; you just caught me off guard for a minute. Gilman School will do anything we can to help. Our community is worried, maybe scared, and that holds especially true for the children, even if they won't admit to it."

"Sir, we appreciate your cooperation. When there are answers, which we hope will be soon, I will inform you directly," Erica assured him. She glanced at me and we both got up. After shaking hands, we took leave of the luxurious office and proceeded to make our way through the throngs of boys shoving, laughing and talking. Once out of the building, we saw only the occasional student.

"What do you think?" I asked.

"This was a good idea, Chica. One of the most important lessons I have learned as a detective is that you can never tell where the relevant information may come from. I believe he will follow through."

"I agree. That was a telling comment about the fears of the parents and their children."

"Robin, I think it would be better to drive over to Bryn Mawr. I said the distance is walkable but even with the lights going across Northern Parkway it is like stepping onto a raceway. It is also too far from the car if a call comes in."

"No problem."

Evidently, single-sex education had seen its way to some gender-integrated classes—Gilman boys and Roland Park Country girls were crossing the footbridge connecting the two schools. I wondered which classes those were—probably something innocuous like theatre. I realized I was being snarky and maybe even defensive about my blue-collar background. What I found curious was that I could not remember ever having similar thoughts while in California. If we had stayed in Santa Barbara, no question, Sean would still be attending a public institution. In Baltimore, I was not so sure, which was a seriously ridiculous thought given I'd already made the decision. He was enrolled in Montessori, an expensive private school.

I reflected on the huge differences between these uniformed female students and my classmates at Our Lady of the Immaculate Conception. Not only did their appearance differ from ours; more noticeable was an overarching confidence. None of us had even a fraction of what these girls appeared to possess in spades as they drifted through a completely different reality.

After talking with the headmistress at Bryn Mawr, who also pledged whatever type of cooperation we needed, we returned to our car, parked unobtrusively at the far end of the lot next to some bushes. A move, I noted, that did not seem necessary at the public school, though it would not have been possible there—no space. We had just gotten into the car when a young girl, 14 or 15, appeared at my closed window and tapped on it with her forefinger. It was as if she simply floated out of the bushes.

Blonde, waif-thin, large dark green eyes overwhelming her fine-featured face, there was something intriguing about her I couldn't put my finger on. She wore no makeup and though her hair was clean, it hung lankly and unevenly to her shoulders. Her blouse was partially outside of a skirt hanging longer than that of most of the other girls on the campus. Her brown loafers were scuffed. Despite the chilly temperature, she had bare legs. Slung over one shoulder was a grungy backpack decorated with peace signs, several Obama campaign buttons, and a rainbow pin. Oddly enough, she looked familiar.

I only partially rolled down the window—trouble comes in unexpected packages. "Can I get in the backseat?" the girl asked quickly, nervously. She didn't wait for an answer and instead pulled at the door handle. "*Please*, hurry! I don't want anyone to see me," she said urgently, trying again to open the door.

I glanced over at Erica, who shrugged. I toggled the switch and the back locks popped up. The girl scooted inside, settling herself in the middle of the back seat. Hunched over, hair falling over her face, she clutched the pack to her chest. And said nothing.

I turned, leaned over the seat and extended my hand. "I'm Officer Crane and this is Detective Moreno," I said, indicating my partner. "What can we do for you?"

"I'm not sure," she said biting her bottom lip and shaking my hand. "Maybe, like, this is a bad idea." With that, she began to make a move to leave.

I stole a glance at Erica; with one hand on the steering wheel, she ran her fingers through her hair with the other. She knew, as did I, that we could get into hot water talking to an underage girl without the permission of her parents or school personnel—we were after all on *private* property. Moreover, I reflected regretfully, we left the head-mistress on such good terms. Now, we may need to see her again, a conversation which none of us would enjoy.

"Here's our numbers," I said, removing a card from the console. "If you'd prefer to call or come in with your parents, you could do that." Erica gave the girl the faintest of smiles and nodded in agreement.

She took it. "Well, I don't, like, think so," she said, slowly tracing one of the peace signs on her pack with an unpolished fingernail. She settled back in the seat.

Neither of us said anything. I was afraid that if we did, we would lose her altogether. On the other hand, I would definitely prefer to speak with her under other circumstances.

She sighed and continued to avoid eye contact. "A friend told me you came here about the dead boy found at Wyndhurst Station ... in the creek." She sat up straighter as she spoke, and tucked her hair behind her ears. "Last week," she clarified, as if a dead child in Roland Park was a frequent occurrence and we might be confused about the body to which she was referring.

I could not imagine how the information about our presence on school grounds had gotten out so quickly, unless Bryn Mawr allowed cell phones. Perhaps someone saw the car but, even so, I was surprised students were aware of *why* we were there. Parents would be unhappy if they heard from their children, before the administration informed them, that the police were investigating a murder potentially connected to their expensive school. I glanced over at my partner—her brow was furrowed.

I asked the question as gently as possible, "How is it your friend thinks she knows why we're here?" The girl stared at Erica with watchful eyes. The car was quiet. We waited her out.

"Well, she … I think I'd better go—I've got a class. If they see me out here, I'll get a detention and then my parents are going to be, like, all kinds of pissed! I am *already* in trouble with them. Sorry."

Before either of us could say anything, she was gone. We watched her walk at a rapid clip toward one of the buildings, backpack over her shoulder.

Erica shook her head. "Robin, I am not sure we could have handled it any differently. She has our contact information—maybe she will call or text. It is unclear whether we should follow up with Bryn Mawr. First, we do not have a name; second, she did not give us anything to justify going to the administration. We'll talk to the boss—he can make the final determination."

"Erica, something's bothering me about her—for some reason she seems familiar."

"Bueno, let me know if it comes to you. Meantime, Chica, after we eat let's go to Roland Park Country. Then we can drive downtown to meet with someone at Transportation and see what hoops some official will ask us to jump through to post flyers on their buses. The light rail as well—there is a stop in the center of Mt. Washington and another on Cold Spring. I am not sure how many students use it, but it won't hurt."

"After we finish, let's head back to the creek and search south from where we left off at Oakdale, though I doubt we'll find anything, since there wasn't anything from there to the culvert. We'll visit the rest of the schools tomorrow."

Chapter 13

Give Me Five and Let's Roll

"Hey, California, you at your desk?" a disembodied voice called out. "Yeah, why?" I hollered back.

"Call on 5. Came to me by mistake."

"Thanks D, I got it." I pressed the button and a vaguely familiar woman's voice asked for "Hello, hello, Officer Crane."

The woman at the other end of the line sounded stressed. "Speaking, may I help you?"

"Officer Crane? I'm *trying* to reach Officer Robin Crane?"

"This is she. Please, who am I speaking with?"

"Thank God!" she said. "This is Marisol Jimenez. You might not remember me—you were at our house in Fells Point last spring. A noise complaint. You gave me your card and said I could call if I needed anything."

I hesitated, still unsure with whom I was speaking. Rossi and I had responded to at least a hundred such complaints. Ty and I, to

141

more than a few. I had left my card at all of them. Still, the urgency in the woman's voice made me think this involved more than a noise complaint or her difficulty in getting through to me.

"Fells Point," she repeated. "We saw you at Jimmy's one night. Getting coffee and fries."

How could I have forgotten? "Marisol, of course I remember you. I'm sorry, how can I help?"

"I need to talk. I mean like in person, not on the telephone. I can come to you."

While I was thinking her request through, she reminded me anxiously, "You said to contact you if I needed help."

"Marisol, I'm no longer at the Southeastern District. I work out of Northern now."

"No, really, I can drive. You're on Cold Spring?"

She not only knew I'd been assigned to another district, she'd gone ahead and pulled up the address. "I am—2201 West Cold Spring Lane. Are you coming now?"

"Is that okay?" she asked nervously.

"I'll stay put." She hung up without saying anything else. I sat there for a few minutes and then walked over to my partner's desk. "Hey, Erica, got a minute? I want your take on something."

"Sure, Chica. What is up?"

"Well … when I worked patrol with Greg Rossi, a call came in for a domestic in Fells Point. Turned out to be a family squabble involving a sister who managed to finagle the rent money out of her brother; the wife suggested the money would go up her sister-in-law's nose. Regardless, she was more concerned about the well-being of her 11-year-old niece than the money. As I do at all domestics, I left my card. Anyhow, the wife just called. She's pretty worried about something and wants to talk."

"And?" Erica asked quizzically, leaning back in the chair. I now had her full attention.

"This thing with nine districts and Headquarters still confuses me. I wasn't sure whether I would be breaking protocol by not sending her directly to Rossi. She's in his district, and we were partners when the call came in."

"Well, unless a crime has been committed, I don't see why it matters. The caller is coming here?"

"Correct."

"You did not contact her?"

"I didn't reach out to her in any way. Didn't even remember who it was when she called."

"Robin, you are not even sure what is going on. Just write up a brief report in case it goes somewhere. If it does, then give Rossi a call and update Sarge. Do not worry about it—you will get things sorted out—the district thing is confusing, but not as rigid as you might think"

"Thanks." My focus shifted to the only framed photograph on Erica's desk. "Is that your mother and children?"

Erica picked up the photograph and gazed at it fondly. "Those are my babies: Natalia and Carlos. And that's my mother—Abita," she said, pointing to an older woman whom she strongly resembled.

"You must miss them."

"I do but I have lived here for many years. Well, Chica, I have work to do—let me know how things turn out." She replaced the picture and focused on her computer screen.

"Will do. Thanks for the advice, Erica." Lesson learned—I returned to my desk, afraid I'd poked my nose in where it didn't belong. I went back to reviewing old investigations. I probably had enough time before Marisol arrived to finish at least one more.

Unlike the two unsolved cases held by the Santa Barbara Police Department when I moved east, Baltimore City had hundreds, if not thousands—I'd been unable to find out exactly how many there were. In the end, I learned the department was actively investigating approximately forty-seven homicides that had gone cold. Even that number was an estimate. After my transfer to Homicide, Sarge informed me that in addition to any active investigations, I would be taking on a cold case. The one of particular interest concerned the death of a man in his late thirties whose siblings recently put up additional reward money hoping against hope that someone would come forward while their parents were still living. I was in another world while reading the file until I realized someone was standing in front of my desk.

"Officer Crane?"

I glanced up to see an apprehensive young woman. "Yes, can I help you?"

"I called earlier. My name is Marisol Jimenez—you said we could talk." Hesitantly, she added, "Didn't you?" My visitor stood there chewing a cuticle—I now remembered her despite the shorter hair and makeup. She was dressed in tight jeans and a crisp pink oxford shirt, over which she wore a black pullover. She carried a brown suede jacket in her arms.

"I'm sorry, ma'am." Before getting up to shake her hand, I closed the file and slipped it into a drawer. I gestured toward the ancient wooden chair parked at the side of my desk. "Can I get you a water or a soda?"

"Thank you. Water would be great." She sat down; back straight, feet placed side-by-side, hands clutched in her lap, the woman glanced about so furtively she appeared to be a criminal. I was curious as to what brought her here.

I went to the machine, bought two bottles of water and when I returned to my desk, did a double take—my visitor was nowhere in sight. I looked up the hallway but didn't see her; next, I checked out the bathroom, also empty, so I walked to the lobby and went outside where she was briskly crossing the parking lot.

"Marisol?" I called out, ignoring the startled glances of two colleagues.

The young woman stopped short and pulled the jacket tightly around her. She slowly walked back. "Detective, I'm sorry to bother you. While you were gone, I began to think that maybe this was a bad idea."

"Why?" I asked. If I had been confused before, I was even more so now.

"Johnny, my husband—I didn't tell him I came to see you."

"Well, Marisol, we won't know whether you made a mistake or not unless you tell me why you're here. In any case, here's your water." The night we'd been to her home, I hadn't noticed the delicacy of her features; she seemed thinner than I remembered. Despite the sunlight and makeup, her eyes were deep pools of melancholy.

"Marisol, if you're uncomfortable inside, we can talk out here. But, truthfully, you seem to need a cup of hot coffee more than a cold bottle of water."

"Thank you, but I guess outside is better. My jacket will keep me warm enough. Sorry, I'm not getting enough sleep."

From the look of it, she was probably correct about that. "Don't worry about it. We all get sleep deprived."

She stood there like a lost puppy. "That's not it—what I know is I'm screwed up."

"Marisol, why don't we start over?"

"I'd appreciate that, Officer," she said contritely.

"First, why don't you call me Robin? Second, let's sit at the picnic table and talk. Then, if you think you made a mistake by coming here, you can leave. No foul." Marisol followed my lead and we sat down. While she unscrewed the top of the bottle, I was tempted to run in for a hot cup of coffee but knew if I did, I would return to an empty table.

As she drank, she seemed to gather up her courage. "Do you remember what was happening with my sister-in-law? She and Joey had been living with us for several weeks when you came to the house. Johnny's a sweetheart, but his sister is nothing but trouble. Officer Crane, I love children—I work at the St. Vincent de Paul Center and am with kids all the time. Our niece is special, despite her crazy mother. Even though my sister-in-law got the money from my husband the night some nosy neighbor called 911, Brenda was angry when she took off. She's returned for more since, but became even angrier when Johnny refused to give it to her."

I tried not to shiver; instead, I took out my notebook and pen—it seemed that I would be contacting Rossi. "Marisol, what's your sister-in-law's name?"

"Brenda."

"Her last name?"

"She's divorced. Her married name was Denney—Brenda Denney. I'm pretty sure she went back to using Jimenez."

"Mr. Denney is your niece's father?"

"No. Brenda was 16 when she got pregnant—nobody knew who the baby's father was. Still don't. Joey's legal name is Jimenez."

"I take it you wanted to see me because you're still concerned about your niece." Without waiting for the expected answer, I continued. "Do you know where Brenda and her daughter are?"

"No. Actually, *that's* why I'm here. The time you came to our house, I expected Brenda would put our rent money up her nose and be back. But since she couldn't get more from my husband the next time, she hasn't returned, and as you've figured out I'm really worried about Joey."

"How long ago—that she came by again for money?"

"At least two months, if not longer. Maybe the end of August."

"Could she have gotten some from Johnny at another time? Met him somewhere?"

"No, we're in agreement about this and my husband wouldn't lie to me. Honestly, even though he won't admit it, I think he's as concerned as I am about our niece."

"Do you have any idea where Brenda went?"

"After you came, I thought she was living close by because it never takes her long to show back up, hand outstretched. But now I'm not sure."

"Did you check with the school?"

"No, but the principal called and left a message—Johnny was the emergency contact—wanting to know why Joey wasn't in class. My husband asked me to call back and I did, although neither of us knew what to say. Robin, I hate lying, so I *sort of* told the truth … I explained we had a family problem and Brenda and Joey were out of town. I went to pick up her work—said I would get it to my niece."

I tried to develop a timeline in my head. "How long ago was that?"

"Sometime in September. It took Johnny a day or two after the school called to work up the courage to tell me. He expected me to be upset. I was."

"And then what? You couldn't just keep picking up homework without returning completed work."

"Detective, Johnny's going to be so mad if he finds out what I did. Please, don't tell him," she pleaded.

"Marisol, I can't make any promises but I won't say anything unless it's absolutely necessary."

Cars came and went out of the parking lot. I waved to D, who was on his way out of the building. He made a shivering motion—I smiled and toasted him with my unopened water bottle, and received a thumbs-up in return.

I thought I had lost Marisol but, after taking a long drink of water, she continued. "Okay, I guess. I did some of the homework and then copied it because I didn't want Joey to fall behind. One day I went to pick up the assignments without calling first and there was no folder. Brenda had called and said they moved and Joey would be attending a school in a different state. It was no surprise to learn she did not say *which* state. Robin, although they expected Brenda to come in and sign the paperwork for the transfer, she never showed. I gave the teacher some story, but I don't think she believed me. Embarrassed and worried—that was me!"

I had a thought. "Marisol, are you acquainted with any of Brenda's friends?"

"Yeah. Two of them. Probably the only ones Brenda has are those two losers—she burned through the rest. I wrote down their names for you." She removed a folded piece of paper from her jacket pocket and handed it to me.

"Thank you. You do understand I'm no longer downtown?"

"I do. When I called, they put me through to Officer Rossi. He said you were working out of the Northern District."

"What did he suggest you do?" There was no way I could work a case that by all rights belonged to my old partner and originated in Southeastern, unless he cooperated.

"Well, honestly, he didn't care. He said there was nothing he could do because I've no proof of Brenda doing drugs or evidence she even lives in Maryland. He also said there's nothing to say she is neglecting or abusing her daughter—Joey could be in school somewhere else. I insisted on talking to you—that's how I got this number. Can you help me?" This time, she implored rather than asked.

"Give me a few minutes." I got up and walked around as I thought through what I'd just learned. A missing person report would not work in this case. Marisol clearly spoke with Greg because he had said pretty much the same thing to me when I wanted to do a follow-up on the girl the night we went to their house. I needed to understand why the woman didn't want to tell her husband she'd come to see me. Maybe there *was* a domestic element and she hadn't been straight with us that night.

I returned to the table. "Marisol, you're worried about Johnny's reaction if he finds out you were here. Why?"

"I love Johnny but, you're right, I am. Though we're both upset about his sister and niece, he does *not* want the police involved. Nothing against you," she stuttered, flushing. "I guess I should have talked with him before I came here." She resumed chewing at a cuticle—it already looked raw.

"Well, it's cold out here. I'll tell you what—I think you should talk with Johnny tonight; meantime, I'll contact Officer Rossi. If you give me your home and cell numbers, I'll get back to you sometime tomorrow. I promise."

My response seemed to satisfy her. "Thank you, Officer Crane. We took out the home line but my cell is 410.555.4372. I work from seven to three-thirty, so it's turned off then. I really appreciate your help. Honestly, I do."

I wrote down the information. "Okay, let's start there. Try not to worry too much. Your sister-in-law seems to keep showing up, so I'm sure she'll be back. Ms Jimenez, if you do see her, attempt to find out what school Joey is attending and where they are living. We need whatever you can get, but do *not* get into it with her. What about the rest of your relatives—have you spoken with any of them?"

"Nothing. They're pretty much done with Brenda but despite what Johnny says about her being okay, everyone is upset about Joey."

We said our goodbyes. Once she returned to her car, I went back inside, grabbed a cup of coffee and returned to my desk. I removed an empty file folder from the drawer, wrote Marisol's name on the tab, tore the pages out of my notebook and slipped them inside before picking up the phone and dialing Rossi's number.

Chapter 14

Settling In

"Hey buddy, how was school today?"

"Good ... Mom, I'm hungry."

"I'm sure you are. What about a turkey and cheese sandwich? Milk. If you finish that, there's a chocolate chip cookie with your name on it."

"Matt made cookies?"

"Yep, a whole bunch."

"Can I watch television?"

"I don't think so!"

"Bummer," he said, putting on his best *life is tough* face.

"I must say, Sean, you're certainly good at looking pitiful! Hey, I've got an idea, let's go to Sherwood Gardens—it'll be a little cool but if we hurry *and* wear jackets we could have a picnic, play Frisbee."

"Yessss!" my ten-year-old shouted at an ear-splitting pitch.

"Why don't you put some cookies in a baggie and take two juice boxes out of the refrigerator; I'll make the sandwiches. Bring your homework folder and you can do some of it in the park. And a pencil and eraser."

He groaned. "Do I have to?"

"Otherwise, it'll be too late by the time we get back. C'mon let's do this. Take everything out of your backpack, except for the stuff you need for homework. Clean out your lunch bag. The Frisbee is in the car."

"Do I have to?" Despite the protests, he went straight for the cookies and took out a fistful.

"Here." I handed him a baggie. "Go ahead; you can eat one or two to hold you over."

Sean returned to the kitchen with his backpack—old food to the garbage, a pile of torn and folded papers to the chair. "Hon, when you're finished, the sandwiches are on the counter. And don't forget the juice and cookies!"

He busied himself with the various tasks, finishing up with an energetic, "All done, Mom."

"Well, then, it's time to go! Oops, give me a minute, I'd better leave a note for Matt—he'll arrive home and not know where we are."

———

I had just sent the Frisbee sailing when my phone rang—Matt was calling. "Hang on, Sean, I need to take this. Go ahead and play with your friends."

"Hi, hon. Where are you?"

"Home. I got your message. Are you still at the park?"

"Yep. We ran into a couple of Sean's friends and they're having a good time. I was going to head home in about ten or fifteen minutes. He's beginning to run out of steam and I'm cold."

"See you soon then."

I no more than pulled up to a stop in the driveway when Sean tumbled out and ran for the house, leaving the car door open.

"Your backpack!" The front door had already slammed shut behind him. My cell rang—work was calling. *Shit!* My husband was not going to be happy if I needed to go back in—tomorrow was bound to be a long day. We were going to York, PA to talk with Sarah Rollins.

Chapter 15

Parental Kidnapping?

We were driving north on 83.

"California, take a look in the glove compartment. You will find the flyer that the York PD faxed last night. By the way, sorry to bother you at home last night."

"No problem. I was relieved not to go in." I removed the paper, which was a request to all departments in the general area to contact the York PD with any information about a Danny Helman. An asterisk accompanied the words "police departments." At the bottom of the page a corresponding reference mark cautioned that the flyer not be distributed to the public or media.

"Erica, why isn't this enough for an Amber Alert?"

"Bueno, when I spoke with them I understood that PA isn't convinced the boy is missing. Alerts are issued cautiously—the public has been unexpectedly responsive to the system, I guess admin does not want them to become routine."

"Makes sense. People can pretty much get used to most anything."

"We will have a better idea about what is going on when we talk with the boy's mother. Wow, two inches over the Maryland Line and the road is a mess—guess we get something for our taxes after all."

Distracted by the flyer, "Hmmm," was all I had to say. Below the photograph was some interesting information that I read aloud: "The child, described as a male Caucasian and ten years of age, was last seen in the company of his father, Dr. Oskar Helman, a German national. Father and son were to return to the United States, the 28th of October, from a vacation in Germany."

A young boy who appeared younger than ten stared out at me from the page. Danny Helman had white blonde hair cut on the longish side, with bangs skating across wide light-blue eyes. He was extremely fair with no visible markings other than a few freckles across the bridge of his nose. "Erica, he's a really cute kid, seems happy and well cared for—I hope we aren't walking into another tragedy."

"That is the truth, Chica. These cases make me even more grateful for my own children."

"How are they doing?"

"Great! I cannot wait to see them next month. They are excited and I am sure Abita is ready for a break. I came up this way last weekend—went to Gabriel Brothers to get clothes and shoes for everyone."

"Gabe's is the best!"

"Can't beat it. Robin, here is the street we want—Lanyard."

My partner took a right hand turn and we drove by enormous house after enormous house. Like Roland Park, not one child played outside—most would be in school, but not even little ones were visible despite most homes having swing sets.

"This is definitely it." I pointed to the house on the right, the only one with Halloween decorations still up. Other than the decorations, the brick-faced home looked like all the others in this upscale community located between Red Lion and York, on what must have been beautiful farmland not so very long ago. Erica pulled into the driveway.

Before either of us exited the car, the front door opened revealing a tall stylishly thin woman whom I figured to be in her early forties. As we approached the house, I took note of the natural blonde hair gathered back into a ponytail, warm blue eyes, and the hint of an engaging smile emphasizing her physical beauty. Dark circles under her eyes and pronounced worry lines spoke to her anxiety.

"Ms Rollins, I am Officer Robin Crane and this is my partner, Detective Erica Moreno. We are from the Baltimore City Police Department." Intentionally, I neglected to mention we were with the Homicide Unit. After we shook hands, each of us showed the baffled woman our badge.

"Ma'am, we're sorry to cause you any inconvenience—we should have called before driving up here," Erica said. In fact, we had discussed it and decided to show up at Sarah Rollins' home without notice.

"I'm sorry, did I do something? I'm waiting for a friend … I thought she'd arrived." Then who we were seemed to sink in. "You're here from Baltimore?" Her voice hit a higher register by the end of the sentence. "If you're from Maryland, I don't understand what you're doing in Pennsylvania."

She seemed genuinely surprised to see police on her doorstep, though I didn't know why that was, given she went to the York police for advice and we were police, albeit from Baltimore. When Erica spoke with York, they told her Ms Rollins was unable to reach her son, who had been in Germany on vacation with her ex-husband and his family. She wanted to find out what her options were.

I felt badly for the woman. "I'm sorry, Ms Rollins, we didn't mean to scare you."

My partner glanced at me and then went on to provide clarification. "Ma'am, the York police sent out a report to all surrounding departments asking for information about your son. Do we understand correctly that your boy is with your ex-husband?"

"That's right. Why?" she asked, seemingly on the verge of hysteria.

"Ms Rollins, would you mind if we come inside to talk? The York police are aware of our visit—our departments work closely together," Erica assured her, carefully maintaining eye contact.

She hesitated. "I'm sorry; I didn't mean to be rude. I just don't understand how the Baltimore police are going to help when my ex-husband, who has my son, refuses to communicate. Danny should be in school—his father needs to bring him back."

"Ma'am, who has custody?" I asked.

"I do. Full custody."

"Ms Rollins, it would help if you could tell us how your ex-husband came to take your son to Europe?"

"Please call me Sarah. That's the easy part. Oskar gets Danny for a month during the summer—I agreed to the arrangement because my son is close to his father's family. We've tried to minimize the disruption caused by the divorce when it comes to Danny, but this time he's over *two weeks* late."

If everything was so good between the couple, I wondered why she had full custody. In addition, a month during the summer made sense, yet we were well into fall. Without saying anything else, she led us into the house and directed us to a couch in a living room that hardly looked lived in—other than a few photographs, I saw no evidence of a child.

"Can I get you a cup of coffee? Water?"

"No, thank you," replied Erica. "Ms Rollins, we have a drawing of a boy we would like you to examine."

"Why? Who is he?"

Erica removed the sketch from a folder and ignoring both questions handed it to the confused woman. Without looking, Ms Rollins set it on the coffee table. She then took her time removing a pair of glasses from a case and putting them on before picking the paper up as if it would bite. While she was going through her routine, I made a mental note about the details of the room. There's no mistaking that a child lives in *our* house—it's a perpetual battle to get Sean to pick up his stuff.

Putting the sketch down, all Ms Rollins said was, "Oh!" The "Oh" encapsulated an unexpected degree of surprise, although it could be relief or perhaps the fear she felt. It was hard to tell. Erica and I darted a glance at each other.

"Oh," she repeated, picking the drawing back up, "I know who *this* is. It's the boy from the Maryland news. I don't remember when, but not too long ago. *Now* I understand why you're here. When I first saw the child, he reminded me of my son, but believe me that is *not* Danny," she said firmly. This time she handed the sketch back to Erica.

It was curious Rollins had not mentioned that the boy discovered in Baltimore was deceased. "Ma'am, could you please take another look?" I pressed. She didn't refuse, so Erica again handed her the sketch.

She seemed to examine it more attentively this time. "No, definitely not Danny. Detectives, a mother recognizes her child!" she said with finality and a measure of relief. "Sorry to disappoint you, seeing as you've come all this way and seem honestly concerned. You don't understand—my son's on vacation with his father. He may look like this poor boy, but I am *absolutely* positive—

"—Detectives, I don't know what I'm thinking. Rather, not thinking. Can I get you a cup of tea or a coffee? A soda?"

This was the second time she had asked. Without looking at my partner, I said, "Thank you." Erica nodded distractedly as she examined the sketch before putting it away.

"I take mine with milk and Detective Moreno has hers black. No sugar for either of us."

"Sarah, do you have a picture of your son we could look at?" Erica asked. "The fax we received from York was not clear. This way, we will be better able to help if we hear anything."

The woman walked over to some curio shelves set into a corner, opened the glass door and removed a small frame. "Here's a good photograph of my son—you can see that your drawing is of a different boy," she said, handing it to me. "Excuse me, I'll prepare the coffee—black and with cream, correct?"

"Yes, ma'am," I said. Once she left the room, I studied the boy perhaps a year younger than our victim. A swing hung from an enormous oak tree: the photograph had been taken while on an upward arc, the boy clutching the ropes and laughing. His mother, also laughing, pushed him. I wondered who had taken the picture. Despite the question of age, I felt sure we had identified our victim. Erica mouthed, "It's him."

True, our victim had brown hair; Sean would call it a buzz cut. The boy in the picture was almost white-blonde and his hair long and shaggy. His eyes were sky blue. Someone could have cut and dyed Danny Helman's hair and, if so, that would suggest the killer must have held him for at least a few days. The child may never have left the country—that should be easy enough to check out. Both boys had blue eyes—the color of the victim's less vivid for understandable reasons. The child discovered in Roland Park had a much darker skin tone, but that might have been for any number of reasons: a trip to the Caribbean or a tanning spray. No freckles were evident in the sketch of our victim. Still, the facial structure was the same. How was it that a mother did not recognize her own son? I again wondered whether Danny's mother had something to do with her son's death—her response to our appearance and to the drawing seemed odd. We would know soon enough whether the boy was, indeed, Danny Helman: DNA would tell the story.

I handed the photograph to Erica just as Ms Rollins entered the room carrying a tray with three matching mugs, a sugar bowl and creamer, which she set on the coffee table in front of the couch where we sat. Erica put the framed picture down without saying anything. Ms Rollins returned it to the shelf and remained standing. "Detectives, why *are* you here?"

Avoiding the woman's question, I responded, "Ma'am, the York police contacted Baltimore because you called them. I understand that you haven't been able to communicate with your son, who has been on vacation with your husband. A vacation allowed by the custody arrangement. Is that correct?"

"Yes," she said, taking a deep breath and sitting down across from us. "Mostly. Oskar has no legal right to keep Danny *this* long—he left

York at the beginning of October and they were due back on the 30th. He *asked* for an extra week—my son's paternal grandmother has been sick and it was important she spend time with her only grandchild. But, Detective Moreno, my son was adamant that he wanted to be home for Halloween, so when another week went by, I became really concerned."

"I'm sure you were. Are. Sarah, what did you do when Danny didn't return in time for Halloween?" I asked.

"I called. And kept calling. Despite all the phone calls—I can show you the bill—I can't reach either Danny or his father. Oskar's family hasn't returned any of my messages. That's why I think they're still together; if they weren't, someone would contact me."

I appreciated her reverse psychology. "Still, if you repeatedly called, they must suspect you're worried about something. Why wouldn't his family return your calls?"

"Truthfully? They don't like me," she said flatly. "They *never* liked me, so the silence doesn't seem odd. I waited until the end of the week and then contacted the York police to find out what my options are. I called them because the divorce and custody arrangement went through the York courts, for all the good it's done me." Her laugh was bitter.

"Ms Rollins, are you suggesting a parental kidnapping?" asked Erica cautiously.

"I suppose I don't want to admit it, but there isn't any other explanation."

"Have you seen a lawyer?" I asked.

"I did … well, we spoke on the phone. I'm meeting with her tomorrow morning." She hesitated, "So now that you know the sketch is not of my son, why the questions?"

"Exactly when did your ex-husband leave Pennsylvania with your son?" Erica had again ignored the woman's inquiry. I wondered how many more times we would get away with that maneuver.

"Oskar picked up Danny in a rental car on the second … of October. In case you are wondering, we are civil with each other—had lunch together before they left for DC. I've contacted Enterprise and they said the car had been returned at the airport—I still have Oskar's credit card information, so I used his name, gave his address in Germany, and made up a story about a gift for our son being left in the car. They, of course, didn't know anything about it but I had my confirmation."

Clever, I thought. "Ms Rollins, you said that under the terms of the agreement, Danny visits his father during summer vacation, so if you don't mind my asking, why is it he took him in October? After all, shouldn't he be in school?"

"You're right. Oskar usually takes Danny during the last two weeks in July and the first two in August, but our son had mono last summer, so this was a special arrangement. To tell you the truth, I wasn't crazy about it, yet Danny missed his father and my ex promised he wouldn't blow it this time, so I gave in."

"What do you mean by not 'blow it this time?' Erica asked.

"He would bring our son back at the agreed upon time."

"Sarah, has this happened before?"

"Yes, I suppose so, but … well, this time Oskar totally blew it! *This* time he's not late by just three or four days. Or, even the extra week he wanted, which wouldn't have surprised me."

She looked from one to the other of us. The coffee sat there getting cold. Nobody had touched it. "I don't understand—are you blaming *me* for this? For the fact that my son is missing?" Then something we said must have registered. "Do you think *I've* had something to do with Danny not coming home?" Her eyes widened; she was almost yelling.

I was no longer ambivalent about Ms Rollins' emotional state. She was now more angry than anxious. I wanted to smooth things over. Our first priority was to identify the Roland Park victim and it was important to get as much information as possible before she asked us to leave. Or, more likely, requested a lawyer because she thought we suspected her of being involved in her son's disappearance.

"Sarah, I'm a mother, so I certainly understand why you're upset at being unable to contact your son. We didn't mean to sound judgmental and I am sorry if we did." As I spoke, I was not at all sure Rollins was listening—she made a move to get up but then leaned back in the chair and gestured toward the tray. I went through the motions of fixing my coffee. While stirring in the cream I decided to ask the question that had been on my mind, praying it didn't set her off again. "Ma'am, please don't take this the wrong way. This is not our case, but since we're already here Detective Moreno and I would like to help you figure out what's going on—it's clear you are very worried about your son."

"It's okay. I apologize, I didn't mean to lose my temper—I hope you realize how worried and frustrated I am. Maryland or Pennsylvania police—I don't care. *Any* help is appreciated."

"Good—we'll do the best we can for you. Ms Rollins, it would be helpful to understand why you didn't report your son missing as soon as his father failed to bring him home on time." She looked blank, so I added, "You expected them to return on the thirtieth, correct? The day before Halloween?" I knew the answer—well, at least as she had told us—but wanted to determine the consistency of her story.

"Officer, you might find this difficult to believe, but I absolutely did not know Danny was missing. I never even suspected he was—actually, I still don't know that he is … missing. But whatever is going on with Oskar and his family, I want my son home."

"Ma'am, we probably can't appreciate your situation but we're trying—it sounds like you and your ex have a pretty complex relationship."

"As Officer Crane explained, we need as much knowledge as possible to be helpful. Where did you think Danny was when he and his father did not return at the end of the month?" Erica asked gently.

"We're divorced, Detective Moreno. It was a nasty parting of the ways, mainly because of the money involved. In the end, I was particularly naïve to believe that it *was* a parting of the ways—a crummy father *and* husband when married, my ex continues to control me through our son. Once the divorce went through, Oskar became father of the year. My son *loves* his father and now that he lives so far away, Danny needs him more than ever."

As she spoke, I unexpectedly found myself identifying with this single mother, having been on the same emotional roller coaster with Stewart, Sean's biological father. Even though he lives on the other side of the country, he persists in making me miserable; however, the advantage I have over Danny's mother is that Stewart has never shown much interest in seeing Sean, never mind taking him off to Europe and then not returning. Moreover, Sean now has a stable father in Matt.

Erica responded, "I understand the difficulty you are experiencing, but that does not explain why you didn't think your son was missing when he was not back on time. As my partner said, we do not want to sound judgmental; we are simply trying to figure out what is going on. The Baltimore police and the southern Pennsylvania force frequently cooperate. That is why we received the flyer from York."

"Sorry, I didn't mean to get defensive again. Oskar … by the way, I reverted to my maiden name of Rollins. Oskar's surname is Helman, as is Danny's. I think I mentioned this, maybe not—my ex-husband is German. Oskar came to the States to attend graduate school at George Washington University—he has a Ph.D. in engineering. GW is where I met him. Oskar has dual citizenship, which means two passports; my son does as well, being the child of a German and a U.S. citizen."

The kid has two passports and she let him go to Germany—despite the physical similarities, I held back a sigh, less convinced her son was our victim. Nonetheless, although I felt for the woman, I wished she would respond more directly to Erica's question about why she hadn't promptly notified the police when Oskar had not brought her son back on time.

"Ms Rollins, I'm not sure how the citizenship issue relates to your concern that Danny may be missing. Let's back up," I suggested. "Is it that you don't know anything *specific* as to why your son is not back home?"

"It must seem strange to you, but this year was atypical. According to the court-approved custody arrangement, Oskar gets our son for a month during the summer and for spring vacation. As I've *already* explained, Danny couldn't visit his dad last summer—he was ill."

"What about school?" I asked. There was an unsettling déjà vu feeling to my question—I thought about Marisol Jimenez's niece, Josephine. Two missing kids—neither clearly missing. Complications arising from the fact they were of school age might have given us an early heads-up, which could help solve both cases.

"When Oskar and I first fought about the trip, I insisted Danny shouldn't be out of school for so long. In the end, Oskar agreed to put him in an international school while he was in Berlin. Danny wasn't thrilled—what boy his age would be? By then I decided that it would be a good experience and, at least, he wouldn't be missing school.

"Once I agreed to let Oskar take him, my ex insisted on keeping Danny longer so that he could spend more time with his grandmother. She's was diagnosed with advanced lung cancer recently. When I refused, Oskar argued that Danny was still weak from the mono and given the length of the flight would need time to rest. That made sense; nonetheless, I guess I wasn't happy about the trip—his family never wanted anything to do with me, Germany is far, he wanted to keep Danny for too long, and—"

"Ma'am, if you don't mind telling us, why did your ex's family have a problem with you?" Unfortunately, I had interrupted her, anxious to ask a question before I forgot it—a bad habit. Later, I was bound to wonder what she had been going to say.

For the first time, she teared up. "From the beginning, my in-laws believed their son should have married a good German girl, not an American. Certainly not someone like me, a girl from a family with no social status—Officer, my ex-husband comes from big money and I come from none. As you can see, I live well. Oskar has been very generous about alimony and child support—the amount I receive is not actually court-mandated, which reminds me, I didn't receive the November check—he gave me October when he picked up Danny. The family thinks I married Oskar for his money and robbed him during the divorce. Anyhow, Oskar hinted that if he didn't get his way, I would receive less money. He supposedly was making the appeal on Danny's behalf. My ex finally wore me down and I agreed to let my son go. That's part of the problem—as the police *clearly* pointed out, I let Oskar take our son out of the country and, technically, Danny is a German citizen."

"Did they fly out of Baltimore—BWI?" I asked, sipping at my cold coffee.

"No. They left here after lunch for DC, where Oskar planned to stay the night—he has close friends there—until they departed from Dulles the next evening. He hoped Danny would sleep for most of the flight. Oskar also planned to spend a couple of days with his friends when they returned to the States. Danny wanted to go to Air and Space and the Natural History Museum. The Spy Museum … I think."

Other than her unsuccessful calls to the Helman family, I wondered how much follow-up Ms Rollins had done. "What do the DC friends say?"

"I spoke with them yesterday. Oskar and Danny did stay with them on their way to Berlin, but even though he and his wife expected them to visit on their return, they never showed. Never called or emailed. *That's* when I went to the police."

I wanted to ask for the friend's contact information but decided to wait. I didn't want to make her suspicious, nor be seen as stepping on the York PD's toes.

"Sarah, let's get back to Danny's schooling." I shifted the direction of my questions in an effort to make it about him and not her. "What did the principal think of Oskar's plan?"

"Surprisingly, they agreed. His teacher thought the experience would be valuable for Danny; something my son could share with his class. Oskar spoke with her directly, and he can be exceptionally charming when it suits him. When Danny wasn't home by the 30th, I thought that Oskar was trying to scare me—pay me back because I filed for full custody—so I kept it low key, thinking he'd bring Danny back a bit late, which as I said he's done before. But after a week went by, I really started getting worried."

"And the school?" Erica repeated.

"They called last week to find out where Danny was. Oskar had maintained contact with them and routinely checked the website to make sure our son kept up with his work, but they hadn't heard from him in over a week—that is when I began to panic."

"What about the website—has there been activity there?" I asked.

"Nothing."

Erica and I looked at each other. "Ma'am, have you spoken with either your husband or your son *since* their departure date from Germany?" I asked.

"Danny and I texted and e-mailed back and forth but he didn't respond the last several times I wrote. If you want, I can check my computer and give you the exact date when I last heard from him. I think it was around the 26th. Could be the 27th. My son was having a great time, but he wanted to come home. Danny said the same thing as the school—he was up-to-date with his work, having submitted his last assignment the day before they were to leave Berlin. Detectives, I have consistently tried to avoid dragging my son into the middle of the problems between my ex and me. At the beginning of the trip we Skyped, but Oskar had problems with his laptop. Then it worked again. Now, it seems it isn't working." With this, Ms Rollins stopped talking. She remained perched on the edge of the seat with her face cupped in the palms of her hands, rubbing her temples in a circular motion with her fingertips, eyes tightly closed.

I wondered whether we had gone too far and should be thinking about leaving. At any rate, it was probably time to call in but, first, we needed something of Danny's for DNA. I mouthed "DNA," and Erica nodded. Even if we managed to obtain an item with the boy's genetic material, how we would obtain approval to run the test was anybody's best guess.

A couple of minutes later, Ms Rollins asked in a measured tone, "Why *are* you here? Is it about Danny?" All the while, she stared down at the rug, tracing the pattern with her foot while carefully enunciating her words. She sounded puzzled. It was as if we had never said anything about our victim. Had not shown her the sketch she denied was of her son. She'd seen the Baltimore victim on the news yet had not recognized him as her son. It occurred to me the woman seemed off because she was in shock.

"Honestly, we're not sure, Ms Rollins," I replied carefully. The questions had to be asked. At the same time I was aware of what a terrible blow it would be if this woman's son had been murdered. That is *unless* she played a role in his death, which was beginning to seem unlikely.

I had an idea. "Ma'am, do you have a picture of Danny and his father that we could take with us? Also, it would be helpful to have Mr. Helman's Berlin address." I figured we could explain the situation to the locals and work out a way to cooperate. While waiting for the DNA results, I would contact Oskar's DC friends and his family in Germany. We could check flight manifests, but would need the travel itinerary.

There was no response, so I continued. "Sarah, you've asked a couple of times why we're here, so let me go over that again."

Moreno nodded in agreement. For the first time, I noticed she was taking notes. It was a good idea; requesting permission to tape the conversation would only have complicated things further.

I took a deep breath and thought about what I might say to bypass her defenses. "Ma'am, we received the York PD's notice asking the Baltimore Police Department to stay alert for anything related to your son. As you acknowledged, our victim looks very much like your son, so we asked our supervisor if we could speak with you. We also informed the York PD of our intentions. We understand you do not think the sketch is of your son, but would you mind if we ran a DNA test to be sure? Ms Rollins, it would really help to rule out the possibility. More importantly, we want to get this child back to his family." By the time I finished, I was almost pleading with her.

The woman slowly shook her head back and forth while avoiding eye contact, but soon relented. "You're right, Officer Crane, the boy is not Danny but I'd like to help another mother, if I can. What do you need from me?"

She actually sounded enthusiastic—the opportunity to do *something* seemed to change her mind. "Could we get Danny's toothbrush or a hairbrush?" If we were wrong, and there were *two* young boys—one dead and one missing—we would have something on file concerning Danny Helman.

Erica said, careful not to suggest the woman's son would be coming home, "Ms Rollins, we will keep in touch. We will also communicate with the York PD."

I got up, walked over to the curio cabinet and looked at the photograph she'd shown us earlier of her son. The body discovered in the Roland Park culvert must be that of Danny Helman—in a day or two this lovely home would be awash in unimaginable sorrow. It was too bad Erica and I were unable to talk in private about how to handle the situation. If our victim was Danny, then we needed to obtain as much information as possible to solve the murder—if *she* was responsible for her son's death, we didn't want her to make any moves that up the road would give us problems with the investigation. I hoped we could get a DNA sample but if not, we would take what we had to the ME—Sarah Rollins' photograph, the one distributed by the York police, as well as the Baltimore PD artist's sketch.

"No problem, Detectives. I appreciate any help I can get, but I don't quite understand why you would need to do a DNA test."

She still seemed confused, so I considered trying again. Erica began to say something, but there was no need for either of us to repeat ourselves. Ms Rollins spoke up, offering more than we had asked for. "If you'll give me a few minutes, I can get you a recent photograph of Danny with his father. Detectives, if I let you take it, you need to return it right away. More helpful might be the Helman family's Berlin address and contact information. That and the flight information are in my office. I may also have a copy of Danny and Oskar's U.S. passports. Anyhow, I'll make copies of what I have. Excuse me, Detectives. It won't take too long to gather everything together—I hope you like the coffee; it's made from a mix of Peruvian and Nicaraguan beans."

"Thank you, it's delicious." I wished it were hot but wasn't about to derail her from getting us what we required to work the investigation.

Once I figured Ms Rollins was well out of hearing, I whispered, "Erica, what do you think?"

"Probably the same thing you do, Chica, but we had better not talk here. How about we speak to Sarge and let him contact the York PD? With his authorization, we can give whatever we have to Huang and the Crime Lab and then decide what to do next. If the DNA confirms that our victim *is* Danny Helman, we will need to return and tell this woman someone has murdered her child."

"I agree, although it makes no sense to me that a child from PA, supposedly with his father in Germany or even DC, is found dead inside a Baltimore City culvert located in a wealthy neighborhood—"

"Shhh," Erica cautioned. "Here she comes."

Ms Rollins entered the room gazing at a small framed photo with something akin to regret. I placed my cup, now drained of the cold coffee, on the table. Erica did the same. Less sunlight came in through the window and the bright and cheerful colors of the room had dimmed.

"Here's the picture of Oskar and Danny, but please be sure to return it," she said to me. "Let me turn on some lights—there's supposed to be a storm. Danny is especially fond of that photograph; he misses his father when they are apart, as he must miss me now. Divorce is a terrible thing for children. I guess that's why I'm particularly worried—my son and I usually talk and email a lot when he's with his father. As bad as things get between my ex and me, we are in complete agreement that it's important for our son to have both of his parents in his life. Oh, and the last time I spoke with Danny was the 26th, which was what I thought. The next day, Oskar sent an e-mail with the travel plans attached, which I printed out for you, along with copies of their passports. I put Danny's hairbrush and toothbrush in separate baggies."

I accepted the envelope, plastic bags, and silver frame. The small photograph was of an exceptionally attractive blonde, blue-eyed man sitting with a young boy who was his mirror image. Father and son were perched on the edge of a dock fishing, a bright green utility box between them. Turned toward the camera, they wore big smiles. I handed it to Erica, who glanced at the picture noncommittally before placing the items in evidence bags that appeared from nowhere.

"Thank you, ma'am," I said. "We'll return your belongings as soon as we can."

More quickly than she will want, I thought to myself, sure that we would be back in a day or two to bring her to Baltimore for an identification. We wouldn't be able to get the DNA results back right away, but Danny's fingerprints should be on the frame and the brushes. CS could check them for a match with what is on file for our victim.

I sneaked a glance at Erica and she nodded. It was time to go.

"Thank you for the coffee, it was delicious," Erica said. "Ma'am, would you mind signing these papers? One details your belongings and the other the tests to be performed by the Crime Lab. Also, please take my card; Officer Crane's number is on the back. Don't hesitate to call either of us with any questions or concerns."

After signing the form, Sarah Rollins saw us to the door but did not follow us out, closing the door once we cleared the threshold. To cry, to figure out what to do, to find out why the friend she was expecting hadn't arrived—I didn't know. It was odd the friend was a no-show; maybe Sarah made a call from upstairs. Once out of the house, Erica opened the trunk and placed the evidence bags inside. We got into the car and she backed out of the driveway and headed toward 83. The rolling pastures no longer seemed so bucolic. It was beginning to rain and Erica turned on the wipers.

Erica groaned. "We *should* stop by the York PD before returning to Baltimore."

"I know." I buckled up and closed my eyes.

Chapter 16

Missing Child or Children?

"**H**ey, Sarge. Can we talk?" I asked.

"Thought you had the weekend off. Ladies, what *are* you doing here? And don't even *think* of putting in for overtime."

"No OT. Closed door, if you don't mind. The trip to PA yesterday took longer than we expected," explained Erica.

"Shit, now what? *Ladies!*"

It was a command, not a request. We followed him into his office— this might be my first time in the hot seat, though, truth be told, it was often difficult to tell how much of our supervisor's response was just bluster. For a minute or two, Sarge sat there giving us the fisheye. He then leaned forward, fingers laced—we had his full attention. "Well, what do you have for me?"

I told him the basics of what had transpired, while Erica set the items we'd obtained from Rollins on his desk. When I'd finished, he examined each item through the bags before sitting back and slowly rubbing his scar, which appeared angrier than usual. I supposed it suited his present mood. "Did you two give any thought to the fact the York PD might not appreciate our interfering in their case?"

"Sir, after their fax came in, I called to let them know we wanted to show Sarah Rollins the sketch of the Roland Park victim and told them why," Erica explained. "They had no problems with that. Honestly, they were not giving the woman's concern much credence. They said she let her ex take their son to Germany and was in touch with them until the end of October. York PD agreed that the father was late returning the boy, but since he pushed for an extra week before leaving, they weren't convinced there was anything to it."

I pitched in. "We advised Rollins that we would be following up with them, but we wanted to update you first."

"Well, ladies, the York PD sent out the request for information in the first place, so somebody there is handling the boy's disappearance if, in fact, that's what it is. I don't think it's up to you, after one phone call, to determine how much *credence* they're giving this woman's concern about her son. You both should know better than that."

I was sure my face was bright red—it didn't take much. "Sorry, sir, I—"

"Never mind. Okay, you two, Huang is always working; stop by his office with your booty and then take it to the Crime Lab. Be sure to give me an update when you've got some results."

"Yes, sir," said Erica.

"Yes, sir," I repeated and eager to escape, headed for the door.

"Moreno, you call York since you spoke with them in the beginning. Keep your contact informed—advise him that he'll receive the ME's report as soon as you have something. No OT but I'll give you a day off if the Lt. approves the request."

"Thank you, sir."

Once out of earshot, Erica burst out laughing. "Come on, Chica, let's get this done! We have gotten ourselves into enough trouble for the day—I do not know which was redder, Sarge's scar or your face! The disadvantage of being white!"

"Moreno, give me a break. You're my partner and all that entails—mostly covering my back. C'mon, girl, you've had enough fun, let's go start with the ME."

"Sorry, Chica, I forgot to tell you I have to be somewhere—it will take me at least an hour. Would you mind taking care of it? I hope the Crime Lab gives you no grief. When I return, we can grab a coffee and you can catch me up."

"Sure."

"*Then*, we'll head to Roland Park."

"It's all good, Moreno. I have waders this time! Let's not forget to figure out our schedule—Monday should work for a day off."

"Definitely.   A   partial   Saturday,   all   of   Sunday   and Monday—¡Caramba!"

———

I stood in the doorway of the Chief Medical Examiner's office. "Good morning, Dr. Huang?"

The ME looked up from whatever he was writing, smiled, and beckoned me into the room. "Please do come in."

We'd met only once and I thought he might be unlikely to remember me, so I approached his desk and extended my hand. "Hello, Dr. Huang, I'm Officer Robin Crane."

"Of course, Officer Crane," he said, shaking my hand. "What can I do for you? I hope you and Detective Moreno are making progress that will allow me to return the little boy to his family."

"That's why I'm here. Erica had an appointment but sends her regards."

"A fine person—please deliver my greetings. You may take a seat."

"Thank you." His office was immaculate and beautiful—an oddity in a department uniformly in need of order or updates as simple as paint. I settled comfortably into one of the chairs Dr. Huang must have personally purchased. Typically, obsolete couches and chairs—stained, foam stuffing escaping and plastic pinching—served as furnishings for most offices.

On the ME's desk was a photograph of him with his arm around a tall, good-looking kid. I remembered Erica saying he had a son and a daughter—the son, premed. "Dr. Huang, your son attends Hopkins?"

"He did. John graduated last spring and now studies at Duke Medical School."

"How does he like Duke?"

"Fine. All is fine, my good detective. My son is doing very well. Thank you. Thank you for asking, Robin. I can call you Robin—this is okay?" The formality plus the strong accent made the man particularly endearing.

"Please. And you, how are you doing?" The ME, who had been exceptionally quiet when I saw him previously, seemed to be in a high good humor.

"We've been busy."

"Busy is good."

Bohai Huang was in his early sixties, short and heavy—almost rotund. Erica said he came from China in his twenties to study at Hopkins and never left. He was an openly gay man; I could not imagine how tough it must have been for him when he came out to his family—a wife and two children. That, however, might be my own prejudice. Despite having spent decades in this country, his English, although technically excellent was thickly accented and sometimes difficult to understand, the bane of the state's attorney when testifying.

"But enough about me, Officer. I see you brought something for me today—something I am confident you need processed immediately."

I handed him the bags. "Dr. Huang, you have me there. Moreno and I think we've discovered something important. We followed up on a fax from the York PD asking for any information about a boy, name of Danny Helman."

"Why did you do that?"

"Sir, the photograph they'd faxed to the BPD looked like our Roland Park victim."

"And what is the story with Danny Helman?"

"The father and son had been in Germany for several weeks, with the mom's approval, but the ex is late in returning the boy to his mother."

"Why a visit when school is in session?"

"The boy had been sick with mono during the summer, so the parents worked out an alternative arrangement. The father is German and the son has dual citizenship."

"Interesting. So, Robin, what do you have for us?"

"Some for you, some for the Crime Lab."

"The evidence may remain with me. I'll see what you collected gets where it needs to go."

"Yes, sir. The framed photograph is from the boy's room—the relevant data are written on each bag."

"How is this working with the York PD? I do not want any problems," he said, with some concern.

"Sir, it's being worked out—we've already spoken with Sarge. Detective Moreno updated the York PD. They told us to follow through with our case. The mother gave the father permission to take the son to Europe, so York is not too concerned about a parental abduction. Sarah Rollins is meeting with a lawyer to find out what her options are but is not putting any pressure on the police.

"Dr. Huang, the mother's fingerprints will be on the frame, but we're hoping the Crime Lab will find at least one or two of the boy's they can compare with our victim's prints. The mother also handled the hairbrush and the toothbrush; both belong to her son, so I'm anticipating there is DNA. Oh, and the hair in the brush is white-blonde. If you remember, you said the Crime Lab could test the victim's hair for dye. Sir, we don't mean to pressure you, but how long do you think the results will take?"

He didn't answer. Instead, he asked, "Did you show Ms Helm—"

"Rollins. Her married name was Helman, as is the boy's—she went back to her maiden name."

"And the mother saw your sketch of the boy?"

"Dr. Huang—"

"Why so formal? Call me Bo, everyone does so."

"Thank you. Bo, even though the mother is very worried about her son, she looked at the sketch of our victim carefully and saw it on television, yet denies it is of Danny. She didn't even consider the possibility—never mentioned the resemblance to the York PD."

"You and Erica seem to have made considerable progress with the investigation. What do you think? You must be suspicious, since you are here with your baggies." His laugh was infectious. I liked the man.

"Dr. Huang—Bo, we believe the dead boy *is* the woman's missing son; we're confused as to why *she* doesn't think so. Denial, I guess, can be a powerful defense mechanism when the pain is too difficult to face."

"So true, Robin. I will let you know when more results come in."

"Thank you, sir." Dismissed, I left shutting the door gently behind me. Once out of range, I dialed Erica.

"Hey, California. How'd it go?"

"Good. I'll update you when I see you. About that—what do you think of going in our own cars? Once we're finished with the creek, we can head home. That'll keep us from being caught up in any new calls. I'm looking forward to the time off."

"Robin, let me know if you hear back from Sarge about taking Monday rather than OT?"

"My guess is there won't be a problem. Okay, let's get this done. Park under the bank and wait for me in front of Eddie's. From there, we can go to Oakdale."

"Right. See you in twenty."

"How about picking up lunch? I'll give you the money."

"Not to worry, Moreno."

Chapter 17

A Tangled Web

"My phone rang. It was Erica. "Sorry, my partner is calling."

"Go ahead and take it," said the Department of Transportation representative.

"Moreno, what's up?"

"Are you almost finished at DOT? Robin, you need to come back as soon as possible. That woman from Fells Point, the one who is worried about her niece, is trying to reach you. She is almost hysterical and *insists* on speaking to *you*."

"Thanks. We're almost done."

"Will they work with us on posting flyers on the buses?"

"Absolutely." I quickly wrapped up my business and left for Northern, wondering what was now up with Marisol Jimenez.

I had no more than returned to my desk when the phone rang. "Crane, Northern District."

"Detective, it's Marisol Jimenez. Fells Point. Brenda, my sister-in-law, says Joey isn't with her—I'm really worried!" She spoke breathlessly, running the words together. Erica was right about the hysteria.

"Marisol, slow down. I'm having trouble understanding you."

"I'm sorry, it's only … I'm scared."

"Did you speak with Officer Rossi?" Even as I asked the question, I knew she probably hadn't even thought to call him.

"Sorry; I am *really* sorry. I called you because Officer Rossi's not worried about Joey."

"I don't know any such thing, but we'll let that go for now and I'll talk to him later. Okay, tell me, where did you see Brenda?"

"Where else but at our house—my crazy sister-in-law came back for more money! Johnny wouldn't give her any … she's pissed and is trying to get at me through my niece. Brenda is a horrible person."

"Marisol, take a breath so I can follow you. You sound rattled, garbled; is there a transmission problem?"

"Sorry." The line fell silent but for her breathing, which was thankfully becoming more regular.

"All right, that's better. "Now, what did your sister-in-law say about Joey?"

"Initially she wouldn't tell us anything, but Johnny insisted and, finally, Brenda told my husband Joey was staying with a friend but *refused* to give him that person's name or a way to get hold of her. We wanted to go to the friend's house but my sister-in-law has *no* idea where this friend lives! Can you believe that?" The pitch of her voice was almost painful to the ear. I put the phone on speaker and turned the volume down.

"What did Johnny say to all this?"

"He begged for information, but Brenda *insisted* she doesn't know! Friggin' unbelievable."

I could picture Marisol's expression of utter disbelief. One that was most likely warranted. It was not sounding good for this little girl and it was too late to second-guess what I *should* have done when Rossi and I took the report.

"What happened about Joey transferring schools?"

"I asked her about that. Brenda says she changed her mind about leaving Baltimore."

"So, she's been here this whole time. Is Joey enrolled somewhere else or back in her old school?"

"Another school … I'm not sure … after she left, I contacted the school—she forgot to remove Johnny as a contact. The principal said she hadn't heard from Brenda … well, since my sister-in-law told her they were leaving the state."

"Marisol, please calm down."

"Detective, I understand I'm asking a lot of you but this is important. Joey is just a little girl. I'm really worried about her."

"Believe me, I appreciate the importance of what you're telling me. What's the number for your cell?" As she told me, I wrote it down. "Okay, give me some time to check in with my supervisor since you're in a different district. I'll call you back and we'll go from there."

"Thank you *so* much, I mean it. Officer Crane, tell your boss Brenda was stoned out of her gourd when she came to the house—we *have* to do something . . . soon. I'll wait to hear from you." She hung up.

It didn't escape me that this was the second time in a week I found myself involved in another district's case. Both concerning a missing child. Once I located him, I gave Sarge the details of the Jimenez complaint, emphasizing the possibility Marisol had information that would get us to a child who might or might not be missing. He enquired about Greg Rossi's role, and I explained *he'd* given her my number. I assured Sarge that Erica was okay with following up the call; I thought we should remain low-key and go out of uniform. In addition, we would keep Rossi posted. He was open to a collaboration but wanted to talk with the Lieutenant.

An hour later, Sarge phoned and approved the request to follow up on the Jimenez call. The case, if there was a case, would be worked out of Northern and we were to communicate with Rossi. Pleased with the resolution, I thanked him and went looking for my partner.

I discovered Erica in a conference room reviewing cold case files. She'd picked up an investigation from 31 years ago: an older woman who'd received a life sentence for murder now claimed her husband sexually abused her and threatened to kill her. Had his hands around her throat. Several weeks ago, the Innocence Project notified her of their intent to take on the case. I listened while she told me of the ins and outs of the murder—Moreno suspected an ex-husband who had never been charged. She stopped midsentence in her description of his previous felony convictions. "Chica, did you want me for a particular reason or are you just hanging out?"

"Sorry, Erica; it's not looking like we're things are going our way today, which is unfortunate because I'd give anything for lunch. The woman who called, Marisol Jimenez—the one with the druggie sister-in-law—thinks she has a possible lead. She's frantic about finding her niece and I've begun to think something's hinky—the girl should be in school but the aunt says she's not and her mother refuses to tell her where she is living. The sister-in-law is Brenda Jimenez. If I remember correctly, her little girl, Joey, is 11. Sarge says to follow up on the call. We can go out of uniform—I thought it would be good to dial down the situation. We're to keep him and Rossi in the loop."

"Sure, let's go for it. Two chicas shaking up Southeastern, I am all for that—should be good times! You want to go now?"

I laughed at her perverted enthusiasm. "Thanks, partner."

"It'll take ten to fifteen minutes to wrap things up and change."

"Take your time. I need to make a couple of calls."

"Bueno, come get me when you're ready."

"Will do." I returned to my desk and called Marisol Jimenez, who answered on the first ring. I easily pictured her sitting there staring at her phone.

"Marisol?"

"Can we talk?"

I turned the page of my notebook and wrote the date and time. Her name. "My partner and I will be at your house in about an hour."

The line went quiet for a few seconds before she began hedging. "Thank you, but that's not such a good idea. Johnny will be unhappy if I get Brenda into any kind of trouble. If the police come to the house again that's just what he's going to think."

I tried to conceal my irritation. "Where did you want to meet?"

"Brenda is staying at a house not far from where I live, I think. I can meet you in the parking lot of the Bond Street Wharf and tell you what I know. Then we can go talk to her and find out where Joey is."

"I'm on my way. See you soon." I didn't bother telling her it wasn't going to be as easy as she expected—Marisol apparently had some idea about riding in with the cavalry to intimidate her sister-in-law and rescue her niece. No wonder she was trying to keep Johnny out of the loop! Unlike her husband, Marisol would be happy enough if we put Brenda in the cruiser and hauled her off to a cell and threw away the key. That was not going to happen, at least for the present.

———

"Chica, you drive." Erica tossed me the keys and walked around to the passenger side. "Why not go to her house?"

"She doesn't want her husband to find out she's talking to the police. Says she knows where Brenda is staying and I'm afraid she thinks we're somehow going to wring Joey's whereabouts out of the sister-in-law."

"Sure, that's us—wringer of necks. ¡Loca!" she laughed. You had better fill me in again on the history and names—what you hope to accomplish with this outing." She giggled and added, "Did I mention I want a caramel frappuccino for my cheerful cooperation?"

"You got it, partner. Here's the deal: Marisol Jimenez believes her niece isn't attending school. Brenda initially left the house with money from her brother, Johnny Jimenez. Marisol thought she was going to use it for drugs. The girl's name is Josephine Jimenez—Joey—and she is 11-years-old. By the way, the *father* is not actually her biological parent, but the man Brenda married and is now separated or divorced from—not sure which and don't know where he is. Anyhow, Johnny and Marisol have not seen their niece since the night Rossi and I received the 911 call for their address. The mother apparently removed her daughter from school sometime after that. She eventually notified them of plans to move out-of-state but never stopped by to pick up the paperwork.

"Okay, Moreno, that's what I've got for history. Yesterday or maybe today, Brenda reappeared with her hand out. Marisol insisted on knowing her niece's whereabouts but Brenda refused to tell her, so they didn't give her any money. After more back and forth, Brenda told them her daughter left the house with a friend but when pushed, claimed she wasn't sure where this *friend* lived. I guess that's what really set Marisol off—she doesn't buy the sister-in-law's explanation."

"Wow, does not sound so good. What is your goal today, Robin?"

"The upshot is to locate Joey and bring Child Protective Services into the mix. Marisol and Johnny are willing to take care of the girl but would need Brenda's permission, which I am sure they aren't going to get. Honestly, Erica, I'm not sure; this case is a first for me—could be a nothing or could be something serious is going on and the clock is ticking."

"Robin, did the mom steal money when you and Greg responded to the first call? If that is how it played out, maybe they could request charges be filed. Bueno ... if she could get her husband to agree. I guess that is unlikely since we're meeting her at the Bond Street wharf!"

"Nope, there won't be any charges. The brother *gave* his sister their rent money. That was the source of the argument triggering the 911."

"Robin, why is Marisol Jimenez calling *you*? Mind you, I am not being critical, but this woman keeps coming to you with her problems. You are too busy to be babysitting her."

"I don't know—maybe because I told her to call if she had any concerns. Of course, that occurred before my transfer to Homicide. You're right, there's a lot going on. It's more likely that Marisol believes Rossi won't follow up on the case and she's right, I've worked with him—he's ready to retire. Greg said I worried for no good reason and didn't want to pursue the matter."

"Bueno, we'll take this little field trip and see what shakes out. Chica, you are definitely going to make a hell of a partner. Hope Rossi doesn't bounce us around ... you are sure we are cleared for this?"

"Yep. When I spoke with him, both this time *and* the last, his take was that he couldn't be bothered. Marisol is undoubtedly chomping at the bit for us to show up. With any luck, she won't do anything foolish before we get there."

The highway morphed into President Street and then followed the curve of the harbor into Fells Point, where I pulled into the Bond Street parking lot. I no more than shut off the car, when a young woman got up from a park bench and came over. At first, I failed to recognize her; she was wearing a hoodie and dark glasses. With that get-up, I second-guessed my decision to be involved and supposed I had better give more thought to the idea of staying involved, never mind dragging Erica into a domestic fray.

Marisol approached and I rolled down my window. Cold air flowed in.

"Thank you for coming, Officer Crane." She removed her glasses, looked at Erica and, reaching her arm across me, extended her hand. "Marisol Jimenez, pleased to meet you."

Erica smiled and shook her hand. "Detective Erica Moreno."

Marisol was not the put together young woman who had come to Northern only days ago: no makeup, hair that could use a shampoo, baggy jeans and what appeared to be her husband's shirt and hoodie. Below her eyes were purplish-black smudges.

"I already gave Detective Moreno the background information on your niece. Where is it you think Brenda is living?"

"Would you mind if I sit in the car with you?" she asked nervously. "I really don't want anyone to see me or it'll get back to Johnny."

"Sure," Erica said. She popped the lock and Marisol slid into the backseat, slumped down, and pulled her hood closer. I swallowed a laugh. Erica flashed a smile in my direction.

"Detectives, you won't believe it. My sister-in-law is living at a rowhouse somewhere on North Glover. I'm sure Brenda is lying about my niece staying with a friend; she has to be with her mother. *If* you can even call her a mother."

I was writing things down as she spoke. Erica remained quiet, keeping an eye on the woman through the rearview mirror. I thought it curious Marisol knew where Brenda lived, though I guess I shouldn't be surprised. What I had learned while patrolling Fells Point was that although frequently packed with tourists, it is essentially a small neighborhood. Most people, for better or worse, are aware of what their neighbors are up to; even at this time of the year folks will sit on their stoops watching the world go by. When it gets too cold, they sit inside by their windows and, intent on tracking their neighbors' activities, peek through the curtains or blinds—a detective's dream when trying to ferret out intelligence. *Avoid snitchin'* is not the mantra here. At any time, there are plenty of feuds and petty jealousies in play for the police to draw from.

"Marisol, how did you come by your information?" I asked.

She removed the hood. "Well, I'm sure you're not going to be happy about this, Officer Crane, but I guess it doesn't matter now because it's done. Remember when you asked me if I knew any of Brenda's friends?"

"I do. I seem to remember you said your sister-in-law had a couple—she had gone through the rest of them. Did one of them tell you where Brenda and her daughter are staying?"

"Not quite," she mumbled, breaking off eye contact and chewing at her thumb.

Erica turned in her seat. "What, then?" she asked sharply, cutting to the chase.

"Well, I talked to both of them. Although they said they hadn't seen Brenda, I thought one of them, Sheila Krasinski, was lying."

"I thought it a good idea to talk with anybody who knows your sister-in-law. We certainly aren't going to fault you for that."

"Well, that's not all," Marisol drew out her words and pulled her hood back over her head.

"Give me the rest of the story then," I said gently.

"Officer Crane, after I saw you at Northern, I did something you're probably not going to like."

Uh oh, we were going to hear something neither Erica nor I wanted to know. "And?"

Marisol leaned forward between the seats and said almost in a whisper, "Once I heard Brenda was in town, I took a couple of days off from work and tailed Sheila as often as I could without making Johnny suspicious. One night I told him I was going out with friends; instead, I followed Sheila downtown to the Power Plant Live. *There* I caught up with my sister-in-law. Brenda appeared fine, maybe a little thin but all dolled up and almost pretty. Anyhow, she and her pal hugged and talked for a while—they were having fun. After about twenty minutes, they went inside. I called Johnny and said I'd be home late. I *hate* lying to my husband," she said, looking at Erica and then at me.

Yet she *had* lied to him. I took a deep breath and waited for the next shoe to fall. Erica stared straight ahead.

Our passenger sat back against the seat and resumed her story. "It didn't matter, he wasn't concerned or even listening to me—Johnny and a buddy had tickets for a Ravens game that night. They always go out afterwards and when they do, Johnny doesn't usually make it past the living room couch when he finally comes home, so if I go in through the back door, he doesn't know the difference."

I was well aware this woman was concerned about her niece, but *concerned* was probably not the right word for what was going on here. It sounded more like stalking. I glanced at Erica and got dark knitted eyebrows; I squelched a sigh and continued with the questioning. "So, what happened then?"

"It was a long night—I couldn't go inside the Power Plant. You can never find parking, so I hung around outside like I had a purpose—it was cold by then. Anyhow, they—Brenda and Sheila—left about 1 a.m. and I managed to follow them—*that* was tricky—to Sheila's house at 140 North Glover Street. I parked down the block and sat in the car. The lights went out about an hour later. Brenda never came out."

Erica spoke up. "Would you have been able to tell whether your sister-in-law went out the back and left through the alley?"

"I could only see the front of the house. You're right. She could have gone out the back, and I wouldn't have known—didn't think of that."

"You stayed parked there *all* night?" Erica asked with a grimace—probably equally concerned about the amateur PI activities. I wondered why Marisol had told me Brenda's friend lived *somewhere* on Glover when she knew exactly where Krasinski lived.

"No, I went home about 3 a.m., got a couple hours of sleep and went back at 6:30. I wrote a note for Johnny about having an early day and not knowing what time I would be home."

"So what happened?" I asked, struggling to keep in mind the possibility that a child was missing.

"Nothing until about 11. That's when Sheila left dressed like she was going to work."

"Why do you think that?" I asked.

"She had on a uniform, like for a restaurant."

"And what did you do, Ms Jimenez?" my partner asked.

"I stayed put. But this time I was prepared," Marisol said proudly.

Not sure that I wanted to hear her answer, I asked anyhow. "Meaning?"

"I brought a book, blanket, some drinks and snacks with me. A good thing because it wasn't until two in the afternoon that Brenda finally came out of the house. I guess, Detective Moreno, it was because I saw my sister-in-law go out through the front door the next day I gave no thought to her leaving through the rear the night before. In any case, Brenda only went to get coffee and doughnuts."

"So how long did this go on?" At that moment, all I wanted was to be somewhere other than where I was. It was bad enough Marisol was sitting in her car watching the house; she had actually admitted to stalking her sister-in-law. "You've been following Brenda's every move?"

"Detective, I need to find my niece. I watched the house for almost a week; Brenda slept there every night. Fine, I was not there *every* night but if not, I arrived first thing in the morning. She has a key to the house. The thing is, only Brenda and Sheila go in and out. Well, that's not true. After Sheila goes to work, men sometimes come to the house. Nobody I recognize from the neighborhood—none with a key. Whoever they are, when Brenda answers the door, they're pretty chummy."

"What about Joey? Did you see her at all?" I asked, although I knew the answer. That was why we were here.

"Not once. That's why I'm so upset and probably why I'm behaving so weirdly—don't worry, Detectives, I understand that I'm off the rails." Marisol faced me. "During the time I sat in my car watching the house, I never once saw Joey." She began to cry.

I handed her tissues. "Marisol, tell me about the conversation you had with Brenda."

"Thank you." She blew her nose and continued. "Well, after about five days of watching Brenda and no Joey, I decided to confront my sister-in-law when she came out of the house on her morning coffee run. Honestly, it wasn't difficult—she left the same time each day. So, I pretended to run into her by accident."

"And how did she respond to your sudden appearance?" Erica queried.

"Surprised. Not happy to see me. Anxious. Detective," she said, focusing on me, "I still think my sister-in-law is doing drugs—I am *sure* she is doing drugs."

We hardly had a reliable witness in Marisol. "What makes you say that?" I asked.

"Brenda wears long sleeves."

"Marisol, in case you didn't notice, it's cold," I said, trying to keep the sarcasm out of my tone, but aware the words probably said it all.

The sarcasm escaped her. "I know it's cold, but she *always* wore long sleeves when she lived with us. Remember the heat wave last spring?—even then. I bet she has tracks. Brenda is most likely paying for the drugs by turning tricks. If not, my sister-in-law is doing a lot of dating, much of it during the day when Sheila isn't home. Ask the neighbors, they'll be able to tell you what's going on—*nobody* in this neighborhood minds their own business."

Erica shrugged almost imperceptibly. The comment about the long sleeves undoubtedly made about as much sense to her as it did to me. "Marisol, I need to talk with my partner privately."

She began to move but then hesitated. "Marisol, it'll only take us a few minutes." Sniffling, she got out of the car without saying anything. The pigeons flew off with an annoyed chatter at her approach; we watched in silence while she reclaimed the bench. I breathed a sigh of relief now that we could discuss the situation out of her hearing.

"Does the story sound legit to you, California?"

"Of course there are no guarantees, Erica, but I think so."

"I am not sure either, even if this is my first time meeting the woman. Bueno, I guess you don't know Marisol Jimenez, but you at least interacted with her, so I am going to take your lead here. As you are aware by now, Chica, I do not like folks messing with children. If the girl is missing, bottom line—we need to find her."

"Thanks, partner, although I must admit I'm a bit worried about the vigilante behavior. Even if she has a legitimate concern about her niece, and I'm becoming increasingly convinced something's happened to the girl, her behavior is out of bounds."

"Well, Robin, let's go to this Sheila's house—*something* is going on there. What do you think we should do about Marisol?"

"Hmmm … well, she doesn't want to be seen with us and I don't think she *should*. At this point, it makes no sense to alienate Brenda, which is sure to be the case if she knows we've been talking with her sister-in-law. We've got the address so there's no reason why she needs to come with us—I'm going to tell her to go home and we'll call later with an update."

"Bueno, sounds like a plan."

"Give me a minute. I'll go tell her she's not invited to this party."

"Good luck. Something tells me she is not going to take this well."

I got out of the car and walked over to where Marisol sat on the bench. Torn, wanting to be present when we confronted Brenda yet not wanting trouble with her husband or us, she agreed to go home.

Chapter 18

Confrontation

Erica parked on Fayette and we walked to the Glover address. I went up the few stairs to the door and knocked. Meanwhile, my partner remained on the sidewalk. Nobody answered. I knocked again. Where there should be a doorbell, there was only a hole with dangling wires. After my third attempt, an irritated woman yelled to hang on and then demanded that I "stop the damn knocking!" With a few choice words, her shrill voice assured me she would be there in a minute.

Despite her assertion that she was coming, it took almost five minutes before the door opened. When it did, out slipped a thin woman maybe 5' 7", with shoulder-length black hair, roots showing. If this was Brenda, I figured Marisol was probably right about her sister-in-law doing drugs—it was not only the possible track marks, but the dilated pupils and sores on her neck and the backs of her hands. She must have used plenty of makeup when she was out with her friends, if she looked "almost pretty."

Brenda stood at the doorway, arms crossed tightly across her chest, jaw set. She caught me glancing inside the house and took several steps onto the concrete landing before shutting the door behind her. I thought about moving down a step to increase the distance between us, but stayed put. Without a word, she stood there looking at Erica and then back to me. Unaccountably, she did not seem surprised to see us. A bit belatedly, it occurred to me neither of us was in uniform and there was no patrol car in evidence.

"*Why* were you banging on the damn door?" she demanded in a tone laced with equal measures of belligerence and scorn. "Whatever it is, I don't want any." She turned to go back into the house.

"Ma'am, I am sorry to bother you," I said, with all the courtesy I could muster. "I'm Officer Robin Crane and this my partner, Detective Erica Moreno." Both of us showed our badges, which she ignored—we might as well be sales people or Jehovah's Witnesses, for all she cared.

I got to the point. "Excuse me, but am I speaking with Ms Brenda Jimenez?"

"Yeah, what of it?" she said, not one whit less antagonistic, despite now being aware the police were at her door. Hand on knob, she remained poised to go back inside. I began to appreciate the nature of the problem between Marisol and Brenda, especially since they had been living together. I also better understood why the "missing" Joey was of such concern to her aunt.

I glanced around and saw a few curtains pulled back. I lowered my voice. "Ms Jimenez, could we talk privately?"

Brenda scanned the area but didn't budge, not in the least interested in allowing us into her home, regardless of the fact neighbors would soon be outside on their stoops. It occurred to me that although the woman might not be nervous about us standing at her front door, she might be wary of roiling law enforcement. I was deciding where to go with that when, without warning, she froze: her jaw clenched and eyes narrowed. She balled her right hand into a fist.

Startled, I looked around to see what had caught her attention. I guess it shouldn't have been a surprise. Marisol had not returned home as advised to do, *told* to do. She was standing on the sidewalk across the street, two houses down.

"What are *you* doing here?" Brenda screamed at her sister-in-law—doors opened, a few people came out. "You fucking bitch, what in the hell!" She looked from Marisol to us and back. "*You* fucking did this!"

Marisol yelled back in a voice matching Brenda's for volume. "It's no secret what you've been up to but believe me, I don't give a damn. I want to find Joey."

"Get the hell out of here! My life is none of your damn business. My *daughter* is none of your business! Marisol, trust me, Joey *hates* the sight of you."

Erica was already striding across the street. She took Marisol by the elbow and led her further down the block. I turned my attention back to the angry woman in front of me. "Ma'am, please, we're not trying to cause you a problem. Wouldn't you prefer to go inside?" I knew that if I couldn't calm her down soon, the few bystanders would grow into a crowd. I had no doubt that if we were unable to keep the two women separated, there would be trouble. I wished Erica well.

"No! I definitely do *not* want to go inside and talk with you! In fact, I don't want to talk with you at all—inside or outside. What I *do* want is a lawyer!"

Great. "Ms Jimenez, I think there has been some sort of misunderstanding—we are not here to arrest you, and have no intention of forcing you to talk with us. All we're trying to do is determine what school Josephine has been attending since classes started this fall. Maryland law requires children to attend school; you notified the principal that you were moving out of state and would be picking up transfer papers but apparently failed to do so. Now, you seem to be living in the neighborhood again; we're only trying to establish whether your daughter has been re-enrolled."

I stole a peek to see what was happening. Erica must have read Marisol the riot act because she was nowhere in sight, and my partner was on her way back. When she got closer, I caught her eye and she shrugged her barely perceptible shrug and gestured for me to approach. Reluctantly, I asked Brenda if she would give us a few minutes. After an update, we agreed we should speak with the school first, rather than taking Marisol's word about whether Joey was attending or not. I went back up the stairs.

"Thank you, Ms Jimenez. We'll be leaving—I apologize for the bother."

"And I want that bitch out of here!"

There was no doubt in my mind who she was talking about. "We told her she can't be here—she's gone home."

"Hell, she has. The bitch is still here."

I groaned; Erica was clearly annoyed. A small knot of neighbors had gathered on the sidewalk. No surprise there.

"Brenda, I really don't want to make things more difficult for you," called out Marisol, who had not only returned but was only one house away, though still across the street.

"*You bitch!* It's not my fault Joey took off. If you hadn't thrown us out on the street none of this would have happened!" She stopped yelling—looked from us to her sister-in-law and back again.

"What in the hell are you doing here?" For a second time, she glanced from Marisol to us. "*You* fucking bitch, you always had it in for me. How did you know where I was? Is my brother aware of what you're doing—that you're responsible for the cops *hassling* me?"

At the mention of her husband, Marisol backed off as if slapped. The sudden movement brought a sparkle to Brenda's eyes—she had hit a soft spot. "You bitch! My brother *doesn't* know what you've been up to, does he? Believe me, he will as soon as I'm finished with these two, and he's going to be sooo pissed."

"Erica, can you stay with Brenda, while I talk to Marisol?" I asked quietly.

"Sure."

I walked over to where the distressed woman stood half-hidden by a telephone pole. "Ma'am, you asked for help and I've made a real effort to do just that—even brought my partner into it. Went to my supervisor. We asked you to go home and let us take care of this and you've ignored us, *twice*." She began to cry.

I softened my voice. "Marisol, I understand you're worried about Joey, but believe me you're not helping your niece by being here and getting into it with Brenda. What I need is for you to go home. You must realize the minute we leave, your sister-in-law is going to call your husband. What I suggest is that you get hold of him first and come clean about what's been going on."

"I'm sorry—please tell your partner. This time, I promise to go. You're right—Brenda will call Johnny as soon as you're gone; I don't need her to tell me how angry he's going to be. I should have stayed out of it. I'll talk with my husband and hope for the best," she said dejectedly.

Marisol *sounded* contrite. I hoped the damage had not already been done because I was determined to find Joey Jimenez and her aunt was making it that much more difficult. "Well, whatever you do or don't do, you need to let us carry out the investigation as we see fit. You came to me for assistance and your being here is not helpful if we're going to locate your niece."

"I understand."

I wasn't sure she did understand what the outcome could be if Brenda insisted on legal representation. Even so, in spite of the problems she was causing, I couldn't help but feel sorry for her. "If you hurry, you should be able to talk with your husband before your sister-in-law gets hold of him—we can delay her, but not for long."

"Officer Crane, when will you let me know what's going on?"

"Marisol, I need for you to go. *Now*. This is not an argument. Your being here is not appropriate and if you don't leave, I am going to charge you with hindering an investigation."

"Okay. Sorry."

I turned and left without another word. Once I returned, I glanced at Erica, who didn't say anything. "Okay, Brenda, she's gone—"

"Officer Crane, Ms Jimenez and I were just chatting while you took care of things—I was telling her about Costa Rica." She turned back to Brenda. "Ma'am, all we want to know is what school your daughter is attending. Are you okay talking with us? If not, we will leave."

"What is it you want?" Brenda asked irritably, as if Erica had not just told her. In this job, you quickly understand what poor listeners most people are if they don't want to deal with the police.

"I'm sorry. We'll try and make this quick, so that we can get out of your business," Erica said in a no-nonsense tone. I hoped Brenda had forgotten about the earlier mention of a lawyer—hoped if things went bad, the prosecutor would not call us out.

"By the way, what *are* you accusing me of? I'm not keeping my daughter out of school, if that's what this is all about."

"Ms Jimenez, we aren't accusing you of anything. We just wanted to make sure your daughter is back in classes—not necessarily her old school, but some school," I said, in an effort to provide her with an out.

Her face tightened and her stance somehow became even more taut. Just when I was thinking about breaking the silence, Brenda mumbled, "Josephine ran away. Since I'm not sure where she is, I can't really help you. I've told Marisol that, but she doesn't believe me." She rallied and continued. "That's *her* problem, not mine! Bitch can't have a kid, so she wants my daughter. Wait until I tell Johnny—putting the police onto his sister!"

"Have you spoken with Joey at all, or has she called since leaving home?" I asked the questions as calmly as possible, hoping Marisol contacted Johnny before Brenda reached him, because all hell was bound to break loose in their house. A runaway, Marisol was unable to have children … maybe we were getting somewhere.

In a soothing tone, Erica said, "Ma'am, we cannot do much without more information." The underlying assumption was that Brenda wanted help, which I doubted.

"Joey called once. That's why I'm not worried—she told me she's staying with a friend. I pushed, but she refused to tell me who the friend was or where she lived. You tell me—what in the hell am I supposed to do?"

I guess her question was rhetorical because she continued without waiting for a response. "I'm telling you, Josephine will come back when she wants to. After all, she's almost 12 and can pick up a phone if she needs something."

Incredulous, I did not dare look at my partner. Instead, I rifled back to an earlier page in my notebook. "Ms Jimenez, I thought Joey was 11?"

"In a few months she'll be 12."

"Did you report your daughter as missing?" Erica asked. We both knew nobody had reported Joey as missing—that, we had checked.

"No, I already *told* you, she's not missing! Shit, don't you get it?" I figured with her increasingly heated tone, we were nearing the end of the conversation because the word "lawyer" was sure to pop up again. "It's simple—this is a family matter; I'm telling you, my daughter will be back. Anyhow, whatever is going on is really none of your business. My ex lives in DC. She's probably living with the son-of-a-bitch to spite me because I wouldn't let her have her way whenever she wanted."

"Did you ask your ex-husband whether Joey is with him?" I wondered why I hadn't gotten any specifics about him from Marisol. Brenda might well be right—many a frustrated child has gone to live with the noncustodial parent.

"Yeah, I did," said Brenda with a self-satisfied smile. "He says she isn't. Believe me, he's a liar. He can get food stamps with her there."

I must be getting cynical—I figured the father for an addict without even meeting him. "Ms Jimenez, would you be willing to give us his contact information?"

She grinned; it was payback time. I wrote down the phone number and address for a Rick Denney.

"When did Joey leave?"

"Maybe the second week of September."

"Ma'am, do you remember when she called?" While I asked the question, I tried to control my dismay as it sank in exactly how long the child had been gone.

Brenda stood there mindlessly picking at a sore on the back of her hand. Just when I thought the woman was going to stonewall us, she continued. "Late September, the beginning of October. I asked her to come back—she refused. Said she was happier living with her friend, but wouldn't give me the girl's name. You know how teenagers are."

It was a statement, not a question. *And no, I guess I do not "know how teenagers are," at least according to Brenda Jimenez's child development expertise. Besides, Joey is only 11—technically not even a teenager.*

"Ma'am, would you allow us to take a look at your telephone records?" Her eyes widened and she pulled back. I hurriedly said, hoping to reassure her, "We might be able to track Joey down through the number she last called you from."

"Nope, *that's* not going to happen. If you're not going to arrest me, I'm going inside—I have stuff to do. Just because you're the police, doesn't mean you get to show up unannounced. If you give me any more trouble, I *will* call legal aid for a damn lawyer. Shit, you think I don't know my rights!" With that, Brenda Jimenez, mother of an unreported missing child, swept back into the house, slamming the door behind her.

I went back down the stairs, trying to keep a check on my emotions, given the many eyes on us. "Erica, thanks for taking care of things when Marisol showed up. Let's head over to Bonaparte's for some privacy, coffee, and a strategy session. I was sure Brenda was going to demand a lawyer before we learned anything."

"Bonaparte's?"

"Coffee shop in Fells Point. Great pastries and bread. Usually, but not always, soup during the winter."

"Sounds good. One of the things I like about Baltimore are the interesting neighborhoods. And Fells Point is definitely unique."

I pulled into a parking space in front of the abandoned building that had been the visual centerpiece for the television series, *Homicide: Life on the Streets.* We walked to the coffee shop currently peopled with walkers and grandparents tending to toddler-age grandchildren. There were a couple of dogs tied outside between parked strollers. Once inside, we ordered two Americanos and several oversized pastries, and left with coffee break in hand.

Settled in the car, I fished an almond croissant out of the bag and washed a large sugary piece down with coffee. "What do you think, Erica?" I brushed sliced almonds, powdered sugar, and flakes of pastry off my jacket.

"Hang around here for too long and I would put on more than the extra pounds I'm already carrying."

I laughed. "I'm with you there. But I was referring to Brenda Jimenez, not the pastries."

"Funny! Bueno, the woman is something else—no wonder Marisol is so concerned about her niece. Robin, *your* friend is probably right about the drug use—Brenda seems ready to jump out of her skin; physically, it looks like she has been doing something on a regular basis. It's not necessary to see track marks to figure that out."

"Yeah, those are some pretty nasty sores on her face and hands. Agitation, irritability, hostility—Marisol mentioned weight loss—she's got it all going on."

"Chica, I think we'd better take this to Sarge—it appears we have another missing child investigation in the works ... and, at least one dead child. What are the odds? Given the amount of time that has passed since the girl went missing—that is, if we can trust what Brenda told us—we should move quickly."

"Why don't I talk with Rossi first? That way I can both update him and find out whether he has any ideas. Maybe he's heard something on the streets that would be helpful. If the dead boy is, in fact, Danny Helman, we still need to learn how he ended up in a Baltimore City culvert. I'm telling you, I'm going to make damn sure the person responsible for the boy's death rots behind bars!"

"I do not mean to be disrespectful, but from what you've said, it doesn't sound like Rossi is much concerned. And even so, it seems like he would contact you if he has something."

"True, but I should call him anyway—Rossi's got plenty of experience; if he doesn't know anything, at least he can keep his ears open and ask some questions. Plus, we'll be doing our due diligence at keeping him in the loop. Two cases involving children; if the media gets hold of this, they'll run with it."

"Well, Chica, other than their age and the fact that Danny and Joey are both missing, I do not see a link. Everything else about their cases is completely different: gender, socioeconomic status, geographic location, family background. Facts, however, are not necessarily of interest to the media. You are right, if a firestorm will drive up ratings, they will run with it."

"*Now*, if the Roland Park victim is *not* Danny and we have a dead child *and* two missing children in the same age range, we've got an even bigger problem on our hands. Erica, let's go see Dr. Huang. I just had a thought—when I was with the Gang Unit, Tyrell Wilson and I picked up one Leroy Nichols. Nichols gave up the name of a guy called Cuz, who was allegedly involved in trafficking.

"Not long after, Leroy was gunned down at his grandmother's home—her house had already been shot up once before. We thought we had the shooter—a something Martinez—but the prosecutor wasn't able to get an indictment for the murder and attempted murders, only for illegal gun possession. I'm not sure what's happened with the case—nothing is my guess, or I would probably have heard something from Ty. After Nichols' death, I'm sure nobody else was going to talk."

"Chica, let's switch. I'll drive and you try to raise Rossi and Wilson.

"Okay."

Chapter 19

A Missing or a Dead Child?

We were ready to leave for Roland Park to continue canvassing the neighborhood when my phone rang. I hesitated, but given we'd had Monday as an extra day off and a holiday was coming up, I picked up the receiver.

"Officer Crane, Dr. Huang, the Chief Medical Examiner—I apologize for being unavailable when you called. Forensic results from your investigation are in. I think you will find them particularly interesting. I must leave soon—do you think you can make the time to come to my office now?"

"Yes, sir. We'll be there as soon as possible."

I knocked.

Erica said through the closed door, "Bo, it's your two favorite investigators."

"Please come in, Detectives."

We entered and sat down. A visit to the ME was inevitably a pleasant experience, being about the only place where one could expect an old-fashioned civilized conversation during the workday. But today, anxious for the results, we only wanted to get on with it.

"Well, my dear ladies, we should do our business. I assume you were trying to contact me about the little boy."

"We were. Dr. Huang, we may have another missing child," I said.

"Yes, I see." All traces of his sweet smile gone, Bo looked slowly from one to the other of us with great concern. "Another case, that is certainly not good. Detectives, I apologize for not having DNA results for you—the proper analysis takes time, as I am sure you are aware." He checked his notes—a move which seemed to be more for dramatic effect than a memory aid. Bo had a rep for a prodigious memory—he might have language problems on the stand but he was amazingly detail-oriented and generally wiped the floor with other experts.

Erica smiled and played along. "Give it up Doctor Huang, give it up—what do you have for us?"

"Detective Moreno, this is not a *final* confirmation concerning your victim's identity but there is something helpful. We were able to obtain several good prints from the picture frame and two partials from the brush. There are two sets on each item—sets meaning prints from two different people—one is surely the mother. You said she handled the items, correct?"

"That's right," agreed Erica. "I guess we need to get her prints for exclusionary purposes."

"That must be done. However, what I especially want to tell you is the partials on the brush and the sets on the frame you brought to me from the Helman home do match those now on file for the little boy. I fully expect the DNA results to corroborate that match. As I said, this is not a final determination I am giving you at this moment, yet I am confident—particularly given the photographs showing structural similarities between the dead boy and the boy you identified as Danny Helman of York, Pennsylvania—there is sufficient evidence for you to bring in the mother for a notification. When she comes to Baltimore, I suggest you first request information—your victim has a scar on his knee and across his little finger. Detectives, it is long past time for the family to bury their child. If the boy is this woman's son, we must return him to her." Bo Huang looked aggrieved—as if it was his personal responsibility to resolve the tragedy facing this family.

"Thank you, Doctor Huang," I said, unsettled by the terrible combination of relief and sadness I was feeling. "We'll call Danny Helman's mother, and see about bringing her to Baltimore today."

"I think that is the right thing to do," he said. "Also, Detectives, the report details the dead child as having brown hair but definitively someone dyed his hair—he was most certainly blonde, probably white-blonde. Furthermore, the child was not by nature as tan as he appears—he was quite fair. Someone used a chemical tanning agent on this boy. I would think he might be of Scandinavian descent—blood group O, his type, correlates with Scandinavian ancestry—but there is no scientific evidence for such a claim. We'll know more when the DNA results come in."

I stood up and shook his hand. "Thank you, Dr. Huang. We appreciate your efforts."

"You are welcome, Detectives. As I informed you, I soon must leave for the day but my assistant will be here. We are going to be with family for the holiday." He closed the file. "Please, you should call when you are sure the mother is to come in for the identification so we are prepared. It is very, very difficult for the parents."

Erica said, "We will do that. Have a good Thanksgiving, sir."

———

"Moreno, Dr. Huang might be right about the Scandinavian background. In the photographs both father and son are exceptionally blonde and fair—though I admit I've no idea what, if any, relationship there is between Scandinavians and Germans!"

"Bo is great at his job. He is right about something else—the child should go home to his mother. He deserves to rest in peace." Erica sat back, sighed and closed her eyes.

"I'll make the call." I looked up the number and dialed. The machine picked up and I left a message. "While we wait for Sarah Rollins to get back to us, why don't you contact Joey's school and I'll try Rossi and Ty again."

"Sounds good, Chica." She yawned and stood up. "And we need to think about food."

"I hear you." After she left, I called Rossi, who answered this time. "Hey, Greg, got a few minutes to talk?"

"Sure. What's up?"

"It's the Jimenez girl."

He laughed. "Sure, it is. For you, California, anything. O'Donnell said you are good police, not to give you shit. Anyhow, the damn aunt is like a flea—anything to get her out of my life."

I was delighted to hear Ken O'Donnell had my back all the way from California—I owed him a call. The last time we talked, he promised to *think* about visiting us. After talking about mutual friends, I went over the facts of the investigation—minimizing Marisol's involvement but giving him the details of our conversation with Brenda. I told him Erica was contacting the school and we planned to speak with the girl's stepfather.

"California, maybe you hit on something when we took the call and there is a case after all. As I said, I don't have a problem with you working it, but it's good you're keeping me in the loop. Unfortunately, I have nothing useful for you, but I'll tell you what …"

"What?"

He laughed and I could hear him lighting up. "Sorry, California, I was thinking. I'll tell you what, I'll ask around and see if I can pick up any street chatter about the girl. Give me the address where the Jimenez broad is living and we'll keep an eye on the place."

"Thanks, Rossi, I appreciate your help with this. The house is 140 North Glover; it seems there are some kinky comings and goings happening there. Maybe one or both women are turning tricks, though it is more likely Brenda is the draw. Probably drugs are involved but we'd like to hold off on that until we find Joey Jimenez."

"No problem. Later—a CI needs some cash. Stay safe, California."

"Same to you, Rossi." The phone clicked before I hung up. I breathed a sigh of relief—he could have been a bear about this, but he seemed to be going out of his way to cooperate. Next was Tyrell Wilson. I explained to him what was going on.

"Sorry, Crane, that I can't give you something more useful. *Absolutely* keep me notified about what's going on with those two kids, particularly if you come up with anything linking them with the intel our buddy, Leroy, gave us."

"Thanks. On a different topic, how about coming over in a couple of weeks—I promise there'll be no turkey."

"I'll check my schedule—don't think the Ravens are playing at home that weekend."

"Good. Well, check with Janie and I'll talk to Matt and get back to you. Again, thanks for your help."

"Wasn't much, but it's all I've got. Later."

Pleased with myself, I hung up, and went to find Erica. After several dead ends, I located her at the machines.

"Hey, Robin, you finished speaking with the boys?" She continued dropping coins into the slot. "Let me treat you to some water," she said, handing me one of the bottles that had clattered down the chute.

"Thanks, I'm thirsty—they keep this building way too warm. Yeah, I was able to reach both—Rossi offered to keep an eye on the house where Brenda is staying and will listen for chatter related to the case. I mentioned there might be some drug stuff going on, but for now we wanted to concentrate on finding the girl. He agreed."

"Can't ask for much more," said Erica.

"True. Rossi and I have a friend in common—not to be cynical or anything but that may have something to do with it."

"And Ty?"

"That's more complicated—nothing bad; we can talk when we see each other. You learn anything about the school thing?"

"Chica, we are on a roll! Last year, Joey attended the Crossroads School, a charter school in Fells Point. I made a few calls. From all accounts, it has a good reputation and no record of any legal complaints. If Ms Rollins does not call back, what do you say to a drive over there after we talk with Sarge? You are aware, as well as I am, that we need more information before going back to Brenda. We will find out for ourselves whether the girl is in school, though the *only* thing Marisol and Brenda seem to agree on is that she is not."

"Once that's taken care of we can contact the girl's stepfather. I guess there's a chance she's with him and going to school in DC. Erica, if I were Brenda's ex, I certainly wouldn't be interested in giving her any information."

"I wonder who has custody," Erica mused. "Oh, Huang's assistant called to tell me the items we took from Rollins' home have been processed and we can pick them up."

"Erica, how about you take Sarge and I'll call Sarah again. If I can get hold of her, I'll be ready to go in a matter of minutes, but her *modus operandi* might now be denial and avoidance."

"You may be right, but it is difficult to imagine her far from her phone. I'll stop by Sarge's office. Call me on my cell if you hear anything."

"Will do."

———

I had just hung up the phone when it rang again—it was my partner. "Robin, did you reach Sarah Rollins? I cleared it."

"I did. Erica, all I said to her was we wanted to return her belongings—nothing about coming back to Baltimore with us to do the identification. Poor woman, I feel for her. She still insists that our victim is not her son but, perhaps, not quite as strongly. I told Matt I would be late. Give me a few minutes to fax Huang's report to York and then I'm ready."

"Pobrecita, she is going to need somebody with her tonight. Bet Matt was not so happy about the long shift."

"No, he wasn't, but he has plans for next weekend and he and I had a *good time* on my extra day off. By the way, Ty and I were talking about a Sunday barbecue at our house—want to join us?"

"Sounds fun. Let me know the time and what I can bring."

———

Danny Helman's mother opened the door as soon as we turned into the driveway. As we approached the walkway, she stepped back and, for an instant, I expected her to close the door. I wouldn't blame her—in only minutes, life as she knew it would end. In my experience, a parent seldom recovers—the death of a child is a betrayal at so many levels. Her son would never have the opportunity to live out his life. And something a friend once said stuck with me: "The worst prison is the death of one's child. You never get out." Murder must certainly be a compounding factor. I found myself wanting to believe Sarah Rollins knew what was coming, and the blow we were about to deliver was not unexpected. I didn't really think that was the case.

"Ms Rollins, do you mind if we come in?"

"I appreciate your returning my things—I hope they were helpful for your investigation. You could have mailed them, though." She looked from one to the other of us and then remained focused on Erica, who was carrying the messenger bag containing the items so recently taken from her home. She continued without waiting for an answer or inviting us in. "I admit I didn't expect you to come back so quickly; I guess that's what threw me when you called, Officer Crane. Thank you both for your thoughtfulness—the photograph of Danny with his father is a favorite of my son's, and he would be very unhappy with me if he found it gone."

"We understand, ma'am—we were careful with your belongings. Please, could we come inside for a few minutes?" Erica asked.

"I *am* sorry—where are my manners? I would appreciate it if you would chalk it up to stress and worry. Please," the obviously exhausted woman said contritely. She opened the door wider and stepped back from the doorway.

Sarah Rollins led us into the now familiar living room where we each took the seat we'd previously occupied. Erica and I avoided eye contact. I had volunteered to give this mother the bad news about her son.

"Can I get you some coffee? A glass of water?" she asked gathering her blonde hair into a ponytail and securing it with a band.

"No, thank you. We had coffee before we left Baltimore. Ma'am, please take a seat and we will tell you what we know," said Erica.

Danny's mother almost dropped into the large overstuffed armchair. A robin's egg blue with a sprinkling of yellow and white flowers—I could picture her reading a children's book, her contented son cuddled closely in the crook of her arm. Now, faced with two Baltimore City police sitting across from her, Sarah Rollins seemed like a lost child herself as she clutched the armrests. How does one survive the death of a child? I woke up several times last night trying to answer that question for myself. When I finally fell asleep, it'd been an unsettled slumber strewn with nightmares.

Erica stood up and walked over to where Ms Rollins was sitting. She placed the photocopies on the side table and silently handed her the bags with the hairbrush and toothbrush, which Sarah clutched to her chest. I was sorry to see her water glass was almost empty. Erica remained standing while Danny's mother set the brushes on the table. She reached out for the framed picture, which she kissed and placed upright next to the brushes. In a measured tone, Ms Rollins asked, "I was right, wasn't I? Danny is not the same boy you found in Baltimore. After all, a mother would know."

Without allowing time for an answer, she continued. "I certainly understand the confusion, though. The two boys look a little bit alike. I thought of his poor mother last night—how horrible it will be for her when she learns her child has died. I know how worried *I've* been, and that's only about Oskar bringing Danny home late. Did you locate his family?"

Erica sat down, the empty bag on her lap. There was no way to soften the blow.

"Sarah, I am so sorry, but we have evidence from the medical examiner strongly suggesting the deceased child discovered in Baltimore is your son, Danny."

For a couple of seconds she stared at me, her expression unwavering. She did not move. "Do you think that's true?" she asked in a flat and formal tone.

I nodded slowly, wanting to look away from widening eyes filled with tears trickling down her cheeks. She began to hyperventilate. Her eyes darted about the room as she looked for an escape. Her breaths were coming in short angry bursts. Her face cupped in her hands, she began rocking back and forth, back and forth; it was during a forward movement that a horrific scream tore through the room and Danny's mother slipped out of the chair onto the floor where she continued screaming until she pulled her body into a fetal position. Sobs and moans slowly replaced the blood curdling screams. I didn't know what was worse. If I still had any suspicions concerning a role in her son's death, this inconsolable mother's response pretty much put them to rest—nevertheless, I would have to avoid jumping to conclusions. Looking for a distraction, I picked up the empty glass and went to the kitchen to fill it.

When I returned to the living room, I found Erica sitting on the floor next to the grieving woman, stroking her hair and mumbling soothing words in a blend of English and Spanish. It took about five minutes to get Sarah Rollins onto the couch. I handed her the water.

"What do I do?" she asked dispiritedly.

"Drink a little," I urged. "We can talk later."

She just held the glass. Did not move an inch. Flushed to the point of looking feverish, I wondered whether we should call for an ambulance.

"Are you sure?"

"Ms Rollins, we're fairly sure, but would appreciate it if you'd come to Baltimore for an identification. Or, a family member can do that for you."

"No!" She sat up. "I want to go."

"Ma'am, if you do not feel able today, you could come tomorrow—" offered Erica.

"I want to return with you," she said insistently. "*Now.*"

"Sarah, you can come with us, but is there someone who can meet you there and bring you home?" I asked.

She put down the untouched water and took a deep breath. "Of course. I … need … need to make a call." She began to cry but left the room.

"Robin, I'm going outside to contact the York PD with an update. I will also tell Bo's assistant we are bringing Rollins with us. Why don't you ask for the computers? We can request her phone when we get to Baltimore."

I groaned.

———

The ride from York to Baltimore was long and quiet. Our passenger said nothing. There were not even tears. Other than periodically responding to dispatch, Erica and I remained silent. I was grateful a friend agreed to pick Sarah Rollins up from Headquarters and bring her back home—the return trip after the identification was unimaginable. Since she was from Pennsylvania, I wondered why she hadn't contacted a family member.

We pulled into the garage at Headquarters. "Ms Rollins, would you mind waiting in the car for a minute?"

"I'll be fine," she replied, releasing her seatbelt.

Erica and I got out and huddled. "Robin, I am going to take the evidence, including her cell, to CS. You take her to the morgue. If she is able to talk with us, we can meet in Conference Room A. I'll let Security know where we are, and friends will be coming to pick Rollins up."

"That's fine."

I returned to the car and opened the back door. "Ms Rollins, please come with me. Detective Moreno will see to your belongings."

"Ma'am, would you mind if I take your cell phone? It's just routine and I'll return it before you leave."

"Of course." She handed it over to Erica without any hesitation. Without any questions, without any change in expression.

"Ms Rollins there will also be someone here to take your fingerprints, so we can eliminate those we found on the brushes and frame." I added, "It's nothing to be concerned about; something we do routinely." She nodded blankly in response. A tech could deal with obtaining informed consent.

———

Danny Helman's mother identified the body of our Roland Park victim as that of her son. She had first confirmed that he had a scar on his knee and across his little finger. I led the grieving woman out of the room into the hallway and to a bench. She had no color—she herself no longer appeared alive. She said nothing. There were no tears. "Ms Rollins, I am so sorry for your loss."

"Thank you, Officer. Please tell me, what is next?" With that, she seemed to pull herself together, which I noticed she was apt to do when acquiring even a little control over the situation.

I pulled my own thoughts together. "Though we have the fingerprints and your identification, we are waiting for the DNA results. As soon as they come in, we will phone you. Also, when you are up to it, we'll need for you to come in for a formal interview."

"Of course. Robin, I do not need a medical test to tell me this is my Danny. What you *can* tell me is what happened to my son. Oskar could never have done this terrible thing. Despite our problems, we both loved our son—he would never hurt him." She broke down and the tears flowed.

It did not seem to be the time to tell her that DNA results, in addition to identifying the victim, often provide information about the perpetrator of the crime. I handed her the small package of tissues I grabbed before leaving the morgue.

Suddenly, she stopped crying. "Where *is* Oskar?"

I had expected the question. Actually, it was late in coming but, still, we had no answer for her.

Erica joined us and returned Sarah's phone; we then went to a conference room where she signed the appropriate identification and release forms. I remained with the grief-stricken woman, asking questions when feasible, until a couple of friends arrived to take her home. I was relieved to hear they intended to accompany her to the funeral home—her son had been lying in the morgue for far too long; she wanted Danny buried as soon as possible. They would stay with her for the night.

After the women left, I made the necessary arrangements to release the body to the funeral director once he contacted us. There was no doubt that Danny Helman was the murdered boy discovered in a Roland Park culvert. A child who was supposed to be with his father, a German national, returning from Germany with plans to be back in York, PA in time for Halloween. I could not help but ask myself whether the outcome would have been different if Sarah Rollins had notified the police immediately when her son failed to arrive as expected.

I now had her in-laws' contact information. After taking a few deep breaths, I picked up the phone and, per Sarah Rollins' request, called Germany to notify them of the child's death. I was also hoping to obtain information that would help locate Danny's father.

According to Oskar's sister- and brother-in-law, he was in DC or Pennsylvania—he left to return Danny to his mother on the 27th Of October, of course. His critically ill mother hadn't heard from her son since he landed in DC. They denied communicating with Sarah.

Somebody was lying. Rollins said she'd called her in-laws several times—cell records confirmed her claim. "Are you sure?" I asked.

"Yes," the brother categorically stated. "Oskar's ex-wife left messages, but didn't say why she was calling. What do *you* want?" he asked sharply. "Tell me now or I will hang up the telephone."

Although uneasy at notifying another family member of the young boy's death, the time apparently had come. I'd consciously avoided explaining the nature of my call at the outset, wanting the advantage. I told him of his nephew's death and explained that the police had no idea of Oskar's whereabouts. There was silence on the line, so I went on tell him that the ME was waiting for more forensic results to come in but was prepared to release the boy's body. Danny's mother had identified her son and they should talk with her about funeral arrangements.

I gave the decidedly unpleasant brother-in-law my information but reiterated that as we pursued the case, my partner and I would be in direct communication with Ms Rollins and they should probably reconsider their decision not to speak with her. I hung up not at all surprised that Sarah had difficulties with her in-laws. Any sane person would. Furthermore, I could not understand how it was that Oskar and Danny were missing for so long and *nobody* had contacted law enforcement for assistance in locating father and son. It could be that family dysfunction was at fault, but maybe it was something more sinister. I went to talk with Erica.

Chapter 20

Codis

"Robin, Bo just** called. He wants to see us. Now."

"I thought he already left for the day? What's going on?" It then occurred to me the DNA results must be in, although even if we had a match it wouldn't make a great deal of difference, other than in court. There was little doubt in my mind that the boy discovered in the Roland Park culvert was Danny Helman. Maybe the ME had something that would get us to a *suspect*.

"Probably the DNA. Whatever's going on—he is pretty anxious to talk with us. Let's go, Chica."

After reaching his office, we found that Huang was, indeed, anxious. There was none of what had become our customary prefatory chat. I pulled out my notebook.

"I see you are ready to take notes, Officer. That is good. I have more to tell you about your Roland Park victim. I previously reported to you that I believed the death of the child may be due to asphyxiation rather than strangulation—we found two cotton fibers in his lungs and no contusions or abrasions or other physical evidence of strangulation. There is, dear ladies, a complication."

My immediate response was one of panic at hearing "a complication," but I quickly reined myself in. The ME was not questioning the identification itself. Rather, he was focusing on the open investigation—*how* the child had died.

"Detectives, despite the microscopic fibers, I do not believe Danny Helman was asphyxiated. The post-mortem and tox results suggest the child was asthmatic, yet the report makes no mention of an inhaler being found with the body. I reread the notes you provided but saw nothing about Danny Helman suffering from asthma. I wonder whether you left out information. Inadvertently, I am sure. Could an inhaler have been missed at the scene?"

Shit! As if there were not enough snags with this case. "No, sir, and Danny's mother never mentioned her son had asthma. To be honest, Dr. Huang, I don't know why it never occurred to me to ask whether he had any allergies."

Erica sighed. "That question should be included in an interview, particularly when the victim is a child. Bo, we searched the area north and south of where the doctor discovered the body: we not only examined the paths on both sides of the creek, above and below the culvert, we went into the creek. No inhaler or anything else of note was found."

"The backpack," I reminded Erica.

"Right. We found a backpack north of the culvert that someone hid in a bush and covered with a large tree branch. We are not sure what we have there—the pack is now with the Crime Lab. There are bound to be fingerprints and DNA, of course, but we do not expect them to be in the system. But the results may be helpful down the road. It probably belongs to a student who ditched school, returned and found no backpack—big surprise," she laughed.

"Anything interesting as far as the contents?" asked the ME.

"Well, that's remains to be seen." I smiled and said, "Erica, you tell him."

"Dr. Huang, I'm sure you can imagine how excited we were to find a backpack hidden in the brush so close to the crime scene. I thought for sure we had something on the suspect."

"So, Detective, what did you find—books, a condom, cigarettes?"

She laughed again. "All good guesses, but none of the above. Robin and I have no idea what to make of it—the Crime Lab techs either, for that matter. There were two complete outfits for an adolescent female—new, including the underwear. Toothpaste, toothbrush, a hairbrush, a small bag with makeup, and a sterling silver necklace with a peace symbol. Oh, dress shoes and sneakers."

"Bo, we wondered whether we had a Romeo and Juliet situation— two kids and a credit card heading off somewhere, most likely an illicit trip to New York rather than spending the weekend with a friend and studying for exams."

"Advise me of the results, please," asked Bo. "Maybe something will come from the discovery later."

"We'll do that." I made a note. "We're hoping for something helpful, but I can't imagine what it has to do with our victim. We'll check with the mother about the inhaler. Do you have anything else for us?"

"Of course, my dear ladies. There is news of the DNA and other findings of which to inform you."

Erica and I said simultaneously, "And?"

Bo laughed and then became serious. "Apart from the boy's, we identified several sources of DNA proving sufficient for analysis: the jacket, which included a hair with a follicle. There were epithelial cells on the skin, from a different source. We found no evidence of semen or sexual abuse. No physical abuse of any kind, except for the coloring of the child's hair and skin, which happened recently as your hypothesized timeline suggests. I checked under the fingernails but did not obtain anything useful."

"Do we dare hope you found a match on the FBI's CODIS system?" asked Erica.

"There is the not *such* good news. I am sorry to disappoint you but we were unable to identify a match. When you find a suspect, however, our data will help convict your suspect."

"Thank you, Dr. Huang. We'll let you go—keep you apprised of the investigation," I promised.

"Be patient, my dear ladies. There is one last result for you." We must have looked surprised because he laughed.

"In addition to the evidence that the child has been using an inhaler, somebody gave him a sedative—a particularly large dose given his size and apparent poor health at the time of his death."

"Dr. Huang, was he asphyxiated or did the drug kill him?"

"Though I at first suspected asphyxiation—the evidence does not clearly support my hypothesis. The combination of an asthma attack, the lack of an inhaler, and a large dose of the barbiturate, amobarbital—by the way, ladies, that is not such a common sedative—would be sufficient to kill a child. I would wonder where the suspect obtained the drug."

"On the report what will be listed as cause of death?" I asked.

"Suspicious death ... for now. You must, my dear ladies, bring me more evidence."

"We will, but Dr. Huang, it *is* time for you to leave for your holiday," said Erica.

"Thank you for everything. Have a wonderful Thanksgiving," I said.

"And to you dear ladies. And to you."

———

Later, the file updated and a report faxed to the York PD, Sarge informed me that I was done for the day. Moreno had headed home an hour ago for a FaceTime session with her kids and mother. All I wanted was to be sitting at the dinner table and sharing a meal with my son and husband; talking about Sean's day; listening to Matt tell us about his; reading to my son before bed; making breakfast and Thanksgiving pies in the morning.

Chapter 21

The Park Service

It was **Matt's** first day at his new job. Given I'd had an especially long day, I was surprised to arrive home before my husband. I paid Magdel, grateful to have finally found a sitter with a car. Once she left, I managed to glean a sliver of information from my son about his day before he bailed to play *Minecraft*, by far his favorite video game.

Though eager for a shower, I decided to fix a cup of coffee. While sitting at the window looking at the stars, I thought about a conversation I'd had with Ty about his grandmother. She had "*expected*" things of her grandchildren, made sure they did their homework, stayed off the streets, and explored dreams for her to nurture. He seemed convinced it was only because of luck that he wasn't a dead gang member on a porch, in a yard or on a street. Luck seemed an awfully fragile commodity to depend on. Sarah Rollins' luck had certainly run out. As had that of Leroy Nichols. With that depressing thought, I rinsed out my cup and hurried upstairs to take a quick shower. Ten minutes later, refreshed and changed, I checked in again with my son who still had eyes only for the screen. I went downstairs to start dinner.

Matt arrived home later than I expected—distance could very well be an issue, at least in the beginning. As soon as I heard his car pull into the driveway, I poured him a beer. Although he appeared to be tired, he seemed happier than I'd seen him in some time. I guess househusbanding *had* begun to wear thin.

"Welcome home, hon! Can't wait to hear all about it," I said, handing him the glass and receiving a hug and a kiss in turn.

"Hi, sweetie—thanks. I think I'm going to like it there. Let me change and check in with Sean; you and I can catch up with each other after dinner." With that, he winked suggestively.

"Okay, but fair warning, he hasn't finished the little bit of homework they've assigned; he somehow managed to talk Magdel into playing games. While you change, I'll go ahead and put water on for the pasta—I made the sauce yesterday, so I just need to heat it up. And I'll pop the French bread into the oven *after* slathering it with butter and garlic. Sound good?"

"Robin, I was hungry before the description. Now, I'm famished!"

"Be sure to leave space for Thanksgiving dinner tomorrow. My mom will have a fit if you don't go back for seconds. Oh, and I'm going to help Sean make two pies."

"No problem there. She's a great cook and I love pie! I'll be back in fifteen, twenty minutes," he said, giving me another kiss before leaving the kitchen.

I do love the man! I poured a glass of wine and continued preparing dinner. While draining the pasta, I could hear my two boys laughing—I thought of Sarah Rollins and felt incredibly grateful for my life. I couldn't imagine what kind of hell she was going through, or imagine the hell her child had experienced before his death. But I didn't want to go there. Instead, I called out from the kitchen door, "Hey, boys, after you finish with whatever you're doing, can you help with the table?"

"We'll be there in a minute, sweetie."

"Coming, Mom!"

I stirred the bubbling sauce a few times more, replaced the lid and turned off the burner. The bread smelled ready, so I removed the loaves from the oven and put them in a breadbasket, covered with a napkin. Finally, I attended to the pasta; grated some fresh parmesan cheese into a small bowl and grabbed the salad from the refrigerator. "Okay, boys, wash up. Chow's on!" I began carrying the food into the dining room—so much for the promised help.

Everyone settled at the table, I handed the pasta to my son. Matt refilled my glass of wine and passed the milk carton to Sean.

My husband now worked with the Department of Natural Resources. His first assignment was to Rocky Gap State Park—a casino had been built out that way and crime was on the increase. The only drawback we could see was the substantial drive. In the end, Matt took the job, expecting he would be eligible for a closer DNR posting if he stuck with Rocky Gap for a while. I passed him the pasta. "Matt, how long did the drive take you?"

"Robin, can you send the sauce and parmesan my way? Back to your question—getting there was about what I expected; getting home certainly took longer, but we can talk about travel issues later."

"Okay." That didn't sound so good; still, Matt seemed in a high good humor. My parents would help—they doted on their grandchild. Maybe he could stay out there a couple of nights a week, if the drive became too much.

"Hey, Sean, how did school go today?" Matt asked.

"Good."

"That's it, 'good?'"

"Yep."

Matt glanced at me with a hint of a smile. "Then let me tell you what happened to me!"

"*What?*" Sean asked with more enthusiasm, putting two pieces of lettuce and half the tomatoes on his plate.

"So, as you and your mom know, it was the first day at my new job. They were shorthanded, so I patrolled on my lonesome. Well, Sean, to tell you the truth I wasn't quite on my lonesome—I had GPS and a map but I still managed to get lost a few times."

"When can we go see where you work?" asked Sean.

"We can't go this weekend. And we're probably having friends over next weekend."

"Who'll be here?"

"Your mom's old partner, Mr. Ty—well, *one* of her old partners— and her new partner, Miss Erica."

"Are Mr. Ty's kids coming?"

"Yep, his whole family, including his grandmother, and your grandma and grandpa."

"Sean, if it isn't too cold, maybe we can camp out and hike in the park." I glanced over at my husband, who nodded. "Now we've got that straightened out, Matt, why don't you finish telling us your story? Sean, you've got spaghetti sauce on your chin."

"Okay, guys. I was hungry, so I pulled over and took out the lunch your mom fixed for me last night. Creative, Robin—it hit the spot— thanks. I had the heat on, so I rolled the passenger window halfway down for fresh air. Anyhow, I was unwrapping my sandwich and opening the chips when I looked up. And *what* did I see?"

"*What?*" we asked simultaneously.

Matt laughed. "A deer with her face *in* my car. Sean, she scared the life out of me! For a second, I couldn't understand what was going on. After we finish eating, I'll show you the picture I took—it'll make you laugh! It seemed like she wanted directions; more likely making a complaint."

———

Dinner over, we began our evening routine: Sean usually did his home- work. I helped him with any problems related to English and Spanish; Matt was the math and social studies whiz. Lucky for me I was off the hook, but Matt was on call for math, which is all he had because of the holiday. He always made sure Sean gave the problem some effort before calling in reinforcements. The call came after about ten minutes. After about twenty minutes that included plenty of moaning, my husband announced triumphantly, "Well, we're done here. This boy has knocked his math homework out of the park!"

"Good job, both of you!" I called out as I went upstairs. "Sean, put your schoolwork in your backpack and get your pajamas—time for a bath." I had already cleaned out his lunch bag. Too often we forgot until morning when I'm scrambling to get us out the door. With Matt now working, there would be even more of a time crunch.

Though he didn't answer, I heard Sean's feet pounding up the stairs. Meantime, I ran the bath water before joining Matt downstairs. He had built a fire in the fireplace and was now enthusiastically poking at it, sparks flying. Once he had it blazing to his satisfaction, and my concern, we cleared the table and began loading the dishwasher.

Sean yelled down. "Mom, I'm done!"

"Brush your teeth and we'll be right there." Some nights I read to him; others, it's Matt, although Sean prefers that Matt tell one of his outlandish stories. Regardless of who does the honors, Matt and I remain in the room—there is a comfortable rocker for the observer. It's a time of day for us all to wind down, to put family first. A time to treasure.

Tonight we were about halfway through the third in a series that my son was caught up in. To be honest, Matt was too. Me, less so—must be a gender thing. Three chapters later, I closed the book. "Okay, Sean, time for lights out. I love you, honey—get a good night's sleep."

"I love you too, Mom. Matt."

"I love you, Sean," said Matt as he left the room. He always gave us a few minutes alone.

I gave my son a kiss, switched on the dragon night light I've used since his birth and flicked off the switch. He was growing up much too quickly; I wondered how long it would be before the dragon disappeared into a drawer and the reading and telling of stories ended.

Probably soon. Matt and I had never discussed having a child. Until now, I never questioned why.

From the very beginning, Matt was thoughtful when it came to Sean. Apparently, when he'd started thinking about asking me to marry him, he'd wondered whether it would be the best thing for us to live in Santa Barbara—he felt there were too many difficult memories for both Sean and me. One night Matt spoke of his frustration—he'd come to realize that we were not only finding the loss of Doug difficult, it was also the loss of his family. I tried, although in retrospect not too successfully, to explain how it was that when you've lost someone you loved—they often took with them an entanglement of relationships, which perpetuated the grief.

I thought Matt was just being kind when he raised the idea of moving, but it turned out he meant it. The more I thought about it, being closer to my family began to appeal to me. Finally, I agreed leaving Santa Barbara might be a good thing, since we would be starting a new life together. And I had a safety net—as Matt had pointed out, moving to Baltimore in no way precluded returning to California. I was surprised to learn that Sean was excited about the thought of living nearer to his grandparents, despite not knowing them particularly well. I hoped that being closer to my parents would blunt the blow of losing the Debayle family. Unsaid, but probably understood by Matt, leaving California would be difficult because neither Sean nor I had managed to make peace with the fact that Doug Debayle, my SBPD partner and our beloved friend, would no longer be part of our lives.

Chapter 22

Rest in Peace

It was a bitterly cold day when young Danny Helman's mother laid him to rest in the small Abbott Cemetery in York, Pennsylvania. The dark sky was heavy with threatening clouds. In the gloom, the leafless branches of the towering trees menaced the mourners—fitting reminders of the tragic loss of a child deserving of protection rather than the brutal death that took him to his grave. His was a life lost much too early.

Erica and I, wearing full dress uniform, were at the cemetery. Despite the considerable time put into the case, we still had no suspects. No official determination of death had been made, and the whereabouts of the boy's father was unknown. During the graveside service, we stood back from the crowd observing and recording as surreptitiously as possible. Afterward, Danny's mother approached us and without a word gave us each a hug.

"Thank you for coming, Detectives. I cannot tell you how much I appreciate everything you have done for my son and me. It is such a miserable day. Would you like to come back to the house to warm up and eat before you return to Maryland?" Her fine features swollen, Sarah's pale tear-stained face, devoid of makeup, made the woman appear even bleaker.

"Ma'am, we are so sorry for your loss. Erica and I wanted to pay our respects to you and your son but, unfortunately, we must get back to Baltimore. Thank you for the invitation."

"I understand. As horrible as this has been, I guess it was even worse when I had no idea where Danny was. At least my baby is home. I wish we knew where Oskar is—his family is frantic with worry. *Now*, they want to communicate," she said dolefully. "But when I get frustrated, I remind myself they also loved Danny. Being so far is difficult; they're reluctant to leave Germany—Oskar's mother is very ill and is in hospice now."

In an effort to provide her with some reassurance, I said, "Mrs. Rollins, we are doing our best to locate your ex-husband."

"Thank you. Oskar must also be dead, but I am glad to hear you're not giving up—I want to know what happened to my son and his father. They deserve justice."

"We will be keeping in touch with you," Erica assured her.

The tears were beginning to flow again. Nonetheless, I asked the question. "Ma'am, I understand you need to go, but would you mind if I ask you something?"

"Of course. They'll wait for me."

"I'll be quick. Ma'am, did Danny have any allergies, asthma, anything we should know about?"

Her face crumpled. "Oh, my God, I can't imagine why I didn't mention that Danny has an inhaler. He didn't need it often, but sometimes he had difficulty breathing if the weather was damp or if he was tired. The pediatrician thought he was old enough to manage it, but he's a kid and periodically left it at home, so there was another with the school nurse. Danny took his inhaler to Germany and I'm sure Oskar would have replaced it if necessary."

She began to cry and we were attracting attention. I hoped she wouldn't ask whether the inhaler was in her son's possession when the doctor found him. "Ma'am, I am sorry to upset you. You should feel free to call Erica or myself at any time—even if something seems unimportant, it could turn out to be a critical lead. It would be helpful if you could fax the prescription for the inhaler. I'm sorry, I forgot to tell you—we will get your computers back to you as soon as possible."

"Thank you. Detectives, you will always be in my prayers. And I hope that you shared a good Thanksgiving with your families." She hugged each of us again, and rejoined the others without looking back. I was relieved that Sarah Rollins did not expect more from us—I had no idea how to respond to so much sadness. And with the Christmas holiday coming up, loneliness.

We headed back to the car. Neither Erica nor I said anything to each other. I'm sure the same refrain played in each of our heads— *What had happened to Oskar and Danny Helman?*

———

"Okay, Robin. You ready to hit the troubled streets of Baltimore?"

"Yep, give me five minutes and I'll meet you outside."

That was my intention until Sarge stopped me on my way out, wanting an update on the Helman case. Though I tried to hurry things along, it took me a good twenty minutes before I made it to the idling car.

"Well, Chica, what happened to a five-minute ETD? Good thing I carry a book with me."

"Sorry. Sarge got hold of me—he's not too happy there's "so little progress," as he put it, with the investigation. I think he's beginning to feel the pressure."

"Straight out irritated or irritation with a vague hint of under-standing?" Erica asked.

"Oh, he is *definitely* straight out irritated. We'll leave the scar and facial flush out of it!"

She laughed. "Couldn't have been too bad, because your coloring is the same—pale. ¡Carajo! Sarge is not the only one who wants answers," she declared sarcastically in a rare outburst. "Well, Chica, let's get back to work."

"Erica, how about we sit here for a few minutes and review the case—we must be missing something. Maybe a brainstorming session will help us figure out where to go from here. I think we need a coherent plan to communicate to Sarge, so that he has specifics for the politicians. Despite the bluster, we both know he would be first to say we should go with 'thorough' over 'speed.'

"True. Robin, you were right when you said your mother was a great cook—she sure is! Please thank them for having me. And, please tell Sean his pies were delicious, I especially like the pumpkin."

"I will—Erica, I'm glad you joined us."

"Me too. *I'm* still full."

"Well, we'd better get working."

"Bueno, I was thinking about the case after I got home last night. Let's work backwards and start with the last time the Helmans were seen. Later we can go through what we know about the time before they left the country. I spoke with Scott from the Crime Lab about the preliminary results they've obtained from the computer and phone. Oh, and everything should be ready for release when Sarah Rollins comes in for the interview."

"Good. There are pictures and videos she's afraid of losing." I unclipped the seat belt, wishing I had brought along my travel mug.

Erica shut off the car. "Okay, Chica. Go!"

I began to tick off the points as they came to mind. "We've evidence the Helmans reached Oskar's family home in Germany. There is nothing on Sarah's computer revealing any difficulties while there, although according to her, Oskar experienced periodic problems with his computer. That appears to be true—the tech identified corresponding gaps in communication on her computer. The arrival and departure dates on the itinerary Sarah gave us are consistent with the information Oskar's brother-in-law provided. Sarah's computer and phone show no evidence of contact with either her husband or son *after* they left Europe, other than the one text from Oskar advising her of their safe arrival in the States. He texted his mother on the same date. We have additional confirmation: according to the German Embassy, father and son left Berlin on the twenty-seventh for the United States, on Lufthansa. That information is consistent with the itinerary he forwarded to his ex-wife and the date of the text. Documentation and footage shows the pair leaving Customs using a baggage cart. We know they departed Dulles with the luggage because there is video footage of them getting into a cab. I'm out of breath. Erica, you take it from there."

"I thought they both looked okay in that footage—maybe tired, but smiling. A long trip, so tired makes sense. Danny seemed healthy on the tapes, heavier than when we found him. He was very blonde and his hair was on the long side. Cannot really speak to the tan given the grainy black and white video."

"Yeah, I now sort of understand why Ms Rollins was convinced in the beginning that the boy in the news was not her son—there had to have been a huge disconnect—a body in a Roland Park culvert and knowledge of Oskar's and Danny's arrival in DC—the marked differences in physical appearance. He'd been gone for a month. I know sometimes when I am unable to see my children for a couple of months, for a few minutes, they do not look as familiar—it does not feel right but it is true.

"I know what you mean. Sean and Matt came months after I moved to Baltimore. Moving on, what we also know is the taxi Oskar and Danny got into at Dulles dropped them off at the Four Seasons Washington—also with their luggage."

"Pricey hotel, isn't it, Erica? We're talking about the one located on Pennsylvania Ave, NW?"

"That is correct. Pricey it is—over five hundred a night! I guess Sarah was right when she said Oskar's family had money."

"Interesting she did not say *he* had a lot of money, rather his family did."

"I forgot about that, Robin. I remember her suggesting the Helmans believed her to be a gold digger. I wonder what kind of hold they had over her husband. If he planned to stay in such an expensive hotel, the money must have mattered to him. We need to get access to his credit card bills for this period—they are really difficult people but I am sure somebody will cooperate."

"Erica, I'll call Germany. Though pretty unpleasant people, they *are* worried about Oskar and were horrified to learn of Danny's death. I need to think about how best to phrase the question. His sister appeared particularly bitter about his marriage and now insists her nephew would be alive if her brother had been given custody." I made a note and added an asterisk. "Back to Oskar and Danny—did the taxi dispatcher put you in touch with the driver who picked them up at Dulles?"

"She did. I spoke with him over the phone. Robin, he did not notice that anything was wrong. Said the passenger seemed like a good father; described him as relaxed, friendly, and a "great" tipper. Oskar had two small black suitcases on rollers, both with red leather identification tags—the type of bags that fit in the overhead compartment; the boy carried a backpack. He is not sure of the color—dark green, blue, or black, but that's irrelevant because we now know it is dark green since we have it in our possession. According to CS, we've learned the fingerprints and DNA on the pack belonged to Danny—I sure would like to identify the owner of the female clothing."

Oskar's DNA is probably present but we need a comparison sample. It's too bad they could not give us more because of the cross-contamination. We told Dr. Huang we would let him know about the backpack, but I figure they took care of that.

"We need to keep that and the missing luggage at the top of the list. Scott said too many people had handled the pack, but there were clear prints on the shoes and DNA on the necklace found inside.

Those results may be useful once there is a suspect. Bueno, this is a good thing we are doing, let's go over what we learned from the hotel."

"Erica, turn on the ignition so I can get warm. I need working fingers for this exercise."

"Will do. I promise to stop for coffee after we head out."

"Thanks. The hotel footage shows Oskar and Danny getting out of the taxi and entering the lobby, but those angles differ from the camera positioned over the reception area—that's the information we really need. Unfortunately, they had already recorded over that tape, which doesn't make much sense since they still had the other angles. Anyhow, the manager insisted that an Oskar Helman never registered nor was there a reservation in the system for him. According to *him*, if Helman didn't have a reservation it would have been difficult finding something in DC. Few rooms were available for the twenty-seventh or eighth—there was a White House gala of some sort."

"Robin, why did he go to the hotel in the first place? Did you call Oskar's DC friends using the number we got from Sarah Rollins?"

"They expected Oskar and Danny to stay with them for a couple of days on his return. The woman I spoke with had the correct arrival date but since Oskar didn't call, she figured something came up with the boy or Oskar's mother and they were still in Germany."

"Did she try to contact him, as Sarah claims?" Erica asked.

"She did. As did her husband. They called and emailed after a day went by but didn't get any response. The calls went to voicemail. It's even more perplexing that Helman didn't contact his friends when he couldn't find a room. I asked whether he'd left with bad feelings, but she said not as far as she knew."

"Chica, what do you say about taking a DC road trip to speak directly with the supposed friends, taxi driver, and hotel manager? I prefer a face-to-face approach."

"I agree. When were you thinking of?"

"Let's run what we have by Sarge—find out what he has for feedback. Saturday would work for me. Since it will be the weekend, one or more of the friends should be home."

I thought about it for a minute. "Okay, I can go if we leave *early*—pick up breakfast en route and get back before one. I was supposed to be off, so Sean and Matt made some sort of plans. Anything else?"

"I think we've covered most of it, Robin. Danny wanted to visit Air and Space. The Smithsonian museums are free but when you check on Oskar's credit card activity, look for any gift shop purchases. After leaving the hotel, Oskar and Danny seem to have dropped off the face of the earth until the morning a doctor out walking his dog in an upscale neighborhood finds the boy's body in a culvert. It makes no sense; the kid did not even live in Baltimore. Or even in Maryland. ¡Carajo! His father is still missing."

"Give me a minute." I leafed through my notebook, silently going over the points we'd covered. "Okay, Moreno, what we appear to have is a father and son who arrived together in DC from Germany, but Danny is found over an hour away with his hair cut and dyed; his skin tanned. The ME has deemed it a suspicious death. His backpack is in our possession but does not contain his computer, phone or, for that matter, any of his belongings. Instead, there is the clothing of a teenage girl. We found it hidden in an area close to where the doctor discovered Danny's body and many schools are located. Someone took the time to paint the date and a teddy bear near the boy's body, all of which indicate some type of personal connection. At least to me. As far as we know, neither father nor son had a link to Maryland. Oskar Helman and the luggage remain missing."

"Chica, we need to concentrate on finding Danny's father and then work backwards. What are your thoughts at this point—the father as perpetrator or as victim?"

"I guess, given what we know so far, we'll learn Oskar Helman was a victim. There is nothing to suggest he would harm his son. Despite her problems with her ex, Rollins trusted him; he sent the itinerary and texted their arrival. Oskar, in fact, according to all of our reports was a good and loving father. He brought his child back to the States on the arranged date—I very much doubt this was a parental kidnapping gone wrong, but I can't make sense of the hotel piece. Anything you want to add, Moreno?"

"Bueno, I also think of him as a victim. I want to know whether his passport, credit cards, and bank account show activity, other than the two hundred ATM withdrawal at the airport. The receptionist gave Oskar the names of other hotels he could try, and there is no record of him having stayed at any of them.

Another thing I find particularly curious is that Helman's phone has a GPS feature but has been untraceable since the day they arrived at Dulles and went to the hotel. No evidence of them having gone to a museum, but Oskar could have taken his son to one of them, while he spent time on the phone looking for lodging."

"Erica, we made some solid progress. Let's go back inside and talk to Sarge"

Chapter 23

HITTING THE PAVEMENT

After listening to our update, Sarge approved the trip to DC, but insisted we also invest time in searching for Oskar in Baltimore. While discussing the pros and cons of a press conference, his assistant put through a call. We were dismissed with the wave of a hand.

"Bueno, Chica. Let's go somewhere and plan what to do next."

"Yeah, I think that went well."

"Give me a minute. I wrote down several questions while we were reviewing the evidence." Erica said as she thumbed through her notes, "Okay, here we go. Robin, we need to find out whether there is a connection between anyone in the Helman-Rollins family and Baltimore—we never brought that up with Sarah. Also, if Oskar was not involved in his son's death, where did they become separated? If in DC, how did Danny end up in Baltimore? Last one ... where is Oskar Helman?"

"Moreno, how about we assume Oskar did *not* kill his son. Maybe he couldn't get a room in DC and for whatever reason didn't want to contact his friends, so they came to Baltimore by train and got a room downtown."

"Bueno," was all my partner said and somewhat unconvincingly at that. She appeared to be thinking it over as she rhythmically smoothed back her hair, brow knit. When I'd about given up on a response, she said, "Robin, I'll buy into those assumptions."

"Since you're onboard, we'll start with the belief Oskar Helman is in the area. He may be dead but, of course, I'm hoping that's not the case. I think the first thing to do is look at all open cases of dead and injured white males in Baltimore—there can't be that many for the time frame we're looking at."

"Robin, how about we go downtown to the CompStat office. If we do not come up with anything, we can expand the investigation to other counties—those closest to DC—Prince George's and Montgomery."

My partner's enthusiasm for what might turn out to be a sizeable undertaking caught me off guard. "Okay, let's start with the City. I'll get you that caramel frappuccino I owe you for dealing with Marisol, and then we can take a look at the crime stats."

———

"California, in addition to the focus on Caucasian males, how about eliminating all victims younger than thirty-two and older than fifty-two? Oskar Helman is forty-two, so that should be a sufficiently broad age range. Since somebody dyed Danny's hair, and eye color can be iffy after death, I think we should forget about those as defining characteristics. This of course for the deaths, not the injured victims."

"Height?" I asked.

"His wife said Oskar is six-foot three, which his passport confirms, although that was eight years ago. Let's go with a profile of six foot one to five," suggested Erica. "Weight?"

"He's a big man—two hundred and ten. Danny must have taken after his mother—I remember thinking he looked to be about Sean's age. Let's go with 190 to 220—lighter because he possibly lost weight."

As we built a profile, Erica entered the information into the computer. "Robin, are there noticeable marks of any kind—*anything* that would make our lives a little easier?"

"Effective program they've got here. I called Sarah Rollins about that. She remembered two scars and a mole. His sister spoke with her mother, who confirmed what his wife gave me. There's one scar in the right temporal area that is pretty much hidden by his hair. The other is larger and runs across his right knee—stitches after a bike accident. The mole is located on his lower back, left. I also requested dental records. They were being sent by DHL—I'll check the tracking number."

"Good work. Crane, now that the physical parameters are in place, you could take the unidentified injured between the 27th of October and today—Oskar may be hospitalized in a coma or have amnesia— and I will take the deaths."

"Agreed."

———

We'd been at it for awhile and I felt bleary-eyed and hungry. "Moreno, if this program is accurate and the data are current—the city has its challenges, after all—I've got three possibilities. One in critical condition. How many did you find?"

"Two. I thought there would be more."

"Manageable. How do you want to handle it, Erica?"

"We could each start with our own lists. I am probably being overly optimistic to think we can get this done today, but we can try. *If* Oskar Helman is alive, he might not have much time."

"That works for me. Moreno, give me a few minutes to make some calls—make sure they all belong on my list and not yours."

"Bueno."

———

"The calls were worth it—one of my injured died yesterday."

"Well, give him to me then, Chica."

"No can do. Dude's been identified. The other two are expected to make it: my first possibility is a John Doe at Shock Trauma. The man suffered a head injury and has a diagnosis of amnesia but is conscious. He had no identifying information on him when found and apparently isn't listed in the missing persons database."

"What about the second man?"

"Well, he was discovered in a car left overnight in the Fort McHenry parking lot. For whatever reason, it didn't raise a red flag with the park police until the next morning, at which time they notified the BPD. This one is at Hopkins—his weight is off but he's of a similar height. We have Helman's passport photo and the picture of him with his son. If there is still a question we can take a photo array to Sarah Rollins for an ID."

"The McHenry victim, he's not conscious?"

"No. The damage from the pills and booze may be permanent. Might be a suicide attempt, though I am not sure why because there was no note and they don't know who he is. Strange case—particularly because there's no missing person's report."

"Who was the car registered to?"

"That's the thing, the guy rented it using a false ID and a cash deposit. He wore sunglasses and a cap."

I waited until my partner finished with her notes. "What do you have?"

"How about we go to Crazy John's first? I need a break from staring at the screen and, more importantly, I am starving. Anyhow, we need to digest your list before we begin mine."

"Funny. I'll call Matt and tell him to go ahead and eat dinner without me."

234

An hour later, we were walking along the section of Baltimore Street dotted with adult entertainment clubs. "Now that we're probably near our daily limit for sugar, grease, and salt, all I can think of is a nap." When I began working downtown, I found it difficult to believe Headquarters, Central, and the courts were neighbors with the likes of Larry Flynt's Hustler Club, Norma Jean's, Club Pussycat, and Power Point Live. Now, I sort of appreciate the fact that the police, the homeless, attorneys, twenty-something partiers, bouncers, strippers and their customers all share the same sidewalk as they go about their respective missions.

"Erica, I'm perplexed as to why I'm so drawn to Crazy John's when each and every time I'm ready to crawl into a hole and go to sleep after eating there."

"I get that, but it tastes *sooo* good! Tell you what, I will make a fresh pot of coffee *and* warm the milk!"

"Much appreciated. Moreno, once we go over your list, I'll head to Shock Trauma. If there's enough time, I'll book it to Hopkins."

Settled back at the computer, we resumed our project. "I understand that we are not excluding Oskar Helman as a suspect in his son's death—he was the last one to be seen with his son of live and could have fled. But this go-round, Erica, our working theory is that he came to Baltimore with his son and he, too, is dead. Correct?"

"That's right. If we obtain something solid, the dental records should help sort things out."

"And, I'll get on it for a source of DNA—Sarah might still have something belonging to Oskar. Thanks for the coffee! Okay, what you got, partner?"

"Well, the first victim will be familiar to you."

"And why is that?"

"Chica, the body found by the window washers when you were downtown has come back to haunt you. The body was in the water long enough for the fish and crabs to get at him, and probably props from a boat or boats. Anyhow, don't get too excited, he only vaguely fits our general description. His fingers have been cut off, so no finger-prints, but there *are* some teeth."

"Sounds more like gang payback or conflict on a ship, rather than a well-to-do German last seen in DC with his son."

"I included him because we found Danny here and Sarge had wanted us to consider the possibility they came to Baltimore."

"I understand. That still Manny's case?" I asked.

"Yeah. I gave him a call but could not reach him. His partner, a rookie I don't know, says Manny still believes something went down on a ship—the killer did not want the dead man traced back to him, so he removed the fingers and tossed the body overboard. Nothing much came out of the sketch they released—with the exception of the possible sighting by Tim Moore. Remember him?"

"I forgot about that. I do remember mentioning something to Ty about there being nothing in the news after the first couple of days."

"We need to find out what came out of Manny's interview with Moore. The rookie said he decided the body was so damaged the sketch probably didn't look at all like the man when alive and its release would just complicate things."

"Erica, how strange would it be if the man pulled from the harbor *was* Danny's father?"

"Manny's a good guy—when I started out, I did a tour with him. I will call again and set up a meeting. Bueno, your floater is a possibility, though the database may not be up-to-date and one or all of our guys has already been identified."

"And your other victim?"

"My second victim may be from Latin America but, Chica, I am not convinced."

"What's his story?"

"Well, this John or Juan Doe is listed as a possible Caucasian *or* Latin American. He's blonde and light-skinned."

"Why Latin American?"

"They believed him to be 'in the country illegally' because he had literature from the Esperanza Center in his pocket. No identification was found."

"Esperanza Center?"

"Esperanza means hope in Spanish. It is an arm of Catholic Charities located on Broadway in Fells Point, a few blocks down from Pratt. They assist people who are in the country without papers. The case file notes state that nobody at the Center recognized a photograph of the dead man. There is a large staff, including many volunteers; the detectives could have missed someone."

"Could be he wasn't here illegally but was involved with somebody who was and tried to obtain assistance for him or her. Maybe a lawyer donating his time."

"Possibly, but remember Oskar is an engineer. California, this just might work. At least we can eliminate some possibilities. Should be easier than I thought."

"I think so. What's next?"

"I'll meet up with Manny and see what he has on his case; maybe talk with the detectives who went to the Esperanza Center. I will take the photographs of Oskar Helman with me."

"Sounds good. While you're doing that, I'll head to Shock Trauma and bring a forensics kit with me. At least in my cases I can start with breathing bodies."

"See you when I see you, Crane. Can you let Sarge know what is up? Finding Manny may take time."

"No problem. Good luck." I returned to the desk we were using and got myself organized before giving our supervisor a call and updating him about our new line of inquiry. I received his blessing.

I went outside; the sun was going down and it was chilly; nonetheless, I set off on foot for Shock Trauma. If it wasn't too late after finishing up there—it was unreasonable to expect the first contact would be our man—I would return and pick up my car for the drive to Hopkins, before heading home. Then, I had a second thought. I had woken up that morning thinking about Seth. After seeing him at Central Booking, of all places, I hadn't spoken with him again, although I'd seen him around. I wondered if he was still sleeping in a shelter at night. If he hadn't already returned to his home, I couldn't imagine how long he would continue his routine with winter around the corner. More importantly, I once again questioned why Seth was out on the street to begin with. To be frank, not only was I concerned about the boy, I had selfishly considered obtaining his help in locating Joey Jimenez. Both kids were from Fells Point. Well, Joey was, and Seth apparently hung around the area. Maybe I would take a quick detour to the plaza before heading home—Matt already expected me to be late. If Seth was not at the square, perhaps someone knew where I could find him.

———

Later, as I made my third circuit around up Broadway and across Thames, who should I see in the street panhandling but Seth. I drove by him without a glance, went another two blocks and parked. Now that I'd located the boy, I sat in the car for a few minutes deciding how to handle the situation—I was determined, at the very least, to learn his last name. As I saw it, I had two options: I could take my time and build some trust with the boy *or* push hard for whatever I could get. After giving the matter some thought, I decided time was at a premium—I needed information. Even so, he had no reason to speak to me. And he didn't. When Seth saw me, he smiled, waved and took off.

Chapter 24

AIR AND SPACE

It was quiet when I got in to the office, so I plunked myself down at my desk and spent the next several hours catching up with my least favorite part of the job, paperwork. Once done, though, up-to-date files inevitably left me with a great feeling of self-satisfaction. At long last finished, I went out for a walk and then to Vaccaro's for some lunch.

After returning to the office, I checked my messages. There were two from Erica. She answered on the first ring. "Hey, partner. Get hold of Manny?"

"I did. Unfortunately, he can't give us much. He *was* interested in the fact that the missing Oskar Helman was last seen in DC, given Tim Moore thought he saw Manny's victim in the capital. Turns out he did not set much store by Moore's *possible* identification because the guy was not sure where he had seen him." She laughed.

"What's funny?"

"Now that his case is getting cold, my pal is okay about working with us. Under the circumstances, he suggested we go back and re-interview the guy. Fair warning, California, he doesn't expect much. Like the rookie said, Manny is convinced somebody threw the man off a cruise ship passing through the Chesapeake. He just cannot prove it."

"Where do ships dock?" I asked.

"Locust Point."

"Interesting … could be a coincidence but that's where the police found one of the individuals on my list. Erica, how about we take a ride over there?"

"Well, since Manny has no evidence of his victim being tossed off a ship, I would not be too excited—Baltimore is a small city and there is limited space for dumping bodies. Anyway, I am game for a drive. I filled Manny in on what we have learned about Danny's death. He will send me everything he has first thing tomorrow. Huang will be able to tell us whether Manny's victim and Danny Helman are related. Bueno, even if one case has nothing to do with the other, he is hoping we will see something he missed. How did *you* do, Chica?"

"All good. I ran our current strategy by Sarge and we have his blessing. Just an FYI: Mr. Shock Trauma's room number is 310. They had a hospital lawyer in the room to protect his rights but it was irrelevant because he agreed to cooperate."

"What about JHH—Mr. Fort McHenry—they also had a lawyer there?"

"Yep. Legal was present but in that case, I could see their point. After all, their patient is in a coma."

"And?"

"In both cases I took pictures, obtained prints, and swabbed for DNA; the samples are with the crime lab. Erica, honestly, I don't think either one is our guy. Same general profile on paper but neither man really looks like Sarah's photograph of her ex or his passport photo. Anyhow, we'll know for sure when the forensics come in."

There was a pause and then she asked, "You still think this is worth our time?"

"I do. Yet the best I can say today is that we're narrowing the field of possible candidates, and we might be able to help someone else clear a case. Erica, I need to get home early. Why don't we drive over to Locust Point tomorrow?"

"Tomorrow is fine with me. I have plenty of work to do—I've got to meet with the prosecutor for another case—but leaving early sounds good, my apartment could use some attention. Anyhow, we probably eliminated two possibilities and the others are in the holding-out-hope column—we are good."

"¡Hasta mañana!" I said.

"Ayyy, I forgot, I have an appointment first thing in the morning. Still, I should not be in too late."

"No problem," I said. "I want to line up the meetings and run down some of the DC leads before Saturday. I'll call Ty and see whether there's anything new on the murder of Leroy Nichols or the child trafficking ring Nichols' pal, Cuz, was involved in. Take your time."

———

True to her word, Erica was running late, but I had plenty to keep me busy.

A couple of hours later my partner slumped into the chair next to my desk and let out a groan. "Hey, Chica. Sorry—my appointment ran long."

"You okay?"

"Yeah, only my routine tune-up—it is that time of the year. I hate the waiting when there is stuff going on and this took forever. Damn doctors see too many patients. Like doing too many tests."

"Don't worry about it, Moreno. You've covered for me plenty."

"Bueno, did you follow up on the events in DC? Anything more about where Oskar and Danny went after leaving the hotel?"

"Yep, while you were pacing the doctor's office and probably irritating the staff and other patients, I think I found something. We may have us a viable witness."

"Wow, you *have* been busy!"

"Erica, I think we've lucked out—despite the thousands of tourists wandering the mall area, this pair definitely stood out—good-looking, exceptionally blonde, and hauling around two suitcases and a backpack. We should be able to spot them easily on the sec cam footage."

"Give it up, Chica. What do you have for me?"

"Okay, here's the basic picture. By the way, Erica, I went back to the Helmans' arrival at Dulles and started there. There were no questions at that point: they arrived with luggage, withdrew money from the ATM, took a taxi to the hotel, couldn't get a room but the manager gave Oskar Helman some suggestions.

"What I do have that's new is a security guard in Air and Space who identified the Helmans; the dad was dragging around suitcases. He remembers a child who seemed to be having a good time. Reported the dad as stressed and looking tired; he mostly sat with the luggage and talked on his phone. Oh, and saw them coming out of the IMAX theatre before it ended. Video should confirm at least some of his observations."

"Robin, given all the parents and kids who go in and out of that place, why did he remember those two? Odd, no?"

"Yeah, that's what I thought. What I did was email a still photo from the hotel footage to the Smithsonian and requested they distribute it to their employees at Air and Space and the Natural History museum via their Listserve. Only the one individual contacted me. I asked him the same question—why those two stood out of the thousands passing through on any given day. It turned out he'd recently attended a DC conference on child abuse that included a training session—the guard and the program deserve medals. Anyhow, the pair had caught his attention and he kept an eye on them. He believed they were father and son, but suspicious of a parental kidnapping. He was thrilled to talk with a "real detective" until he learned the boy may have died. He's willing to come here for an interview or meet with us in DC. We can bring the photograph of Danny and his father."

"Did he have any idea how long they were in the museum? Where they went next?"

"He's fuzzy about time. At least an hour, he thinks. When I pushed for specifics, it turned out he hadn't actually seen them leave. He just couldn't find either of them when he looked."

"He must be beating himself up pretty bad," Erica said.

"He is, poor man."

"Well, put him on our list. We should also talk to the Metropolitan Police Department."

"Right."

"And Ty Wilson?"

"No luck."

Chapter 25

Oskar & Danny

"Hey, Ty. Reached** you first thing—hope the rest of my day goes as well!"

"How's it going, Crane? I must say, I miss you. My new partner doesn't measure up but, then, you left the bar set pretty high. He's not concerned about the kids' homework—no children. Plus he's not as good-looking and, worse, he's a grease and sugar junkie. I've put on a few, which is making Janie *and* my doctor irritable. Otherwise, *I guess,* the dude's not so bad."

He sounded so forlorn that I couldn't help but laugh. "I miss working with you too, buddy. How's the family?"

"Everyone's fine. Matt and Sean?"

"They're both well. Matt seems to like his new job."

"Are we still on for Sunday?"

"We're looking forward to it. Ty—my parents will be here. Oh, and Erica Moreno is coming."

"Great. Janie said to tell you we're bringing a pasta salad and baked beans. Grandmom is making her famous chocolate cake—wait 'til you try that! Let us know if you need anything else."

"No, that's more than enough! Sounds delicious, especially the cake."

"It is, but I'm sure that's not why you called. What can I do for you?"

"We need your help with our Roland Park investigation."

"Yeah, heard you got an ID on the boy. Good work."

"We did. Ty, we're trying to figure out how Danny Helman came to be in that culvert. Last time he'd been seen was with his dad in a DC museum; they had just arrived from Germany." I went on to give him the details.

"You got anything on the father?"

"We're still trying to locate him but that's not exactly why I called. I wanted to find out whether there's anything new on the Leroy Nichols murder. I have one dead pre-adolescent white male and one missing pre-adolescent white female. That seems like too much of a coincidence in a city this size. Dude, it got me to thinking back to our interrogation of Nichols, the possibility he raised of a Baltimore-based human trafficking ring, and his subsequent murder. Did you get an identity for Cuz? Or find out anything more about his activities?"

"Wow! That would be interesting—a connection between your Roland Park case and the Nichols case. Honestly, Robin, we haven't made much progress. It makes some sense though; victims being trafficked come from somewhere. Crowded areas like museums are close to perfect: kids are running around, and worn out parents don't always watch them closely. Guards have their hands full."

"Well, I've certainly been there—I guess I operate with the assumption that a child is safe in a *museum*. Ty, though we have a witness and probably footage placing the pair in Air and Space, there's nothing after that. How would someone get a child out of the building without raising an alarm? Never mind into a vehicle without anyone witnessing the abduction. There are always hordes of people on the mall."

"You've got a kid, Robin. We raise our children to be polite and respectful of adults. The same things making them good citizens, children we can be proud of, may leave them vulnerable to the evil wandering among us. Guys like Cuz frequently have a woman troll for kids. *So*, a woman is trolling for your son, overhears you use his name and picks up on additional bits of personal information. She is patient. You become worn out while trailing after an active kid, sit on a bench trying not to nod off, or go to the restroom after cautioning him to stay in a circumscribed area. The woman is experienced. Motivated by love, money, fear, or perhaps all of the above, she sees her opportunity and swoops in like one those falcons living on top of the Transamerica building that target unsuspecting pigeons at the harbor. She approaches the boy, tells a lie—something like, '*Danny*, your daddy went outside because he's feeling sick. The suitcases were so heavy, so he's resting in my car out front. Danny, your daddy asked me to bring you to him.' Danny never asks how she knows his name. The child is aware his father is tired and has been dragging around suitcases. He accepts her extended hand and out of the building they go. As they approach, the van door opens and somebody pulls the child inside before he can say a word; before anyone notices something is amiss. She may or may not return for the father, but since he is missing, we'll assume they did for whatever reason. That wouldn't be difficult; he's been caught off guard and she has his child. They come back around. The vehicle pulls into the traffic and father and son are lost to the world they've always known."

"Thanks for that, Ty—I will *never* take my eyes off Sean again. Ever! And, he's at the age I'm supposed to be giving him more space."

"Sorry, but that's how it is. *That* is why I drive my kids and Janie crazy."

"No, really, despite being the stuff of nightmares it was a helpful scenario. Ty, I gotta go, a call is coming in. Can I get hold of you later?"

"Of course. California, you and Moreno just might have hit on something. I know you were upset by the Leroy Nichols murder and feel we let him down, but we'll see it through to the dismantling of

Cuz's business, whether or not he trafficked your two kids. If they did, we're too late to save the boy but maybe we can locate the girl."

Ty hung up and I clicked over to the other line, which was flashing. "Officer Crane, Northern District."

"Oh, thank God. This is Marisol Jimenez ... you *need* to come right away!" She said something else, but between the tears and hysteria, I didn't have a clue as to what it was.

"Calm down, Marisol. I can't do anything if I don't understand what you're saying." How many times had I said the same thing to this woman? I was becoming tired of it, as I'm sure would soon be the case for Erica. As was clearly the case for Greg Rossi.

"There's a girl at the plaza who knows Joey. *Please*, you've got to talk with her."

"Plaza, what plaza?"

"Fells Point—Thames—by the pier. Robin, I've been coming here most days. I talk with the kids; bring them food, a little money. I made friends, of a sort, with a girl who actually lives up your way. She hasn't been down here lately but called me today."

Maybe Marisol really had something this time. All along, I thought the kids hanging out in Fells Point could give us useful information. "It might take me half an hour; will she stay that long?"

"We'll go over to Bonaparte's and I'll get her a sandwich. I think she knows something and is worried or scared. But I need to go, I'm around the corner and afraid she'll take off."

"See you soon." I hung up and wrote a note for Erica.

———

I made it downtown in record time, parked and walked directly to the coffee shop. It is no exaggeration to say I was shocked. Sitting in a far corner by the fireplace was Marisol and the girl who had been in our vehicle at Bryn Mawr. Now I knew why she had seemed familiar, she'd been hanging out the first night I had stopped to talk with the kids. They had food, so I went over to the counter and ordered a coffee and several large cookies. It wasn't until I had the tray in hand that I joined them.

"Hello, Marisol, it's good to see you again."

"Thank you for coming. Rachel, this is Officer Crane—she's been trying to help me locate my niece."

The girl recognized me. She had the deer-in-the-headlights look reminiscent of the one I saw at Bryn Mawr before she bailed out of the car. Afraid she would bolt, I quickly sat down and put a large chocolate chip cookie on each of their plates.

"Nice to meet you, Rachel. I am sure Ms Jimenez is appreciative of your help." Not only didn't I say a word about our last interaction, I avoided shaking the girl's hand or asking for her last name. Nonetheless, she failed to respond.

"You're right, Detective, I'm very grateful Rachel called me."

I could not imagine how this girl had Marisol's phone number but remained quiet. I stirred some milk into my coffee and nodded encouragingly.

"Joey was sitting on a bench at the plaza one day. Rachel told her she was too young to be out there—some people did bad things. Robin, this sweet girl attempted to help my niece; she took her for frozen yogurt more than once and they talked. My niece told Rachel she was afraid of her mother and wanted to run away."

Marisol tried to relate this news calmly, even though I figured she was about to erupt from a combination of hope and fear. Once I understood what was going on, I could call Erica and ask her to get a search warrant for Brenda Jimenez's home. I would also contact Ty.

"Please tell the detective what you told me, Rachel. You can trust her."

She said this reassuringly. I was surprised and impressed by the thoughtfulness of her behavior, under the circumstances.

"But first, maybe you can tell Officer Crane how we came to talk."

"A girl—the same one from the plaza wanting to run away, Joey— gave me a phone number to call if I got away. I gave her *mine* in case she escaped. I did."

I was lost. "You did what?"

"I did escape." She seemed sheepish. A flush was spreading across her cheeks, making her look even younger than I believed her to be.

Marisol placed a hand over Rachel's; I was surprised the girl allowed her, a stranger, to touch her with such intimacy. "It's alright. Tell the detective."

"I don't know why, but I didn't call until today. Ms Marisol, I am sooo sorry."

"You have nothing to be sorry about, hon. You're helping now and *that's* what counts. Are you sure you don't want us to reach your mother?"

"No!" she replied sharply. She glanced at both of us. "I'm sorry, but *please* don't call her."

"Okay. Hon, can you tell the detective about your time in the basement?"

"Time in the basement." What in the hell is going on?

Her voice strong, she said without hesitation, "Detective, there was a girl named Claire with me for a little while but, like, she was taken away and never came back while I was there. It was awful for Joey because her *mother* lived upstairs with another lady—they never came into the basement. They brought a little boy and his father there. The man seemed drugged—maybe he was hurt. One man was *really* scary; I don't know his name. He wanted to throw the big man down the stairs—said they shouldn't have brought him—but the boy started screaming. The father was locked in a room, but they left his son with us. The boy said his name was Danny Helman and he lived in Pennsylvania. I heard Cuz and Bro talking—Bro wanted to get money from Danny's father. I guess he has a bunch of it because he said he would pay whatever they wanted. Officer, he must be from a different country because he was hard to understand."

I was finding it difficult to process what I was hearing. She could have been telling us about a tough day at school. My brain was spinning as the possibility that Oskar was still alive, and that we might get

Cuz. "Rachel, were Cuz and Bro considering Danny's father's offer to give them money?"

"They had his wallet and cell phone. A laptop. They could have done it. I think. But Cuz and another man were mostly mad they brought him with the boy."

"Honey, I know you are aware that Danny died. Now, I understand why you were so upset when my partner and I spoke with you at Bryn Mawr."

A surprised Marisol put down her sandwich. She looked at each of us searchingly but said nothing. I forgave the woman for her previous craziness. Rachel was nibbling at the chunks of chocolate in her cookie. There were crumbs everywhere. She seemed to be somewhere else. Her hair was much shorter and appeared blonder than when we'd last seen her, but she was just as thin. Her large green eyes had dark shadows underneath.

"Rachel, the offer Danny's father made—do you know what happened?"

"Nah. This is, like, hard."

"Hon, I understand. Please, just do the best you can." I picked at my cookie and took a few sips of coffee, hoping to maintain calm and not pressure the girl, even though we didn't have much time.

"In the end, I guess they didn't wanna—Bro wanted the money but the others said the man was going to cause problems and it wouldn't be worth it. When they stopped fighting, Bro and the mean guy took Danny's father away. I was terrified."

We had stumbled onto something truly awful. Although Rachel must have experienced an unimaginable fear, her voice was eerily flat as she continued speaking in what was almost a whisper. I glanced around—nobody sat near enough to hear us. "What happened to Danny after they took his father away?"

"He couldn't stop crying even when the man guarding us yelled at him to quit it. I don't know *his* name. The yelling just made Danny's breathing worse and trying to get him to cry into the pillow didn't help—a couple of times he started choking." With that, the girl covered her face with her hands and began to whimper. "I think he needed a new inhaler," she mumbled.

"Sweetie, I am so sorry for what you went through and how difficult this is." Marisol put an arm around Rachel's shoulders and looked at me helplessly.

I knew by now her fear for Joey must be all-consuming yet somehow she'd managed to be there for this girl living through a nightmare. Marisol Jimenez had been right all along to be worried about her niece. On the one hand, I was glad I had stuck with the case; on the other, I regretted not pursuing it more vigorously earlier on. We had missed the big picture, despite Leroy Nichols having set the pieces out for Ty and me months ago. And paying with his life for doing so.

"I should have saved that little boy." the girl said, taking a quick glance around the room and wiping away her tears.

"Rachel, you have nothing to blame yourself for—you are not much more than a child and have been extraordinarily brave," I assured her. "Hon, I am truly sorry for Danny and his family, but with your assistance maybe we can save Joey." *The time has come to go. Such a traumatized girl surely doesn't need this type of responsibility on her shoulders.*

"Ms Jimenez, thank you for calling me, you've been a great help. I'm going to take Rachel with me now. Is there somewhere I can reach you?"

Marisol remained sitting. "Is that okay with you, hon?"

"Yeah. I guess," the girl mumbled. She stood up and pulled her backpack out from under her chair. Pinned to it were the social messaging buttons.

"Rachel, I'll call your parents and ask them to meet us downtown." I handed her my pen and notebook turned to a clean page. "Could you please write down their phone numbers for me?" She began to protest.

I had a terrible thought. "Do your parents know what happened to you?"

"No. Do they have to?"

An unbelievable response that could only come from an *adolescent*. The girl had my sympathy but there was no way I would continue this conversation without parental permission. "I'm sorry, hon, but they do. Who would you prefer I call, your mother or father?"

"My mother. *Please* don't call my father. Here, I'll write down the numbers for her cell and the office. She'll be upset but it's better than calling my father. He'll be a complete mess—my mom should talk to him first." She started to cry but wrote down a name and several numbers.

We were now attracting attention. I pocketed the notebook, stood up and turned toward Marisol. "Ms Jimenez, thank you again for your considerable help. I am going to leave with Rachel. It's essential you wait for me at home."

"I understand."

I hoped she did. "Do you have a home line?"

"No, just my cell, but I'll keep it with me."

"Thank you—it's important that you do."

The three of us gathered up our belongings and left the coffee shop.

Chapter 26

Rachel

Instead of taking notes, I turned on the recording equipment and concentrated on observing Rachel Corey while she answered our questions. Time was limited, so Ty had agreed to sit in on the interview while Erica obtained the search warrant. We had located Rachel's mother in Annapolis and I expected her to arrive in a little more than an hour—it would be a tough conversation. When I explained that we were trying to locate a missing child and Rachel might be able to help us, she voiced confusion and concern but faxed her permission to talk with her daughter, as long as the girl agreed. We already had one dead child and didn't want another. There was only a narrow window of opportunity or I would never have asked.

"Miss Corey, Officer Crane says you told her two men seemed to be making decisions—Cuz and Bro. Is that right?" Ty asked.

"Yes, sir."

"Who was the man who held you captive most of the time?" I asked.

"*Who* was the man?" At that supposedly simple question, the girl was almost screeching but surprisingly, given her age and what she had gone through, she managed to control her emotions and lowered her voice. "Who was he? The man was a perv … the asshole who must'a killed Danny," she finished sadly. "The dude who thought he would get money for letting some perv diddle me—that is who I, like, talked to Miss Marisol about. *I* showed him though!"

The girl's anger caught me off guard—the first I'd observed of either, but I guess it shouldn't have surprised me. Ty and I exchanged glances.

Until now, Ty had said little; he sat there attentive and calm. "Miss Corey, let's back up if you don't mind. I'm sorry," he said gently, "I may be a little confused because I wasn't present when you spoke with Ms Jimenez and Officer Crane."

"O … kay." She pulled herself up straight and took a breath.

He smiled at her encouragingly and shifted gears, catching me off guard with his question. "Thank you. Could you tell us how you happened to end up with the man or men you escaped from?"

She took so long to answer that despite Ty's measured approach, I thought she might be lost to us before we'd barely begun. "This is my fault," the girl whimpered. "All my fault. My mother is going to be so mad when she finds out. I'll be like grounded forever."

"Rachel, I am sure that she will be more worried than anything," I said reassuringly, although I could only imagine what her mother would go through for a long time to come. I certainly wouldn't rule "mad" out.

"Like, I was in Fells Point and it was getting late. I waited and waited for a friend who promised to pick me up but she never came back. When I finally got hold of her, she said something came up and she couldn't get me, so I went back to my friends."

"Where did your parents think you were?"

"The Hopkins library. Studying. I like Fells Point and they never let me have any fun." She said the last bit with a whine.

I wonder why! It seemed to have escaped Rachel's notice, even after what happened, that her parents had a legitimate reason for their concern. I found it interesting, the difference in emotional response while talking with Ty, compared to the earlier conversation with Marisol and me. She sounded more her age, more vulnerable. I wondered whether her mother had contacted her father—to recover she would need a particularly resilient family.

"Where did your friend go?" asked Ty.

"She knows someone who lives in Silo Point."

"Excuse me, but where is that?" I asked.

"In Locust Point, by Fort McHenry. Stephanie drops me off in Little Italy before she goes over there. In two hours she, like, picks me up."

"Where?" I asked thinking I had misheard or she was confused.

"Little Italy."

"Rachel, isn't it a long walk from Little Italy to Fells Point and back, within a couple of hours? Or, does she pick you up in Fells Point?"

"No, where she leaves me off."

"Is it worth it?" I asked, but it must have been because she apparently made the trip a routine.

"The walk's not far. I don't like going to the gym, so it's good exercise."

Ty laughed. "Wouldn't it be nice to be young again, Officer Crane?"

I tried to lighten up. "True, I must be getting old because it sounds like a lot of walking to *me*! Did you call your parents for a ride … once you knew your friend wasn't coming?"

She looked at me as if I had lost my mind. "They would kill me!"

"Okay. So why not take the bus?" She wouldn't have to walk much farther than Little Italy to catch a bus that would drop her off only a few blocks from home.

"A bus!" This time the look said *horrified*. I squashed a smile. Ty cocked an eyebrow and swallowed his own smile.

"So how did you plan to get home?" Ty asked, keeping it low key but pushing the conversation along. I had forgotten how good he was at interviewing suspects *and* victims. They quickly came to trust him.

"After I went back to Fells Point, a guy who hangs around the plaza offered to drive me home. Big mistake," she said sadly.

"Do you know his name?" I asked hopefully.

"Seth."

My lungs constricted. Seth … the kid I was so worried about. He had fooled *me*, a seasoned detective. No wonder Rachel, a young girl who unexpectedly found herself in a pinch, took off with him without a concern in the world other than her fear of taking the city bus. When finished, I would call Greg Rossi first thing.

"Hon, do you think you can work with our sketch artist?" *Between the two of us, we should be able to come up with a hell of a rendering.*

"Yes. *I* could draw the picture."

Ty smiled encouragingly. "Miss Corey, do you think that if you looked through pictures of car models, you could identify his?"

"No need—Seth drove a 2013 Porsche 911, metallic blue. Go figure, *that* should've been a dead giveaway—kid who panhandled with such a great car."

"Did you happen to notice the license plate?"

"Not really."

"Maryland or a different state, maybe—"

"Oh, I remember, one of those special plates. I think … the red one—"

"With a barn?" I asked. Lot of red—it sounded like the agricultural tag—the western Maryland plate.

"I'm not sure." She perked up. "If I saw it, I could tell you then!"

"Very good. That's easy enough." Ty said. "Do you remember any of the numbers or letters?" He asked the question again, ignoring the fact that she had already answered in the negative.

"Sorry."

"So what happened after you left Fells Point with Seth? By the way, do you know his last name?" I asked as casually as possible, all the while wanting to get this girl to the hospital. She needed a medical check-up and to be set up for counseling—all these questions were certainly going to stir things up for her. Her parents were going to want to take their daughter home as soon as they discovered what had taken place. Marisol and Johnny wanted Joey home. *I* wanted her home, and anyone else these people were holding. *I* needed to understand what had happened to Danny and his father. And to the mysterious Claire.

She shook her head back and forth. "You don't know his name? Or, you don't know what occurred after you left for home with Seth in his Porsche?" I asked carefully.

"Seth was only called Seth. It sounds bad but I was thirsty and he gave me a Gatorade to drink. It must have been drugged because I woke up in a basement with the other kids. Officer Crane, I never saw him again."

Though our time was short, I needed to be patient. After all, she wasn't much more than a child. "Rachel, we're sorry about what they did to you, and realize this must be difficult, but we really appreciate your help. Is it okay to continue?"

"I'm fine."

"Miss Corey, do you think you could describe the basement for us?" Ty asked. "For example, were you all in one big room?"

"No. There was a disgusting bathroom, the one large room and a small one with a lock. There were a few filthy mattresses—I'm lucky I didn't get bedbugs—and a table with three chairs. Oh, a crummy refrigerator with a microwave on top. I won't even tell you how awful they were."

"So once they brought you to the basement what happened?"

"I don't know. I slept till the next day and felt sort of out of it for awhile. Sick. Claire treated me really nice though. Joey tried to help Danny. Just a few times he could be with his father."

"The man, *Bro*, said if I didn't help out I couldn't eat. He brought me clothes, makeup and other stuff. I told him there was no way I would put on such a skanky dress and such ridiculous shoes. He, like, *slapped* me." She put a hand up to her right cheek and winced. "Hard. He called me a 'hoe' and told me that would be the first and last time I 'disrespected' him. And if I didn't believe him, I should ask Joey whether that was a good idea. Said he would be back after I got my head on straight and there would be a price to pay if I didn't look good by then. I believed him—he was scary; he'd even threatened Danny's father."

"Did you talk with Joey about what was going on?"

"Yes, but she mostly tried to keep Danny calm—he couldn't breathe. Before Bro left the room, he yelled at Joey to clean up Danny—he needed to go on a shopping trip."

"What about after Bro left?"

"We went to a corner to talk—Joey thought the inhaler wasn't working. I wanted to know where they were going to take me, but she said not to ask. If I didn't do what the man said, he would like hurt me. Hurt me bad. Joey said to get dressed and she would help with my makeup and hair. She told me it wouldn't be too bad because they would give me a drug—not the kind like before but I wouldn't remember much."

Appalled, I asked, "Rachel, what did you do?"

"I did what I was told. It was *so* awful! Joey helped fix me up—a skanky dress and my hair in pigtails but, like, the makeup wasn't bad— Sephora. Joey put my own clothes into Danny's backpack. Detectives, you might blame me for getting myself in trouble, but I'm *not* stupid. I *knew* what they wanted me for."

"Not at all, Rachel," I said in what I prayed was a supportive tone. "I think you're a courageous young woman and we are very grateful for your help. What happened next?"

"After a while, Bro came back and looked me up and down—dirty old man felt me up and then grabbed me by the elbow and dragged me up the stairs. We went out the back and there was *Seth's* car!"

Ty sat up straight. "Rachel, when you came outside, did you have *any* clue where you were? Anything you can tell us might help find Joey."

"They kept us in the basement of a rowhouse. When he drove out of the alley, I saw a sign that said Fayette, so I hoped I was still in Fells Point and not West Baltimore. We took a left on Fayette and after a while passed the Hopkins hospital on the right—I went there when I broke my leg playing soccer—I knew where we were."

"And then?" I asked, concerned about staying on track.

"Sorry. At one of the stop signs, Bro pulled over. He handed me a Starbucks coffee in a bottle and told me to drink it. The cap came right off. Joey was right, he gave me some kind of roofie."

"I am so sorry, Rachel," I said. "Ty, I'll give Erica a call." If there was any difficulty applying for the warrant, this information should do it.

"Okay. We'll wait until you return." He smiled. "I'm sure Rachel would like to talk about something else. Like, Rachel, is school still a drag?" he asked with a contorted face and desperate tone.

She laughed. At this moment, Rachel Corey looked like the young girl she must have been before she unwittingly got into Seth's car that ill-fated evening.

I returned to the conference room ten minutes later and took my seat, placing a Coke and two packages of fig bars in front of Rachel. In retrospect, I wondered why I had worried about choosing healthy cookies. "Detective Wilson, I've taken care of the matter. Sorry Rachel, is it alright to continue?"

She sat up straight and rested her hands on the table, one on top of the other. I felt for her. "I can do this. Detectives, my heart is broken for Danny—he was just a little boy who wanted his parents. They told Joey not to worry because they would take him to the doctor. That's why I was *so* shocked—I *knew* Danny died when I heard about it on the news."

She had knocked the breath right out of me. "Rachel, honey ... did you paint the little teddy bear?" I tried to keep my voice steady as I asked the question, aware Oskar Helman must be dead. Recognizing that when Danny's mother and Oskar's family learned of their loved ones' last days, they would experience more pain than they could ever have believed possible.

"I'm so sorry. I wanted to do something for Danny and didn't want to call 911—I knew they would blame me for what happened. The police had left and they'd taken the yellow tape down."

Ty let her words hang there for some seconds before proceeding. "Rachel, it's okay. If you don't mind, let's back up again. Once Bro told you to drink the coffee, then what?"

We suspected but didn't know with certainty whether Rachel had been raped before her escape. This had to be the last question. I could no longer justify keeping her here. We'd surely gotten enough for the judge to sign us a warrant.

"Detective Wilson, I didn't want to drink it, but Bro said he'd slap me harder if I didn't. We were passing the post office when he put on his signal, so I sipped at it and pretended it tasted good. Bro needed to slow down to take the right onto 83. He would be watching the road—there are always homeless people wandering the streets because of the tent city at St. Vincent's and traffic goes different ways. My mom always gets confused. When he got on the highway, I threw the bottle at him; he hit the brakes but it was too late and I jumped out with the backpack and ran down the ramp to the post office." She then said … oh, so simply, "On an Oprah show, she said to get out of the car."

Shocked and amazed by what this young girl did to save herself when faced with so much horror, I said nothing until it occurred to me an armed guard sits at a desk in the center of the post office. "Did you tell the police officer what happened?"

"No."

"Why?" Ty asked, with as much surprise as I felt.

"I expected Bro to get off at the first exit and come back, so I didn't have much time to get away. Besides, I didn't want anyone to find out how stupid I'd been; they would think I did drugs because of the drink. When my ride didn't pick me up in Little Italy and I would be late getting home, I'd texted my mom to tell her I planned to spend the night with a friend because we had an exam and I would be going to the library after school. Then Bro made me text my mother again and give her another excuse for the weekend. My mom was, like, not very happy about it. I guess I wanted to get home before I got into too much trouble.

"Anyway, I left the post office and ran to Vaccaro's in Little Italy—on Albemarle. Like, my family goes to that restaurant a lot for dessert when we have visitors and it's always crowded, so I hoped nobody would pay attention to me. There *were* lots of people, so I went into the bathroom and tried to clean up my face and fix my hair—took out the stupid pigtails. I changed into my own clothes from the backpack."

"Then?" I could not understand, for the life of me, why she hadn't asked someone for assistance, but didn't want to sound judgmental.

"I was leaving when Miss Ana came over and asked if I needed anything. She's always very nice."

"And?" I asked. I often ate lunch there—Ana *was* "very nice."

"Detectives, I lied—sort of. I told her I came downtown without my parents' permission and a mugger stole my purse. I begged her not to get the police; I would do that when I got home. She made me promise to wait while she fixed me a sandwich. I was scared but really hungry and I guess I trusted her."

Again, no police. I couldn't believe it. "Did she make you the sandwich?" I asked gently.

"She did. A turkey sandwich and some pasta salad. A drink and even cookies. Miss Ana came out from behind the counter, handed me the bag and walked out with me. I got scared the cops would come and I almost ran away but Miss Ana said a taxi would take me home. When he came, she paid him—thirty dollars *and* a tip! I went there today to pay Miss Ana back but she wouldn't take the money for the food or the taxi. She said she was happy to do what she could and I should do something for someone else, which made me cry. That is why I texted Joey's aunt and then said she could call you. Officer

Crane, Miss Marisol says you can get Joey away from those terrible men—is that true?"

"Hon, we're doing our best, and you've been an enormous help. Can you give us a minute to talk? Officer Boyd will stay with you."

"Sure. Thank you for the soda." She popped it open and concentrated on unwrapping the cookies.

Not until we were outside of the room did I feel I could catch my breath.

"Damn," said Ty. "She's one brave girl."

"Smart, too. You do need to keep your wits when driving through that intersection. Only yesterday, I almost hit an elderly homeless woman walking in the road when her cart tipped over. Brave, that's also true but, honestly, I'm surprised Rachel didn't go the postal police. Or, for that matter, ask this Ana to make a call. Ty, we have to get these child traffickers but, more importantly, right now our priority is to locate Joey Jimenez. And Oskar Helman, although I very much doubt he's still alive—I think someone went out of bounds when they snatched him and that wiser heads in the organization decided he was too much of a liability. Marisol must understand what's going on because I haven't received one call or text from her and she's understandably anxious. Erica believed, given the information we'd obtained from Rachel, that she could get a warrant for a search of Brenda Jimenez's house. That has to be the house Rachel is referring to—geographically, it fits the bill and it's the last place Marisol saw her sister-in-law."

"Tell Moreno to try Judge Walsh if she's having trouble—I saw her in court not too long ago."

"Will do. Ty, I think we should stop the interview. I'll contact her mother again, and if she's not already in the building, she should meet Rachel at Hopkins. I received a text from Special Victims and they're waiting to take her there—they can better explain to her mom what has happened, and can work with the folks in the prosecutor's office. Then, I'll call Rossi to find out whether he can locate Seth. I can't believe I felt sorry for the boy; now I've learned he's involved in trafficking children and who knows what else. Greg told me I was too soft—might want to consider a social work career. He could be right."

"Crane, Rossi was just giving you shit. If you hadn't kept at this, we wouldn't be where we are today with the case. Is it necessary, after so much time, for SVU to take Rachel Corey to JHH? Tough girl—she appears to be pulled together."

"We've got what we need for now, Ty. According to the professionals, it's never too late. A psychiatrist will meet with the girl and her family and set up long-term counseling. Rachel deserves all the support she can get, and it will take professional intervention to help the family deal with this awful situation. I think it will take Rachel a long time before she can let go of the guilt she is feeling about Danny's death. Also, SVU is trained in how to carry out these kinds of interviews—we're not even sure whether she's been sexually assaulted. This is going to be a huge case and I don't want anyone to walk."

"I agree. Contacting Rossi is a good idea—maybe he can come up with Seth's last name. The shelter might have something. He could put out a BOLO on the vehicle."

"If she's not here, I'll advise SVU that the mother will meet them at the hospital and they can send someone down to pick up Rachel."

"I'll check in with Erica about the status of a search warrant."

We went our separate ways. I thankfully reached Rachel's mom. I then made the necessary calls and returned to the interview room where I explained to Rachel what would happen next. She appeared relieved. I know I was.

Chapter 27

Joey

parked in front of the house at North Glover, walked up the steps and knocked on the door. The bell hadn't been repaired. After several minutes and considerably more knocking, the door opened a crack. "Oh, it's *you* again! Whadaya' want this time?" she asked, joining me on the landing and closing the door behind her.

"Ms Jimenez, have you heard from Joey since we last spoke with you?"

"No. She's living in DC with my ex."

"No, ma'am. Mr. Denney says he hasn't been in contact with her."

"Well," she cackled, "I'm friggin' sure he knows where Josephine is. He can get food stamps with her living with him."

"No, ma'am, he doesn't. We believe him."

"Who's *he?*" Brenda asked, with a belligerent thrust of her chin toward Ty who stood on the sidewalk.

"Ty, could you come here?"

"Ma'am, I'm Detective Tyrell Wilson," he said to Brenda with an outstretched hand offering the search warrant, which she ignored. Erica and another car pulled up.

Brenda looked around. "What in the *shit* is going on?" She took the document but just stood there without reading it. I beckoned to Erica.

Ty moved up the stairs and held the door open. "Ms Jimenez, what you're holding is a legal document giving us the right to search your house. You should know that any person interfering with the search is subject to arrest and potential criminal charges."

Short of patience, I brushed past the woman. "Ma'am, I need for you to let us do our job." Ty followed, leaving Brenda on the landing. Erica remained on the sidewalk in case the woman had any ideas about skipping out. Minutes later, neighbors gathering, a seething Brenda came inside, trailed by D and Erica.

Glad to see D, I quietly asked him to keep an eye on Brenda, explaining she was likely to run and if we could find *anything* to hold her on, I damn well would do so. If Joey Jimenez wasn't here, Brenda must know where her daughter was. "Erica, let's go downstairs."

"Sorry about the mix-up, Robin. A prosecutor needed to see me about another case."

"No problem. Thanks for getting the warrant to Ty first."

Just then, he hollered up. "Crane, Moreno, come down here. Lights are out; be careful."

He had smashed the locks and splintered the wood of the basement door; it now swung by one hinge. In single file, we went down the steep narrow stairway, hesitating at the bottom while our eyes adjusted. There in front of us was a young girl wrapped in a grungy blanket and huddled against the wall. Thin, she appeared sick but was *alive*. Erica and I looked at each other—we had found Josephine Jimenez, the 11-year-old girl whose mother refused us entrance only one floor above. I could barely contain my outrage. Brenda, whom we had suspected of turning tricks, trafficked children while taking drugs and coming and going as she pleased—getting coffee and donuts. All the while, in the basement below sat her abused and terrified daughter.

I walked over to the girl, knelt down and gathered her into my arms. "Joey, I promise you, you are going to be okay. I'm Officer Robin Crane, this is Detective Erica Moreno; your Aunt Marisol asked for our help." She clung to me and wept.

"Have you called for a bus?" Erica asked Ty.

"I did. They'll be here from Hopkins in a matter of minutes."

"Moreno, could you come over here?" I asked.

She knelt next to me on the filthy mattress. "Hello, Joey—you're safe now. Robin, what can I do to help?"

"Would you stay with her?" I whispered. "I'm going upstairs for a minute."

"Sure."

"Honey, I'll be right back—Detective Moreno will take care of you. I need to talk with someone."

She sniffled an unintelligible response, and Erica and I switched off. As I headed up the stairs, Ty came over and said quietly, "There's a locked room but I want to remove the girl first."

"Understood. None of the men holding the children were here?"

"I was taking the door off at the hinges when I heard someone downstairs and broke through instead. Unfortunately, I was just in time to see a man bailing out of a basement window. Sorry."

"We'll get him—there are probably prints. Ty, I'll be right back." I took the stairs two at a time, intending to arrest Brenda Jimenez—she would not remain in the same house with her daughter for one more minute. D was blocking the kitchen door. He nodded; she *had* tried to make a break for it. I advanced toward the woman who I could hardly bear to look at and with enormous satisfaction, said, "Brenda Jimenez, *you* are now under arrest for child abuse. D, would you mind reading Ms Jimenez her rights and then take her to Booking? She obviously needs cuffing. I'm going to make a call."

"My pleasure, *Detective* Crane," he said with a grin. "Lady, turn around, you are a definite candidate for cuffs."

Pleased with Brenda's arrest, knowing the prosecutor would add to the charges, I went outside and dialed Marisol's number. Not surprisingly, she answered in one ring. Without preamble I said, "Joey is with us—she'll be okay. Meet us at the Hopkins ER waiting room in a couple of hours—it'll take some time to finish up here and make the arrangements necessary to get you in to see your niece." As I spoke, I saw D bringing Brenda out of the house. "Marisol, please do what I ask. It is important there be no trouble."

Brenda must have overheard me because she wrested free of D in an attempt to get to my phone. "You fucking bitch. You will *fucking* pay for this, Marisol," she screeched. "Don't even think that you won't!"

I covered the phone, *probably too late.* "D, would you get her out of here?"

"Absolutely. Sorry—she's high on something."

Once he removed the still screaming Brenda from the immediate area, I resumed the conversation. "Marisol, your sister-in-law has been arrested. You should tell Johnny what's going on immediately. I'll call you back but, for now, please follow my instructions. Do *not* come over to Brenda's house, and give me a good hour before you leave for the hospital. Marisol, there can't be any scenes. Trust me."

"God bless you, Robin." She hung up, and I was sure she did so with the feeling her nightmare was over. In many ways it had just begun. They would also need support. Although my heart ached for Danny and his father, Joey and Rachel were alive—I felt unbelievably grateful for that. Now, we needed to locate Claire and Seth. As I waffled with the decision to call Danny's mother, a cacophony of sirens announced the arrival of two ambulances. The EMTs and individuals from Crime Scene, who had also just arrived, followed me down to the basement. I stood to the side and signaled to Erica.

"Ty, we're going to see what's upstairs while you manage this. I gestured toward the locked room and mouthed, "Brenda Jimenez is gone; we'll be back after Joey is removed."

"Understood."

In the room where Joey apparently had lived at one time, several textbooks with her name written inside the cover rested on a side table. A search of the dresser and closet revealed few clothes and two pairs of shoes. No photographs. A ratty old blanket that when pulled back exposed stained sheets. A grungy pillow with no case. We looked through the bathroom but other than a broad array of pharmaceuticals, found nothing of interest. We left everything in place for Crime Scene.

It was in the kitchen that we discovered what helped tip the balance in this investigation. I changed gloves to examine a well-used address book that not only contained names, addresses and phone numbers, but also dated notations written to the side of many of the names. I didn't recognize any of them until I made it to the letter M. Totally unexpected, there it was—an entry for Manning, Bernard J., the Roland Park doctor who reported "discovering" our young victim in the culvert. The man who had no alibi and we'd not eliminated as a suspect—someone we somehow managed to overlook for much of the investigation.

"Erica, look at what I've got!"

"What?"

I showed her the entry. "¡Ayyy, Dios mio! I can only imagine why the doctor is in this book," she said with equal measures of anger and sarcasm.

"Your case, partner. Do you want the pleasure of notifying the prosecutor's office and obtaining the search warrant for his home and office before word gets out? He found the body, does not have an alibi, and his name is in a black book discovered at a home where children were being held captive. You shouldn't have any trouble getting it, but call if you need something. I don't think Rachel was imprisoned long enough to give us client names, but Joey might. Can't imagine Brenda will be of any help. At least for now."

"Absolutely, Chica! I'll give you a call as soon as I have them."

"Meantime, I'm going back downstairs. Ty said no sounds were coming from the small room; he'll open it as soon as they take Joey out of the basement. Then, I'll head to the hospital and arrange for Marisol and Johnny to see their niece. Erica, I'm going to suggest they file for temporary custody. I don't know about Joey's father or stepfather, whatever he is, but he didn't seem too concerned about her. He'll probably sign off—that is if he has any legal rights whatsoever."

"I hope so. Robin, it looks like all Marisol's craziness was warranted—after seeing Joey, I feel bad for not taking her more seriously."

"Me too."

"Well, let me know what else you find that will give us probable cause. I will keep you or Ty posted about the search warrant."

"Will do. Okay, I'm heading back to the basement."

Chapter 28

Leroy Nichols

"Ty, **I really** believe Leroy Nichols was truthful with us. His fear of snitchin' mushroomed into a terrible reality. I still feel guilty—we were supposed to protect him."

"It's a problem; I'm not sure what to say. Robin, *he* opened the door and got into the life. I feel bad, too, but I don't take it home with me. Sometimes, it's a nasty business."

"I guess," I said, not convinced.

"What did they get from the Jimenez girl about Cuz?"

"We've got the transcript from the Special Victims Unit interview down at the hospital. Cuz seemed to be 'the boss,' which is pretty much what Rachel Corey told us. We've got to find him."

"We will, California. We will."

"On a slightly different topic, Ty, I swear you were a mind reader when you gave me your take on trafficking."

"Meaning?" he asked.

"We got more or less the same information from Joey Jimenez and Rachel Corey. The traffickers are using other young people to snatch their victims: we know Seth brought in Rachel. Joey said the young woman named Claire somehow managed to pick up Danny Helman, and probably Oskar, in DC. Bro drove and someone else she'd never seen before accompanied them."

"Crane, we need to find Seth and Claire—those kids should get us another step closer to Cuz. But my guess is there's somebody above him pulling the strings and we're going to be in this for the long haul. Anything from Rossi about Seth?"

"Nothing. I'm sure the boy is long gone—he flat out avoided me the other day. Although he must have been a victim at one point, he is now a perpetrator and I'm finding it difficult to feel much sympathy for him. Claire apparently disappeared not too long after the traffickers nabbed the Helmans, so *she* could be dead. Neither Rachel nor Joey knows Claire's last name. Could be 'Claire' isn't actually her first name. As for age, they agree she's in her late teens."

"Robin, any idea how they pulled off the kidnapping? Oskar Helman was a big man and Claire, per the girls' descriptions, was small."

"I'm not sure. Helman and his son visited Air and Space, as Sarah told us her ex had promised Danny, and as the guard reported. The girls were unaware of the details, just knew the little Danny told them. Claire wouldn't talk about it."

Ty looked like he was going to say something, but only rubbed the side of his face. He sighed.

"What? Just say it."

"Robin, are you sure that Rachel wasn't a part of the scheme? Well, I mean, in the way Claire was, which I understand probably involved duress."

"Like I said, it's confusing—I've never handled a human trafficking case involving children. Ty, given the complexity of this investigation it's difficult to be sure of anything, but I don't think so. Why?"

"I've been thinking—why didn't Rachel Corey go to the police when she escaped? You brought that concern up. That is, *if* she escaped. I accepted her story without question. Now, I'm wondering why it took so long for her to come forward."

"Ty, she's a victim! A frightened kid at that. She seemed scared when we saw her at Bryn Mawr."

"Bryn Mawr? You've come into contact with her before?"

"Yep, what makes sense now, but didn't at the time, is what happened when we went to the Roland Park schools asking for information."

He looked confused.

"I'd better back up. Ty, there was tagging at the crime scene, which we thought a kid might have done. We checked out schools, thinking that just maybe we would see similar artwork. Anyhow, we were leaving Bryn Mawr when a girl showed up out of nowhere. She scuttled into the back seat of the car; sat there hunched over like a turtle with nothing to say. The girl *looked* as if she had problems—she definitely wasn't taking care of herself. Just when I thought she was going to disclose something, she panicked and bailed. We gave her a card but never heard from her."

"Are you *certain* Rachel Corey is the same girl?"

"Absolutely! I recognized her immediately. I can't account for the delay—denial, fear—maybe she thought Cuz and Bro would track her down. Hell, Ty, her fear makes sense to me—after all, Leroy Nichols is dead. The suspects are aware Rachel can send them to jail for life—by the way, they accessed her phone, so we should let her parents know they should get new phones and change their numbers. Erica and I are really concerned about the safety of both girls."

"Well, I hope you're right about Rachel," he said, sounding unconvinced.

"We are. You'll see."

"Anything else on Cuz?"

"Nothing—but we'll find him. Ty, we're pretty convinced that he doesn't oversee daily operations—that's what Bro and the nameless dudes are about. I think Cuz is over them and has a layer of protection.

Honestly, I'm surprised they even saw him at the house. It seems he was mainly at the Glover address over what they were going to do with Oskar. Other than that, Cuz was more of a threat if the kids didn't do what the traffickers wanted."

"Anything from Brenda Jimenez or Sheila K., whatever her name is?"

"Nope, but Moreno thinks Krasinski will eventually take a deal."

"I hope so. Well, California, I'm outta here. Let's keep in touch." With that, Ty left.

"Be safe, Ty," I said, but by then he was out of earshot. I hoped I was right about Rachel. After all, I'd been wrong about Seth.

———

"Come on in, ladies." Sarge literally bellowed the greeting—we went in and sat. "What can I do for you?"

"Sir, we wanted to let you know the man discovered in the Harbor, Manny's case—the one the three of us were working on—is, in fact, Oskar Helman," Erica said.

"Huang's positive?"

"Not a doubt," she said. "He has Helman's dental records and a DNA sample obtained from a jacket left at Sarah Rollins' house, as well as his son's DNA."

"Any thoughts as to what happened?"

"Cuz or his minions must have killed the father and disposed of his body in the harbor—there is still plenty of work to do," I said, holding back a sigh heavy with frustration. "Sarge, we've *got* to locate the traffickers before we have more dead and traumatized children. We have eyewitness testimony, supported by the forensics, showing they held Helman in the basement, but he was no longer there by the time we moved in, and there is no evidence of his having been killed there. We found the suitcases, phones, including Rachel's, and the Helmans' passports in the room where they held him. Oskar Helman's wallet and phone are still missing, but there's been no activity on the cards since the airport. Sir, his family wants the body shipped to Germany, but we're holding off on that."

"Ladies, I understand there's still a ways to go to determine the cause of death for Helman, but what's the point of hanging onto the body if they want it returned?"

"I know ... I know," I said. "Despite the nastiness of some of the Helmans, I feel for them, especially the mother who is critically ill. We're still trying to sort out the details—locate as many victims and suspects as possible before the case hits the news. I guess we were thinking that this is our last chance for any further tests." By then I was almost pleading our case and Moreno was nodding.

Though not looking persuaded, I thought he was going to acquiesce. "Okay, ladies. You can maintain the news blackout on the investigation for two days but then, I don't want an argument, the body is to be shipped back to the family and we'll hold a press conference."

"Yes, sir," we said simultaneously, grateful for the reprieve.

"But work with the ME's office *now* to make the arrangements, which are bound to be complicated. And you're to convey my sympathies to the family."

"Yes, sir." I said.

"So what have you got so far ... Moreno?"

"Sir, we believe Danny Helman was trafficked to the doctor living in Roland Park who called 911 about discovering a body near his home—we found Dr. Manning's name in an address book at the house. We think *that* is how the victim came to be in the culvert: Manning may have driven up there at night, parked close and carried the body to where he *purportedly* found him next morning. At first, we were unable to get a search warrant for his house and office. Sir, by the time we did, a cleaning service had been to both locations; he had his car detailed—we did not find much. Despite all the precautions, the CS techs uncovered evidence of the boy's presence but, Sarge, he admits to that. No semen or blood."

"What does he say? I'm getting a lot of calls from *very* important people complaining the police are harassing an innocent man."

"Sarge, *nobody* is harassing Manning," insisted an aggravated Erica. "But I am sure he has juice—a well-known surgeon and long-time resident of the neighborhood who has nothing but a few traffic cam tickets! According to him, 'It was an accident—the boy suffered an asthma attack and died.' He insists he tried to help him."

"And what's his explanation for having an unrelated boy at his house? The child, I'm sure, begged for his father and mother, repeatedly, and wanted to go home."

"Well, there's the rub, sir," I said. Dr. Manning admits to a drug problem, 'OxyContin, only since my divorce,' is what he told us. He insists the 'young woman,' Claire, sold him the pills. She brought the boy to him because he was unwell—"

"—so, Moreno, the drugs found in the boy's system, they're from Manning?"

"Sir, he claims *not* to have given Danny drugs. He blames the traffickers for the drugging, claiming the boy stayed at his house 'for less than a day and slept most of the time.' I imagine that Manning is going to want a deal. If the prosecutor is willing, I would hope he would have to give up something really big to receive any kind of consideration. The man is totally driven by self-interest, so who knows what will come out of those negotiations."

"Why didn't he call 911 when it was clear Danny Helman was in trouble?"

I responded, trying to remain dispassionate. "Dr. Manning insists the boy came to him with his hair and skin dyed. He admits that he knew something was wrong but didn't want to be a part of it. For good measure, he says they threatened to reveal his drug use and, if they had, his life wouldn't be worth much. Sir, he insists that he thought things were under control—that he could help the boy."

"Ladies, are you positive Manning isn't one of the traffickers?"

"Positive? Not by a long shot," retorted Erica. "Sir, what did he think would happen to the child when he was returned to whomever?"

"Good question. Let's see what the State's Attorney's office says. What comes next?"

"Erica, Ty, Manny, D, and I met several times. There are differences of opinion about which suspect was responsible for what and about the strategy moving forward, but we are of the same mind when it comes to building a strong case. Oh, and we wanted to advise you of the FBI's offer of assistance."

"Thanks, I spoke with the local office. It will probably come to that given the DC connection and the transport of minors across multiple state lines. Could be DC is where this Cuz is lying low. By the way, don't even think about suggesting a deal to Manning. Anyhow, that's ultimately up to the prosecutor—I'll give them a call." He sat back, arms folded, overlapping chins resting on his chest, obviously finished with the conversation.

"No deals, sir," said Erica. "We will get them. All."

"Thank you, Sarge," I said. We left the room.

Chapter 29

Joey

"**Robin, are you** sure we are covered to talk with Joey Jimenez?" asked Erica. "¡Caramba! It's complicated with her mother charged in her kidnapping."

"We're good. State's Attorney approved it."

"Is she living with her aunt and uncle now? I cannot imagine this going very well with Marisol sitting in."

"They went to court just a few hours ago, and the judge granted an emergency decree of temporary guardianship. I've explained to her that it would be easier on Joey if we spoke to her alone. Now that the girl is going to live with them, her aunt has calmed down but is coming anyhow. Marisol did agree to remain in another room; she'll 'be available if needed.' Anyway, they signed the appropriate forms. Erica, I know she behaved a bit wacky early on, but she's trying; she understands if she screws up, they might not get a chance at permanent guardianship."

"It's okay, Chica. I guess if something so terrible happened to one of my children, I would act like a loca. Ready?"

As much as I dreaded questioning a sexually and physically abused young girl, the time had come for a formal interview. Apart from learning what occurred with Joey Jimenez and the Helmans, I hoped speed would help us to find other victims. "Erica, she trusts us, so I think she will reveal more to us than she did to SVU. Someone from the unit will remain behind the one-way glass. When we're finished, now that the formalities are taken care of, they'll talk with Marisol and Johnny about support services."

"Good job, California."

"Thanks, but I couldn't have done it without you. My preference is a big dose of frontier justice for anyone trafficking children. However, since I swore to uphold, etc., let's go talk with Joey Jimenez and see what we can learn."

"How about we stop by the machines and buy the girl something. In the end, she is a child ... not even a teenager, despite what her mother believes."

As we entered the interview room, we saw a small girl dwarfed by a large table; her head rested in her arms—I thought of Leroy. Boyd sat on the other side of the table. I closed the door and she raised her head; I was concerned. Gaunt and pale, Joey Jimenez appeared decidedly unwell. We wanted information for all the right reasons, but the girl had been through hell and being in this awful room was probably the last thing she needed.

"Detective Moreno, may I speak with you?"

"Sure." She set the snacks in front of the girl and turned to leave.

I nodded to Boyd and we left the room. Once the door had closed, I said, "Erica, I can see why Marisol is worried. I think we should keep this short. You okay with that?"

"I agree—the girl, she does not look so good. Robin, Joey is going to need time and that *we* don't have."

"I know." I held the door open and we went back inside.

"Thank you, Officer Boyd," said Erica. "We'll take it from here."

"Miss Josephine, take care of yourself," said Boyd and turned to leave.

"Thank you. You're a really nice person." She might be young but she sounded like an old soul. He smiled.

"Joey, it's good to see you. In case you don't remember who we are, this is Detective Erica Moreno and I'm Officer Robin Crane. Please feel free to call us Erica and Robin."

"I remember you. *Thank you* for everything you did for me. My aunt says you saved my life and helped Rachel."

"Hon, I am sorry about Danny," said Erica.

We hadn't even begun the interview, and the girl seemed ready to burst into tears. "Joey, are you up for this?" I asked. "Your aunt and uncle gave us permission to talk with you, but your Aunt Marisol can join us if you want. I wasn't sure whether you would want privacy, though we won't be asking you anything too personal—just some general questions today."

"I'm *fine*," she said sharply and then, just as quickly seemed to crumple into herself. "I said so to the other policeman," she whispered. She reminded me of Rachel the day she sat in our car at Bryn Mawr. Without eye contact, the girl continued in a now raised voice. "*They* can't get away with this, it is just so wrong."

The mood swings—I wondered whether Joey was suffering with PTSD. "Who are they?" I asked, even though I was sure we knew to whom she referred. Still, we needed confirmation—a name or a description we could pursue. Anything that would get us to Cuz and Bro before they were in the wind and setting up somewhere else—doing further harm to innocents.

"I never knew any of their real names."

"That's okay, Miss Joey. Do you remember what they called each other?" Erica asked.

She perked up at that question. "Bro. He was so mean, but he wasn't there all the time." She hesitated and then said, "Bro was mostly the one who drove us places. "The other man seemed more important

... I forgot his name. He was really mad about Danny's daddy being there."

"Thank you, you are doing a fine job," Erica assured the girl.

I was unable to imagine what the girl had gone through but before going into the details, we had to start with the basics. We wanted a rock solid case that would send the traffickers to prison for as long as possible. "Joey, could you tell where Bro took you?"

"No, ma'am. The van didn't have windows and they took me in and out after dark—sometimes Claire came with me. Sometimes it didn't take long. When I got out, it never looked like Baltimore—big, really *big* houses and yards."

She had not mentioned Danny, I thought with a measure of relief. "They took you in a van, not a car?" I asked, thinking of the Porsche.

"Yes, a van. Is it okay to open the soda?" Her dark blonde hair fell in soft waves below her shoulders. Long bangs called attention to beautiful brown eyes, larger I suppose because of how thin she was.

"Of course. The cookies, too," said Erica with a smile.

"Thanks for the food—we were always so hungry. Now, it seems like I want to eat all the time."

"Well, let us know if you want more. Joey, the detectives who spoke with you at the hospital said that sometimes they took you from Baltimore. Did you know where you were?"

"No. We would stay in one place for a few days and then they moved us again. It was hard to tell because they made us take drugs."

"Do you have any idea how long you traveled before stopping?" interjected my partner.

"No, ma'am, but sometimes we went really far," she said, licking off the frosting from the two halves of the cookies. "Maybe two hours to the next place. Long enough I needed to pee really bad." She opened the soda and sipped at it.

That timeframe could have gotten them to somewhere in DC, Philadelphia or Wilmington. Big houses, landscaped yards—in Baltimore, that could be several neighborhoods—Roland Park, Guilford,

Homeland, and Greenspring Valley. Those areas are consistent with the direction Rachel's captor was driving when she escaped. With Ty's help, Erica and I could explore the possibilities and then come up with unique characteristics, which might tap into something she would remember. We also needed to bring in a sketch artist.

Erica tried again. "Miss Joey, did you think of any other names?"

"They called the two guys that were there a lot Man Man and Black—stuff like that. My main man. My mom and Sheila, but I don't want to talk about them."

"That's okay, hon, you don't need to," Erica reassured her. "Did you hear *anything* about the others? Something describing the person?"

Joey seemed calmer and more thoughtful about answering my partner's questions; I supposed that was a hopeful sign. When she had finished with the cookie, the girl gazed around the room while playing with her hair. After winding and unwinding it round a finger, she separated it out strand-by-strand and chewed off split ends until her eyes suddenly widened. Erica raised her eyebrows.

"Do you remember something, hon?" She asked the question softly.

"I think so. One time Bro was yelling at us and Claire was really upset because we were taking so long to get ready. Bro said *Cuz* would be pissed and it wouldn't take him much time to drive to where we were from *Towson*," she said triumphantly. "I guess Bro and he were cousins. Does that help?"

"Honey, it sure does!" I said. Left unsaid—we would find her captors.

"Every piece of information helps," said Erica. "A name, a description of a neighborhood, the distance from Baltimore to the next house—it all gives us something to go on, which will lead us to something else," said Erica. "*That* is what detecting is all about—we are extremely grateful for your help."

Joey smiled proudly, and I wanted to hug her. She had gone through more than I would ever comprehend, certainly more than any child should. "Honey, can you describe the woman who worried about upsetting Cuz, Claire?" Almost instantly, her expression changed and she seemed to close up.

Erica looked concerned. "Did we upset you?"

"I don't want to get her in trouble. Claire was really scared and *I* don't blame her—they hit us and forced us to do horrible things."

Erica said, "We do not want to cause her any problems but, Joey, we need to find her because she also could be Cuz's victim."

"Oh." She twisted her mouth and pulled at her earlobe, as she mulled over that information. She began to play with her hair again.

"Do you know the woman's last name?" I asked.

"She told us to call her Claire. She wasn't, like, a woman."

"No? How old do you think she was?" Erica asked.

"I'm not sure—eighteen?"

Eighteen was consistent with the age she and Rachel had given SVU. "Joey, do you by any chance know where Claire is?"

"No. After Bro and his friend brought Danny and his father to the basement, I only saw her a few more days. Danny said she took him from the museum and she was, like, nice to him, but he wanted his mother. He would tell us his father was tired. When he got really sick, Claire told him not to worry—she would go with him to the doctor. Bro took them somewhere like he did before, but then I never saw her or him again. She *never* said her last name."

Chapter 30

Bpd Press Conference

After **Rachel Corey** and Joey Jimenez provided as much information as they could, Sarge insisted the time had come to hold a news conference. Media Relations made the arrangements and e-mailed the marching orders to all of us who were expected to attend.

The next day we met and reviewed the case at Headquarters before gathering in a small conference room adjoining the media relations briefing room. Once the media finished setting up, we entered. Present on the dais were the BPD Commissioner, the Lieutenant and Sarge, as well as the members of our informal task force: Erica, Ty, Rossi, D, Manny, and me. The prosecutor working with us on the case stood next to a woman from Child Protective Services. The mayor should have been present but was out of town. Marisol Jimenez sat in a chair at the back of the room. Johnny had remained home with his niece. Joey's aunt looked like a new woman: barrettes held her now shiny hair back from her pretty face and her eyes once again sparkled.

She made an effort to suppress a smile, a good idea given the serious nature of the event.

Sarge approached the podium and adjusted the microphone. "Good morning and thank you for coming today. The Commissioner has asked me to speak with you." Sarge gave his superiors a nod of recognition and then began by introducing everyone; as he did, we each acknowledged our name. He then continued. "As is evident from my introductions, there are individuals from several districts and city offices who have been engaged in a cooperative effort to solve these horrific crimes. We now need more assistance. I have called this press conference to ask for the community's help with what is an *active* investigation of a child trafficking ring purportedly run out of Baltimore City. We also want to provide you with an update regarding the case. Due to exceptional police work by the BPD, a warrant was issued for Mr. Marcus Winter for human trafficking, child abuse, and drug distribution. Mr. Winter goes by the moniker of "Cuz." We are asking for assistance from the community in locating Mr. Winter. A reward of $10,000 is being offered for his arrest and successful prosecution. Thank you—I can now take questions."

Every reporter's hand shot up. "The Sun," Sarge called out.

"There are rumors about two East Baltimore residents who are involved in the trafficking ring. Is the information accurate? And, if so, how are they connected to the case?"

Sarge hesitated. I couldn't imagine how the reporter had gotten the information and hoped to God that we could shield the girls' identities from the press, at least for now.

"In answer to your question: Yes, several local residents are alleged to be involved in the trafficking scheme."

"Can you speak to the rumor that two of them were addicts and one prostituted her daughter?"

"For privacy reasons I cannot discuss the health status of suspects. Any individuals arrested in our city, however, who have drug habits, are treated while incarcerated."

The reporter persisted. "What are the policies of the Child Protective Services when it comes to cases in which a parent is involved—would they regain custody if out on bond?"

I didn't look but could only imagine that the smile had disappeared and the color had leached from Marisol's face. I wasn't sure how Sarge was going to put the question to rest—too much information was out there. What I did know was we weren't off to a good start.

He glanced at the CPS representative but didn't ask her to step forward. "We don't discuss victims and would ask you to respect the privacy of minors," our boss said in no uncertain terms. "Simons, City Paper."

"Thank you, sir. Has there been an arrest in the murder of the little boy discovered in Roland Park? Is that why the press conference?"

"Not yet. What we do suspect is that the trafficking ring under investigation had a role in the child's death. We currently have several individuals of interest in his murder, as we do for the death of his father, a German national, whose body was found floating in the harbor. Dr. Helman's body was returned to his family. They asked me to communicate their appreciation of the BPD's efforts to bring justice to those responsible for the kidnapping of their loved ones."

He took several other questions from different media outlets and then concluded with "That's it for now, ladies and gentlemen. Thank you for coming. When we have additional news, we *will* make it available to you. Again, I want you to recognize how grateful I am for the hard work of this team, as well as the members of the community who worked closely with us to solve this case. Please contact the BPD with any relevant information. You *can* choose to remain anonymous."

Reporters began to pack up and camera operators were dismantling their equipment when Sarge abruptly turned back to the microphone: "Before you leave, there's one more message I want to get to your readers and viewers." Heads swung in his direction. "And I want to be crystal clear about this—the crimes we are investigating have been particularly horrific. Ladies and gentlemen, as one of the members of our team said the other day, "We *must* do a better job of protecting our children, as individuals and as a society." Thank you for your help with that and have a good day."

"Well done, sir," I said, shaking his hand. His face was unusually flushed—I hoped he was taking blood pressure medication.

"Sarge, that was good work," said Erica.

"Well, ladies, as far as it went—we've still got quite a way to go with this case."

"We're working it hard," she assured him. "That's a big reward, maybe something will come in."

"Are you and Crane busy right now?"

"No, sir."

"I'd like to see you in my office in ten."

"Yes, sir!" We, unfortunately, sounded like the Bobbsey twins.

Marisol wanted to talk but I told her I would call later; meantime, I said she wasn't to worry. Under the circumstances, I wasn't sure what else to say. Erica and I took off with just enough time to grab a drink before heading to Sarge's office.

———

"Come in, ladies."

"Sir, do you think the Sun reporter has knowledge of Joey Jimenez being trafficked by her mother?" I asked before even sitting down.

"I do. I'll give him a call and offer an exclusive in return for protecting the girl's identity for a while longer. I think he'll bite—there's a lot yet to come out and he's surely aware of that. In any event, the information originated from somewhere, so it's liable to leak anyhow. You should meet with Josephine Jimenez's aunt and uncle and the Coreys to inform them of that very real possibility. If they don't already have professional help, they're going to need some."

"Both families are receiving support services," said Erica. "Joey's aunt was in the room and heard the question for herself. Sir, if the details come out, I can't imagine what kind of problems these girls will experience at school."

"Okay, ladies, now that we have given and will continue to give the press something to keep them at bay, let's see where we stand. I sure as hell am going to get every son-of-a-bitch involved in this thing. "Crane, Moreno tells me you're familiar with the kids hanging out at Fells Point."

"Yes, sir."

"What about the one who kidnapped Rachel Corey—the panhandler. You got anything on him yet?"

"There's an open warrant for Seth Doe, but Rossi and I keep running into dead ends with this kid. On the other hand, it was while looking for him that we came up with Cuz's legal name, Marcus Winter."

"You may be having difficulty locating the kid because Seth isn't even his name. We don't even know whether he's from Baltimore," said an exasperated Erica.

I said, "Sarge, like the missing Claire, he in all probability was abducted or a runaway at some point."

"Well, keep on it. We may need to go national. A street kid who panhandles and drives a Porsche—*someone* knows who and where he is. He may have been hanging around Central Booking to target vulnerable individuals for his bosses. We *will* find him. Crane, you really think he's as young as fifteen or sixteen?"

"I do, sir," I said, shifting in the uncomfortable seat. "Also, Rachel Corey independently told us she thought Seth was fifteen. I guess that's why she felt comfortable getting into a car with him after her friend failed to show, though to say she was surprised by such an expensive car is an understatement. I doubt he even has a license. It occurred to me he might be in a selfie—kids that age are constantly taking them, but he wasn't in any of the photos on Rachel's phone, which we found in the basement."

"I don't know what to say, ladies, except I want the kid brought in. We'll figure out the rest later. Actually, his life history is *not* our problem—let the legal beagles take care of it. Anything about Rachel Corey's friend who met *someone* at Silo Point and just happened not to return for her the day she was abducted?"

"Not yet, she'll only give up the girl's first name," Erica said.

"Well, get on it then. Now, about Tony Greene. You're picking him up tomorrow?"

"That's right, sir," I said. "After he leaves his house for school."

"Good. Let's go over what his role is in this—I don't want the little shit falling through an unanticipated crack. Crane, you dealt with Tony Greene and Darren Antek while partnering with Ty Wilson. Correct?"

"Yes, sir."

"Well, give me the rundown."

"Actually, I was patrolling with Greg Rossi when I first met Tony Greene. He regularly hung out at the plaza in Fells Point—good-looking, outgoing, he was at the center of things. The first time I approached the group, an older kid ran off before I spoke with him—he turned out to be Darren Antek.

"Sarge, it may be that Greene is the 'rich white kid' Ty Wilson's CI gave up for the grandmother shooting, but the prosecutor says there isn't enough to charge him with, at least right now. Later, the grandmother's grandson, Leroy Nichols, who initially gave us the trafficking information, was killed, but there is *nothing* to say Greene was involved in that. Crime Lab says the bullets are from different guns."

"What about Antek?"

"When I first heard his name, it didn't mean anything to me. When I mentioned it to Ty, he reminded me of a minor stop we'd made. The kid had been drag racing on Boston Street—at the time, he said he was on his way home to Dundalk from Fells Point. He's seventeen, though I thought he was older. Anyhow, since then, he's acquired some drug-related charges. "Ty and I spoke with Antek and his folks about making the more serious ones go away; in the end, he was willing to give up Tony Greene for a promise from the prosecutor's office of no jail time—probation and community service only. With the proviso, of course, that the prosecutor will reinstate the charges if what he gives us doesn't hold up.

"What we've got Greene for is possession and distribution. Sarge, what Darren Antek says is that he and others who routinely hung out in Fells Point had been buying marijuana and pharmaceuticals from Tony for almost a year. The transactions between the two always took place in Fells Point. He didn't know Tony's last name but picked him out from a photo array. Antek sold the drugs at the Dundalk high school. My guess is Darren was carrying the night we stopped him. What Ty and I think is that *Greene* got the drugs from someone in Cuz's gang—so we've got something to negotiate with, though that's out the window if Tony shot up the grandmother's house and car."

"Why would Greene jeopardize his future like that? He seems to have a pretty privileged life."

"According to old news reports," said Erica, "his father lost a lot of money in the crash. When we spoke with Tony, supposedly to obtain information about Seth, the father was present and he mentioned his son had a full ride to Stanford, *his* school of choice—could be his son lied to him and found a way to cover the tuition. Or, maybe Tony dealt drugs because he liked the thrill *and* the money—whatever the case, we'll know more once we bring him in. All we have now is what Darren and the girls gave us; bueno, and the bit from Mr. Greene."

"I'm surprised the father didn't march in with a lawyer," said Sarge. There was a threatening squeak as he settled back in the chair.

"Tony Greene is eighteen. He probably made it about Darren—we did."

Erica added, "Sarge, I think this investigation is going to take time, and the community will need to help before we develop a solid case against Marcus Winter, even if we *can* find him. Though the man seems to have his fingers in everything from human trafficking to serious gun and drug distribution to witness intimidation and undoubtedly murder, he has managed to keep a pretty low profile."

That was an accurate statement—Leroy Nichols' death remains with me. He gave us good information and deserved our protection, though it may turn out that he worked with Cuz, and did open and walk through the door that brought about his own demise. I hoped not, but Baltimore is a complicated city and making a living with little education has its challenges. When Ty followed up on some of the witness statements, he discovered Leroy's grandmother somehow had learned about the trafficking and pressured her grandson to go to the police. It might have been Leroy's love for his "Gramma" *and* his fear of being sent back to Hagerstown that accounted for his willingness to talk. The first volley of shots at her car and house must have been an unheeded warning that finally resulted in Leroy's death. We're making progress, though we haven't gotten anywhere near Cuz for this, and there has to be someone even higher up in the organization who directed what appeared to be a complex system of illegal activities. I very much doubt he would've been in the basement of the house where the children were held. It was clear we are nowhere near *that* individual.

"Sir," I said, "you should be aware that Tony Greene and Rachel Corey regularly hung out together downtown and have friends in common—unfortunately, he wasn't there at the time Seth gave her the ride. Anyhow, he attends Gilman and she, Bryn Mawr—the schools are in the same neighborhood. In our initial interview, Tony mentioned Rachel as someone he knew who spent time in Fells Point. He doesn't know Joey or Claire. He admitted to knowing Seth but claimed they didn't get along, and this is a quote, "Dude, Seth is bad news." *This* from a drug dealer. Sarge, that's another reason for locating Seth pronto. Any lawyer worth his salt defending Tony Greene is going to put this off on the missing Seth Doe—I can already hear a strong reasonable doubt argument. As of now, Greene is not giving up anything, but the prosecutor is willing to work with him. We're hoping as the system moves forward he'll at least get us to Cuz."

Erica asked, "Robin, does Ty Wilson think he can get his CI to talk—maybe he can identify Greene as the individual involved in the initial shooting at the grandmother's house?"

"Nope." That was a repeat of his answer to me. I couldn't get any more from him—something I wouldn't tell Sarge.

"Well, he needs to keep at it," Sarge insisted irritably. Put more money on the table. "Work with him to bring the informant around. Remind me—why the timing for picking up Greene?"

"Sir, the last time we spoke with him, he told us he'd gotten his wish to go surfing—his parents are sending him to live with his aunt in California for his last semester before graduation. Honestly, I'm not sure what we're going to get from him regarding the trafficking. About the drug distribution charge, we *are* expecting to learn something during an interrogation that will get us a search of his house and car. Not sure whether schools still have lockers—I'll call the headmaster. But with only Darren's say-so, a good lawyer is sure to get Greene off. Meantime, D and Ty are working hard to locate other clients. If they do, or we find something through the searches, I'm almost positive Tony Greene will deal."

"Crane, Moreno, I don't want this privileged bastard taking a walk while we put some boys from the hood in jail, which I anticipate will be the case. Give it two or three more days but, meantime, keep a close eye on the kid and don't let him leave town."

Chapter 31

Name of the Game is Change

Ddragged a chair from an adjoining desk over to mine. "What do you chicks have for me?" he asked. "Sorry, what do you *good cops* have for me?" He threw a wink my way.

"Hey dude, where is *my* honey?" said Erica.

"Not to worry, Moreno, I'm saving something *special* for you!" She broke out laughing.

"Okay, D, if you can reel it in, we'll give you what we've got," I said. He leered, nodded, and swung his long legs onto my desk. "Go ahead—give it to me."

Ignoring the double entendres, and pushing his legs off my notebook, I proceeded. "Moreno and I re-interviewed Rachel Corey to find out whether she would be willing to help nail Tony Greene. Though a shot in the dark, it turned out to be a good move. It seems she went to see Tony after returning home—the girl apparently had a thing for him before the kidnapping. Somehow, Rachel got the idea they were going away to discuss "things." She had Danny's backpack with her when she escaped; that's what she packed for their weekend, hiding it in the bushes before school, which is where Erica discovered it. But, as you are aware, it was already at the crime lab when she went to pick it up. Scared, she called Tony; all *he* had to say was she would be sorry if she spoke to the police. After that he wouldn't return her calls. To say the girl is bitter is putting it mildly. She *wants* to cooperate with us. Her parents will let her cooperate. They believe Greene is responsible for her having been trafficked—I can't speak to that. Their lawyer's good with it—a winning combination, or as Ty would say, 'a bing, bang, bong.'"

"You think we can break this trafficking ring?"

"Well not with what we have learned so far, but every piece of the puzzle gets us there. This has been tough for Rachel and Joey—they are just kids."

"You're right, Erica," I said. "Healing is a slow process. It's just that I'm afraid these guys will lay low for only so long and then they'll get back to business."

"Be patient," D said seriously. "I'm mindful of the fact that you two and my boy Ty have worked nonstop on this thing—don't worry, you'll get some of the bad guys off the street."

"Thanks, D. The deciding factor, I think, is that the Coreys are leaving Maryland." I had been surprised at the news but figured it would be best for Rachel, who needed a sense of security if she was ever going to recover from the trauma she'd experienced, surely still experiences.

"Find out anything more about why Helman was looking for a hotel room? That decision seemed to be at the crux of the matter—he was dragging his kid around looking for a hotel room, instead of staying with his friends. I don't know, it seems odd, is all. Did you find any evidence to show he stayed in a DC or a Baltimore hotel or a B & B?

"Nothing. But after we called for information, the friend found an email in her spam folder from Oskar—it went to spam, I guess, because of some oddball German attachment. Anyhow, Oskar apologized to them for the change in plans but explained that his mother was dying—he wasn't sure that he would see her again and Danny was upset. He thought it better to spend whatever time he had left with his son, before returning the boy to his mother. Oskar planned to stop in for a day on his way back to Germany. D, it must have been a last minute decision and it probably never occurred to him that getting a room would be a problem. When the guard saw him on the phone, he might have been calling hotels. I guess we'll never know for sure, but we have put in a request for his phone records. I don't know if we'll be successful given we're dealing with a foreign country."

"Well, that's an interesting possibility—keep me posted. Good work getting the girl to cooperate."

"Oh, did we tell you that she gave up the friend who dropped her off in Little Italy before heading over to Silo Point to meet someone?"

"The one who did a no-show, leaving Rachel Corey with Seth who kidnaps her?"

"That's the one. Seemed pretty suspicious to us, too."

"And?"

"And now, D, here is some hot off the press news to brighten your day!" Erica declared cheerily.

"Well, other than getting to hang out with us," I added.

"*C'mon*, give it up, Moreno."

"Rachel's friend, Stephanie Cohen, insisted she never met Seth and so far we have no reason not to believe her."

"Well, what was her role in this?" D asked.

"She claimed to be taking care of plants and the cat of family friends who own a Silo Point condominium and are in Europe," I explained. "Stephanie's mother called the condo owners, who agreed to let us take a look at their place. And, Ty, *who* should we find in a closet but the missing Claire. Both girls were absolutely terrified. Someone from SVU is interviewing them as we speak—separately."

"Fantastic! Keep me posted."

"Will do," Erica assured him.

"D, we showed Rachel the facial sketch of Seth I'd worked up. She tweaked it some, so we've got something solid to work with there. Joey Jimenez didn't recognize him, but several kids hanging out in Fells Point identified him from the poster, so Erica released it to all Maryland PDs, as well as those in the surrounding states, the FBI, and the Center for Missing and Exploited Children. None of the kids knew Seth's last name. Rossi said there was no record of him at the Fellowship shelter he told me he was staying at."

"Though we have no new leads getting us to Cuz, aka Marcus Winter," Erica said, "the reward has increased to fifteen thousand, thanks to Sarge's press conference and the Missing and Exploited organization. Maybe *that* kind of money will bring somebody out of the woodwork. D, you get anything on the one they're calling Bro? Ty said you expected something from the prints on the basement window, the luggage and the phone."

"Yup, I got my own news. The prints from the basement gave us a Mr. Calvin Colson, age 25, whose last known address is a boarded up house in the Western District—I checked it out myself. Mr. Colson has a sheet dating back to age 12—he'd already left school by then. His grandmother, who raised him and his two sisters, told me she could never control him—that family was one of the lead poisoning cases. Ty and I canvassed the area and spoke with any willing informants. The last time anyone saw him was before you found the Jimenez girl. The police pinched Colson in DC, *twice*, so it could be that's where he and Cuz are hiding out. Sheeit! Once we arrest them, I don't understand why the judicial system can't manage to put the bad guys away for longer than they do."

"Well, it appears we're making progress. D, you hear we're holding Sheila Krasinski?" I asked. "Neither she nor Brenda Jimenez will give up any names, but Rachel Corey and Joey Jimenez are willing to testify against them. That said, I think Joey is pretty angry with her mother right now. Even so, I don't think she'd actually take the stand."

"Anyhow, Robin, I don't think she should be put in that situation unless the prosecutor absolutely needs for her to testify," said Erica.

Bueno, I believe Krasinski will deal, but I don't know what her role in the trafficking was—she *must* have been aware of the comings and goings. Brenda was thoroughly involved and I'm not sure we're going to get anything without putting her in a witness protection program, which Crane and I are totally against—we want her in prison."

"D, Sarge said the prosecutor has enough to take multiple charges to the Grand Jury against Cuz, Bro, Seth, in absentia, as well as Sheila and Brenda. We'll see what falls out of the interrogation with Claire. Sarge is talking about turning the cases over to the Feds—more resources and longer sentences; their reach from prison—if we can get the lot of them there—won't be so long."

"Lot more to do, California, but good work all around! You chicas got time for a beer before heading home?" asked D.

I glanced at Erica who laughed and nodded. "Sure, let's go!" I said. It had been a good day.

Epilogue

Costa Rica, December 2014

"Erica, have a great vacation. This has been one tough case."

"That it has, California, but there is still a way to go with the investigation."

I laughed. "True, but you shouldn't think about the case—you're leaving things in good hands. And don't forget to send a postcard infused with a healthy dose of sunshine and a picture of a beach or an animal or two. Sadly, I'll need to stay warm and be a tourist by proxy this winter."

"I will do that, Chica, but one day you must tell me *why* you are living in Baltimore instead of Santa Barbara. The *real* explanation. I say that because what you told me about moving east makes little sense, bueno, except for Matt wanting to start a new life. Sounds to me like there is an old boyfriend in the mix. By the way, why did Matt want to come to Maryland? Isn't he from the Midwest?"

"He is. Moreno, you are such a conspiracy buff—no wonder you grew up to become a real live detective! Fair's fair though, if I come clean, you have to tell me why *you* came to Maryland."

"That is the truth about being a conspiracy buff," she laughed, ignoring the comment on her personal history. "Seriously, Chica, we'll get Cuz, Bro, and the rest of them. I will say a prayer every day to the Blessed Virgin for Baltimore to remain calm while I am gone. Robin, I understand you are no fan of winter, but what I have learned is the heat drives the bad guys out the door and the cold pushes them inside, well other than New Year's Eve—the harbor activities seem to draw the crazies out no matter how bad the weather is."

I laughed. Though D and I work well together, I was going to miss my partner. "Your prayers will be much appreciated, Erica. Be sure to double up on them for the holidays."

"Bueno. California, do not give D too much grief—remember it is only a temporary assignment and I *need* my mommy time. My *mother* needs for me to have my mommy time. I will be back before you know it—first week of January."

"Yeah, Moreno, that'll be the day when *I* give *him* too much grief. That boy can definitely take care of himself. All I want to say is that if you don't come back, I promise to track you down and drag you back by that braid of yours." Despite the quip, I had registered my partner's words about "mommy time." "Just giving you shit, partner. Enjoy your family. Everything will be okay here; D's the one you should worry about."

"D will be fine, you will be fine. Robin, remember to wish Sean a Merry Christmas. Tell him my kids will be in Baltimore in a few months and we'll go to Hershey Park. Thanksgiving and the barbecue at your place with Ty and his family were fun—we need to do more stuff like that. Bueno, amiga, Feliz Navidad y Prospero Año Nuevo to you and your family, and thank you for the presents. I hope you enjoy your visit with your Santa Barbara friend. And congratulations, *Detective* Crane—a well-deserved promotion, and an early one at that!"

"Thanks. Yeah, we're excited about Ken's visit—Sean's full of plans. Greg Rossi is an old buddy of Ken's, so he'll be joining us—ought to be quite the time. Merry Christmas, partner. Be safe." I gave her a hug and she took off.

As I watched my partner and friend leave, I realized just how long the two weeks would be. Matt had suggested a family vacation next Christmas to Panama (Matt wanted to visit only if they completed the expanded canal) or Costa Rica (Erica had pushed that idea). I'd been ready to accompany Erica *this* winter, but Matt thought we needed to be more settled first—finish unpacking the boxes. Chief Bartolo called from Santa Barbara a couple of weeks ago and I mentioned our plans—well, I guess he is now *ex*-Chief Bartolo—anyway, he and Suzanne were thinking of sailing to Central America in the summer; they would check things out for us.

Acknowledgments

A heartfelt thank you and appreciation to members of the Baltimore law enforcement community who shared their experience and expertise with me. I hope all will forgive the literary license taken with the Baltimore City criminal justice system. Moreover, any mistakes are absolutely mine and mine alone.

I am greatly indebted to Barbara Crain for her significant contribution to both the development and editing of this book (and nudging me along when a nudge is called for). By all rights, if aggravation were the measure of authorship, you deserve a co-authorship!

Thank you to Mary Bamberg for being a first-rate reader, willing to pitch in when those deadlines loom—your eagle eye and ideas are much appreciated. Barbara Larcom, the time and thought you gave an earlier version of the manuscript certainly strengthened the book. Thank you.

My appreciation goes to Diane Toby and Jeff Lea (and their kitties) for sharing their beautiful home—a wonderful sanctuary for a writer. Thank you to Marianne and Mike Moran, exceptionally good friends who never fail to support whatever project I have in the works.

Marianne, thanks for untangling the sentences I sent your way. I am indebted to Mary Keating, Esq. for your friendship and legal expertise.

I am exceedingly grateful to my family and friends for their love and support. A special thanks to Rachel Smith for lending her name (though not her experience; nonetheless, the fictional Rachel and her namesake share an important characteristic—courage) to a new character in the *Robin Crane Mystery* series, and to Sean Smith for his enthusiasm for my writing.

For further information on human trafficking, you can go to:

http://ww.soroptimist.org/trafficking/faq and https://polarispro-ject.org

If you suspect an incident of sex trafficking in the United States, call the National Human Trafficking

Resource Center's 24-hour toll free hotline: 888-373-8888. Callers can receive a variety of services.

About The Author

B A Smith received her doctorate in psychology. She carried out research in infant development at the Johns Hopkins University and studied healthcare delivery in Costa Rica. Smith is a proud mother and grandmother who has lived in Central America and across the United States. She enjoys travel and gardening and is currently at work in Maryland and California on a sequel to *Green Grows the Grass*, a work of historical fiction set in Latin America. *Floater in the Baltimore Harbor* is the second novel in the Robin Crane Mysteries series; the first being *Death at Painted Cave*.

www.robincranemysteries.com
basmith@robincranemysteries.com

Made in the USA
Charleston, SC
01 March 2017